Mayur Patel has a diploma in Civil Engineering and has done a course in Computer Aided Design (CAD). He is currently working in the field of architecture.

Though he is passionate about writing, he enjoys a wide variety of activities like reading, gardening, watching Hollywood movies and travelling.

The author lives in Valsad, Gujarat with his family. He can be contacted at mayurpatelwrites@gmail.com.

Vivek and I

MAYUR PATEL

PENGUIN BOOKS

PENGUIN BOOKS
Published by the Penguin (
Penguin Books India P
New Delhi 110 017, India
Penguin Group (USA) Inc.,
Penguin Group (Canada), 9
2Y3, Canada (a division of
Penguin Books Ltd, 80 Str;
Penguin Ireland, 25 St St
Books Ltd)
Penguin Group (Australia), 250 Camberwell Road, Camberwell, Victoria 3124, Australia
(a division of Pearson Australia Group Pty Ltd)
Penguin Group (NZ), 67 Apollo Drive, Rosedale, North Shore 0632,
New Zealand (a division of Pearson New Zealand Ltd)
Penguin Group (South Africa) (Pty) Ltd, 24 Sturdee Avenue, Rosebank, Johannesburg
2196, South Africa

Penguin Books Ltd, Registered Offices: 80 Strand, London WC2R 0RL, England

First published in Portfolio by Penguin Books India 2010

ISBN 9780143067924

Typeset in Sabon MT by InoSoft Systems, Noida
Printed at Chaman Offset Printers

To my lovely mom
For loving me so much & believing in my talent

one

It was lush all around with tiny blossoms and plenty of dry leaves scattered on the pebbled way that I was walking on. It was a sunny day with the air filled with the fragrance of various flowers. The dew soaked leaves of the trees looked like glowing diamonds in the sunshine. And even though I liked all these divine elements of nature, none of them were interesting me at that moment. My eyes were fixed on the figure that sat on a bench at the far end of the garden. Even the vague sight of that person filled my heart with excitement and elation. Though the image was a blur, I had a strong feeling that I knew who the person was. I was eager to see the face, but it remained indistinct despite my reaching quite close. I walked on.

Now I was within reach of touching the shoulder, but the figure still wasn't clear. I stood there, steady and silent, not knowing what to do. And then the figure rose and turned . . . the face still blurry like the morning haze of winter, was very close to me. I peered, but my eyes were unable to identify the person. A hand slowly went up to wipe away the mist from my eyes, the image of the person was to become clear. My curiosity to recognize the face doubled and . . .

. . . A loud noise broke my dream. I woke up with a start. Irritated and angry, I opened my eyes. It was Sukhi, my maid, who had dropped some vessel on the floor which had made that annoying clang. I cursed and closed my eyes. The same figure appeared in my subconscious mind again. But the face wasn't clear even now. It didn't matter because I knew who it was. I could well imagine that pretty, innocent face.

'Saabji, tea.' I heard Sukhi say and opened my eyes. She was going back into the kitchen. Sukhi, a skinny, thick-lipped, average looking woman in her mid-twenties, was a great cook and I admired the magic of her hands. The aroma of the hot tea filled my nostrils and I didn't feel like staying in bed any more. I put on my spectacles and picked the cup from the side table.

'Hmm . . .' I murmured satisfyingly as I sipped. Nothing in the world is better than a cup of hot tea to make one feel refreshed, I thought, as I walked towards the living room with the cup. There was a large window there which opened towards the west. I flung it open, reclined on the rocking chair, and gazed outside.

The prettiest thing around my house was there, right in front of my eyes, the neem tree on the hill. A few yards away from my house, this majestic tree stood alone on the hill that wears a lustrous blanket of soft, downy grass in the rainy season. I could see no plants, weeds or any other undergrowth around it. It seemed as if the fully grown tree was behaving autocratically and wouldn't let anything else grow in its realm.

Though this place didn't offer the best view of Valai, I liked to go and sit under that tree and enjoy the greenery around. It is said that if you want to know yourself, be solitary, and I knew I could be both alone and peaceful there. The tranquillity of that place gave my thoughts wings. It was always a pleasure to catch a strong gust of the cold wind on my face while sitting in the lap of the old roots of that tree. Being a great lover of nature, I would forget all my agonies in its company

Since it was evening, the sun was in the west and the large, shadow of the neem tree stretched over one-thirds of the hill. Its jovial leaves danced in the wind and the periphery of the tree glittered in the golden rays of the sun giving it a somewhat enchanting character. Both the edges of the crumpled but not so thick stem seemed to be aflame. The sweet twittering of the sparrows hidden somewhere in the thick grove of the tree poured into my ears and took me back to my hometown, where hundreds of pigeons used to gather on the terrace of my apartment to eat the grains we offered. The chattering of the pigeons never sounded as sweet as that of the sparrows, yet I had liked it so much as a kid. As I enjoyed the spectacle nature had spread before me, that sweet face flashed in my mind again and I longed for it. It was Sunday and I wasn't going to see it until tomorrow morning. Oh, how I hated waiting like this!

After finishing the tea, I thought of going out since there was nothing to do at home. I left the cup in the kitchen and went to the bathroom. When I came out after freshening up, Sukhi was cleaning the vessels. She looked at me expectantly. I don't know how her senses were so powerful. She always knew when I was going to talk to her. Almost in response to her questioning look, I answered, 'I'm going out, Sukhi. Don't know when I will be back. You leave when the cooking is done,' and headed for the bedroom.

'Bara, Saabji.' I heard her respond behind me.

Bara means 'okay'. I couldn't utter this word the way she did even if I wanted to. She used this word and many others from her language quite often. It felt good to hear these words from the local people. But when I tried to pronounce them the way they did, I failed miserably because of my urban accent. However, my vocabulary of the Dangi dialect was getting richer day by day. I put on a white T-shirt and a pair of blue jeans and without caring to look in the mirror, I left. Ripples of a pleasant breeze began to caress me as I walked down the streets of Valai.

Valai is a beautiful place. Set in the south of the state of Gujarat, this small town is at the heart of the primitive district named the Dangs. The smallest district in the entire state, it is set in the ranges of the Sahyadri hills that expand into two more states, Maharashtra and Madhya Pradesh. The hilly ranges throughout the district are covered mostly with bamboo and teak wood trees. The thick jungle has hundreds of other species of trees and vegetation, but I could name only a few. Wild animals roam freely in the sanctuaries because hunting is prohibited. Divine greenery, salubrious air, and a pollution free atmosphere are the assets of this corner of the world. Famous for its deciduous forest, the Dangs wears a fresh, new look in the season of monsoon. In fact, the word 'Dang' itself means a woody, mountainous region. The climate here is always extreme with bone chilling winters and nightmarish summer afternoons. It doesn't just rain here, but pours. Most of the population here is tribal and the rest, like me, are those who have come here because of their occupation. Two years back I had shifted to this place for a job, little knowing it would help me heal the wounds of my past.

The Dangs has a total of 386 villages scattered around the Sahyadri ranges. Most of them are diminutive. Some of the villages, set on high mountains, are so remote that they are bereft of even the basic facilities. The government has often tried to persuade the rural people to leave their villages and settle somewhere down on the plains, but they are so attached to their land that they can never ditch it. The poor tribals live a pitiful life, in tiny huts with practically no money. Whatever they earn is from farming and cultivating some vegetables and grains, mainly rye. There are no jobs. Neither is there any industrial activity that can provide them employment. Water is the biggest problem of the district despite the fact that the place is blessed with maximum rain in the entire state. In Valai, however, there was no shortage of water because we had a huge lake in the middle of the town.

At first, I thought of going to the sunset point, about a kilometre from my place. But then I thought about meeting Mr Desai in the garden, the only green expanse alongside the lake that was known as Bandharo. He was generally there every evening. This garden was so small that one could easily take in the view of the entire garden from any corner. I first looked on all the benches, but it seemed that Mr Desai had not arrived yet. So I sat on a bench in a corner and waited for the old man.

Breathing in the heady fragrance of the newly bloomed flowers, I thought about the day. Unlike every morning, I had been a bit listless today because I had no one to share it with me. The whole day had loomed large in front of me. I had taken more than my usual time for my morning routine and by the time I was dressed, it was ten. The newspapers had taken an hour and then I had busied myself in studying the plants. Although the heavy downpour of early monsoon had ruined my little garden, I had managed to save some of the plants by planting them in pots and keeping them inside the house, under the shade in the backyard. Then the monsoon had taken a break and it hadn't rained for about seven days. Having had a light lunch, I lay down in bed reading a James Hadley Chase thriller. It was fun but I couldn't stand it for more than half an hour. I put the book aside and started to think about the love of my life. Without whom I liked nothing and the feeling that I wasn't going to get to see my love until the next morning was a little torturous. I don't know when I had fallen off to sleep. Then the sweet dream happened. Unfortunately, I couldn't see the face of my love in the dream as Sukhi played villain by dropping some stupid utensil.

'Hello, Kaushik,' a rough voice broke into my thoughts and I turned around. It was Mr Pratap Desai, one of the trustees of the local library that I was a member of. The fair and healthy old man in his early seventies was smartly dressed in crisp, white kurta pyjamas. He was almost bald and sported a thick, white moustache. Though he was friendly by nature, he had became callous about minor things. I guessed it was his age.

'Good evening,' he said and sat by me on the bench.

'Very good evening,' I welcomed him with a warm smile. He sounded as if he had a cold, so I asked, 'How's your cold? Are you feeling better?'

In reply, he turned his face away and blew his runny nose as noisily as he could. I looked away to avoid the unpleasant sight. 'It's bad, I can see,' I said keeping my eyes averted. 'Better keep taking your medicines.'

'I am. And don't try to sound like a wife,' he quipped irritably. 'I already have one at home for the regular doses of advice.' The man was of an irascible nature. I laughed to myself.

After clearing his nose, the old man started with that most common of subjects, the weather. 'Is it going to rain or what?' The tip of his nose had turned a bright red because of him rubbing it with a handkerchief.

'I bet it will,' I said. Though the clouds were flimsy, it was likely to rain.

'I hope so,' he said and added, 'Unlike most other places, rain isn't unpredictable here.'

'True.' I looked up at the sky. 'By the way, India was playing South Africa today. What happened?' Though I knew the result, I asked to tease that die-hard cricket fan. Mr Desai was fond of throwing a party whenever India won. It was obvious that there were no celebrations because of the defeat that day. Had India won, I would have been enjoying beer and chicken at his place.

'The bastards lost as always!' he uttered angrily. 'It's a total waste of time to watch cricket these days. They seldom win. And the worst thing is that they lose even the lollypop matches. Batting second, with a mediocre target of 206, we were 107 for three and then all out for 161!' A filthy abuse in local language fell from his mouth. 'How many times have they made such blunders in the past years, one can't count.' The face that was peaceful before was red with rage now. 'Hell with them! They should be punished badly for such failures!'

This happened time and again. Every time India lost, he would curse and revile the cricketers. But when we won, it was a different story. He would be ecstatic that day. He would throw a party in the evening and drink a lot. I'd have to have my dinner at his place on such occasions.

As he went on castigating each player and comparing them with the veterans of his young days, I thought about him. I wondered why he watched the matches when they disheartened him most of the times. But there was little he could do at the age of seventy-one. As a trustee of the only library of Valai, he had very little work to do. He had two sons—both worked in Ahmedabad and visited Valai occasionally. His daughter was married into a rich family settled in America. He lived here with his wife. I was a friend to Mr Desai whereas Mrs Desai called me 'son'. Though we represented different generations, we had become friends. He was a great personality, and a great husband. And above all, a good human being.

In Valai, he was one of the few people who could communicate in correct English. As a friend, I talked to him about current events since he had a great knowledge about happenings around the world. I discussed my problems with him and the solutions he gave worked most of the times. From him, I'd learned so much. His talk was always full of old age wisdom and experience. He and his wife had become such parental figures that I revered them. Away from home, I went to them whenever I felt alone.

'. . . And despite the adversity, he brought victory to our nation single-handedly which is . . .' He stopped suddenly and asked, 'Are you even listening to me?'

'Yes, of course, I am.' I replied, pulling myself out of my thoughts and concentrating on what he was saying. But the way he raised his hand, I understood that he knew I had lied.

'Ah! You don't like cricket, I know,' he said. 'Tennis. Tennis is what you watch, don't you?'

'Hmm . . .' I replied, for there was no way I could fool him.

'What for? For the long, bare legs those bitches show?'

His language didn't surprise me as I was used to his foul language. I just tittered.

'I know that is what you see. You are a young man, full of passion. It's obvious that you like women. Well, good for you. But I don't understand this game, tennis. I'm okay with cricket. But I'm not going to see the next match on Tuesday. They'll lose again.'

Oh yes, you will! I thought to myself, chuckled and set my eyes on the three waterfowls frolicking in the lake.

Mr Desai also stared at those happy creatures, 'You like them very much, don't you?'

'Ah . . . huh.' I didn't feel like replying.

He smiled and turned sideways to look at me, 'You are a person anyone would fall in love whom.' I looked at his face as he went ahead in my praise. 'There's always a scarcity of gentlemen on this earth and you are one of the few. If I had another daughter, I would have liked you to be my son-in-law.' I guffawed loudly. He went on, 'No, really. Sometimes I wish I had another daughter for you.' Like most other people in Valai, he too was impressed with my personality.

'Thanks, but I'm comfortable being your son and friend,' I said jokingly. We talked about other things for a while until he got to his feet and said, 'It's getting dark. Let me get back home.'

'I can walk with you if you want me to . . .'

'Oh, no. I'll be fine. I'm not *that* old as yet. Just seventy-one, you know,' he said winking with his left eye. I smiled and he walked away saying, 'Then I'll bore you again with my everlasting commentary on cricket.' I could hear a faint laugh at the end of that sentence.

Thinking about my love, I sat there alone until twilight merged into complete darkness. Then a sudden burst of bells chiming in the nearby temple drove me out of my reverie and I got up to go back. The way home was engulfed in darkness, but there was nothing to be afraid of. The charming face I was in love with lit up in my mind again.

It was Sunday, the day for having 'some good chicken and a drink' as Mr Desai used to say. Sukhi had prepared chicken for me and as always it was great. I sat down for dinner and switched on the television. I had my eyes on the screen and food in my mouth, but my attention was elsewhere. I finished my dinner and switched off the TV. It was just nine and there was no sign of sleep in my eyes. James Hadley Chase came to my rescue again, but for no longer than an hour. It was that face that kept coming before my eyes again and again. I'd left the bedroom window open for fresh air and lay on the bed with my thoughts. I remembered what Mr Desai had said that evening, 'You are a young man, full of passion. It's obvious that you like women.'

Women! I smiled wryly. *What if he comes to know the fact that I don't like women?* It will surely come as a terrible shock to him. But then, there's nothing he or I or anyone else could do. I smiled again and thought about the face again. How adorable and innocent! How charming it was! The face that had appeared in my dream was clear now, there was no mist. It was him—Vivek.

Vivek, the love of my life. He was going to get back tomorrow morning. He was just a night away from me. Oh, how desperately I longed for him. Tomorrow is going to be great . . . tomorrow . . .

two

The next morning, I woke up early. I wanted to be ready and waiting when Vivek came. He was expected to be back by the 9 a.m. bus and I would have a chance to chat with him until school time at 10.45.

Unlike the unhurried pace of yesterday, today's quickness in my routine surprised Sukhi. Watching me rush around, she at last asked, 'Are you late for something, Saabji? I could have . . .'

'No, no,' I replied, trying to calm myself down. It was so stupid of me to hurry around like that. It seemed as if I was a young, eager girl waiting to meet her lover. *Idiotic! Childish!* I cursed myself for behaving so in Sukhi's presence. *What must she be thinking? God, I'm a twenty-six year old man! Such behaviour doesn't suit me.* I locked myself in the bathroom and took deep breaths to control my panic. Once I felt calm, I started to shave.

While I was applying foam on my beard, I remembered what Vivek had once said, 'You look great in a day or two old beard.' *Vivek likes me with a stubble.* Should I keep it? I asked myself. *No, it's too grown to be kept any more.* I took the razor and shaved. Had I shaved it yesterday, it would have grown well by now. However, I was gentle with my razor which kept my face from looking extra clean shaven.

By the time I had finished bathing, it was 7.35 a.m. There was still a lot of time left to meet Vivek. I told Sukhi to do what she was doing in the kitchen, and engaged myself in making my own breakfast. That didn't surprise her because she knew I liked cooking and was good at it. I took my time to prepare tea and omelette, thinking about Vivek all the time.

'Tea will be cold by the time the newspapers arrive,' I complained to Sukhi as I sat on the dining table with my breakfast. One thing I hated about this place was the late delivery of the newspaper. I loved to read the newspaper over a cup of hot tea. Whereas, the dailies here were never delivered before 9 a.m. It bothered me more now that I was failing in my battle of not thinking about Vivek. I took some more time in finishing the breakfast. Sukhi sat on the floor and finished her breakfast before I did. When she returned, I could see perplexity writ large in her eyes. Minutes ago, I was making haste as if I had to reach somewhere urgently, and now I was so relaxed that I hadn't even finished eating. *What kind of impression am I generating? Whatever, she's just a maid. She's not going to ask for an explanation. I'm not bound to answer her or anyone else.*

That I took longer to get dressed was obvious because I was to meet the love of my life. It took me five minutes to decide what to wear. I thought about several shirts. *Which one would he like?* I tried some and finally I chose the one in olive green. The trousers were black. Actually, I was lucky that God had bestowed me with a handsome body I had to do little to make myself look good. Everything suited me. In Baroda, my hometown, I was always so conscious about what I wore, but here it didn't matter much since people here weren't that fashion conscious. Glamorous clothing and great hairstyle can earn one love—following that belief of mine, I used to be very conscious of my looks and dressing style in my younger days. It took me time to realize that, to achieve true love, it takes only one's inner ability to love one's beloved and nothing else. But then looks do matter and what was wrong with polishing the beauty I already had! Vivek liked my chic and trendy sense of style and that day I wanted to impress him. I wanted him to praise my looks. I wore the best perfume I had in my collection and applied some gel to my hair. Then I wore my leather shoes and slipped on a wrist watch to complete the picture.

Wow! I watched myself in the mirror for a long moment. *You look gorgeous, Kaushik.* I couldn't help praising my appearance. *Had you not got glasses, your looks would have been perfect!* Nevertheless, I still looked good and in some people's opinion the rectangular frame of my spectacles actually complemented my face. I removed the glasses from my face and the handsome reflection in the mirror turned blurry. I put it on again and gave myself a closer look. For a moment, I felt I'd gone overboard. But then I thought that this was all to impress Vivek. I was a handsome man, fair, tall, slim, sharp features—everything that's necessary to make a lady killer. *A lady killer!* A scornful smile flickered over my face. Girls had always been crazy about me but I was never interested in them. It was men who interested me. Always. And the latest one I was getting crazy about was Vivek, a sixteen year old boy from the school where I worked as a teacher.

I had nothing else to do except waiting until the watch showed 9 a.m. so I left my place and kept sauntering around aimlessly. It was a fine July day with no sign of clouds overhead. I took a long, leisurely walk so that no one would recognize the anxiety in my behaviour. I kept roaming till 8.50 a.m. Valai was such a small place that one could easily walk around most of the city without getting tired. Mr Gavit, my neighbour, had a motorbike he seldom used. He allowed me to use that bike but that rarely happened. I knew that Vivek liked bikes and so I took it only when I was going out with him.

Situated among hills, Valai was one of the highest points of the district. The entire place could be seen from the sunset point. From there, it looked like a large bowl full of houses. It was open and spacious, and buildings were nowhere to be seen. There were some restaurants too but no hotels at all. Besides the only quality Chinese restaurant of my choice, there were some cheap eating places where people liked to go. The tourists had to stay at the government guesthouse, but most of them preferred to stay at Sapttara, the famous hill station of the Dangs about forty kilometres from Valai. The central area of Valai was known as Shaheed Chowk, the place where martyrs had fought and died for the independence of India. Sadly, fast-food carts were occupying this area now. There was a bus depot, a small garden, two hospitals, a high school, a college of arts and commerce, a radio station, and a reservoir called Bandharo, which supplied water to the entire town. The town, however, lacked in many things such as a town hall, a college of science, and a proper drainage system. At the eastern end of Valai, there was an open field, a maidan that was used for public gatherings. A large concrete stage had been built on one side of the ground and the audience had to sit on the bare, uneven, grassy land. Time and again, the people of Valai had demanded a town hall, but they had received only empty promises from their municipal candidates. Our school offered the science stream, but education level in that particular stream wasn't up to the mark. The percentage of success was very low and the facilities available at the school for the students of science were not as good as it should have been. No further study in science was available in the entire district of the Dangs and students had to go to neighbouring towns for graduation in science.

The population of this beautiful place was nearly four thousand. It surprised me in my early days here that almost everybody knew everyone. It was very much like a large, extended family. For someone like me who sought complete isolation, sometimes it felt suffocating because you had to greet every single person you met on the way. One could try and avoid them, but it was considered rude not to greet the people you knew. Then again, I was a teacher whom people respected. The kind of looks and personality I had was very rare in this primitive area. In the two years of my stint here, I'd felt that people adored me more than I could ever imagine. I didn't know what they particularly liked in me but I think more than my physical appearance, the ease with which I connected with these simple people drew them to me.

Socially, there were many class distinctions, but being an outsider, I could afford to ignore categorizing people. I treated all of them in a similar way and tried to be friendly. To them, I was like a complete man who had a secure government job, great looks, and knowledge. I had received some marriage proposals too. Besides, ever since I had set my foot in Valai, women had been approaching me with different propositions—some decent, some not so decent. They tried to impress me in different ways. Both the married ones and the spinsters, indirectly asked for a physical relationship. This was surprising since I had the notion that people here were not so bold and open as they were in bigger cities like Baroda. But later, I found that my judgement about the people here was quite wrong. In fact, extramarital relationships and premarital sex are not taboo amongst even the most primitive tribes.

I work as a teacher of English language at the Jeevan Bharati School, the biggest high school of the district. There were seventeen classes from class eighth to twelfth. I taught English to the eleventh and twelfth grades of commerce, arts and science streams, and my colleague, Ms Patel, taught classes from eighth to the tenth. There were two primary schools in Valai. Our school accommodated all their students after the seventh class. Since I was young and broadminded in my attitude, the students got along very well with me and my interactions with them was quite affable. Unlike other teachers, I treated my students as friends. I was utterly satisfied with my occupation and what I was earning from it. Being at the school with the young ones was something I absolutely adored. Had I been in some other profession, I wouldn't be as happy. Besides my amicable nature, my good looks and personality had made me popular in school since the very first day. Many girls at the school also liked me. I could see the admiration in their eyes, but the poor girls didn't know that the object of my affection was someone else!

Behind the large school compound were two hostel buildings, one for the boys and the other for girls. Individual compounds separated both the hostels and what kept the boys from peeking into the girls' hostel was an enormous, evergreen banyan tree. But the biggest problem for the boys was not the tree, or the compound wall. It was Mrs Dalvi, the matron of the girls' hostel who was known as 'Hitler' because of her strict nature. But just like a river that hollows out even the biggest stones in its way, the boys had found out their own ways to meet the girls.

Vivek lived in the boys' hostel since his village was about thirty-five kilometres from Valai. To the left of the two storeyed school building was a staff colony surrounded by huge trees where I had my living quarters along with sixteen more. Including mine, only eight of them were occupied. All of us had been given a similar house—walls made of stone and concrete, with roofs of corrugated, concrete sheets. An enormous gulmohar tree spread over my little house that was second from the end of the colony. The beauty of the gulmohar in summer was simply ethereal. In fact, all the quarters were under the shade of the vast canopy of the gulmohar trees. And the grandeur of the grove turned into something of a breathtaking visual feast when nature crowned the trees in a bright orange glow.

The quarter behind mine was not occupied. Since I had a big house in Baroda, the place I was given felt very small to me. There were just three small areas divided into a hall—not big enough to actually be called a living room, a kitchen and a bedroom. In the name of furniture, I had a double bed, a cupboard, a small dining table for three, a settee, a writing desk, two cane chairs, a TV table, and a storage cabinet in the kitchen. I could have purchased more but there was not enough room for more. The furnishings were plain and simple, cheap and unimpressive.

Since I wasn't sure of how long I was going to survive in this small town, I had bought all that second hand furniture from the local market. The most expensive things that I had purchased being the television and the refrigerator. Though my salary wasn't that good in the beginning, I could have afforded to rent a place of my own choice. Unfortunately, there were no such places in the entire town. People were used to living in petite houses. Not just in the size of the residences, but also in other luxuries such as fashion and comfort. Other than the bare necessities, their purchasing power was limited. Most people belonged to the middle and lower classes, but even those who had money liked to refrain from showing off.

In my early days here, I used to wear trendy clothes and artificial accessories that I used to wear in Baroda, but then I realized that people of Valai were uncomfortable with such things. Most of them would stare at me when I went out dressed like a fop, so I limited my dressing style. I avoided wearing the funky T-shirts I had always been crazy about and tried to look sober. My sunglasses remained locked in my wardrobe and artificial accessories were forgotten. The only thing I couldn't give up were perfumes. I had a large collection of branded perfumes which was no less than a treasure to me. And despite discarding all those fashion supplements, I still remained the tidiest person in Valai.

When I had come to this beautiful land of Valai for the first time, my knowledge about this far-flung land had been almost zero. I knew little about the customs, rituals and lifestyle of the locals. It took me a while to get acclimatized to the atmosphere and lifestyle of this place because I had to deal with something so different from my hometown. I hardly had any thing to do here, whereas in Baroda there were so many activities going on all around. How busy I used to be in Baroda! Swimming, tennis, long drives, movies, college . . . the day flew by instantly. Here, in Valai, there were no avenues for enjoyment at all. There was a video theatre, but watching a movie on its tiny screen was a terrible experience. Then again, I wasn't so fond of watching Hindi movies and they never showed English ones. I liked Hollywood flicks but there was practically no audience for foreign films. There was a movie library which was always short of the latest Hollywood films and one wouldn't find anything else but those exaggerated action flicks of Jackie Chan, Arnold Schwarzenegger and Sylvester Stallone. I had seen them all when I was in college.

Valai was such a remote place that there still was no provision of satellite channels. The only way to pass time was to go to the public library, but no one can read all the time. I needed a change, but there was little to be entertained with. I had travelled through the district and by now, there was almost nothing left to be visited. I'd never been idle, but the sluggish lifestyle of this place made me inactive. And to kill time, I had slowed down the pace of my activities. Swaying between Valai and Baroda, present and past, I didn't know which life I wanted. I used to tell myself, 'Boy, you've got into the wrong place! You definitely deserve a better place than Valai.' I really felt like a fish out of water. Baroda had everything for a person like me and I could have moved to some other city similar to my hometown but the thing that kept me from leaving Valai was Vivek.

The bus was due at 9 a.m., but I didn't want to be at the bus stop. I stood at a distance from the stop and waited. It was Saturday afternoon when I had last seen Vivek before he had left for his village. He was away from me for just some forty hours, but it seemed like he had been gone for weeks. The separation of even a second from your beloved seems ages long in love. I counted every second until the bus appeared at the far end of the road.

Okay, he's back! I took a few deep breaths and began walking towards the bus stop. My walking pace was so well controlled that I would hit the stop exactly when the bus stopped there. From a distance, I had my eyes on only the exit door of the bus and there emerged in my view the lovely boy disembarking with a few other young ones of his age. But while passing by the bus stop, I pretended to be unaware of his return and kept walking.

'Sir!' Vivek called me from behind. Even though I knew he was going to accost me, I turned around as if I was surprised to see him.

'Hi,' I greeted him exercising great control over my excitement.

Vivek was dressed in his school uniform, a white half-sleeve shirt and khaki pants. The clothes didn't complement his beauty yet he looked attractive as always. At five feet eight inches, he was one of the tallest boys of his age in school. By exercising regularly, he had built his structure well. The well-toned chest and biceps were easily visible through his shirt. The features on his triangle-shaped face were not great, yet captivating. Had the nose been a bit small, his looks would have been just so perfect. But it was his brown eyes that truly reflected the purity and gentleness of his heart. In all, Vivek was a good looking boy who radiated warmth and affability. However, strangely enough, he was not so confident of his appearance. He was disappointed with the shape of his nose and the complexion of his skin which was wheatish. It was my looks, he believed, that were impeccable.

'Good morning.' Jovial by nature, he greeted me with a lovely smile. That was what I was crazy about! His smile—warm and innocent.

'Good morning,' I replied and added, 'I was just passing by.' *Damn it!* I bit the tip of my tongue unseen. He hadn't asked me where I was going. I had expected him to and

Mayur Patel

that's why I had blurted out even before he had asked. 'So you're back.' I tried an artificial smile to conceal my embarrassment. 'Great to see you!'

'Same here,' he said and added, 'see you at the school!' Then he turned back towards the hostel. He hadn't noticed my appearence, hadn't praised my clothes. That was unexpected! I wanted him to be with me for longer than this but he seemed to have no such interest. *He hadn't missed me!* I sighed with disappointment. *Why should he? He's not gay. He's not in love with me. He doesn't even have any idea about my intentions for him. He doesn't know that one of his teachers is deeply in love with him.* I kept thinking about him on the way back home. My enthusiasm was gone. It was so stupid of me that I had thought so much about Vivek.

At home, I locked myself in the bedroom, lay on the bed and remained there until it was time to leave for school. I changed my shirt and put on a regular shirt, for I didn't want to be the centre of attention of other people. The day was no longer as warm and positive as it had been in the morning. Vivek hadn't noticed my looks and I felt really bad. I had no intentions of meeting him anymore!

Other than Saturday, the timing of the school was 10.45 a.m. to 5 p.m. and I had a lecture in Vivek's class on all days. On Mondays, I had to take his class in the sixth period but I wasn't excited about it that day. *He hadn't missed me; he wasn't as excited about seeing me as I was.* My thoughts disheartened me, and even my colleagues noticed it. Mrs Dhondi, the social studies teacher, even asked me if I was sick. The bleakness of my temperament was transparent in public and it had to be controlled. I tried to behave normally but it was with an effort.

It was recess when I happened to meet Vivek again. I was on my way home for lunch while he was coming from the other direction.

'Good afternoon, sir,' he greeted me. It was I who had taught him to greet people this way. He made it a point to wish me in the morning, afternoon and evening.

'Good afternoon!' I beamed at him, trying not to let him know how dejected I was with the early morning meeting.

'Are you free after school?' he asked.

'Yes, I am,' I said with a sudden leap of joy.

'Okay. Then I'll see you at your place in the evening,' he said. Then before leaving with his friends towards the playground, he asked, 'Why did you change that shirt you were wearing in the morning? It was looking nice.'

He ran away, leaving me pleasantly surprised. That was what I had expected him to tell me in the morning! Better late than never, I thought and chuckled. *That means he had noticed my looks, and had liked it. It was just that he didn't say that when he should have. Oh, man!* I smiled and walked away. *It just takes a single thought to perk you up, Kaushik.*

The rest of the day was again full of cheer.

The first thing I always wanted to have after getting back home from school was the evening tea. As Sukhi came at around 5.30 in the evening, I had to prepare my tea by myself and I had no problem with that. For a while, I thought of waiting for Vivek to come and have tea with me, and then I remembered that he didn't take tea. It was milk that he liked. I left some milk for him in the refrigerator and made tea with the rest. He had never been punctual, so I had no idea when he was going to come. After having a nice ginger tea, I changed, took a quick shower and slipped into my shorts. Then I sat with the newspaper in the veranda.

Born in an upper middle class family, I had had a great childhood with my elder brother, Smit, and younger sister, Ridham. My father, Ramanlal Mistry, was a well-known lawyer in Baroda. He had earned well in his profession and had wanted me to become a lawyer too. I don't know why, but I had never liked that profession. Since childhood, I had wanted to become a teacher, a profession my father saw no future in. He had always told me that there's no money to earn in teaching, but money was never of prime importance to me. I deeply respected my teachers and believed that they were doing a great service by giving a good education and teaching the ethics of life to children. The other option in my father's mind for me was to join the family business that my uncle owned. Chachaji, my father's younger brother, owned a chemical factory at Ankleshwar and earned much more than my father did. He also wanted either Smit or me to join his factory since he did not have a son. But my goal was different. It was English language I wanted to specialize in. It was a shock to my teachers when I took the arts stream in the eleventh class despite standing fourth in the entire school in the Senior Secondary Certificate Examinations (SSC). In their opinion, I had made a mistake, while according to my father, I was the biggest idiot. But I knew my goal. I was determined about what I wanted to do. I respected my father and understood his perspective, but then, as an individual, I had a right to choose my career and I did so with the moral support of my mother.

I had to fight to convince Smit and Ridham but there was no hope of doing the same with my father. His stubbornness didn't let him give up even after the endless debates we had. I have a feeling that there was no way I or anyone else on this earth could win over his obstinacy. From my side though, the decision was made and it wasn't going to change. I had studied English in high school and college for seven years. My father was never happy with my level of education, but my mother always backed me up.

Like my brother and sister, I was very close to my mother who was a person of great poise and deferential mannerisms. She was a housewife and a great cook. Being intuitive, she knew the mood of her children very well. She was a kind-hearted, spiritual woman, and believed that every thing happens by God's grace. She took life easily whereas my father was a strict man in terms of values and etiquettes. He was not an atheist, but hardly gave credit to the Almighty for anything he had achieved in his life. A believer in assiduousness, he always said that a man can choose and change his faith by hard work. And he was right because he had begun his life empty handed and whatever he had achieved by hook or by crook, had been the result of his fight against odds such as poverty and scarcity. He was proud of his hard-earned wealth because he and my uncle had struggled a lot in life. From him, I had inherited the qualities of punctuality, courteousness and practicality in life; while a legacy of kindness, honesty and spiritualism was a gift from my mother. My mother's values had always meant more to me and it was with her that I felt connected.

I got along well with my brother and sister too. Smit had studied commerce and worked as an executive in a local firm, while Ridham, respecting father's wish of having at least one lawyer in our family to inherit his experience, became a lawyer. She had agreed to take up our father's profession on one condition that she wouldn't practise with him in the beginning of her career. She wanted to learn the basics of law on her own.

Within a year of my shifting to Valai, Smit had married Namrata. An independent woman, Namrata was fairly good looking and was so nice by nature that people told Smit that he was lucky to have such a spouse. All of them wanted me to marry one such girl. Though Namrata and I were two different individuals as far as our likes and mindsets were concerned, we shared a healthy relationship. She worked in a travel agency where her charming personality made quite a difference.

Baroda, the city where I grew up and studied, was a big place and there's no comparison between Baroda and Valai. Famous for its number of gardens, Baroda is a rich place. There are high-rise buildings, cinema halls, sports clubs and many such things that were missing from Valai. Sometimes, I miss those luxuries, but then, it was my decision to take up a job in this under-developed town. There was a reason for that: I had finished my studies at the age of twenty-three and taken up teaching in a local high school. In the mean time, I had received an offer to join Jeevan Bharati School in Valai. Initially, the thought of going to an unfamiliar place had excited me. My family though was against my idea of shifting to a remote corner in a tribal area. My father had already been unhappy with me working as a teacher, so it was obvious that he was angry when he came to know I was serious about the new job. According to him, there was no future in an underdeveloped place like Valai and he argued with me on the several disadvantages of living there. Getting a mediocre salary of Rs 2,500 per month and that too in an area like this, was according to him both insulting and frustrating. The truth was that unlike my father, brother and sister, I was never too ambitious. My aims in life were limited, or I could say my life was aimless. Having a large bank balance and owning luxurious things had never been my idea of a successful life. Family, friends and love mattered more to me. Though I'd indulged in all the luxuries of life in Baroda, I had never let them be my weakness. At Valai, I missed them but then, it wasn't as if I couldn't live without them. After having seen the limited lifestyle of the people of the Dangs, I had decided to live like the average Indian.

However, not just my father, but Smit had also been negative about the Dangs. And he actually fought with me when he came to know I was thinking of giving that offer a second thought.

It was strange that all my life I had been timid, not wanting to get out of my unchallenging life, and when I dared to get out of my shell, all of them were against my will. I tried to convince them but they seemed to be deaf to my pleas. My mother was the only person who understood my point of view and was ready to allow me to fly alone.

Unexpectedly, Smit had become as tenacious as father, and at that time, I had to surrender to their wishes because I knew that they all loved me a lot and didn't want me to go away from home. Being separated from my family surely would be tough on me as well had I accepted the job. So, I worked at Baroda for about a year, and then something happened that forced me to give up not only the job but the place too. By then the circumstances had turned so unsupportable at home that none of my family members tried to stop me the second time. It took just a phone call and I got the job after the formality of an interview. I had shifted to Valai two years ago.

In the beginning, everything was fine, but then I missed my life in Baroda. Trendy clothes, fast food, entertainment, family and friends—my life was colourless without them. Away from home, I felt lonely and alienated since there was nobody I could easily relate to. It took me a while to draw myself out of my cocoon and begin to mingle with the locals. The lifestyle, the routine, everything here was calm and slow. Accustomed to the throngs in Baroda, I sometimes got irritated and bored of the openness and emptiness of Valai. But I somehow managed and oriented myself with the new circumstances because I didn't want to go back for certain reasons. Time elapsed and I fell in love with this place as it had its own specialities that were rare in Baroda or any other major city. The best things about this place was its honesty, purity and simplicity. At Valai, I didn't need to impress anyone. While Baroda lay shrouded in layers of hypocrisy, and artificialities. I had to dress up well most of the time. People were very concerned about your looks and the way you presented yourself. 'Showing off' was a widespread disease and I had been a part of it for years. I had to be aware of countless etiquettes and manners while going out. Like others, I presented myself with false facades, as if I were ashamed or displeased with my real self. I was thankful to Valai and the people here, because of whom I could reach my self. The place and the environment had helped me meet the real person inside me.

It was 6.05 p.m. when Vivek came running. 'Sorry, I'm late.' He apologized panting.

'Always,' I said and welcomed him. 'Come in.'

He had a polythene bag in his hand which he offered me as we stepped in. He sat on the settee to catch his breath.

'What's this?' I opened the polythene bag which was crammed with vegetables, green onions, fenugreek, gourd and beet. Since the soil of Valai was porous and stony, vegetables and fruits were hard to cultivate. They had to be brought from the nearby villages and towns, so the prices were always high. Vivek's father was a farmer, so Vivek often brought me fresh vegetables from his father's farms. Underneath the vegetables, there was a small steel vessel that contained besan laddoos, the round sweets made of gramflour. My face lit up. 'Thanks,' I said and put one in my mouth and offered him one.

'I have had it,' he said. 'My mother told me to share them with the people I like.'

For a moment I stopped chewing. *I'm one of the people he likes!* I was feeling on cloud nine. I put the rest of the laddoos in the kitchen and asked Vivek if he would like to have some milk. When he said no, I insisted but he wanted me to go out with him instead of staying at home. I changed quickly and set out with him. We spent a lot of time together. I was accustomed to taking an evening walk and with Vivek, it turned out to be a treat. Usually, we would take a long walk in the woods or go to the sunset point or we would just sit under the neem tree on the hill by my house. He wanted to go to the hill, so we moved in that direction.

All the residential houses in the staff colony were surrounded by trees of all sizes. It was just the beginning of the monsoon and once it would start raining regularly, the land would be blessed with uncountable species of weeds.

'Watch out for the snakes,' I said as we slowly paced through the grassy land.

Once after the first rain, when the burrows of the reptiles were submerged in water, a snake had come in our way when we were going towards the hill. I had been so scared when Vivek had bent down to catch that five feet long, brown snake known as Dhaman. I had cautioned Vivek, but he hadn't listened and I had watched horrified as he grabbed the tiny head of that hissing reptile! He knew it wasn't poisonous. He had told me that a reptile, caught by its head, was helpless even if it was poisonous. Meanwhile, the snake had wrapped itself around Vivek's hand and I gaped at the fearless boy. How relaxed he had been! He had told me to touch it but I couldn't dare until I was fully convinced that it wasn't poisonous and wasn't going to harm me. It was the first time in my entire life that I had touched a snake. It had felt cold and my fingers reeked with its smell. We had picked it up and left it in the jungle. I was surprised to know Vivek had such skill in catching reptiles. It was his uncle who had taught him the art.

'So, what's the story at home?' I asked as we sat under the tree.

'Everything's fine. I had fun there,' he replied and then added excitedly, 'actually, a buffalo gave birth to a calf a couple of days ago.'

'That's nice,' I said. *You had fun, but I was totally lost without you.*

'What did you do over the weekend?' he asked, my eyes fixed on his animated face.

'Just routine, nothing special,' I answered but couldn't help but say, 'In fact, I missed you so much.'

'Oh, really?' He sounded as if he liked that. 'I also remembered you there.'

He thought about me! I found myself flying.

We stayed there for about an hour talking about the weather, and about the defeat of the Indian cricket team in the previous day's match. He loved cricket and was dejected with that loss. By the time we got back, it was dark. The half moon was cloaked under a thick quilt of bleak clouds.

'Thanks,' I said when we were to part.

'For what?' He asked.

'For spending your time with me and for the laddoos.' I grinned.

He nodded and walked away wishing me 'good night'. I kept my eyes on him until he disappeared into the darkness. I wondered if I would ever be able to tell him that I loved him.

three

Vivek was the first child of his parents. Thirty-five kilometres from Valai, was a small village named Kurkas, where his family lived. His village was known for the apiaries on its outskirts. Like most villages of the Dangs, Vivek's village also had a primary school where his two younger sisters studied. His father was a farmer and grew grains and seasonal vegetables. They were not poor but there was a shortage of money in his family. Vivek's father spent a lot of money on Vivek's old, asthmatic grandmother.

Vivek, a student of arts, was not a topper but he was above average. He was good in maths and average in English, the subject I taught. He wanted to graduate so that he could have a decent job and earn for his family. He was crazy about cricket and was good at it. His place in the school cricket team was fixed and like most young players, he idolized Sachin Tendulkar and loved to watch cricket on TV. It was always a red-letter day for him when India won. Besides cricket, he liked to roam around with friends and with me too.

I can't remember exactly when I had seen him for the first time because he was in the ninth class when I came here. Last year, Ms Patel, the senior English teacher was involved in an accident which had forced her to take complete bed rest for about a month and, since there was no other teacher of English, I had to take up her classes as well. I knew it was going to be tough, but I couldn't disrespect the principal's request. As Vivek was a student of the tenth class, I taught him too. In the beginning he was just one of my thirty-five students. Then I began to feel that he was the most charming boy in his class. In fact, I had not seen a more charismatic young boy in entire Valai. It was hard not to notice that tall, wheat-complexioned, brown-eyed, athletic lad. Besides having eye-catching features, he had an attractive, muscular body that complemented everything he wore, especially half sleeve T-shirts. He had everything in his conspicuous personality to make a strong impression, but I had never been a believer in love at first sight. I feel that love can bloom anywhere, anytime and it can be anything—a pleasant glance, a warm smile or a scent that attracts you towards a person. But true love shouldn't happen impulsively. The phrase 'love at first sight' should be changed to 'affection at first sight'. I have witnessed many such instances of love in my college days—even experienced some. Girls would propose to me without knowing my true self. Such attractions had a short life. In my opinion, two people should take their time to know each other better.

Vivek and his fellow student had come to me with a grammatical problem one day. He had diffidently asked me for help and I had been unable to take my eyes off his sexy, brown eyes. 'You've got beautiful eyes,' I had told him. That had been our first meeting when we had actually talked to each other. My solving his problem had been the beginning of our relationship. When he passed the SSC examination and had taken up arts in the eleventh class, he became my regular student.

One day, he had stopped me in the passage with another problem in grammar. I was on my way to meeting Mr Solanki, the principal, and as the problem would have taken more time, I asked Vivek if he could come to my place after school. He agreed and we met at my place in the evening. It was the active–passive voice that was troubling him. I took my time to teach him and gave him a little exercise. He was to came back with the solution the next day.

That's how we started meeting at my place, much like private coaching. He'd asked me if he could bring his friends along. I said no because I had no intentions of giving tuitions. Also because, by then I had begun to like him and didn't want anyone to disturb the two of us. Other pupils did try to be in my good books, but it was only Vivek I was partial to. And for obvious reasons. Most times we met at my place but sometimes, for a change, I took his lessons under the neem tree. I not only helped him in English but also in other subjects. History lessons were a big bore to him. I had faced the same problem in my school days. But as a teacher now, I could make the lessons easy and interesting for him. I narrated the history of the Mughal era and the East India Company in such a way, that it was far more comprehensible to him than what was there in his text books.

The more we met, the more we liked each other's company. From a teacher–student, our relationship developed into a genuine friendship, but I must admit that being a homosexual, there had always been this feeling of physical attraction since the beginning. Then a time came when we started meeting even without a reason. We would sit under the neem tree, visit the sunset point, the Valai dam or go to the jungle. We would spend hours together. Being with Vivek were moments of happiness in my daily life. I adored talking to him and as time passed, I realized that I couldn't help but think about him all the time. He filled my life with joy; otherwise there was a time when I had felt terribly alone in Valai. I had prayed to God to send me a true friend, a good companion, and what he had gifted me was this boy. That's why I called him Lord Shiva's blessing.

We kept meeting every day and a time came when I found myself going crazy about him. I woke up every morning wishing to see him first. That was love. I was in love with him. I was in love with my student. People who knew me considered it unusual that I had befriended Vivek. Nobody dared ask me on my face, but I could read the question in their eyes: 'What the hell are you doing with this boy?' In the beginning of our friendship, I would ask myself if Vivek was suitable for me because we were at variance in many ways, age, culture, family background, education, rearing and many other things. But one thing we had in common—we genuinely liked each other and our feelings were true in every sense. People believed that the rustic boy wasn't worthy of my companionship, but only I knew how deserving he was. And wasn't it enough that he was loyal to me! The boy who was ordinary for others was special to me. Perhaps, that's what love is—whatever is ordinary to others is extraordinary to you.

Vivek wasn't the most handsome guy I had ever seen in my life, but there was strong magnetism in his personality which attracted me to him. I was fond of seeking out his face in the crowd and even a brief glimpse filled my heart with delight. A slight brush of his body or a pleasant smile from him brought me great excitement. I must say that he had a great smile. His smile, as innocent as of a child, brought a smile on my face and made me forget all my miseries. A fact I had told him several times.

Then again, it wasn't as if everything about him was good. Being an intellectual, I'd always liked intelligent company. Vivek was not a fool, but neither was he very bright. I felt that many a time he was unable to understand me. Probably my thoughts were too deep for a sixteen year old.

Yet I got attracted to him because there was some kind of magic in his personality which was hard to ignore. He had some other qualities that are rarely found in people of his age—he believed in 'forgiving and forgetting' and he never lied. The purity of his heart was reflected in his eyes. I had taken a lot of time in recognizing these virtues in him, but the thing I'm not hesitant about admitting is that what really attracted me to him was his good looks. For me, his physical appearance was the biggest inducement. Everything else came after that.

He was clumsy and there was still a little childishness in his disposition. Besides being clumsy, he lacked in good manners too. I drew his attention towards them and always told him to work on his bad habits but, he forgot most of the time. I had taught him table manners and other routine etiquettes. He was so amazed with all that since he had never learned anything like that before. According to him, he had learned more with me than he had in his entire life.

Sometimes I felt that I advised him too much, and even though he never showed his displeasure about it, I tried to hold back. I loved Vivek, but didn't want to dominate him. I liked him for what he was, but then I felt that if I helped him to change, he could be a better person in many ways. I wanted him to progress and to have a flourishing career. And I believed that it was my responsibility to help him to become refined. I wanted him to grow in his life in every possible way. When he would go to college, I wanted him to be richer in mannerisms and that's why I was keen to teach him things he'd never learned before.

Vivek belonged to a caste lower than mine, but caste or religious differences were never an issue with me. Many of my friends at Baroda belonged to lower castes as well, but I never had a problem in being with them or even eating with them from the same plate.

However, the thought that I had fallen in love with a student bore through me, giving me a feeling of indignity. I told myself that it was wrong and that I must refrain from rearing such feelings for him. But I was helpless! I couldn't kill my burning desire of attaining his love someday. Neither could I put him out of my mind. The more I tried to forget him, the more he pulled me towards himself. Finally, I accepted that I was madly, deeply in love with him. But the guilt always remained with me that it was dishonourable.

Vivek was a health conscious boy. He exercised regularly and therefore had a good physique. He was immensely strong too. He could alone do physically demanding jobs that required two men. I had seen him doing so and was surprised to know what a strong bull he was! He could lift heavy things that I couldn't lift at all. Be it the ease with which he could lift three or four heavy cricket kits or the ease with which he shifted the writing table single-handedly at my place, his physical strength never ceased to marvel me. Almost every morning he went for a jog with his friends. One day, he had asked me if I wanted to join them. I got ready and jogged with them for a few days but couldn't keep up with it. I hated to wake up in the small hours of the morning everyday and even Vivek's company couldn't change that habit. We later changed it to something more convenient, I would tell him at night if I was interested in going the next morning and they all would come to wake me up at dawn. We would then take a longish run through Valai. People at school would find me yawning the day I did that!

There was a cricket match between India and South Africa on Tuesday. Vivek hadn't come to see me in the morning because he was watching the match at his hostel. The students had to follow the hostel rules. There was a TV but they were only allowed to watch cricket matches and a weekend movie on Sundays that Doordarshan, the national network, showed. They could watch news broadcasts but there were very few who liked to do that. My TV remained switched off because I had no interest in cricket. I never had, but just because Vivek played the game and liked it very much, I had begun to take interest in the sport. When you love someone deeply, you start to like things your beloved likes. You want to do things of your lover's choice. You want to develop new interests and hobbies so that you can have a chance to be together more often. It helps to strengthen your relationship. Watching cricket was my attempt to get closer to him and to let him realize how important he was to me. My knowledge of cricket was only that I knew the senior and key players of the national team. It was Vivek who had familiarized me with the basic rules of the sport. I invited him to my place to watch and even though he liked to watch it with his friends at the hostel, he joined me for a few hours at least. Sometimes, I invited his friends also and on these occasions, my place would be full of young men. But most of the time I went to Mr Desai's house to enjoy a nice party.

At school, I had come to know that India had elected to bat first and the opening pair was doing great. When

I was having my lunch at home during recess, Mr Desai called me up. 'It looks like we are going to win!' he said enthusiastically.

'Great!' I showed some excitement. 'What's the score, sir?'

'We've scored 314 and so far they've lost two wickets for seventy-one.'

'Fantastic!'

'Do join the party at my home in the evening.'

I knew it was coming.

'If we win . . .' I tried to be naughty.

'What do you mean?' His voice hardened for a second. 'Of course we're going to win.'

'Sure, we will!' I laughed.

'Come early.'

'I will.'

Pratap Desai was amongst the first few people I had become acquainted with in my early days here. We'd met at the public library and the daily exchange of smiles had turned into friendship. He was older in years but young at heart. His thoughts were open and secular, and whatever he said was always full of wisdom. We continued to meet at the library. Then he invited me to his place for a match one day, and our friendship began. He had no close relatives in Valai, but was good at winning friends of all ages. I was the youngest, but always enjoyed the company of older men as much as they did mine.

Pratap Desai had worked as an engineer in the Public Works Department, for thirty-seven years. And when he retired, he chose not to go back to Ahmedabad, his native place. He was used to the serenity of this town and wanted to spend the rest of his life here. His children had asked him to live with them many times but he had no intentions of leaving Valai.

While having tea in the evening, I switched on the TV to learn the score. Bad light had stopped the game for more than an hour and a half after noon, that's why it was still on. The opposite team was batting on 260 with three wickets in hand. Seven overs were yet to be bowled and the way Hansi Cronje was batting, it was anybody's game. After having my tea, I decided to leave for Mr Desai's. I washed my face with a face wash, wet my hair with water and looked at myself in the mirror. For a while I couldn't take my eyes off my face which looked handsomer than ever—no sunken cheeks and pimples anymore. Acne had been my biggest enemy in youth and despite trying nearly every remedy suggested, I was not able to get rid of them. They did vanish over a period of time and now there was nothing to be bothered about.

All of Mr Desai's old friends were there at his place. Greeting them all with a loud 'hello', I went straight into the kitchen where Mrs Desai was busy cooking. Gayatri Desai, a short, slender and fair woman in her late sixties, was a pious soul and unlike Mr Desai, had a quiet, gracious, and content nature. A woman of great sympathy, she called me 'son' and I addressed her as 'mom'. I had with me a polythene bag which contained some chocolates and pastries in a box. Those were the things they liked, but never bought for themselves since they believed they had passed the age to be indulging in such things. I placed the bag in the fruit basket that lay in the middle of the dining table. Then I talked to Mrs Desai for a while before I joined the bunch of pensioners who were enjoying every moment of the match that was getting more and more thrilling with each ball. Every dot ball brought a smile of relief, whereas every boundary or a six disappointed us. It was fun to hear the oldies curse the South African captain whenever he hit the ball for a boundary. The fall of wickets created an uproar of joy among us. Then came the climax—the last over, six balls remaining, eleven runs to be scored, just one wicket left and Cronje was still batting. The tension was at its peak when he hit two boundaries back to back—lots of abuses for the bowler, Javagal Shrinath.

With the fourth ball, our heart was in our mouths as Cronje went for a six. The ball sailed in the air towards the boundary and then fell straight into Saurav Ganguly's hands. The final cheers rattled the house! India won and our party began which was going to last for at least two hours.

Mrs Desai was a great cook. She had prepared chicken curry and rice. Rotis, Indian bread, had been ordered from the bakery and alcohol was always available in Mr Desai's storeroom. Everyone, other than me, took whisky. I took a bottle of chilled beer. We got drunk and enjoyed ourselves on the terrace under the moonlight. Throughout the party, they kept talking about the brilliant match and all I did was to listen, smile and nod in agreement.

When I was to leave at 10.30 p.m., Mrs Desai suggested that I stay back for the night since I had had quite a lot to drink.

'I'm fine, thanks. I'll be okay!' I wished them 'good night' and made for my home. The town was under the blanket of the night. The road home was as deserted as a crematorium. Valai had no nightlife—no pubs, no discos, nothing. Even the word 'nightlife' was alien here. A feeling of loneliness and emptiness pervaded the place. My place was within ten minutes' walking distance from Mr Desai's. While walking back I realized that I had had more beer than was good. It took me longer to reach my home, but I finally reached safely. There was nothing to be afraid of except the wild animals as they sometimes intruded into residential areas late at night.

I unlocked the door and went straight to the settee in the hall. Mrs Desai had asked me to call her as soon as I reached home, but I forgot all about it. Neither was I capable of making a phone call. I fell into a deep stupor as I slumped onto the settee.

four

Every morning I woke up with the sound of the prayers by the girls in the girls' hostel. They would wake me up at 7 a.m. daily. That day, the first thing I did right after leaving my bed was to call up Mrs Desai and apologize. I felt guilty that she would have waited for my call until midnight. She said she had called me but I had probably not been able to hear the ring in my inebriated state. Before we ended our conversation, I apologized again. Mrs Desai was like a mother to me and I had troubled her. I promised myself that I'd never drink that much in future.

This was not a good start and during the rest of the morning, nothing happened to make it better. I had to take tablets for a massive headache. Then I saw Sukhi who was sweeping the floor. She had a lump on her forehead.

'What happened?' I asked and touched my forehead with a finger to indicate as she looked at me. The unfortunate woman had a wry smile on her face. 'What else would it be? Babu beat me up.'

By now I was close to her. 'Let me see,' I said and she showed me her wound. There was a big swelling on the right side of her temple.

I visualized her slovenly-looking husband. 'Bastard!' I cursed and then asked, 'Why?'

'He wanted to party with his drunkard friends and I

didn't have any money. He wanted to celebrate India's victory in the cricket match. I said I had nothing to give him and he hit me with an empty bottle of wine.'

'What a brute!' Indignant, I cursed him again. 'Massage some balm on the lump. It's in the–'

'I've done that,' she said and got back to sweeping again.

'I don't understand why you tolerate his cruelty? Why don't you leave that . . .' I swallowed the invective but Sukhi knew it. She just smiled and busied herself in her work.

Sukhi, a poor, lower caste woman in her mid-twenties, worked as a maid in three houses including mine. She had parents-in-law, two little daughters and a drunkard of a husband to feed. She laboured hard to keep body and soul together while Babu drank her money away. Her name Sukhi means 'happy'. Ironically, she was leading a miserable life. Whenever they fought and Babu beat her, I advised her to throw him out of her house but she never responded positively. She just smiled sullenly which probably meant it was easier said than done. A traditional Indian woman can't live without her husband even if he drinks, abuses and beats her up. Blame it on the customs of the society. Babu was going from bad to worse day by day. I told myself, *I'll have to take that black sheep to task someday.*

While I was brushing my teeth, Jalpa, Mrs Gavit's teenage daughter, came in with a vessel in her hands. The good looking, slim, dusky fifteen year old girl studied in my school. I had a sense that she had a crush on me. She was always looking for a chance to touch me. I would be alert whenever she was around me. The way she looked at me every time we happened to meet, I knew she would be an easy target to take to bed, but I wasn't interested. I always preferred to keep a safe distance from her.

'Mom's sent this for you,' she said and smiled at me.

'Thanks, put it over there on the dining table,' I replied without a smile and, before she could go on with the conversation, slipped into the bathroom. I could sense that this had disappointed her. I kept my ears on the closed door.

'How long would he take to bathe?' I heard Jalpa ask Sukhi.

'Half an hour, at least,' was the clever answer from Sukhi.

'Okay then!' I heard Jalpa.

Moments later, Sukhi announced, 'She's gone.'

I came out smiling and thanked her. Jalpa wasn't aware that I never took a shower before having breakfast. Mrs Gavit had sent delicious, dhoklas, steamed snacks, for me. It was great having them with tea.

While I was getting dressed, Vivek dropped in.

I greeted him with a 'Hi handsome!' and he smiled shyly. That's how he usually reacted when I praised his looks. I did so time and again to see that bashfulness on his face and to make him happy. *Or was that an unconscious attempt to make a place for myself in his heart?* Maybe it was so, but indeed there was no flattery.

'I was just passing by, thought I should see you,' he said. 'By the way, I'm heading for the library.'

'What a coincidence!' I said excitedly. 'I too was thinking of going there.' I lied. 'Great minds think alike!' I had not even thought of visiting the library. It's just that I wanted to be with him. 'I was thinking of shaving first. Give me five minutes.'

'Don't,' he said immediately. 'You look good with the stubble.'

Now it was my chance to beam. *He likes my looks, he is concerned about how I look! He has always been.* I didn't shave and got dressed. He had always admired my looks as I did his. I generally wore what he liked. All I wanted was to impress him with my personality. I remember once he hadn't liked the shirt I had worn. It was the colour he disliked. I had given away that shirt to Sukhi for her husband, for Babu was the man I sent my old clothes to.

As I stepped out, I noticed a half eaten guava in Vivek's hand. I had never done this before, but suddenly I had a strong urge to take a bite of that fruit. I couldn't help myself and blurted, 'Could I have some?' pointing to the guava that had been bitten from almost everywhere.

'This?' Vivek frowned 'but it's half eaten?'

'So what? I wouldn't mind.' I took it from his hand and took a bite.

'Delicious! Where did you get it from?'

'Ah . . . from the orchard behind our hostel. I stole it!' He replied without any hesitation or feeling of guilt or shame.

Though what he had done was morally wrong, I liked the fact that he hadn't lied to me.

'It's really tasty!' I enjoyed the fruit as we walked down the road. It was unbelievable for Vivek that I had no problem in eating his leftover. Though I had always been finicky about hygiene, surprisingly it just seemed like the most natural thing to do!

Emboldened by his confession of stealing fruits, he told me how he and his hostel mates stole fruits from that small orchard. Then he chatted on continuously, discussing the thrilling cricket match of the previous day. I was busy thinking about myself: *Is he as excited about being with me as I am to be with him? Is he falling for me the way I have fallen for him?* There seemed to be no such possibility. Not yet.

At the library, Vivek immersed himself in the newspapers and I dug into the racks of novels. It had little to offer, especially in English literature. There were only a few readers of English in a small place like Valai. I didn't like reading heavy literature and most of the fiction there I had already finished. For a change, after a long time, I chose to read something in Gujarati. I picked up Harkisan Mehta's *Dev-Danav*, a gripping tale of a young, troubled man from Nepal. I had read it in my college days, but decided to give it another go because, in my opinion, it is one of Mehta's best creations.

Though Vivek was not an avid reader, he liked to visit the library frequently. Books were too lengthy for him, so he went through magazines and dailies. When I returned to where Vivek was seated, I happened to see what he was reading in the newspaper. It was an article about a lesbian couple—two girls from New Delhi, childhood friends, who had got married against their families and society. Finding him deeply engrossed in that article, intrigued me. *Was there a small possibility that he too was . . .?*

That day in school, Miss Vidya Parmar, a teacher of Sanskrit and Hindi languages came to me when I was alone in the staff room.

'Hi, Kaushik!' She sat in the chair by me.

'Hi.' I gave her a warm smile. Vidya was not beautiful, but was attractive and young. I'd say she was one of those many women who had a crush on me.

'Why didn't you come to my place?' she asked complaining. She lived in a nearby village. She had invited me for her cousin's wedding that had taken place two days ago, but I had given it a miss. The other teachers going there had asked me to join them, but I had avoided it. By now, all the teachers and students had come to know that Vidya liked me. They talked about us and I didn't want to give them any more to gossip about by visiting her place.

'I'm sorry, Vidya,' I apologized, keeping my eyes on my book. 'I was busy in . . .'

'Pretences!' She cut in and sneered. 'Always!'

'No I really . . .'

She didn't let me lie. 'It was a Saturday. A half day in school. You could have come like everybody else had, but you didn't.'

I had to give up arguing. 'I'm sorry,' I replied.

For a while she stared at me and then uttered in a whispering tone. 'Oh, I missed you. It . . .'

'How was the marriage?' I interrupted to divert her from getting romantic.

'Oh, it was great!' She smiled as she told me about the event in brief. 'You know, everybody from the school was there and we had a great time. I wish you had come, Kaushik.' She sighed. I knew she had been staring at me all the while, so I kept my eyes on the book. I wanted her to talk, instead she her eyes were fixed on my face. Before I could do anything to get rid of her, Mrs Nayak entered. Seeing the two of us alone in the staff room, she raised her brows, 'I hope I'm not disturbing you.' I could see the sarcastic curve of her lips.

'No, not really.' I stood up. 'Actually, I was about to leave. I have a class. You two chat.' I smirked at Mrs Nayak and found my way out. *Damn it! The old lady would be spreading rumours now.*

It wasn't like I didn't like Vidya. I liked her for a number of reasons. Though not a rare beauty, she was still charming and had something very likable in her personality. She had silky hair and her big eyes looked nice on her oval face. Though it revealed the shapelessness of her teeth, her smile, in my opinion, was her biggest asset. She was a good conversationalist and it was fun to chat with her. Despite being gay, I had always enjoyed the company of women, be it my friends in Baroda, my relatives, my sister or my mother. I liked women who were well turned out. They, in turn, had always appreciated my dress sense. My mother always took my advice before a special occasion and my suggestions always meant a lot to her. Vidya wore beautiful saris and preened herself like no other teacher at school. She always wore makeup and matching jewellery. I liked her dramatic expressions. She used the ends of her lips artistically while talking, her eyes danced and she smiled elvishly —all complementing her character and beauty so well. I would have thought of marrying her had I not been gay.

In turn, my presence excited her. She was after me, while the other male teachers, married and unmarried were after her. Some of them were jealous of me because she used to give me so much attention, whereas some were happy that I wasn't interested in her. All said, everybody at the school knew that she was fond of me. But I liked her only as a friend. And I tried to keep her off, careful not to let any rumours spread. On the contrary, Vidya didn't care if people gossiped about us. She continued to approach me fearlessly. It wasn't that her behaviour was unabashed but her efforts towards befriending me were so loud, open and obvious that everybody knew. Every time we happened to meet, she would behave as if we were seeing each other after weeks. Sometimes, she sounded childish and sometimes, overexcited. Once I had told her to control her excitement about me, but she seemed not to care.

It didn't make sense to my male colleagues why I didn't make 'the most' of this relationship. Mr Richards, a disrespectful man who taught science, made fun of me sometimes, 'Why don't you give her a *chance*? I bet she's ready to get into bed with you. Go for it, man. If I were you, I would have . . .' he would opine and guffaw pointlessly, his paunch shaking disgustingly.

'I'm not that type of a man,' I'd say with a wry smile. 'And she's not my type.'

'Oh? What type of a woman do you want, Mistry?' he'd ask with a mocking smile.

I was one of the youngest teachers at the school, and now all my colleagues were my friends, but things were not as positive in the beginning. In my early days at the school, my abilities were questioned and the seniors didn't think I would stay in Valai for long. It was probably because of my urban personality and attitude that they took me to be an outsider for a considerable period of time. While the female staff began to like me, a few of the male colleagues were uncomfortable in my presence. They called me 'hero' and made fun of me. But I ignored all that and tried to be nice and friendly to everyone, and soon became a popular figure among my colleagues as well as the students. Things had been easy and supportive ever since.

I was under the neem tree in the evening. The blue sky lay open and there was no sign of rain. Putting my left arm behind my head, I was lying among the roots of the tree. I was thinking about Vivek when my attention was caught by two sparrows gaily playing hide and seek on the branches laden with inestimable tiny leaves. They fluttered out of the grove and disappeared among the leaves, twittering all the time. As I enjoyed their innocent game, I thought of myself and Vivek in their place. Yes, I wanted to make merry with Vivek the way the sparrows were having fun. And I was sure, sooner or later, that this wish of mine would come true.

In school that day, I had asked Vivek if he could come to see me in the evening. But he had to go for cricket practice at the school ground. He was a key player in the school team which was going to take part in the Inter-School Cricket Competition to be held mid-November. I was confused about the feelings I had for Vivek. It'd been about five months that I had been in love with him, but I had no idea how to tell him those three words, 'I love you'. In the past, I had given him hints about my interest in him by holding his hand for long or telling him that I liked to spend my time with him. I had even told him that his smile was a great healer for me and also that the sight of his face made my day beautiful. But he was too juvenile to understand the substance of those remarks. He was born at a place where something like same-sex relationship was presumably an unfamiliar terrain to most people. He, I understood, had no idea about the meaning of words like 'gay' and 'lesbian'.

This morning when I had found him reading about a same-sex relationship in the newspaper at the library, I had decided to check his knowledge by asking him questions. But he wasn't coming to my house today. Maybe some other time, I consoled myself.

Half an hour later, he presented himself at my place! Mr Imran Sheikh, the sports teacher, had fever and the practice match had been postponed by a day.

'Why don't we go to the sunset point? It's been days since I've been there,' he proposed.

'I don't think we will be able to catch the sun going down. It's too late,' I said looking at the reddening sky. My wrist watch showed 6.12 p.m. In no time, the sun would be gone for the day.

'Oh, come on sir! We can try,' he said in a pleading tone. 'We'll have a great view since the sky's crystal clear.'

I agreed and we set out for the sunset point. Fortunately, we got a lift on the bike of an unknown man who left us at the base of the sunset point within a minute or two. Now this place, like in most other mountainous places, was the most beautiful and the most visited place in Valai. From this highest point of Valai, one could have magnificent views of the sunset and the sunrise. The sloppy road climbed uphill all the way to a vast, uneven ground that was surrounded by a three feet high steel fence. The steel had rusted and the concrete pillars that supported the steel were damaged. There was a garden lying in neglect. Weeds had grown all around. The swings, seesaws, slides and the benches were in no better condition and so was the thirty feet high observation tower. Going up the tower was prohibited but prohibition in India is discretionary. So people went up and enjoyed the sunset nonetheless. The tower, waiting for a disaster someday, needed to be demolished. Despite all these flaws, people loved to be there because when the sun sank beyond the hilly ranges in the west, the entire atmosphere turned magical. From a dull, sweaty noon, like an over-exhausted man after the labour of an entire day, it metamorphosed into a glistening, tender evening, like a newly-wed woman. It was here in Valai that I had enjoyed the rare magnificence of sunset for the first time in my life.

There were two ways to reach the sunset point: one, that most people used because it was an easy climb, and the other, a tougher one that only the young, mischievous boys took. Actually, it hadn't existed till about a decade ago. Some adventurous guys had discovered it to fulfil their appetite of the thrills of trekking. But it was risky to climb from the other side of the mountain because the rock was steep and it made the climb more treacherous. I had once accepted the challenge of climbing up this route with Vivek and his friends. It had been a fine evening and they had asked me to join them at the sunset point. At the base of the mountain, they told me about the other way that I had not really known about till then. And about how unsafe it was. Still I had shown my interest in hiking and we'd set out for it. It had rained the previous night and the ground was slippery. Since the boys belonged to the villages and had many such adventures climbing cliffs, they were pretty comfortable in dealing with the path which was not only slippery but full of weeds too. It was I who had struggled throughout the climb. They had told me to dig my toes in the muddy soil, but I proved to be an amateur at that. I had fallen, stumbled and slipped my way up. By the time we had reached the top, I was smeared with mud from head to toe and had mild bruises all over my hands and legs. It took me a few minutes to catch my breath and be able to talk.

'How was that, sir?' one of the boys had asked.

'Awful,' I had answered. After that, I had climbed that route with Vivek twice. It was much easier to trek when the path was dry in winter and summer.

The place that remained deserted when it rained was crowded today as there was no cloud to hinder the mesmerizing spectacle the setting sun was offering. The high rocks, where I liked to sit to watch the sunset, were all occupied, so we had to go far, towards the edge of the cliff where nobody could disturb us. Enjoying the headwind, we sat on a rock and talked. An eagle floated high above us. I smiled. Being a great admirer of nature, I felt energized whenever I beheld a blissful bunch of trees or a flock of birds or any beautiful element of nature.

Seeing me smile, Vivek asked, 'What?'

'See that bird?' I asked. 'How blessed it is to have wings! It might sound crazy, but I have always dreamt of flying like a bird.' I saw Vivek watching and listening to me intently and continued, 'A pleasant breeze creates such sensations for us, imagine how exciting it would be to float in the air. I pray that God makes me a bird in my next life.' Then I asked Vivek, 'You must be thinking what an absurd thought this is!'

'No, no. Not at all!' he replied. 'In fact, it's nice to imagine being able to fly.'

'Yeah,' I said and thought that he hardly disagreed with me. *Is it that he can't differ from me or he really thinks I'm always right?* I watched him intently as he combed his hair with his fingers. The wind had left his hair messy. Mine was in no better state, but I didn't give a damn.

'I read a joke in today's paper,' I said. 'Listen. A couple goes to an astrologer to know the future of their newly-born son. No sooner does the astrologer take him in his lap, the child pees and spoils his clothes. With a snigger the seer says that the child's going to have a great future. He'll "go ahead" very well. Wherever he'll go, people will say, "go ahead"!' I finished the joke and laughed. Vivek looked at me smiling, a confused look on his face. He had been attentive to me throughout the joke, but didn't get the humour.

'What?' I asked. I knew he hadn't understood the joke.

He managed a smile and said, 'See? My brain doesn't work. It's been proven again.' Many a time he had complained to me about the same thing.

'Oh, come on. It's just a joke. Many people don't get the wit.'

'Whatever.' He sighed heavily, 'I wish I had a few things like you have.' He had always admired some qualities in me.

'Don't compare yourself with others,' I responded. 'You've got things you are not aware of. You might be a bit weak at mental exercises, but then, God has blessed you with such a beautiful heart! You are a good human being and that's what matters to me, and only because of that you're sitting here with me.' I tried to make him feel good and it worked.

This time when he smiled, it was honest.

By praising him time and again, I was trying to make my place in his heart. It was a selfish attempt but whatever I ever said to him in his praise came straight out of my heart and there was no exaggeration.

I watched Vivek as he concentrated on the bird. Every now and then, my eyes turned to his face. His face, even if it was expressionless, was so captivating that I couldn't take my eyes off him. No matter how pure a heart he had, it was his beautiful face that had interested me first.

After a while, I asked, 'Is there any secret about you that you might like to share with me?'

Apparently, the boy didn't understand what I was up to therefore, I had to make it clear. 'I mean is there something I still don't know about you.'

'I guess not. Why?' he asked staring back at me.

I looked into those brown eyes. They were ingenuous. A tongue can lie; not the eyes. And his were as truthful as a newly born child's.

'Well, there are secrets in almost every heart,' I said as he tried to understand me fully. 'And there is a secret about me I need to tell you.'

'What?' the eagerness in his question was apparent. 'What secret?'

'That I'll tell you when the time comes.' I wanted him to know that I loved him.

He smiled and said nothing but I still could see keenness on his face to know my secret.

To divert his attention, I gave an even more interesting subject a go, 'Do you discuss sex with your friends?'

'Hmm . . . yes . . . Sometimes,' he said somewhat hesitantly. Obviously, my question was a bit awkward for him. But he hadn't lied. I chuckled to myself. My second question was, 'Have you ever seen a porn film?' The subject I wanted to actually discuss was still a secret. I was making a base for it.

He looked confused. He hadn't understood the word 'porn'.

'A blue film.' I tried to make it easy.

'Ah . . . hmm.' Again, he sounded a tad hesitant.

'Good, a boy of your age should see one. It could be a good teacher.' He smiled back as I smiled at him naughtily.

'Have you ever had sex?' This is what I'd been meaning to ask him for long. We had talked about girls and romance before. Sex was the new subject.

'No.' He replied promptly and vehemently as if sex was a bad thing.

I grinned. From his expressions I could make out that he wanted to ask me the same question, but my status of being his teacher held him back.

Coming to the point then, I asked, 'Do you know the meaning of words like "gay" and "lesbian"?'

He hesitated for a while then said, 'Not much but . . . a boy with a boy . . . is called gay . . . and for girls . . .' He found it hard to pronounce the word.

'There you are!' I wanted him to be familiar with these words. 'When two men have sexual relations they are called gay. And when two women are involved, they are called lesbians.'

His attention encouraged me to go on. 'Then there are some who like both men and women. They're called bisexual.' We were staring into each other's eyes.

'Aren't these relationships, you just told me about— unnatural?' he asked after a short while.

'Well, in my opinion, they are not. They've been in our society since ancient times. The ancient texts, for example *Kamasutra*, are the proof. The best examples are the temples of Khajuraho—you must have heard of them. Everything from gay and lesbianism to animal sex has been engraved on the walls of the temples there. It was highly acceptable in ancient India. It was only during the Mughal era and then the British Raj that our culture changed. Even today, these types of relationships are widespread in every class of society. And one can't deny it.' It was like I was hammering my thoughts into his head.

He remained silent and thoughtful, so I went ahead, 'Same-sex relationships happen when people of the same sex stay together for long. A hostel is that kind of a place. In your hostel, maybe some boys share such intimacy.'

Keeping his eyes averted from me, he picked a small pebble and tossed it far into the valley. From the expressions on his face, it seemed like it was way too much for him to digest.

'I knew some boys at my friend's hostel who liked all that, you know?' I didn't say I was one of them.

He appeared contemplative for a while as if he was remembering something. 'I don't know if this is true or not but I've heard of one such incident.' I was curious but didn't interrupt him.

He continued, 'A few years back . . . a barber and a

tailor were caught red-handed by a bunch of boys behind the building of the old post office at dusk.'

'Here, in Valai?' I couldn't believe that.

'Yes, it's an old story. Somebody at the hostel told me. Don't know how much truth there is in it though.'

'Well, I didn't know that!' I said smiling. 'But if it's true it certainly is interesting as well as shocking.' The story had certainly piqued my interest.

'They were caught having sex in a public place?'

Vivek giggled in reply and I laughed, 'Mind-blowing!'

Clearing his throat, Vivek asked a little later, 'Do you think there's anything wrong in having such relationships?'

'Of course not.' I was looking at him expectantly. But he was too innocent to understand my intentions. 'Why should we have a problem if two people of the same sex like to get physical? It's their life. Let them live on their own terms. We've no right to interfere in their personal lives, do we?' I kept pushing more to make him talk on that subject.

'I think you're right.' Vivek's answer was positive.

He's understood! It was the first lesson in the process of driving him into bed with me. He was convinced about what I had said. But it was not the right time to let him know I was gay and was interested in him. It was not the right time, yet.

five

The previous day's conversation with Vivek kept reverberating in my mind till the following morning. It wasn't the first time we had discussed a mature subject. We had talked about girls before. And the day was to lead us to one more such conversation. While taking the class, I found a girl ogling at Vivek. All eyes, except hers, were on me as I was teaching an important lesson.

'You, on the fourth bench,' I called out to the girl and startled her. She immediately looked at me, frightened. I inquired, 'What's your name?' For a moment she found it difficult to answer. 'Stand up and tell me your name!' I demanded sternly. I seldom punished any student and my image among the students was of a very affable teacher. For a change, I decided to become harsh. *Or was it because it concerned Vivek?*

'Chandni,' the girl replied—sweat beads appearing on her forehead.

'I've found that you're not paying attention to what I am teaching.' I had seen her stare at Vivek several times before.

'No sir, I was listening to . . . you.' The girl replied apprehensively. I studied that healthy, fair girl. Though she looked lovely in her khaki frock, she was not the most beautiful girl in the class.

'Let's see then,' I tried hard not to sound contemptuous. 'Tell me what you have learnt. What topic was I on when I called you?'

She was unable to reply. She stood quietly, her eyes fixed on the floor. I squinted at Vivek who shifted his eyes from me to his book instantaneously.

'I want your attention to be on *me*, Chandni. Your eyes should be on me and not anywhere else. Is that clear?' I asked sternly and she, terribly humiliated, nodded. 'You may sit now, but keep that in mind!' Before I proceeded with the lesson, I glanced at Vivek whose eyes were still on his book.

I am sure my behaviour that day surprised the class because, never before in the past had I been that ruthless with any student. *Was I jealous of the girl for ogling at my love interest? Yes, I was.* This was something I couldn't control.

During recess, I asked Vivek if he would accompany me for lunch. I was doubtful he would join me since I believed he knew that I would ask him about Chandni. But he came with me for lunch to my house. On the dining table, I told him about how Chandni's eyes were constantly on him. He didn't react at once.

'It looks like she likes you,' I said, trying not to sound jealous. 'Don't tell me you don't know that!'

I knew that girls adored him and he did talk to them rather fondly. He had told me that many girls stared and smiled at him and invited him for friendship, but he liked very few of them. His friends had told him to take advantage of his looks, but the boy never did. He was very particular about his choice of a girl. He didn't like girls who were taller than him. His dream girl was not to be very short, fat or thin. Unfortunately, Chandni fitted his criteria of a beautiful girl and that is what bothered me.

Vivek looked at me for a long while before he admitted, 'I know she stares at me but . . . I'm not here for these things. I'm here to study.' He didn't look away from me when he said that. I could see nothing but truth in his eyes. They weren't lying. I liked his answer. That's what I had wanted to hear.

'Your friends and the boys you sit with were smiling when I was scolding Chandni,' I said as I filled our glasses with water.

'They also know she likes me. They make fun of it,' he said and took a mouthful.

'Do you like her?' Now this was a critical question. I found my heart racing to know the answer.

He answered hesitantly, 'Everybody in the class likes her. She's a beautiful girl.'

'I'm not concerned about *everybody*. I want to know about *you*.' I wished he would say 'no'. Instead, he remained silent which meant 'yes'.

'Whatever, I have got the answer,' I said, and he laughed coyly. He had no idea what was going on in my mind. 'Knowing the fact that you *like* her,' I wanted to know how badly it had hurt Vivek, 'you must not have liked what I did to her. I mean, my scolding her.'

'Honestly, that didn't upset me at all.' Vivek's eyes again reflected the truth.

'Oh, really?'

'Yes.'

'Do you talk to her?' I wanted to ferret out how things were, between the two of them.

'Rarely. Only when she approaches me. I don't want

her to get any ideas. She belongs to a well-to-do family. I'm poor. We can't even be friends.' He drank some water from his glass and shrugged. *Was he disappointed that he couldn't have a rich girlfriend?*

'Okay.' I sighed heavily.

'May I ask you a question?' Vivek asked me to fill the emptiness after lunch. I nodded. He asked me the question tentatively, 'Have you never had a girlfriend?'

The question took me by surprise. I could see strong curiosity shining in his eyes. It was unexpected, yet I had to answer it. It would be unfair to avoid replying. 'No.' I spoke the truth.

'You must. Such a pretty face and no girlfriend! I can't believe it!' He seemed deeply curious and interested in knowing about my love interests.

'Such a pretty face!' It was a sensational feeling to have heard that. *That means he likes my appearance.* 'Okay, I had.' I took off my specs and concentrated on cleaning up my glasses. They came to my rescue whenever I lied. I lied without looking at Vivek. Those eyes were so innocent that I couldn't face them. 'Her name was Zeenat. She was in my college. She had proposed to me on my nineteenth birthday.' It was true. 'Our affair lasted till we were in college.' *That* was a lie. The truth was that I was gay and had no interest in Zeenat who claimed to be madly in love with me. She had left the college as she couldn't bear the pain of facing me every day after I had turned her down. Later, I had tried to have sex with a woman to check on my manliness. I had failed because no part of her body had excited me.

'Anyone after that?' Vivek wanted to know more.

'I had a short affair with one of my second cousin's friend.' Another lie. I cursed myself. *What the hell are you doing, Kaushik?* I was telling him that I was straight. *Why are you doing that? To prove that you are a man? To hide your homosexuality?*

'Well, you can have one more,' Vivek said naughtily.

'What do you mean?' I asked, now thoroughly confused myself.

'Ms Vidya Parmar.' His face lit up with a sly smile. 'She's crazy about you!'

I laughed out loud. 'I'm not interested. She's not my type.'

'You don't like her?' He asked disbelievingly, as if he very much liked her.

'I like her as a friend, a colleague. Not as you think.'

'Oh, come on sir!' he said sincerely. 'You're alone here. You should have someone.'

I became serious. I looked into his eyes. *Yes, I'm alone here. And I should have someone. I want you to be that someone. I want you!*

At school that noon, I got a phone call from my mother. She asked me how things were going. As soon as we finished chatting, she gave the receiver to Chhaya, my cousin. Chhaya's new boutique was being inaugurated in Baroda next Wednesday, and she was inviting me to it. Chhaya was one of my few cousins with whom I got along well. Though I had no intentions to go there, I couldn't say 'no' directly. I said I would try. She insisted that I would have to be there. Without promising, I said 'all right'. Then I talked to my mother for a while. It felt good to talk to her. She was one person I could do anything for. She told me to take good care of my health and, before she hung up, I asked about my father. Mother said he was fine, and though I wanted, I couldn't ask her to give my regards to him. Having placed the receiver back on the cradle, I wondered if my relations with my father would ever be normal.

That reminded me of something . . .

One morning when I had been heading to the library, I saw a man and a little girl passing by. The beautiful, young girl in her school uniform, was holding the finger of the man who I guessed to be her father. And I knew that my speculation was right when a few sentences of their conversation fell on my ears as they passed by me. A smile flashed on my face as I realized how happy the two of them looked. I couldn't remember when I'd had had a chance to hold my father's finger like that! It was always my mother who took us out to parks and fairs. My father was always so busy in his practice that he hardly had time for his kids. But my mother took great care of us and never let us feel alone. Our upbringing was entirely her responsibility. Maybe my father had thought he'd be a good father by earning good money for his family. But then, kids need more than that. I didn't know if my relationship with my father would ever be normal again, but I earnestly wished that Smit and Ridham would be with him and he wouldn't feel alone.

Vivek talked a lot about his father. Despite the fact that his father was just a farmer and didn't earn much, Vivek idolized him and he meant everything to Vivek. He told me about how his father had carried him on his shoulders and wandered through his orchards and fields when he was a kid and how they had enjoyed swimming in their village pond. He said he had learned so many things from his father—growing vegetables and grains, taking care of domestic animals, and repairing electric devices such as tube lights and fans. It surprised me because I hadn't been able to learn even the basics of electric devices. He respected his father a lot and dreamt of giving his father a hand by earning good money for his family after studying.

I felt Vivek was lucky to have such a father who held his hand while teaching him. When I compared all that to what I had received from my father, all I found were those 'dos and don'ts' that rolled off his tyrannical tongue. He had lived his entire life under rigorous rules and regulations, and expected his children to be a part of that. He, who knew the cost of everything, had no idea how priceless the relationship between a father and son was, or how his and mine, was getting worse. I didn't know about Smit and Ridham but I couldn't like him because of his strict, patronizing nature. Being the judge of all things and saying 'this is right' and 'that is wrong' was what he did every now and then. As a kid, I couldn't oppose him, but it started to irritate me as I grew older. Because of his incessant advice on every little thing from morning to evening, I felt as if he had dedicated his life to restraining my adolescence. It was nearly impossible to have a normal talk with him since his tone was always incompassionate, if not harsh.

I had become the object of despair for my father since the time I had taken up the arts stream against his wish. Later, I realized that he had begun to hate me in a way. Studying arts and not commerce or science was a shameful thing to him. He was not as hard on Smit and Ridham since they were doing well in their careers. And it was so especially because both of them had chosen the fields that my father approved, commerce and law respectively. He was always proud while talking about them in his friends' circle. When people asked him about me, he'd put up an act of being equally pleased about having a son like me. My mother tried to talk to him about it, but father believed that he knew better and was always right. Slowly but steadily, the discordance and incongruity mounted between us. I was unable to help the situation, he probably didn't want to help things either . . .

A practice cricket match was due in the evening, but the clouds in the sky were bothering the players. All of them were so excited about playing the match, but the clouds seemed to be playing spoilsport. It was a complete waste of time to wait for the sky to clear. The match, between the two teams of our school, began after five. Fourteen of the twenty-two players were to be selected for the match with the other school on Sunday. The teachers were seated in a row of chairs under the mango trees at the boundary line. The sports teacher, Mr Sheikh, was the umpire. I was seated with Mr Richards, the scorer.

The weather was bleak. With the sky overcast it was likely to rain any minute. Thick clouds were casting dark shadows on the ground. The match was being played under these threatening circumstances. Vivek's team batted first and set a mediocre score of eighty in twelve overs for the opposite team. Vivek, who came one down and was one of the most reliable players of the school, was caught behind the wicket on a score of only eight. He was really disappointed with his performance. The selectors also seemed disappointed with him. The rival team started off well, but then Naman, the best bowler from Vivek's team, struck and took four wickets. Vivek's team fielded well and got wickets at regular intervals which brought them a thrilling victory. The losing team could only score seventy-one. Yet Vivek was upset for not having taken any wickets. He had failed in batting and in bowling as well. But he had taken two good catches and a run-out wicket, which was probably enough for him to get into the list of eleven for the Sunday's match. He had also performed consistently all of last year. The result of the team selection was to be announced in the first period the next day.

It poured that night. It was a beautiful night because it hadn't rained for more than a week. With a novel, I sat on chair by the window and enjoyed the smell of wet earth in the air. I strained my eyes to take a look at the neem tree, but the darkness and the thick blanket of rain had made it completely invisible. Sukhi had prepared fish curry and rice, and I was about to sit down for dinner, when Vivek came with his roommate Paresh. They had an umbrella, but it wasn't enough to keep them both from getting wet in such stormy rain. I gave them a towel to wipe themselves.

'Sorry to bother you at this hour, but I couldn't help coming over because of my mental agitation,' Vivek said, apologizing as they sat on the settee in front of me.

'What agitation?' I asked.

'About my blunder in today's match.' He sounded pathetically distressed.

'You were not that bad, okay?'

'But I disappointed the selectors, didn't I?' While talking, he was continually wringing his hands nervously.

'Well, yes,' I said and he sighed. 'But let me tell you again that you were not *that* bad. You took two catches of the top batsmen of the opposite team which helped your team win.'

'And a run-out also,' Paresh put in. He was the boy Vivek called his best buddy at Valai. They weren't in the same class but were hostel mates. Vivek had told me how much they liked each other's company. The impression I had of the boy was that he was a reticent soul.

'Oh, yeah!' I said. 'You are fretting pointlessly. Just relax!'

'He,' Vivek signalled towards Paresh, 'and my other roommates have been telling me that everything will be all right but . . .' he shook his head, 'I wanted to know what the selectors had been discussing throughout the match and afterwards. I tried, but couldn't control my anxiety. So I came here to ask you if anyone of the selectors were positive about me.'

I grinned,' I had asked Mr Sheikh about you after the match and he said "we'll see".'

'That's what he said?' Vivek's expressions were pitiable.

'Uh . . . huh.' I couldn't control my smile. 'Don't you worry, everything will be all right. The selectors have to make their final decision by tomorrow morning. I'll see if I can put in something in your favour.'

A slight expression of satisfaction spread across his face. I asked them if they wanted to have a meal with me, but they humbly refused, and left.

I returned to the dining table, and while serving in my myself, thought about him absent-mindedly. *I wish he gets selected.* I prayed inwardly. *I wish all his dreams come true!*

six

The neem tree, bathed in rain the whole night, looked aglow in the tender rays of the morning sun. It radiated such an abundance of divine magnificence that no other tree around could match up to it. The clouds had shed themselves fully, so the sky was all clear and it promised to be a warm day.

I had finished bathing when Vivek came and requested me to do whatever I could to get him into the cricket team. Earlier, I had enquired from Mr Sheikh if Vivek had made it or not. He had replied mysteriously, 'He might have; he might have not.' I had told him about Vivek's anxiety and requested him to let me know about his selection. He still didn't tell me and left me guessing. But I believed that Vivek would be selected as he had been consistent in school cricket in the past.

When the team was declared, Vivek was on the list. When he came to thank me in the recess, I said I had done nothing but he didn't believe me. He believed that I had used my influence to get him into the team. The Sunday match was only two days away, so the chosen fourteen started to practise from recess till late evening.

In the evening, I was absorbed in reading a science magazine when Mr Gavit, a fat man of around forty-five years, with a balding pate, invited me over for some tea. To the right of my quarters, a few feet away was Mr Gavit's house which did not belong to our colony. A low level compound wall separated our houses. In Valai, I had a passing acquaintance with many, but had become intimate with only a few. The Gavits were the first people I had developed a close relationship with here in Valai.

I had already had my evening tea, yet I accepted the invitation because it was always fun to be with him.

Manohar Gavit, Jalpa's father, was a chatterbox. Never in my entire life had I met any man who talked as much as he did. An intellectual person, he was an executive in the tourism department of the district. His job demanded a lot of travelling, and hence he was never short of experiences to share. His wife and daughter never believed his stories, so he liked to share them with his friends and neighbours. I was quite fond of his company because he had a great sense of humour. He could make fun of anyone and anything. And the most important thing was that he could laugh at himself easily.

'Welcome, Kaushik!' he said to me with his perpetual warm smile.

'Nice to see you after days, bhai,' I said and took a seat across him on the sofa. I called him bhai, brother and his wife, bhabhi, sister-in-law. His house was larger than mine and was well-furnished. I liked the way Mrs Gavit kept things in perfect order. Jalpa must be out, I assumed. *Thank goodness!* Had she been home, she would have been in the living room by now. She'd sit in front of me and pretend to read a newspaper or a magazine while peeking at me over and over again, which would become terribly uncomfortable after a while.

'I was busy hunting for women,' he spoke loudly so that Mrs Gavit in the kitchen could also hear. The place was filled with the delectable smell of something being fried.

'Hunting for women?' I raised my brows in surprise.

'Yes,' he turned his face towards the kitchen and said, 'hunting for tall, slim and fair women.' His wife Sarla was short and obese. Mr Gavit often cracked jokes about her appearance.

'But bhabhi is fair . . .' I whispered. I knew Mr Gavit would make something out of it.

'Oh, really? I have never had a close look!' To make me laugh, he made faces while talking.

While I laughed at what he said, Mrs Gavit appeared from the kitchen with a plate full of hot samosas. *She must be busy preparing a retort to that!* I waited eagerly for some crackling reply side.

And sure enough, having placed the plate on the glass table, the jolly woman spoke in a similar fashion as her husband, 'Dear Kaushik, I'm also searching for a handsome man who has long, black hair, and a flat belly and who doesn't wear headlights.'

Her comment made me laugh out loud. Mr Gavit was bald, pot-bellied and wore spectacles. Even Mr Gavit revelled in the joke that was aimed at his undistinguished looks. He couldn't resist a laugh.

'Well said, bhabhi.' I took her side and picked a samosa from the plate. It was delicious. 'Nice samosa,' I praised as she went back into the kitchen.

'I know the man you're looking for . . .' Mr. Gavit said loudly as he relished a samosa. 'You don't have to go far. It must be Kaushik.' His comment caught me by a surprise.

'But I too wear headlights,' I pitched in.

'I'll manage,' Mrs Gavit cooed from the kitchen. 'At least, you're much better than what I have at present.' She was as wayward as Mr Gavit was. I couldn't help a guffaw.

'You are free to elope with him any time.' Mr Gavit didn't let go. 'I'd be greatly obliged.'

It seemed like it would go on for ever and ever. The two of them were always like that. They loved each other so much. Making fun of each other was their way of expressing love. What a perfect couple they made! Both of them were lucky to have each other and they knew it very well. I sometimes thought: *would I ever have such a life partner? I don't think I would. I'm not as lucky as they are.*

While we were having tea, Jalpa turned up. She seemed thrilled to see me. I looked for reasons to take leave, but Mr Gavit wouldn't let me. I asked about Jaydeep, Mr Gavit's son, who was studying engineering in Ahmedabad. I was feeling awkward in Jalpa's presence since she was peeking at me again and again. But I didn't let the uneasiness appear on my face.

'Jalpa's not doing well in English,' said Mrs Gavit appearing from the kitchen. 'She's telling me to tell you to teach her.' She started to untangle her hennaed hair with her fingers.

'Sure,' I said reluctantly. Jalpa just wanted to be with me. *Damn her!* I could see that my answer brought great happiness on her face. Mr Gavit was still sharing the tales of his last tour, while I was in search of an escape. It had started to drizzle and luckily for me, none other than Vivek came to my rescue. He was calling out to me from my veranda and I left Mr Gavit's place quickly.

'The rain must have played the villain in your practice,' I said as I joined the boy.

'Yes,' he replied.

In a brief second, I observed that he was wearing a pair of black jeans and a grey half sleeved T-shirt through which his muscles were partly visible. His hair was wet and water was dripping down his forehead. Though he wasn't looking his best, I liked him as always.

'You're looking charming, dear,' I couldn't help praising him. In return, I got to see my prize—a reticent smile. I hardly missed complimenting him and he was so down to earth that he never took any of my compliments seriously. He believed that he didn't deserve my praise and I did so just because I was a friend who didn't see his weaknesses. I told him that I genuinely appreciated him and certain things about him were really praiseworthy. I remembered that misty evening when we had been sitting under the neem tree, and had been talking and the memory of a funny occurrence had made both of us roll with laughter. At that time, I had admired his smile saying, 'Do you know that you've got a beautiful smile? And you look even more handsome when you laugh openly.' He had reacted with a mocking smirk and a shrug of his shoulder.

'What?' I had asked, 'do you not believe that?'

Giving me a long stare, he had said, 'You tell me so only to make me feel good, I know.'

'Oh come on, Vivek. It's not like that. You can ask anyone,' I had said.

'You're not the first person who's seen me laugh. Nobody's ever appreciated my smile. Why?'

'Because they're fools,' I said as he began to laugh. 'No, seriously. You know the people here. They don't, can't understand such little but important things. Besides, most people are miserly when it comes to praising someone. I've got many vices but thankfully, I'm not one of than. I never admire a person or a thing unless it's worthy of my appreciation. And let me tell you that you've no idea what you've got. Look around you. Most people here are average-looking or have below average looks and you must be grateful to God for giving you such a nice physique and features. Value your pluses and look at yourself through others' eyes. Only then you will realize what a nice human being you are!'

Vivek had smiled at the end of my long speech and it had been a genuine smile. Seeing him nod positively, I assumed that he'd got me right. The boy could be aware of his plus points but the best thing about him was that he was never pompous. And that's the quality I valued the most.

While Vivek sat in the hall, I went to Sukhi in the kitchen. 'What's being cooked?' I asked.

'Would you like eggs with onions?' she asked in reply.

'Eggs will do great. Make them with tomatoes instead.' Then I went to Vivek and said, 'You're going to have dinner with me.' He opened his mouth to say 'no' or something, but I didn't let him. 'Please, I'd like to have your company.'

He smiled his consent and asked, 'Why don't we go out for a while?'

I agreed. We took our umbrellas and went out. It was only a quarter past six, yet it had gone dark because a thick layer of clouds had shrouded the evening sun. The recitation of the Friday evening prayers at the Catholic Church reached our ears as we walked down the road to the east. It was great to take a walk with him in the drizzle. I always loved the rain and with Vivek, it was more pleasurable. He was the one who made my present a present. I liked him for many reasons. People do change with time and I realized that in Vivek's company, I was a different person. I became just like him—I behaved like a young boy. He too changed in my company. The earlier roughness was gone from his character. He uttered abusive language while being with his friends and classmates. But with me, he was always careful. It's because he respected me. He talked a lot but he was always cautious about not being immodest. I never told him to behave in a certain way with me, it was what he'd chosen himself. In fact I wanted him to behave with me the way he did with his friends, but perhaps the age difference and me being his teacher, kept him from being so free with me. But I liked him anyway.

I always accepted people the way they were. Never did I wish that a person should change for me. If I couldn't change myself for others, how could I expect them to change themselves for me! Also, I believed that the only way one can win friends is to accept them with all their vices and virtues. Vivek's personality changed with me just the way mine had changed with Krishna, my best friend in college. Krishna had made me talkative and an extrovert. Otherwise, I was the kind of boy who liked to stay away from strangers.

We wandered around for about an hour and then returned home. Sukhi had left, so I opened the door with the duplicate key I always carried in my wallet. Though we had umbrellas, our trousers had got drenched in the rain, so we immediately changed into shorts. While getting back, we had purchased some Chinese food to add to the dinner. Once or twice a week, I ate out with Vivek, and since I knew people's mentality, I had asked Vivek not to tell anybody about our eating out and other excursions. I had also asked him to keep our discussions to himself. And Vivek had successfully followed my instructions but then there was little to be kept hidden. People did see us together and our closeness was the envy of many, but I didn't give it any importance unless they bothered us about our being together.

'At home in Baroda, I used to take my meals with my

Mayur Patel

family,' I said while eating. 'So in my early days here, I hated to eat alone. I still don't like it, but I'm used to it now. And when you have company, you always eat more than what you do while alone. It's a fact, at least in my case.'

The food was great. Sukhi had prepared boiled eggs in tomato curry. The Chinese noodles and dry Manchurian were superb too. There was only one place in Valai where Chinese food was available. It was cheaper and better than what many restaurants in Baroda served. I knew Vivek couldn't afford to buy it, so whenever I happened to eat it, I called him over. And he simply loved it. He was fond of eating and ate more than what I did. That was because he worked out regularly and played cricket for hours. At home he was used to working in the farms and that had probably enhanced his appetite. He was always ready when it came to food. His eating habits reminded me of Krishna, who also used to be forever hungry. My prize was the satisfaction that reflected on Vivek's face after a nice meal. Hostel food was not that bad, but it definitely wasn't as good as the home cooked stuff. And since Vivek was fond of eating, I liked to treat him to good food.

After dinner, we sat in my bedroom and chatted. It was raining harder now. I opened my cupboard and took out a plastic box. He watched me eagerly as I opened it and took out the greeting cards I had received and preserved since my school and college days. He was very happy to see those exquisite cards. I told him how precious they were to me.

'This indeed is a treasure,' he said, impressed. 'I don't have such friends.'

'Well, you may have someday. Maybe in college,' I said and took a pink envelope from the heap in his lap. 'This isn't worth reading.' There was a letter inside. The letter carried a secret I didn't want him to know.

'I certainly hope I shall,' he said wistfully, without showing any curiosity about that envelope. While he was going through a birthday card, a photograph slipped out from the envelope. He picked it up and found me with my friend.

'He must be your close friend,' he said.

'He was. How did you guess?' My eyes were fixed on the picture Vivek had in his hand.

'It shows. The smiles on your face tell what a great time you two shared.'

We really had had a great time. I spoke wistfully, 'He's Krishnaraj. I called him Krishna . . .' Hundreds of pleasant memories flashed in my mind in an instant as I looked at Krishna's laughing face. 'Hey Kaushik, come here!' Krishnaraj Swami's words echoed in my ears. That's how he used to call me.

'He was a south Indian, hailing from Kerala. He had a nice family, a father, a mother and a younger sister. We had taken these pictures when we had gone on a college trip to Goa.' I slipped into the memories of my college life until Vivek asked me about another greeting card. After he was done with the cards, he started concentrating on the photo albums that were like glimpses into the life I had left behind.

Besides these, he liked the photos I had taken of the sunset point. Even the leafless trees of midsummer looked beautiful with the background of the sinking sun. I had given those lifeless trees a new charm. Then there were photos of green valleys and enormous falls one would find in the Dangs during the monsoon. He was also surprised with the photographs of the tribals I had taken in this year's 'Dang Durbar', the fair that was organized in Valai every year for festival of Holi in the beginning of summer. The

'Dang Durbar' was so famous that many tourists visited Valai during the celebrations which lasted seven days. It was the only time of the year when the place would be overcrowded. The usually silent streets became busy and rowdy. Such crowds were an uncommon sight in a small place like Valai.

Many officials of the state government too visited the fair. Performers from other states were also welcomed to show their art. The local people earned well by selling things such as toys and decorative artefacts made of wood, especially bamboo. They had so much to offer to the outside world. For example, they would make traditional clothes, vessels and ornaments for the whole year and bring all of it to sell at the fair. The government took an active part in organizing the festive event. Extra vehicles for people and goods were made available. Additional police forces from the neighbouring districts were called on duty to keep peace and prevent any anarchy during the festivities. There at the fair, I got a chance to get familiar with the brighter side of tribal life, otherwise, the only impression I had of them was that of exploited and underprivileged people. They had so much more to offer for ignorant people like me. It was the time when the people of the Dangs got to show their skills to the rest of the world.

The prime attractions at the Dang Durbar were the songs and dances performed by the tribals. They expressed their daily life in their dancing and singing. I was fascinated with the bright colours of their costumes and the rare musical instruments they used while performing. Then there were plays and magic shows, merry-go-rounds and the circus and food and fun! The first ever Dang Durbar of my life had surprised me a lot and I had a nice collection of pictures of saffron clad monks, beggars, rope dancers and even eunuchs from that one. Of course, I had pictures of acquaintances as well like the Gavits, the Desais and my colleagues. But the most photographs I had, featured women, children and men wearing colourful, traditional outfits decorated with small mirror-work. All their limbs—from the ears, nose, neck to the wrists and ankles—were covered with outstandingly beautiful ornaments. And while I was fascinated enough to take a large number of photographs of them, the local people believed that I had 'wasted' my film on the tribals. Even Vivek was of the same opinion.

'Oh, I had taken this one last year.' I pointed at the photo in his hand. 'During the fair, I came across a man who was looking at me with a lot of curiosity. He had recognized me, but it took *me* a while to identify him as one of my school friends because he had become fat and had grown a thick beard. Both of us were pleasantly surprised to see each other as we were meeting after about ten years. He had his wife and a two year old baby with him. He had come to visit the Durbar without having any idea that I would be there. They stayed at my place for two days and we happily talked about the old times. It was wonderful because none of us had imagined we would ever meet again. Life surprises us sometimes, doesn't it?'

Vivek nodded and went through the other photos that I had taken during my early excursions through the Dangs. He found himself in some photos and said, 'I hate to look at my old pictures. I look so bad!'

'You're not that bad. Just a bit thin,' I said and whispered something that probably didn't reach his ears, 'You always look good. Ask me.'

While going through the stack of pictures, he expressed amazement at a photograph. 'Oh, ho, ho, ho.' He laughed as we discovered it was Vidya and I—ice-cream in one hand—together in the picture.

'Well, this was taken in this year's Durbar.' I shook my head. 'You know how she sticks to me! She forced me to take a picture with her.'

'I smell something . . .' Vivek tried to tease me in vain. It took him half an hour to go through all the stuff. We were so close that my body was touching his all the time. The warmth I felt in his closeness was something I had been craving for so long. His sweat smelled bad, something he had mentioned to me before, but I found the odour of his body extremely stirring! It was one of those things that drove me crazy about him.

Having found him excited about my collection of photographs and cards, I decided to show him something else. In one of the drawers of my cupboard lay a cardboard folder that contained some fine sketches made by Krishna. I took it out and displayed those sketches that were very precious to me. Vivek was so amazed at those marvellous pieces of art. Flowers, children and trees were sketched on paper.

'My God, these are wonderful!' Vivek exclaimed as his eyes scanned the sketches. 'You made these?'

'No, they are by Krishna. I just gave a few of them a final touch.'

'Look at this. Superb!' He was completely fascinated. I didn't know that Vivek appreciated art so much. He liked the one that showed the landscape of the outskirts of a village.

'It's awesome, but don't you think they still could have been more detailed? I mean some of the shapes and figures are not as clear as they should be. Isn't that true or am I wrong?'

I was surprised at the way he had studied the details of the drawings. 'No, you are right,' I said to make him understand. 'But a sketch doesn't need to be as clear as a finely portrayed painting. You should recognize the object by the way it has been drawn. Clarity isn't that important and that's why it's called a sketch and not a painting.' With eyes glued to the sketches, he was listening very carefully to me. 'A sketch is something that doesn't take as much time as a painting does. You wouldn't believe it, but Krishna hardly took more then five to seven minutes to complete one, no matter how detailed it was.'

He was astonished. 'It'd take me a whole day to finish any of these!'

'Take a look at this.' I flipped through the pages and found the one that had my portrait. 'This is me, but not exactly like me, as you can see. The man on the paper looks more like a European. This was done within three and a half minutes.'

'It's hard to believe!' Vivek exclaimed.

'Krishna had swift hands,' I said and recalled how tactfully Krishna had used his hands in *many* things. I found myself drifting towards his memories when Vivek asked, 'You said you gave them a final touch, how's that?'

'Some of the sketches are coloured. I did that since Krishna wasn't good with colours. He made a lot of sketches and I was allowed to take what I liked. He liked them black and white while I liked to fill them with colours. I used water colours and wax pencils for that. Here I must say that by using colours, I killed the beauty of some of them such as the one which had two dusky women working in a farm. I attempted to colour the sketch and the result was so terrible that I apologized to Krishna for murdering his hard work.'

'Where's that sketch?' Vivek asked eagerly.

'I tore it into pieces.'

'Well, but the other coloured ones, aren't bad. They appear much more alive in colours.'

I was delighted to hear that. I knew he had said so because he was a good friend and liked most things about me. He had liked all the sketches. Collecting them in an order and giving me back the stack he said, 'Tell me something else about your friend.'

'What can I tell?' Putting the sketches back in the folder, I remembered Krishna. 'He was exceptional. So bright and enthusiastic. Besides making sketches, he knew skating, was fond of photography, and could play football like a pro! And I visualized Krishna's masterly kicks on the grounds. 'I also played football in college but I never was as good as he was. I was better in tennis. Krishna's talent as a footballer was enough for him to become a professional, but he couldn't because of some reasons.' With eyes fixed on nowhere in particular, I was completely lost in the past.

'I was slim, whereas he had an athletic body. He always defeated me whenever we raced to reach that old, decrepit fort situated on the outskirts of Baroda. The fort was about two hundred feet from where we parked my bike. I never won even a single race.' I chuckled as I remembered how once I'd played a cunning trick. I said, 'Oh, yes, I'd won once.' I laughed again. 'I won when I tricked him, pushed him on the ground and ran ahead. That was all a lot of fun. And Krishna took that desperate attempt of mine sportingly. He was happy to let me win by fair means or foul.' I heaved a heavy sigh. *You feel content to lose to a person you love the most.* I was talking to myself. There was a long silence in the room and I was still lost in the bygone days. When I got back to the present, Vivek was staring at me. 'You two had some great times together!'

'Yes, we did.' I sighed again and rubbed my eyes as they had begun to shed tears with the memories of my closest friend. Vivek saw that, but I had no problem with that. I knew I cried easily and wasn't ashamed of it at all.

'We were the best of buddies,' I said, getting nostalgic. 'We both were so fond of wandering together that we used to go on long drives on my bike almost every day. We often went for walks too. Just the way you and I go. And I must thank you for bringing me the same joy I used to experience when being with Krishna. You've filled my life with fun.' I put my hand on his and pressed it gently. But the significance of those sugary words was beyond his juvenile understanding.

'You are lucky,' Vivek said. 'I would have loved to have such a friend. He had so many talents—sketching, photography, football! Just like you. Painting, gardening, reading, tennis—you are just so perfect! I feel like a big zero. I wish I had such merits.' He couldn't conceal his sigh of disappointment. 'I wish I was like you.'

'Who said you have no talent?' I asked compassionately. 'You are a cricketer. And such a good player at that! You have a sound knowledge of the sport. Square-cut, mid-on, LBW, I know little of these words.' I sniggered at myself and went ahead, 'I do gardening, you've worked on farms back home. That's an art! And you have a lovely voice. I'm a bad singer and Krishna was even worse.' He was looking into my eyes all the time. 'God gives us all certain gifts but we don't learn to appreciate and value them. Don't belittle yourself, look at yourself through my eyes and you'll realize that you're not inferior to anyone. You're a special person—to me at least.' The last sentence seemed to have worked on him and he nodded gratefully.

From my face, his gaze went back to the paper in his hand and he requested politely, 'Would you make one such beautiful piece for me?'

'It's been a long time since I stopped painting,' I said. 'I think I should start painting again. I'll surely begin with your request.' I enjoyed watching the beauty of his face as he took his time to look at those pieces of art.

'Where's Krishna now?'

Vivek's question took me by surprise. I didn't have an answer. I didn't know where my one time best friend lived! A reply like 'I don't know' might have made him ask more questions so I decided to lie. 'He's in Baroda. In the teaching profession.' *I can't tell you the truth, Vivek.* To keep him from further questioning me about Krishna, I said, 'Tell me about your best friend.'

'Paresh?' he answered, 'what do I say about him? I can't say we're as close as you and Krishna were, but we sure are fond of each other. He's good. Actually, the best among the boys of my age I've met so far.'

You two better not be as close as Krishna and I were. I advised Vivek silently. *It hurts a lot.*

When Vivek was about to leave, I asked, 'Why don't you stay here for the night?'

'Maybe some other time,' he said and left with a smile. I watched him disappear. *Maybe some other time.* I sighed. *I'll wait for that time.*

I went back to my room and began to arrange the cards and letters and photographs that we had left on the bed. They had stirred something deep inside me, something that I had left far behind. My eyes were set on a picture of Krishna, and layers from my past came off as I remembered him with such passion after weeks. I was not surprised to know that nothing, not a single thing, related to Krishna was lost in oblivion even after this length of time. *How could one forget someone one had fallen in love with?* I put my fingers on Krishna's face and a tingle ran through my body from head to toe. I felt as if my fingers had really touched his face. I could visualize his broad chest, I could smell his odour and I could feel his warm breath on my neck. My eyes closed as the sexual urge aroused the man in me. *Krishna*. I remembered every single thing we used to do to each other in bed. I loved to kiss him on his lips, cheeks and neck; he was fond of biting me. I liked it to be slow and rhythmic; he was always aggressive and dominating. For me, sex was more mental, for him, it was more physical.

Leaving the stuff on the bed as it was, I switched off the lights and lay down. Outside, it had begun to rain harder. The musical sound the heavy raindrops created on the corrugated sheets in the backyard of my house took me back in time. Caressing Krishna's memories, I relived the passionate time I had spent with him . . .

Long, so long ago I knew a man whom I had genuinely loved from the bottom of my heart. Krishna was his name. Krishna, a tall, dark, and brawny, young, spirited man with average features, was a south Indian who had shifted to Surat a couple of years ago. He had curly hair that I didn't like and he too disliked his hair so much that he used to wear a cap to hide it. In Baroda, he lived in the college hostel where I used to go to meet my other friends. I had first met him there and had a brief interaction with him, but I didn't want to develop it into a friendship since I believed, the two of us were different personalities and wouldn't do well with each other in the long run. The initial impression he had left on me was that of a loud, chatty, and extrovert person, that's why I'd taken him to be in total contrast to my disposition. But this impression hadn't lasted long as I'd learned more about him and started to like those very attributes I had disliked in the beginning.

Before we actually started to like each other's company, we used to go for movies and outings in a group. Thus, we had a chance to understand each other and we really did. Though we were different in many ways, we began to get along very well with each other. It is said that opposites are not contradictory but complementary, so the attraction was obvious. I liked him for a number of reasons. He was enthusiastic, amiable, energetic and helpful. And the thing I liked the most about him was that he loved to live life to the fullest. But above all, he was a great friend. It didn't take us long to become friends since we had a few things in common too. He started to come to my place, I would often visit his hostel, and our friendship grew.

One day, all of us had gone for the movie *Basic Instinct* for a late night show. Since it had become really late and my house was about twelve kilometres from the cinema hall, Krishna asked me to stay at his hostel. I liked the idea so I called home to tell them that I was going to stay at the hostel. Two of Krishna's roommates, who hadn't gone for the movie with us, were asleep on their beds. I was sleeping with Krishna on his. It was a cold, late winter night and we were under a single blanket. We whispered about how Sharon Stone and Michael Douglas had done nude scenes in the movie. Krishna had said, 'I liked the scene when they were in the bathtub . . . naked.'

'I liked it when she tied him on the bed,' I said. 'That was hot.'

'She played a brilliant bitch, didn't she?' he had asked. 'She was a lesbian, a bisexual in fact.' I had been lying on my back, while he lay facing me. His face was so close to my right shoulder, that I could feel the warmth of his breath on my skin.

'Hmm . . . but Michael didn't look that hot. He looked old.'

'True. I wish it was Mel Gibson or Harrison Ford.' He started to brush my hair with the fingers of his left hand. His right hand was across my belly.

'I'd have liked Richard Gere there,' I'd said, whispering.

'Richard . . . hmm . . .' From my belly, his right hand had slid to my waist and rested there. 'Do you like Richard?'

'Yeah, he's sexy. I loved his performance in *Pretty Woman*.'

'What was so special about his performance? He was in bed all the time!' His joke had made me giggle.

'They showed Michael totally nude from the back. I wish they'd shown him from the front,' Krishna had said. Krishna had never spoken so boldly. That's the first time the thought struck me that he might be gay. I didn't say anything to that. His toe had been continually playing with mine. We kept talking for a while.

I was drowsy when I felt his hand slipping inside my pants. My back had been turned towards him then. I turned to face him and asked, 'What do you suppose you are doing?'

He hadn't flinched. He'd brought his face closer to mine and said openly, 'I want to make love to you.'

I had never expected him to make such a blatant proposal! When there had been no protest from me, he'd kissed me on my cheek. I made no movement until he detached himself from me. I had liked it. I really did. There was no light in the room, so none of us could see each other. We could just feel the heat of our bodies. He had kissed me again. This time on the lips and it was tighter and more passionate.

I'd never experienced that kind of kissing before. It was warm, deep and pleasant. And suddenly, I had become more aware. *Something like this shouldn't happen between best friends!* I'd pushed him away saying 'no'.

'Why?' he'd asked urgently, his voice no more than a whisper. I could feel that he was quite ready to go ahead.

'We're friends. We shouldn't . . .' I had said and shifted a little away keeping a safe distance from him. Behind me, I heard a heavy sigh. He was disappointed, but I couldn't have helped it. However, it didn't take me long to forget.

In the early hours of the morning, I felt my body being stroked. Drowsily, I had opened my eyes and found that Krishna was hugging me from the side. This had taken me completely by surprise. He was giving me pelvic thrusts and since his eyes were closed, I believed he was doing this in his sleep. I thought he was having some erotic dream. He had his hands on me and I was caught in an awkward position. The thrusting went on for a while at regular intervals. I wanted to move but couldn't, for the fear that he would wake up.

I believed he was asleep until he made a swallowing action. At that time, my eyes had been on his face, watching him. When I found his eyelashes trembling, I was sure he was fully awake and was just pretending to be asleep. He wanted me to believe whatever was happening was spontaneous, but I knew it wasn't.

'Krishna,' I whispered in his ears to wake him up fully, but he acted as if he hadn't heard. Surprisingly, I was enjoying his hot breath on my neck. Even I was stirred by then. I couldn't control myself and to make the experience more pleasing, I'd turned my back towards him. From behind me, he slipped his hands on to my hips to hold me tighter and went on with the thrusting even faster as there was no distance between us now.

It was my turn to get naughty. I turned to face him, held his hips and gave his body a little lift. At once, he was upon me as if he was waiting for something like that. The thrusting, even when our bodies were still parted by what we were wearing, was so pleasurable that I was fully aroused. The more I responded positively, the more he went wild. My eyes were open as I wanted to watch his face and what he was doing to me, but he had his eyes closed all the time.

In a while, he revealed his organ and opened the zip of my half pants. After a brief masturbation, he went in between my thighs. It was almost like a complete intercourse since I had tightened my thighs as he'd gone on with ceaseless thrusting. Then followed the kissing, on the lips, cheeks, neck, shoulders and chest. Sex had never been so pleasurable in the past. For the most part, I'd remained under him enjoying his warm breath on my skin. And even though I had hated stale breath all my life, that day it hadn't bothered me. I was under him and he was upon me, thrusting harder and harder. The thrusting and kissing went on until he came. He then took me to an intoxicating orgasm by giving me a quick masturbation. What an awesome experience it was! Finally, the moment of ecstasy was over. With feelings of shame and guilt, we had parted and turned our backs because we were too embarrassed to face each other.

That had been the beginning of our homosexual relationship.

seven

'I wish I was like you,' Vivek had said last night. While brushing my teeth in the morning, I remembered that particular line and murmured, 'Don't you ever wish to be like me, Vivek. It's tough to live the life I'm leading. It's tough . . .'

I knew Vivek had said so because he was fascinated by me. In his opinion, I had everything a person could have, good education, great looks, an attractive personality, ethics, manners and etiquette. He had enumerated all these attributes before me one day, and I hadn't been able to stop laughing. I remembered the early days of our friendship when I had received a phone call from Smit in Vivek's presence. The entire chat had taken place in English. When I had hung up, Vivek had said, 'That was impressive! I was trying to understand what you were talking about, but it was a complete bouncer for me. I wish I knew English as well as you.'

I often talked to my colleagues in English, so this had not been the first time he had heard me talk in the language, but it was just that he had been taken in by my personality at that moment.

'Well, you can be fluent in English if you work hard at it,' I'd said.

'I'm ready to work hard, but my mind wouldn't help.' He had smiled while saying that. 'I wish I was as perfect as you are!'

'What makes you think I'm perfect?' I'd asked frowning. *I'm not perfect. I'm gay!*

'Everything about you is just so perfect! As a matter of fact, I've never seen anyone as perfect and as intelligent as you are.' He was praising me unabashedly. He'd done so many times before. In fact I had heard the same praise from many of my acquaintances in Valai. While I wasn't sure about the sincerity of others, I knew that coming from Vivek it was genuine, and it meant a lot to me.

'God has endowed you with everything. You're handsome and fit and well educated, a good human being, a great friend and . . . what else or more do you need to be complete?' *I need you to be complete. I need you . . .*

Since the beginning of our friendship, Vivek had been impressed with me. Initially, he had known me just as a teacher who was smart, well dressed and friendly with his pupils. Later on, as he came to know more about me—my looks, dressing sense, mannerisms, my friendly nature, and the way I presented myself to people—everything was perfect in his opinion. He believed so because he hadn't known me fully. I knew my flaws, I was the kind of person who thinks he knows everything. I would get worked up about trifling issues and would frame ideas about things and people beforehand. My habit of prying into others' lives was also something I hated, but couldn't give up. Thankfully, so far I had been able to surmount two big enemies in my nature, one, my short temper, and the other, my squeamishness. These two devils had troubled me the most in my adolescence. But the one still to be overcome was my being an avid advisory. I simply couldn't help myself when it came to advising people. I felt that God had given me a brain and being a knowledgeable person, I could think of the solutions to most problems easily. I did try to work on this weakness of mine, but it was not of much help. Krishna was the one who hardly advised people unless asked and it was one of the pluses that made me like him.

Sometimes I thought I advised Vivek too much but he seemed to have no problem with that since he believed my advice was always correct and acceptable. Vivek had taken me to be an ideal person because these shortcomings of mine never surfaced before him. Or he wasn't mature enough to understand those insufficiencies of mine.

The boy, unfamiliar with the *real* man in me, didn't mention it to me openly, but I knew that he liked me more than anyone else in school. I could see trust and adulation for me in his eyes. In me, he saw an impeccable personality—beauty as well as intelligence, but he had no idea that there was something very amiss behind this perfect image of mine. I knew he wouldn't be able to guess that I was gay unless I told him. And I had no idea what his reaction would be when my reality would come out of the closet.

On Saturdays, it was a morning school. Vivek was to be at the playground for his cricket practice. I talked to the sports teacher about the schedule of the cricket match our school team was going to play the next day. I had only two classes to take on Saturdays, so I was at ease. Having visited the playground, I got back home at twelve thirty. While I was having my lunch, the phone rang. It was Mr Desai who had called to invite me to his place since it was a match day. It was a day–night match at Mohali and India was the favourite to win.

'What's up, sir?' I asked.

'Nonsense!' he began as usual. 'The match has been cancelled. It's been raining there since morning. It wouldn't stop. Hell!' He sounded really disappointed.

'That means I've lost a party?'

'Damn you. I can throw a party for you *anytime*, you bastard!' he swore at me. 'I'm free in the evening. What's your plan?'

'Nothing as yet.' I laughed at his gruff manner.

'Same here. Come to me, we'll have a party. Just you and I.'

I had no reason to say no. I wouldn't dare.

I knew the afternoon was going to be boring since Vivek was going to be on the grounds. A game of cricket was playing the villain between the two of us. I lay in bed giving a free rein to my thoughts. I didn't like being without Vivek. I loved the boy so much that I always found myself sorely craving for his company. I wanted him to be with me all the time. *How stupid of me to wish for something so impractical!* But it is said that love doesn't know any logic. I was seriously in love with the boy and constantly yearned for him. On the contrary, Vivek didn't seem to be longing for me that desperately. And why would he? He wasn't in love with me! He just liked me as a good friend. The innocent fellow was unaware that he was more than just a good friend to me.

Each morning started with thoughts of him. I actually talked to him in my mind, no matter what I did. It was only reading that helped me put him out of my mind. Time passed quickly in school, but I felt alone at home. And even though I liked to be alone, sometimes I got irritated with the solitude in my life. The Gavits and the Desais were angels for me since they filled the emptiness of my life. But then, ever since Vivek had come into my life and I had actually begun to like him, my life had changed. Once I came to know him better, I started to believe he could fill the place in my life, the place that Krishna had left vacant. We met, we talked, we ate, and we wandered around together. It helped us bond well with each other. Earlier, the memories of the time I had spent with Krishna would keep coming back to haunt me every now and then, and made me despondent. After Vivek's entry into my life, there were no more gloomy moments. My mind was always filled with the happy times I spent with him and I dreamt of having a pleasant future in his company. I was grateful to Vivek for bringing a new spring to my dull life.

Initially, even though I was sceptical about my feelings for Vivek, I found everything about him was adorable. Then I'd thought it was just physical attraction that had driven me to him, but I knew I was wrong when I realized that he was the one I really longed for so desperately after Krishna. I liked to watch his face, to hear him talk, and to be with him. I had told him to join me whenever he was free, but it wasn't easy for him. He had his friends at school and at the hostel also, with whom he had to be. He had his family whom he had to go visit every other weekend. Besides all this, he had to do his homework and study. There were lot of things that kept him away from me. Unable to say 'no' to me, he always tried to give me his time, but it always seemed insufficient to me. I wished he would be with me most of the time, or rather all the time. It happened several times that I would call him but he couldn't come. I would wait and wait with no sign of him. I really hated to wait for anyone, but you have to do everything for your loved ones. Vivek's memory was not sharp, so he forgot things easily and I had to remind him about our plans again and again. Although his habit of forgetting things irritated me, I never admonished him harshly, the way I had Krishna. Krishna, a regular late-comer, could never be punctual. It took me a while, but finally I accepted Vivek with all his habits and flaws. After all, accepting your beloved with all his vices and virtues is what love is all about!

It was a sunny Saturday, so I thought of doing some shopping for the house. Finishing my lunch, I left for the small vegetable market nearby. From a distance, it looked like an ocean of large umbrellas. While shopping, I bumped into none other than Vidya. Both of us were surprised to see each other.

'You do these kind of things by yourself?' She was the first to start the conversation.

'Anything wrong with doing "these kind of things"?' I asked.

'No, but I thought it was your maid who did . . .'

'Well, I was free so I . . .'

'How sweet!' She smiled. 'I can't expect something like this from my father or brothers.' Then she looked into my bag to see what I had purchased. We did the rest of the shopping together.

'You do often shop from here?' I asked as she leaned down to pick carrots from the basket.

'I had gone to Ms Bhoye's home. I had lunch there.' She continued to pick carrots while talking. 'Then I thought of buying vegetables since my bus was late. How much for these cauliflowers?' She asked as the vendor put the carrot in her plastic bag. The vendor quoted a price and she tried to bargain, but he wouldn't agree with her. She wasn't interested in buying at his price.

'What about the vetch?' She haggled for it and the vendor agreed this time. I had my eyes on her all the time.

When she was buying green onions from elsewhere, her sari slipped from her shoulder, revealing her clevage. For a long moment, I gaped at it and she was clever enough to notice. A wily smile flashed on her lips. While heading out of the market, she asked the same vendor if he was ready to sell the cauliflower on her price. When he said 'no' with a smile she walked away saying, 'How mean!'

I had a cauliflower in my bag. For a second, I thought of giving it to her, but fearing that she'll make something else out of this gesture, I changed my mind. She expressed the desire to eat panipuris as she spotted a handcart by the road.

'Will it be safe to eat them in this season?' I asked. 'I mean they don't give a damn about hygiene.'

'Even I don't give a damn!' She gave her nose a playful lift and hastened towards the handcart. I had to follow. She told the vendor to serve us paninpuris, those spicy, crisp balls of flour filled with tangy tamarind water and eagerly waited to be served. I watched her as she put the first one in her mouth and savoured it slowly with her eyes closed. I just watched her. She was a different person today. Like a child, she was naughty yet charming. She was not like that when she was flirting with me.

She took another panipuri and offered it to me.

'I don't . . .' I protested.

'Have it or I'll have to stuff it in your mouth forcefully,' she said obstinately and I had to eat.

'How's it?' she asked.

'Too spicy!' I replied, sniffling.

'Spicy food for spicy people!' She squinted at me and winked.

You really are hot and spicy! I thought.

She didn't let me pay and we almost quarrelled over it. Finally, I had to surrender. 'Girl power. Nothing like a woman's obstinacy.' I tried to irritate her.

She looked ebullient instead. 'Very true.'

'Your panipuri might make me sick,' I said as I accompanied her to the bus stop.

'My constitution is not that weak.' She gave her brows an unusual lift. I wondered how she could change her expressions so well with every new sentence.

'You'll have to take me to the doctor if I fall ill.' I was hell bent on teasing her.

'Anytime,' she laughed, and asked a bit later, 'by the way, did you hear about the leopard attack last night?'

'A leopard? Where?' I was surprised to know.

'In Kalamkhet,' she said. 'A couple was heading to their village from the ghat at dusk when the animal attacked the woman who was sitting on the carrier of her husband's bicycle.' I was listening attentively to her. 'They fell on the road and death seemed imminent, but fortunately, the brave man had a strong stick with which he attacked the leopard back. The hungry animal wouldn't leave though. So he took off his shirt quickly and set it on fire with the matchbox he had. That made the devil run. Throughout the encounter the couple kept screaming to frighten the beast away.'

'My God!' I was taken aback. 'Brave people, indeed!'

'Oh, yes.' Vidya was happy telling me about the incident.

'If I'm not mistaken, this is the third time that a leopard has attacked this season. What's the forest department doing?'

'They have set cages around the jungle, but the animals are not dumb, unless they are too damn hungry they won't eat the goat placed inside the cage as bait.'

'There must be more than one. Don't you think so?' I asked.

'They say there are four. And the one that was seen last night is the most fearless of them all. She must have cubs. Maybe that's why . . .'

'I don't think so. If it was a she and not a he, she should have attacked the man!' I said smiling.

Vidya laughed out loud, and it began to rain as if even the rain wanted to be our company in that happy, carefree moment. There was no place around where we could take shelter, so we had to run to not get wet. The pipal tree nearby became our shelter, but not for long. It drizzled through the sparse canopy of the tree and left us soaked. We stood there talking. I watched her as she enjoyed the rain. And all of a sudden, I was aware that Vidya had never looked so beautiful. Water was streaming down her wet hair that were stuck to her face. Her plain silk, sky blue sari clung to her fair body making her curves more visible. *How the hell had I not noticed the delicate curves of her body till now?* She was aware of my eyes glued to certain parts of her body. And she probably wanted me to notice her. I was not sure if the smile I had seen in the curve of her lips was triumphant. The wind had begun to blow and she was shivering with cold. Everything was cold, the rain, wind, her body, and mine. For the first time in years, I longed for a female body. She was right in front of me, sensual, sexy. But I couldn't get excited. Had I been a man, a *real* man, I would have done something. Had I been a man . . .

In a short while, she got her bus and I walked homewards. I had never been with her the way I had been that day. She had always been after me and I had always been running away from her to avoid any kind of controversy.

For the first time, I felt what fine company she was and how good a friend she could be! In Baroda, I had many female friends, but Valai was a different place. It wasn't possible to be friends with a person of the opposite sex in such an orthodox society. Tongues would wag immediately. Despite all the odds, that day I decided to have a good time with Vidya.

Back home, Jalpa was waiting for me.

'Shit!' The word suddenly popped out of my mouth. Seeing notebooks in her hands, I understood that she was going to stay with me for at least an hour. I greeted her with a fake smile and found that her gaze was fixed on my chest which was clearly visible through the damp shirt clinging to my skin.

'I had some problem in grammar,' she said as I walked up to her. Clad in a white frock with small black dots, she was dressed up as if she was going out for a special occasion. Her hair were neatly combed, and she had worn make-up and a nice perfume. She always did these things to impress me, but my response was cold at all times. She looked pretty, but unfortunately, the ignorant girl was wasting her energy.

'I know,' I said somewhat sarcastically. 'Sit,' I said and went into the bedroom to change.

After changing into dry clothes, I returned to her in the hall. I sat across her on the settee at a safe distance. Throughout the lesson that lasted for about half an hour, I noticed Jalpa staring at me time and again. It not only diverted my attention, but also made me feel uncomfortable. Twice while teaching, I had to ask her to keep her eyes on the books. I wished I'd get a phone call from school or Mr Desai or from anywhere for that matter, but the damn phone didn't ring! Finally, when I realized she wasn't there to learn anything, I had to end the session. When she asked me why, I said, 'This is enough for the day.' Only when she left, could I heave a sigh of relief.

I was in my second year of college when I had decided to try getting close to women. It was because of a slim, dusky, beautiful girl who had asked me to spend time with her. In the library which was almost deserted, I was looking for some additional material on Shakespeare when she, a new student, came from behind pretending to search for something on the same shelf. I looked at her and she introduced herself. 'Hi, I'm Sheetal. First year. And you are?'

'Kaushik Mistry,' giving my name I'd taken her outstretched hand in mine. She'd pressed my hand gently and looked at me. The touch of her tender skin and the gaze of her brown eyes was magical. I was charmed by her gorgeous face and couldn't take my eyes off her. 'I know you,' I said. I had seen her before. Actually, her face, figure, and her sex appeal had caught the attention of many boys at college. It was thrilling for me that the girl every boy was interested in was eyeing no one else but me.

'Really?' she'd asked, smiling mysteriously, her eyes dancing from my eyes to lips. We'd talked about our subjects and when I was to leave, she held my hand and asked passionately, 'May I kiss you?'

I had found it hard to respond to that. Though I had not been excited about the idea of her kissing me, I wished to experience it just because she was so attractive. Looking around, I'd said, 'We could be seen.'

'I don't care!' She was bolder than she looked. 'Neither should you. Just don't think about the rest of the world.' Talking in a seductive voice, she seemed at ease, whilst I was at a loss for words. And before I could say anything, she'd come nearer and pressed her lips on mine. She had my hair in her fists, and if it was not wild, it was not gentle either. The kiss had lasted for some twenty seconds and I had nothing to do in response, because it brought me no pleasure.

Moving apart, she'd kept her eyes closed for a few seconds as if she was savouring the experience we'd just had. I was looked around to check if someone had seen us. Nobody seemed to have noticed.

'Sunday noon. Come to my place. I'll be alone.' She'd smiled sensually, writing her address on a piece of paper, and then had left.

With the paper in hand, I stood there transfixed. That was the first time I had experienced the heat of female breasts. When Sheetal had kissed me, her breasts had been against my chest, and I had felt their shape blossom and their tenderness. There were still three days to Sunday. I wanted to get naked with that desirable girl, but was not sure about my performance. So I decided to test my manliness. I wanted to know how far I had gone with my homosexuality. It was necessary because I didn't want to fail in bed with Sheetal.

It was risky to pick a girl from my college because if I failed, it would be news. It was better to go for the experienced. And who would have been better experienced than a prostitute. Many college guys went to prostitutes to test their manliness, and talked about their experiences. Next day, I picked a young, attractive girl from the railway station area and drove her to a mediocre hotel on the state highway. She was more experienced than I had expected, more aggressive too. In the beginning, it seemed like I'd have to do nothing but be a mere witness. We went for kissing first. However, despite a long foreplay, I was not stirred when she reached inside my pants. 'Never mind,' she'd uttered and got naked. Even the sight of her nakedness had failed to turn me on. I had pressed myself close to her body and waited for my weapon to stir. Even that hadn't helped.

Not knowing the reason for my frigidity, she said, 'Don't get nervous. It happens. Just relax and cooperate.' She'd gone for oral then and continued it until I told her to stop. She looked at me, puzzled. I had felt nothing in the whole process.

Frustrated and tired, I paid her the decided amount and left her where I had picked her up from. Without bothering about what Sheetal would think of me, I decided to say no to her. I was sure then that I was gay. Girls continued to approach me, but even the most beautiful girls of my college didn't turn me on. Not even the sultry, 'film actress' types. The only thing that worked for me was the image of a bare, male body. There was nothing else needed to prove I was gay. An absolute gay.

eight

Our day began early on Sunday. We were scheduled to leave at 8 a.m. Gavachi, the village where our team was to play, was forty-four kilometres from Valai. Our bus left a little after eight. Most of the staff members and teachers sat in the front seats of the bus, while the boys occupied the rear. Their enthusiasm was worth watching. The roads that passed through the mountains were always in good condition, so it was fun to drive through the Dangs.

It was lush everywhere. The summits of the high mountains were eclipsed by thick, grey clouds. The tiny falls that streamed down the mountains added a distinctive splendour to the bamboo jungle—thin, white streaks running down the cheek of a great, green mass. What a picturesque spectacle it was! I had always been fond of being in the vicinity of nature and the sort of natural beauty God had lavished on this fortunate land was celestial, especially in the monsoons. I had been to hill stations in my life before, but nowhere had I seen such abundance. The region still had a certain purity, probably because it was a forsaken, neglected land. There were very few places I hadn't visited in the Dangs so far, but the scenery still stirred and thrilled me the way it had done in my early days here.

In Valai, Mr Gavit was the first person I had befriended. It was he who had taken me on the tour of the Dangs. On

Sundays, we would hire a jeep and explore the remotest areas of the province. His family, Mrs Gavit, Jaydeep and Jalpa, who was just a kid then, joined us sometimes. We would meander through the jungle, visit the secluded villages, and prepare our meals on the banks of shallow rivers.

I did the same thing with Mr Desai and his old friends too. It was they who had told me about so many new things related to this land. One such thing, albeit unpleasant reality, was the illegal deforestation. During one of our earlier outings, I had happened to see vast expanses of denuded hills. When asked, I was told that the cutting of the trees was prohibited but on paper only. Cheats and touts spilled a lot of money to get the valuable teakwood, and bribing the local officials was never a problem. People of the Dangs knew everything, but the mafia was so strong that nobody could protest. It was sad but true. There was lack of awareness about the importance of preserving nature. The illegal activity was done in the remotest corners of the district so that there wasn't a chance of getting caught red-handed.

Still those outings had been special. I had a huge collection of photographs of those memorable excursions. Once I became friends with Vivek, I started to take him with me on such trips. My memory is still fresh of the time when I, on his request, had joined Vivek and his friends on the visit to the falls of Mozira somewhere on the border of Gujarat and Maharashtra. To give me a surprise, they had not told me where we were going. And when I beheld that massive sight of the roaring falls, I was dumbstruck because nowhere in the Dangs had I seen such a huge waterfall. We had spent the entire day swimming in the large pond the falls had created, and how sensational it was to be bare with Vivek! I still remember the sight when he had removed his shirt before my eyes. My God, what a gorgeous physique he had! While swimming, there were brief moments when our bodies had touched. A tingle would run down my body every time that happened. There were others but my eyes remained glued on Vivek the entire time! After a long time, I had genuinely liked someone.

We reached our destination well before time, but we had to wait for long for the match to begin. It was a sunny day and there was no sign of clouds in the clear, blue sky. The match promised to be a great entertainer as the opening pair of the host team hit three boundaries in the first over. The spectators were screaming with joy for both teams. The whole atmosphere was quite friendly, nevertheless, charged, with the host team receiving a better response as they continued to hit fours and sixes. I cheered for our team, and especially for Vivek. Even there on the ground, I found that Vidya, sitting in a chair not too far from me, was peeking at me again and again.

The host team was to come to Valai to play another match the next Sunday. This whole exercise was for the Inter-School Cricket Competition, which was slated for November in six different venues of the district. Thirty-two teams of the district were going to compete for the first prize which was five thousand rupees cash. The tournament, the biggest school cricket competition in the district, was just eight years old and our school had won the title twice; the first, when it had begun in 1989, and the second two years back, in 1995. Last year, we had lost in the semi-finals.

The host team put up a good score of 142 runs in 120 balls. After a break of fifteen minutes, our team came to bat exuding confidence. They started off well and kept the scoreboard moving, but the opposite team took wickets at regular intervals. After ten overs, our team was on seventy-one with five wickets in hand. Vivek was still at the crease with a total of twenty-six runs off seventeen balls. Another wicket fell and Kaushal came to bat. He began to hit the ball hard all around the field. That surprised everyone as so far he had been recognized as a fast bowler, had seldom done well with his bat and was supposed to give the strike to Vivek. Vivek also played well, but it was Kaushal who turned out to be the hard hitter. He made forty-four off just twenty-six balls, making Vivek's job easier. They led our team to a comfortable victory in the end. Vivek had scored a half century, fifty-three runs. But the Man of the Match trophy was given to Kaushal for his splendid innings and the three wickets he had taken of the key players of the host team. It had ended well. Despite losing the Man of the Match award to Kaushal, Vivek was happy because he had lived up to the expectations of the selectors who had shown faith in his talent. The principal announced a party for the boys at his place that night.

It was time for evening tea when I stepped into my house, but I preferred to take a nap since the day had drained me. When I woke up after a nice slumber of an hour, the last rays of the sinking sun were entering my room through the splats in the window. I lay idly in bed and let the rays bathe me with their energy. Then I had my tea with the soothing view of the neem tree. Because of the busy morning, I hadn't read the newspaper, so I sat with it and read the news of the leopard attack Vidya had told me about.

At night, I had to go to the party at the principal's house which was at the other corner of my colony. Only the members of the winning team, the teachers and the staff members had been invited to the feast. Everybody was in high spirits that night. I sat on the swing in the courtyard of the house with a cup of vanilla ice-cream. By my side were Vivek and his team mates. Under the open sky, we were enjoying our dessert while talking about this and that. Most of the time, I preferred to remain silent and just enjoyed the loose talk of the boys.

Vivek was behaving freely with his team mates. He never behaved like that with me because of our age difference. Though we were friends, he respected me and that's why his true personality—that came out with the boys of his age—had remained repressed in my presence. In fact, I preferred him to be restrained rather than being garrulous and overdemonstrative. He called me 'sir', but when we began spending more time together, I once had asked him to call me by my name in private. He had disagreed humbly and said that he'd be uncomfortable doing so. I had understood his feelings and hadn't insisted on it. Thus, I could say that we were close friends, yet there was a distance. I wanted to exterminate that distance from our relationship!

In bed that night, I thought about the party. From those pleasant thoughts of Vivek and his friends, my mind slipped to the memories of Krishna. One of our common friends had thrown us a party at a nightclub a few days before he was to leave for the United Kingdom. We'd danced, drank and ate there until midnight and then I had gone to Krishna's hostel to drop him. I had wanted to borrow a jumper from him, so I went to his room which was deserted. Since it was a hot summer night of late March, all his roommates were sleeping on the terrace. Krishna told me to stay with him and I agreed because I was tired too. We went straight to bed, but after a while, he had started fooling around. I told him not to do so, but it was useless. We were drunk but were well aware of what was happening between us.

This time, it had started very gently as he had held my hands and started to kiss my face all over. I joined in licking his lips slowly. He'd slipped himself over me and our kissing had gone on and on and on. He had gone for my cheeks, neck, shoulders, and chest while I'd remained passive, allowing him do whatever he liked. He even bit me on my neck, and shoulders. Although it hurt, it made me yearn for more and more. Still not in favour of having sex, I'd tried to shove him aside but he was stronger than me. He didn't surrender to my protests or stop his attempts to turn me on. And finally, when his hand had reached my undergarment, I had given up as the touch was so irresistible. The heat in the bed had turned extreme as we got naked and our limbs touched. It had made me feel like a girl as he went between my legs. The kissing and biting made me wild. He had incessantly whispered vulgar abuses in my ears and though I was uncomfortable with something like that, I'd gone along.

Later however, unlike the first sex we'd had that day in the early morning, I hadn't remained a mere receiver. I had decided to enjoy those incredible moments, forgetting what was right and what wasn't. I'd became aggressive and taken him by surprise. That was the first time I'd actually gone crazy in bed. For a while I had forgotten that he was my best friend and then I was above all ethics and morals. There was a nude male body before me and I wanted to play with it to get the satisfaction I had never had before. I didn't know how long the intercourse had lasted, but it seemed to me as if it was eternal. He had come first and taken me to climax in no time, and only then the stormy waves of ecstasy had abated. Catching our breaths, we'd remained clinging to each other for long. The fatiguing copulation had bathed us in sweat, so I got up to open the window by the bed to let the wind in. As I threw the window open, a cold breeze had wafted in and hit my bare chest. I went back to lie by Krishna.

'Thanks,' he whispered. 'That was great!'

So mentally and physically saturated with love I had been that I was not sure what to say. Besides, there was nothing to say. It had been beyond description. Perhaps 'great' wasn't the right word to describe what I had experienced that night.

nine

I was confused and a little ashamed of what had happened between me and Krishna that night. It hadn't been the first time that we'd done it. The first sex had been accidental and that's why it hadn't bother me too much. But the second one hadn't been impulsive. Though intoxicated, we had been fully conscious of what we were doing. Still I felt whatever had happened shouldn't have happened. But years had gone by in longing for a suitable guy, whom I could have a physical relationship with. Since Krishna's appearance hadn't interested me, I had never thought of getting physical with him. More than that, the guilt was caused by the fact that I had sex with my 'best friend'. While the incident kept bothering me all the time, Krishna had looked normal as if nothing had happened. He had however, been perceptive enough to notice my uneasiness the next day in college. He took me to the garden. We sat on the bench and he asked, 'What's the matter? You look disturbed.'

It had taken me a while to arrange the words in my mind and then speak. 'Whatever happened last night was wrong. We are friends. Best friends. This latest development in our relationship could kill our friendship and I don't want to lose a friend like you.'

'Relax, yaar!' Krishna was bolder than I had imagined. 'It's just sex, plain sex. Don't let it reach your heart or mind. There's nothing to worry about in our friendship!'

'Whatever . . .' I'd said. I still couldn't get over it. 'It should—must not happen again.'

'Okay. That's fine.' He had jeered at me. 'Now cheer up! You're not a girl who's lost her virginity or who is going to get pregnant!' I'd watched him aghast as he guffawed shamelessly about what he'd said.

Krishna wasn't the first man I had had sex with. It was Mr Mark Abraham who had taught me the first lesson of sex in my life. I was a kid then, hardly about eleven, when Mr Mark Abraham and his family had come to live in my neighbourhood. A tall, well built Christian, he had a neatly cropped moustache and a thick beard that looked fine on his fair skin. He had a wife and two school going kids—a son and a daughter, both younger than me. Mr Abraham's family was Catholic. The Abrahams soon got acquainted with my family. They never failed to attend the Sunday morning and Friday evening prayers. With my brother and sister, I sometimes went to the church where I played in the garden with his children. Mr Abraham would buy us chocolates and mints which was why I was always ready to go out with him.

Mr Abraham worked in a bank while Mrs Abraham, a beautiful, kind hearted woman, was a beautician and ran her own beauty parlour in the middle of the city. Their children, Valentina and Russell, studied in a convent school. Everything in that well-to-do family seemed just so perfect till the afternoon when I knocked at their door. Mr Abraham was alone, watching TV in his bedroom. He took me in with the sort of expressions that I had never seen on any other face. Being a child, I was unable to read them at that time, but now I can understand how noxious and lustful they were.

'Don't we have something to play with, Mr Abraham?' I had asked innocently. He didn't like to be called uncle, so every child in the society called him by his name.

'Oh, yeah. We have a new game to play. Let's see if you like it,' he said in a cunning tone. How unabashed had he been while lifting me up in his arms and rubbing my abdomen with his! He had then taken me into the bedroom where a porn film was being played on a video player. I had never before seen a blue film. Neither had I any idea about sex.

'Don't you know what this is?' He had asked, playing with certain parts of my still undeveloped body while I, confused and dumbstruck, hadn't protested. 'This sure will be fun.' He'd dropped his pants and forced me to touch him. He had then done a few other things to me and all that had lasted until he was done.

Then from his refrigerator, he had brought me some pastries and told me not to tell anyone about anything. I did as he told me, for I had always been told to obey elders. At that time, what he had done to me didn't trouble me much because I was too young to understand how terribly it would change the path of my life. I had infact liked it. Afterwards, he had continued to do it with me whenever he was alone at his place. I cannot deny that a certain kind of attraction for him had developed in me too. He used to tell me how much he liked me to all the other children in the colony. I felt I was special. The feeling that I was a favourite kid to the man whom everyone in the society respected had made me feel superior among the other kids of my age. I had no idea that I was being abused and what he frequently did to me was going to have a lasting impression on my mind.

One noon, while Mr Abraham was 'playing' with me in his bed, Mrs Abraham had come home. She was having a terrible headache, so she had taken an early off from her work. She opened the main door with the duplicate key she always carried in her purse. Neither Abraham nor I had any idea of her arrival until we found her, stunned, standing at the bedroom door. It must have been a terrible blow for a spiritual woman like her that her husband, who pretended to be a religious man, had this dark side of a paedophile in him. I had been sent back to my place immediately. I never came to know what was discussed between the two of them. They must have fought but nothing—no screaming, yelling, wailing, or reviling each other—reached beyond the walls of their apartment. The next morning, the Abrahams had left without telling anyone, anything. Nobody knew where they had gone.

Feeling that I was responsible for whatever had happened to the Abrahams, I remained despondent for quite some time. And my family believed that it was because I missed Valentina and Russell. Nobody knew the truth! It took me several days to get rid of the pleasant memories with that family. I wondered what had happened to them. Mrs Abraham was a strong, independent woman. She must have divorced her husband. The biggest loss for me was that I had lost friends like Valentina and Russell. I couldn't even bid goodbye to them . . .

That's how I believe the seeds of homosexuality were sown in me. After that, my way of looking at men changed. Any handsome, good looking man caught my attention. Be it Mr Shailesh Patel, the attractive looking friend of my father, Mr Paras Shah, my school teacher, or Kamlesh Bhanushali, the owner of the grocery store at the end of our colony. And a few others, I didn't know personally. In the face of every attractive man, I saw Mr Abraham's face which never let me go further with any of them. Being a sexually abused child, I was the first in my group to have actual knowledge of sex. I used to tell the younger boys of my colony how they would be as adolescents one day.

My memory has always been sharp. I scarcely forget things. There was no way I could obliterate Mr Abraham's memories from my mind. The memories, I can't say, were bitter. Even today, I can recall every single thing that man used to do to me. All that could have been terrifying to a child, but I was fortunate that it didn't cause me any mental trouble. In fact, I had liked the way I had been treated. And for several years, I actually longed for that sort of pampering.

My sexuality almost remained in the closet till I met Krishna and the night we saw *Basic Instinct*. For years, I had repressed my sexual desires because of not getting the right partner. My covert sexuality needed just a nudge and Krishna had done it that night. I had never had such a wonderful sexual experience before I had it with Krishna. Oh yes, I had! But a lesser one. When I was fifteen, my mother, and my siblings, Ridham and Smit, and I had gone to my maternal uncle's place at Nagpur, to spend our summer holidays. There I had befriended my uncle's two sons, and with one of them, I had sex one night. His name was Pranav. All four of us were sleeping in one room. We were in bed watching TV and Smit and Rahul, Pranav's younger brother, had fallen asleep. After midnight, when I was going to switch off the television, Pranav asked for a pillow fight. I had no reason to say no. We took our pillows and started to beat each other up. During the fight, he'd thrown himself upon me and I, unable to bear the weight of his body, had lost my balance and both of us had fallen onto the floor. At first, we were stunned. Then finding that neither of us had been injured, we'd broken into a laugh and then grown serious all of a sudden. I was under him, he was on me, and the heat was on. We looked at each other and it was I who had made the first move. His response had been positive and we did it on the floor. There followed some more such pleasant 'fights' between us while we stayed there. We used to meet occasionally. Later, he would refuse because he already had a girlfriend whom he didn't want to cheat. I forgot that relationship very easily because it was just physical from both sides and I was too young and immature to fall in love. Otherwise, Pranav was definitely better looking than Vivek or Krishna.

As far as physical appearance was concerned, Krishna wasn't the type of guy I would have normally liked. There were some hunks in my college I couldn't help myself thinking about, and Krishna was nowhere in my list of favourite faces. He had a likeable personality, but never had I imagined getting into bed with him. Had he not made the first move, I wouldn't ever have gone for it. I regretted the first two encounters we had had and had no intentions of going deeper into that anymore. Not just because his looks didn't interest me, but also because he was my best friend. But then, it happened again and I had to give up. I allowed myself to drift to wherever that development took me.

I was a bit shy and an introvert in my early adolescence, so I was drawn towards Krishna's boldness and talkativeness. Apart from such differences, we had a lot in common. Many of our hobbies like sports, movies, and sketching were similar. We thought alike in many ways. Our mode of looking at most things was similar, so there was no reason we two couldn't be the best of friends. We studied in different classes, but when there was no class, we liked to spend our time together. Then came a time when we couldn't stay away from each other. And once we got physical, it was impossible for us to stay apart. We started to bunk our classes to go for outings. We tried to be alone, away from the rest of our group. Our common friends at the college and hostel sometimes complained that we didn't have time for them. We tried, but the truth was that we enjoyed the most when it was just the two of us.

Even though Krishna and I had a lot in common, he was exactly the opposite of me when it came to money, career and success. He was an ambitious person. He was better than me in studies and worked hard to score the best marks. He used to laugh at my laidback attitude many times. But I didn't mind. Everybody has their perspective and it was obvious that Krishna hankered after big money since he had been living a life devoid of all luxuries, because of his father's small earnings. He wanted to be rich, whereas I had never given a damn about material possessions. Instead, I always remained in search of love. True love. Eternal love. Gay love.

It's true, what tempts man is what's most out of his reach.

In others' presence, we were the best of friends, in private, we were always something else. He treated me as if I were his girlfriend and I liked that a lot. He liked the gentleness of my face and told me that often by suddenly hugging me from behind my back, holding my hands while roaming, kissing me while we were alone. Gradually, I had started to believe he was in love with me. Never in our initial days together had I asked how serious he was about our relationship and even he had never told me about it himself. I was oblivious to the fact that those self-indulgent thoughts were taking me far away from reality.

He'd often came to my place and we'd enjoyed sex in my bed. We remained in each other's arms for hours without getting tired. How wonderful it had been to feel the warmth of his body! How lucky and secure and complete I'd felt while by his side under a bedspread! How arousing the sweaty odour of his body had been!

He'd stay over at my place to study many times. Besides studying, we did much more. None of my family members had any idea about what was going on behind the closed door of my room. That was the time when I believed I couldn't live without Krishna. I started to think of living my entire life with him. Poor me! I had no idea how devastating it was all going to be!

ten

It was Mr Richards whom I fell out with on Monday afternoon. I was in the staff room, alone, when he came upto me. Giving me a friendly slap on my shoulder, he asked aloud, 'Enjoying monsoon with a *special* company, eh?'

I couldn't understand who he was talking about. Seeing the confusion on my face he said, 'Oh, come on! Don't pretend to be so innocent. No need to hide from me.'

'Would you please make clear what this is all about?' I put the register aside and asked.

'As if you don't know, Mistry.' He addressed everybody by their surnames. 'Valai is a small place. You can't hide your affairs here.' He emphasized 'affairs' and giggled.

Has he got a whiff of my crush on Vivek? He couldn't have. Nobody could. I had never told anyone about . . . I panicked so much that my palms began to sweat. But I didn't let him know. *He must be joking or . . .*

'You still need an explanation?' He was making it worse. *Why don't you bark it out, you idiot!* I cursed him in my mind.

He explained, 'Quite an interesting sight it was! You and Miss Vidya, soaking in the rain, under the tree, in the middle of the town. Huh?' He winked and giggled.

Thank God! It wasn't what I was thinking! I took a deep breath of relief and tried to smile. 'It's not what you're thinking . . .'

'Don't fool me—'

'We just met at the market and I went to see her off at the bus stop. When it rained, we took shelter under the tree. There's nothing remotely romantic or interesting about it as you think.' I said firmly.

'I didn't know you are such a good liar.' He was there to vex me.

'I'm not lying! I have told you the truth. And I request you not to make stories out of it. I don't want any kind of controversy. I have nothing to do with her, understood?' I spoke harshly as I had never done to any of my colleagues before, and left the staff room. He was taken aback because such rudeness from me was quite unexpected. I fumed not only because he had joked about the incident, but also because he had tried to defame Vidya, whom I had genuinely begun to like as a friend. The rest of the day was a burden as Mr Richards's comments gnawed at my mind constantly. I took my classes abstractedly. I was so disturbed that for the first time in months, I did not look at Vivek even once while taking his class.

In the evening when I was preparing for the lesson I was to teach in school the next day, Jalpa came with her books. To avoid her, I contrived a lie immediately. 'I'm sorry. I've got to meet someone in a while.' My words, I could clearly see had killed the radiance on her face.

'Okay,' she said, trying to mask the disappointment in her tone unsuccessfully, and left.

I knew that even then, she would be watching to see whether I go out or not, so I got dressed and went out. At first, I thought of going to the sunset point but then the urge of seeing Vivek took me to the boys' hostel. It happens in love many times that you feel lonely despite having your beloved before your eyes. The same thing was happening to me. Vivek was there in my life but I couldn't express my true feelings to him. I was confused and clueless. Only I was loving and dreaming and going mad in that one-sided love. Vivek was totally unresponsive. It was like one-way traffic. My love wasn't *with* me despite being with me.

The boys playing football in the narrow playground by the hostel building, seemed quite surprised by my presence there. The grassy ground was full of rain water so the boys were soaked in the muddy water. Seeing me, all of them, not less than fifteen in number, stopped for a while. I lifted my brows, and shrugged my shoulders, 'What? Keep playing!' They busied themselves with their game and I paced down the rest of the paved road from the gate to the entrance of the hostel building.

When I entered the building and went upstairs to Vivek's room, few of the boys I met in the passage were in their towels or knickers only. The realization that they were almost nude before one of their teachers, put them in an awkward position and the embarrassment forced them to hide themselves in any of the rooms. I sniggered at the sight of those half naked bodies which took me back in time to when I had seen the shocking sight of bare bodied, young men for the first time in my life. I hadn't known Krishna at that time and had gone to his hostel to get some notes from one of my classmates who was coincidentally, Krishna's roommate. It had been early in the morning and many boys, preparing for a bath, were roaming in the passage in knickers and towels. With a mixed feeling of dislike and shock, I'd watched. It had taken me a while to realize that all this was a part of hostel life.

Vivek, exercising in his room, was taken by surprise to see me there. With him in his room were Hardik, Bhikhu and another boy I didn't know. Vivek welcomed me with a warm smile—a smile that took away all my miseries. While he seemingly had no problem in being topless in my presence since we were friends, the other boys in the room scurried around to put on their shirts. And I wished they would because none of them had a physique to display with pride.

'That . . .' he set his eyes on my yellow shirt and said, 'That looks good. I've never seen you wear it before. A new one?'

'Oh, no. It's old. Just that I don't like the colour much. It's a bit too bright, I think. That's why I never wear it outdoors.'

Though everybody knew us as friends, other boys in the room were surprised to see how at ease Vivek and I were with each other.

'But it looks good on you. You make everything look good.' He mopped his sweaty face with his palms.

I always waited to hear something like that from Vivek. People had always praised my looks and admired my fashion sense since my adolescence. It hadn't mattered so much, but the same thing from the one I loved, always brought me a great sense of elation. It made it all worth while. Years ago, I used to ask Krishna what he wanted me to wear. And all that I wore depended on what he liked. Being a village boy, Vivek didn't know much about fashion, neither was he overly concerned, but he did dress well. I gave him some important tips for looking more elegant and sober.

Vivek quickly began to clean up the unkempt room. His roommates joined him in that attempt.

'Don't bother,' I said. 'I'm used to such disorder. We lived the same way in our hostel. I mean in my friends' hostel.'

Vivek was in shorts and I just loved the sight of his

muscled upper body, but I was always so concerned that my gaze shouldn't linger too long so as to make others suspicious. Sweat running down his broad chest, evoked the memories of Krishna who was equally fond of working out. Krishna's well built body had inspired me to exercise, and several times I had thought about exercising regularly. I sometimes joined him, but my idle nature never let me continue with that. Instead, I preferred jogging, which Krishna hated because he couldn't wake up on time. Krishna used to tell me about how I could get a great personality with regular exercise. I believed I didn't need to own a muscular body. There was a kind of vulnerability in my looks which attracted people to me. And my biggest asset was my face.

While putting things in order, Vivek's hand accidentally touched the glass of water that was on the windowsill above his bed. The glass fell on the bed, spilling the water on the mattress and soaking it. He cursed under his breath trying to wipe dry the mattress with a dirty piece of cloth. When he realized it was of no use, he threw the cloth in a corner. I smiled and consoled him, 'It happens.' He smirked back.

Time and again, Vivek had shown his clumsiness. He had such strong hands that knew no way to be tender to things. Dropping and breaking things was usual with him.

By the time I took a seat on a stool, they had done a pretty decent job of cleaning things up. I had been in this building before, but I had never visited the students' rooms. None of the teachers ever bothered to go and see how the students lived in the hostel which was an old structure and needed repairs. The medium sized room had four single beds, one in each corner. Two cupboards, reaching up to the ten feet high ceiling, were against the wall next to the entrance door. To my surprise, I found that there were no study tables. The boys were expected to study in bed. Thankfully, there was a good arrangement of lights and fans. The walls of the room, in fact the whole building, needed a paint job. The hostel boys themselves were responsible for such a pathetic condition of the building. Most of them didn't care about cleanliness. The walls had been defaced with slogans, posters of film stars and cricketers, names of girls, and even swear words. And the staircase seemed like an art gallery where all the corners were painted red with spitting of tobacco.

'Do you play football?' I asked Vivek.

'Sometimes,' he said.

I suggested, 'Why don't we go and join them?'

'In that muddy water?' I had never seen him that surprised.

'What's wrong with that?' I asked in reply.

'Are you sure?' He tried to confirm that I was not joking.

'Do you want it in writing?' I asked, smiling. 'Now come on. Let's have some fun!'

The faces on the ground were equally surprised when Vivek told them that I wanted to join them. Some of them looked at my neat clothes.

'I don't care about getting dirty,' I said as I began to fold my pants up to my knees. 'I don't even remember when I had last played in the mud. It sure will be fun.' It took me just a few seconds to fold up the sleeves of my shirt above the elbows. Some of the youngsters still couldn't believe that I, their teacher, was going to play with them in the dirty water.

Like most other boys, Vivek was also wearing shorts. Giving my wallet to Bhikhu, who was not playing due to fever, I moved onto the ground which was submerged in water up to my ankles. Though the small ground was unable to hold all the players, I enjoyed playing football after years. We splashed in the dirty water, shoved, rammed, hauled each other, and did everything that was forbidden in the game of soccer. In comparison to the young boys, I felt old because I wasn't as good as they were in the game. They were kind enough to let me score a goal.

I spent about two hours of which more than an hour was spent on the ground. My hair, clothes, and my entire body was soaked with the grubby water. And it seemed like I'd have to take a bath in the boys' hostel before leaving. Fortunately, it started to pelt down heavily in the middle of the game. Rain completely washed any body. By the time I was ready to leave after an exhausting hour of fun football, the boys had been so enthralled with my playing with them that they asked me to come back to play again.

I had always been uncertain about whether my feelings for Vivek was love or just physical attraction. As at the same time, while I thought was in love with him, I was physically attracted to other guys too. The thing that had attracted me to Vivek was his credulity. I had fallen in love with him and my love for him overrode everything else.

On my way home, I enjoyed the drizzle. Then impulsively, instead of going home straight, I went around and though a bad singer, I couldn't help but sing in such a romantic atmosphere.

I chanted while slowly pacing the deserted road. On the roadside mulberry tree, I spotted some nightingales trying to protect themselves from getting wet. For a few moments, I stood still watching those innocent beings and remembered Krishna who was so fond of nature photography. He had a nice camera that he had got from one of his relatives abroad. The results of the camera were always excellent and Krishna made the most of it by using his photographic skills. Had he been there, he would have captured those birds from various angles. Just a couple of yards ahead, I saw another beautiful scene, two kids were busy playing in the gully, the lane, with their tiny paper boats. They were paddling barefoot after their boats which were full of tiny flowers. I slowed down to watch them make merry and remembered how I used to have such fun with Smit and other friends from our colony, when we were children.

The memory of the wonderful time that I'd had just now at Vivek's hostel, made me remember his bare body and my cold body yearned for the heat of his brawny one.

'Aren't you proud of your body and face?' I had once asked him on a hot summer afternoon at my place. He had unbuttoned his shirt since it was hot and there was a power cut.

'I don't think it's worthy of taking pride,' he had replied. It wasn't that he was being modest, he actually didn't know that he had something to be proud of.

'Poor boy, Vivek,' I had uttered smiling, 'you've no idea what sexy physique and features you've got. You need to learn to value your assets and attributes.'

In response, he had shrugged carelessly. I had given his innocent face a long stare and thought, but you know what? that's what I like about you the most, your childlike nature. Credulous. Ignorant. Stupid. And I had inwardly thanked the Supreme Being for sending a soul like Vivek into my life.

As I was walking, at the end of the turn near Hanuman temple I saw Babu, Sukhi's husband, smoking a bidi, a local cigarette made of leaves, at a tea stall. The bony, dark coloured man with disgusting features was dressed in threadbare pants and a stained shirt. He was a tramp and worked at will. His paltry earnings were spent only on drinking, a habit that made him look much older than his real age. The sight of that coarse person carelessly puffing away his wife's earning provoked me even as I remembered the bulge on Sukhi's temple. I stopped singing and went to him. Babu welcomed me with a simper, revealing an almost toothless mouth. His eyes as usual, were those of an inebriated man.

'Another tooth is missing, huh?' I asked rubbing my palms together as it was really cold.

'Saab . . .' the slave to drink smirked again and threw away the bidi without stubbing it out. I shook my head in displeasure and asked the man at the stall for two teas. I looked at Babu again—drunk, he would fall on the road or collapse against a street pole or a wall. Unlike Sukhi, he was always in dirty clothes and with unruly hair. A distasteful odour of cheap wine emanated from his scrawny body. The blotches on his charcoal face caused by falling here and there, the redness in his big, round eyes and a stumbling gait had become his identity. What had Sukhi seen in him? How could she put up with such an animal? I asked myself. *If I were a woman, I wouldn't have married him even if he was the last man on this earth!* All his friends who weren't with him at that time, were just like him.

'Will it do or should I ask for Mahudo?' I asked jesting, as Babu took his cup from the stall. Mahudo was the local wine he drank.

'Saab . . .' he uttered. He never had answers to my sharp questions. His smile made me snigger. The hot tea was a great relief for my shivering body.

'Saab, are you . . . a . . . coming from the sunset point?' he inquired.

'No, why?' I asked, sipping tea.

'A tiger was seen there yesterday . . . You shouldn't go there in the evening,' he advised. Babu had called the leopard a tiger, so I asked the man at the tea stall. He confirmed the presence of the beast.

'Okay,' I said and came to what I wanted to ask. 'Why did you beat Sukhi the last time?'

'I didn't beat . . .' he tried to conceal his embarrassment.

'Last Tuesday, if I'm not mistaken. She earns for you and your family and you beat her. Why?' I fixed him with a hard stare.

'Saab . . .' He avoided facing my piercing eyes.

'Everything has a limit. I have warned you in the past. You beat her one more time and I'll send you to jail, understand? And then you will know how severe their beating is!' I threatened him. I could have told him what a mean life he was leading and what a useless person he was, but I knew all that would have fallen on deaf ears because there was no way I or anyone else could change Babu's attitude. I had even helped him find a job, but he hadn't stuck to it.

'Saab . . .' he kept on uttering as if he had no other word left in his vocabulary.

'You understand, right?' I asked. He nodded and I said, 'Good. Now go home. It's getting dark.'

'Saab . . .' I paid for the tea and walked down the road singing the same song.

eleven

I was enjoying the cold and crisp morning air. The canopy of the neem tree above was swaying slowly like a melodious, flowing stream. Nature took me closer to the almighty and inspired me to have a chat with Lord Shiva. I thought of God as my dear friend and talked to him. I told him about my problems and other things. I prayed to him to be with me, to help me achieve everything I had ever wished for. I also prayed to him to bless the people who loved me and the people whom I loved. I visualized the face of my God in the grove of the neem tree and had a conversation with him. Someone might find it crazy, but that's how I was.

Mr Gavit was giving his motorcycle a wash when I returned home. As I greeted him, he invited me over for morning tea and asked me to bring a hammer.

'Sorry, but I don't have a hammer,' I apologized as I walked up to the patio of his house.

'Never mind, I have one,' he said leading me in.

I followed him inside wondering why he asked me for a hammer if he had one. Being familiar with his sense of humour, I had a feeling, he was up to something. I gave him a quizzical look as he mysteriously squinted at me through his thick glasses. I tried to guess what he had up his sleeve until Mrs Gavit came with a tray of tea and biscuits.

'What did you say, Kaushik?' Mr Gavit asked me as his wife took a seat by me.

'I said . . .' By now, I knew he was trying to make fun of her. '. . . I don't have a hammer. Why did you ask for one?'

Mrs Gavit had a puzzled look on her face since she had no idea what was going on.

'Madam has prepared some biscuits.' He pointed to his wife with his right hand and to the biscuits in the plate with the left. 'Homemade biscuits. You'll need a hammer to break them!'

Mrs Gavit gaped at Mr Gavit for a while and then snapped, 'How mean!' She looked at me for support and I nodded. 'Well then . . .' she picked up the plate and placed it on the sofa between the two of us. 'Go out and buy yourself whatever you like because you're not going to get anything from this plate.' she said with a plastic smile. Then she instructed me, 'Don't let him have even a single biscuit!'

'Oh, thank you very much! You are doing a favour to me and to my teeth also!' Mr Gavit laughed aloud as she went back into the kitchen.

I stopped laughing and tasted a biscuit. 'You never praise her cooking, do you?'

'Of course, I do.' Mr Gavit winked at me and whispered, 'In the bedroom only!'

I couldn't stop laughing at that. Mrs Gavit heard the whispering between us, so she asked from inside the kitchen, 'What's he saying, Kaushik? Joking about me?'

'No, no.' I stopped laughing. 'It's just male talk,' I answered, offering Mr Gavit the plate. 'The biscuits are great bhabhi,' I praised as they really were delicious. 'And by the way, bhai is also having some.'

'Don't let him! I'm coming with a hammer to hit him on his head,' she roared from inside the kitchen.

I thought about what a nice a couple they made—cracking jokes at each other without taking anything amiss, enjoying every bit of life, being happy all the time. That's what life ought to be about! The two of them always seemed to be at odds, but I never knew if they ever fought seriously. Mr Gavit, on my asking, had told me once that it wasn't that they never fought. They had their share of serious fights. But they never let their fights out of their bedroom. He was proud to say that for years when they had led their conjugal life in a joint family with his parents and brothers and sisters-in-law back at their native place, never did anyone of his family members find them fighting. Neither did their children, Jaydeep and Jalpa. I felt that was commendable.

On the first night of their marriage, Mr and Mrs Gavit had promised each other that their differences would never cross the threshold of their bedroom under any circumstances—and they hadn't. I had never seen such understanding between couples. I had witnessed fights between my parents over trivial issues since they thought differently. Although they were not at loggerheads all the time, they were visibly paradoxical in their dispositions. Mother listened to her heart while my father always took his decisions practically. He brought home the stress and failure of his office which, most of the time, became the cause of the quarrel. He was the kind of person who liked to swoop upon weak people around him, so mother had told us to keep away from him whenever we found him distraught. Mother was more composed by nature.

'Hello!' Mr Gavit snapped his fingers before my eyes as I was busy with my thoughts. 'Where are you?'

'Huh?' I was suddenly back in the present. I cleared my throat and said admiringly, 'I was thinking what a great couple you two make!'

'That's the fun of marital life. Such pranks and teasing rejuvenates marriage and you never lose interest in your better half,' he said smiling. Then he asked, 'Tell me, when are you going to get married?'

I found myself unable to answer.

'Do you want me to find a girl for you?' he asked.

I was hoping he would not ask me to marry his daughter who was not there at that time.

'Why will he tell you? He must have his own choice,' said Mrs Gavit, appearing from the kitchen. 'I don't see a proper girl in this place for such a sweet, well-bred young man. The girl he'll marry will be very lucky indeed.' Mrs Gavit had always considered me a very wise and nice human being. *What if she ever comes to know I'm gay?*

'Like you, huh?' Mr Gavit asked and Mrs Gavit retorted as usual, but my mind was somewhere else. I remembered how excited my mother had been about my marriage. She had so many dreams! Since my elder brother's marriage had taken place in a hurry, she hadn't been able to fulfil all her wishes in Smit's wedding. She hadn't been able to invite her relatives from abroad because the date the pundit, our local priest had given for the marriage had been less than a week, away and unfortunately, there was no other auspicious day for marriage until the next year. We were short of time and every arrangement had to be made in a rush. None of us could really enjoy the wedding fully, especially my mother, who had then reserved her plans for my wedding.

My wedding. I sniggered to myself as I stepped out of Mr Gavit's place. I remembered Mrs Gavit's words, 'The girl he'll marry will be very lucky'.

The discussion on my marriage reminded me of an incident. It was the wedding day of one of my cousins who was younger than me.

'See, even the younger ones are getting married. When are you going to marry?' One of my aunts had complained to me in my mother's presence. Mother's face had lost all its colour. The aunt obviously didn't know that I was gay, had no idea how terrible this question was for a woman who knew her son was gay. I felt so ashamed of myself but couldn't do anything except leave the room whilst my mother wore a mask of fake smiles. While leaving the room aunt's last words addressed to her fell on my back. 'Veena, I didn't know your son was so shy that he can't discuss his marriage in the presence of elders! Indeed, this is a virtue.'

A virtue! A faded smirk had appeared on my pallid face. Being gay was no virtue, but a shame to my parents! All the dreams that my mother had dreamt for my marriage had been sabotaged. For years, she had made plans of doing this and that on the occasion of my marriage, but the disclosure of my homosexuality had smothered all her desires. I regretted that so much! I had failed her as a son. I couldn't live up to the expectations of my parents. I was a failure. Devolving my responsibilities on my brother, I had escaped from my family like a coward. I was worthy of what my father did to me. All his frustration, wrath, repugnance and dislike were reasonable. I was guilty and deserved the worst punishment any person could ever get for murdering the hopes and trust of his parents!

I reached home disturbed and picked up the newspaper. From the front page of the newspaper, I learnt that the final match of the India–South Africa series was on that day. India was leading the five match series 2–1 and the last match, the fourth One Day International, on Saturday had been cancelled due to bad weather. This was to be a defining match. Mr Desai had already called and reminded me that there was a party at his place in the evening. He had sounded so sure about the result of the match. Vivek and his friends were equally excited about the game, hence they had tried to take a half day leave but their class teacher, Mrs Nayak, hadn't okayed their request.

In the cloudy evening, I set out for Mr Desai's with a cake. An hour's match was still to be played, so I hurried. A putrid smell drove my attention to the communal garbage bin that was overflowing with rubbish. Next to the bin was a big puddle of stagnant water. I cursed the municipality and strode ahead. On my way, I saw Jalpa standing with a young boy at the far corner of the college road. I slowed down a bit to identify the boy she was with, but I couldn't recall if I'd seen him before. Since they were too busy with each other, neither saw me pass by.

The tall, slim, wheatish boy had a bike by his side, while Jalpa had her books in her hands. He seemed to have said something hilarious and Jalpa burst into a laugh. I was busy guessing who the boy might be but was pulled out of my thoughts by a voice on a loudspeaker. It was an announcement being made by a government vehicle that a leopard was seen at the sunset point the last two days, so the people of Valai were instructed not to go there after dark for their own safety. These animals had become so fearless of humans that they had actually begun to come to residential areas frequently. They were seen in the ghats, relaxing on the outskirts, and even sitting in the middle of the road at night. I had always wanted to see a leopard, but my wish had never come true. Last year, when one had been trapped in a cage at the village Lavchali, I had set out to see it. Unfortunately, it had been taken away by the forest department by the time I had reached there.

The atmosphere at Mr Desai's house was lively. His hall was full of familiar, wrinkled faces. They welcomed me with a loud shout of joy. Before I took my seat, I went into the kitchen to meet Mrs Desai. 'How's my dear mom?' I asked.

Mrs Desai, busy with her cooker, complained without giving me a look. 'It's been three days since I last saw your face. Where have you been, son? If this goes on, you will not be here even the day I die!'

'What rubbish! Why would you die?' I took the cooker from her hands as she was struggling to fix its lid. 'Mutton, wow!' I exclaimed as I saw mutton inside the cooker. I put it back on the stove.

'I'll die because I'm old.' She was not only old but she had also been ailing for a while now. She walked towards the backyard, saying, 'Take some sweets from the refrigerator.' She had always showered me with her love. Inside the fridge I found *halwa* and my favourite *jalebies*.

The spectators in the hall applauded as Rahul Dravid hit a boundary. The target for the Indian team was 269 and so far they had scored 233 with four wickets in hand and nine overs to go. It was a win-win situation until Shaun Pollock struck in his last spell. When Rahul Dravid was caught behind, our team was left with tail-enders only. Anil Kumble was given out for an LBW. Then it was Javagal Shrinath who was clean-bowled, and the last wicket was Venkatesh Prashad's. The end came abruptly. India was all out for 251! What a pathetic end to a near triumph! The air was filled with acute despair. No one had any words. The South Africans had managed to draw the series two-all. Moments later, the disappointment burst out in the form of abusive words from most men there. They cursed every single member of the team and I nodded every time I was asked for my opinion. To me, it was quite amusing to listen to their invectives. Meanwhile, Mrs Desai came in and ordered, 'No one's going to leave. I won't let you people spoil what I've prepared for you. The party's still on even if we've lost!'

We had a party, but it wasn't as lively as it used to be when India won. Everybody ate and drank but it was all over soon and by nine, everybody had left. This time I didn't have much beer. On my way home, it began to pour and I was completely drenched. The first thing I did was to rush to the bathroom to change. I dried my wet body with a towel. This was the thing that people loved—my body. I too loved my body. For a while, I enjoyed my nakedness as it reminded me of how I used to have sex with Krishna in front of a full-length mirror in my bedroom. The reflection of the nakedness of our bodies was so stirring to both of us. None of us had any problem with nudity. Now alone under a blanket in my bed, my cold body longed for the heat of another human body. I remembered the exquisite time I'd had with Krishna. My nostrils were still full of the lingering odour of Krishna's body. I missed those warm hugs. I missed the rough touch of his whiskers on my skin and that perfect merging of our naked bodies. I still remembered even the minute details of our lovemaking during those sex-saturated nights. My mind flashed back to one such evening when I had taken a bath with Krishna for the first time.

After playing a football match in the hostel ground one summer noon, we had gone to Krishna's room. He was going to take a bath and had asked me to join him. Since I was not happy about whatever had happened between us in his bed some days ago, I had refused. He asked me to at least come to the bathroom so that he could talk to me while bathing. I had gone with him and stayed outside as he got under the shower. We'd talked about how we had played.

'If you don't mind, uh . . . would you come in and rub my back? It's really sweaty and sticky, and I can't reach,' he asked from inside. After thinking for a bit, I got in. He had been only in his underwear and I hadn't been able to help but steal a glance at his covered organ. By now I had become fond of the lustrous texture of his body and he knew that well—too well. His astute eyes had probably caught me stealing a look. The sight of his nudity had stirred me completely, and all of a sudden, I wanted to be with him—physically and emotionally. I began rubbing soap on his back as he kept talking about sundry things. When I was done, he had turned to face me to say a thanks or something like that, but his eyes expressed something else. We had stared at each other. It hadn't taken me long to understand what it was, but before I could protest, he'd pulled me towards himself and I was in his arms.

'I love you,' he whispered in my ear after the first kiss. It wasn't as if I didn't like him; I just didn't want to have sex with my best friend one more time. But he had made me helpless and I got carried away. He had embraced, caressed and kissed me. Every action of the heavy foreplay had pushed me to the height of exquisite contentment. The heat was on, passion was in the air, and I was in his arms, fervently longing for more, more and more of those moments of self forgetfulness. He had got me undressed and we'd done it. Dirty words falling from his mouth through warm breaths played the role of a catalyst since I had become fond of them. We had gone for oral sex for the first time and for me it was like being on cloud nine. Stimulating all my erogenous zones, he had done it so skilfully that it had taken me to another level where nothing but only pleasure, heavenly pleasure existed. Those were ecstatic moments when I had been beyond worldly worries. Nothing was important, nothing held any meaning for me. I only knew that I was lucky to have such a wonderful time. And I wanted to make the most of it by offering and receiving the ultimate delight of life.

Taking a bath together was not uncommon among the hostel boys, so there was nothing to worry about anyone arriving there suddenly and finding us together in the bathroom. In a relaxed mood, we had enjoyed sex under the drizzling shower.

twelve

Dressed in a white T-shirt and brown shorts, I went for jogging early the next morning. Last night I hadn't thought about jogging. It was just in the morning when I woke up early that I decided to go for a run. It had rained torrentially till the crack of dawn, so the roads were wet.

When I used to go for jogging in shorts in my early days here, people would laugh at me as if I were an alien. It amused them that I went out in public in half pants. Some of them even asked, 'You wear shorts?' Mr Desai was one of them. In the beginning, he called me the man in *chaddis* (underwear). Mr Solanki, the principal, had stared at me strangely when he had seen me in shorts for the first time. 'Don't you think it's uncomfortable?' he had asked somewhat disdainfully.

'Not at all! Nothing is more comfortable than this,' I had replied. His eyes had stared at my bare legs. I couldn't understand what was wrong with wearing shorts. The people here had seen adult men in shorts on TV only and I was the first man to go bare legged in public in Valai! Even then, I never thought of forgoing my shorts.

When I reached Vivek's hostel, everything was calm because it still was a quarter to six and most boys didn't leave their bed until seven. Standing on the pavement, I called out his name with my eyes fixed on the window of his room. Paresh peeped out of the window.

'He's still sleeping. Should I wake . . .' the skinny boy asked.

'Uh . . . no, no. Let him sleep. I was just—just tell him I was here,' I said and left the place.

The sun was still under the quilt of grey clouds in the east when I reached the sunset point. I had been here at daybreak with Vivek many times before. He would come with his friends to wake me up in the early hours and we would reach this place jogging. We would sit on the rocks that appeared to be jutting out of the breast of the earth, and enjoy the rising of the sun. The best thing here were the gushes of cold wind while we watched the mesmerizing strokes of various colours splashed across the vast canvas of the sky.

Had Vivek been there with me, he would have taken his shirt off and started exercising and I would have enjoyed watching his muscular body. *What a feast the sight of his bare body was for my eyes!* I did some stretching exercises and then I sat on the high rock with a desire to watch the sunrise, but the clouds, playing spoilsport wouldn't let the sun out of their huddle. I saw only a faint, orange glow on the edges of the clouds. Whenever I came to this place, I remembered Krishna, who was so fond of going out. There was no place in Baroda we two had not visited: gardens, movie-theatres, restaurants, amusement parks. But the one place where both of us simply loved to be was the old ruins of the fort located twenty-six kilometres from central Baroda. The ancient castle of much historical value had regrettably been left derelict. Most of its walls were damaged and moss covered and there was no chance now that anything would be done to preserve that lonesome legacy. We would go there and perch ourselves on the tallest tower of the fort from where we could see the villages and vast fields around. We would sit on the filthy, old stone walls for hours and wait for the sun to set, or just wander aimlessly in the fields hand in hand. *How beautiful those days had been!*

Suddenly, I remembered that it was dangerous to be at this place alone since a leopard had been seen around. But I didn't take it seriously and enjoyed the daybreak, inhaling the salubrious air of the morning.

Later, while taking a bath, it suddenly occurred to me that I had seen Jalpa with an unknown guy on the college road. Should I talk to Mr Gavit about it? I wondered. *Or maybe it is too early. The boy could be just a friend. Maybe my perception is wrong.* Keeping that in mind, I decided to erase the scene from my memory.

While I was having my breakfast, Vivek came looking as fresh as ever. For a moment I stared into his brown eyes until he suddenly asked, 'Paresh told me you came for me. Is there something you want me to do?'

Yes, I want you to love me. I wished I could say that aloud. 'Oh, no. Just . . .' I motioned him to sit in front of me. 'I had gone for jogging in the morning and thought you could have joined me. That's why I had come to the hostel but you were asleep.' My eyes rested on the wet hair on his forehead. Whenever he went out, he preferred to wet his hair to style them. I liked the way he combed his hair with his fingers.

'Hmm . . . we have not been jogging for the last few days out of sheer laziness,' he said. 'I would have joined you had you let Paresh wake me up.'

How nice of him! My mind began to think. *You surely would have joined me, I know.* He was so concerned about me. Always disposed to doing things for me. When

I was busy, he did the shopping for me or anything else that I asked of him. *He really likes me and that's why he does . . .*

'Should I go now?' Vivek's voice dragged me out of my thinking.

'Oh, no. Stay,' I said. 'Have some breakfast.'

'I can't.' He made a face of regret which made his innocent face look even more innocent. 'I've yet to brush my teeth.'

That meant he'd come for me no sooner had he woken up!

'Okay,' I said and added, 'by the way, since it's a holiday today, I was thinking of going out. What do you say about exploring the jungle of Mahal?'

'Ah . . . well,' he said hesitantly. 'I'm a bit short of money these days and . . .'

'That shouldn't be a problem,' I said instantly. 'Money is not a problem.'

'Yes, but . . .'

'Say yes, please,' I pleaded.

'I wish I could, but the sports teacher has been calling us for practice every day. And due to this cricket practice, I have a lot of pending homework too. I was thinking of using today's holiday to finish that. Besides, I don't think any of the boys would be ready for such an unplanned trip.'

There was a feeling of disappointment, but then, he had other things to deal with. How could I wish him to be free for me every time I asked? I didn't let the sigh out. The disappointment didn't last for more than a second or two. In the past, it had bothered me a lot when things didn't go according to my plan, but as years passed, I learnt that not all things can always go the way we wish. Krishna was also not a yes-man, but to please me, he used to do as I said. I couldn't take a 'no' from him. And when he did, I would fight with him like an immature child or an obstinate girl. As I grew older, I controlled that weakness of mine. A denial did not exasperate me as much now. Perhaps, it was a learning process.

'Okay, maybe some other time,' I said, trying to smile. 'At least you can come here with your homework. I'd like to have you here. I won't disturb you, I promise!'

'Sure, I will.' He looked up at the cloudy sky. 'After the practice,' he said, and left with a joyful smile. I looked at the sky and wished it would rain.

Since it was a national holiday, I began to think about how to kill time till Vivek turned up. Spreading a mat on the floor of my bedroom, I did yoga and lost myself in meditation. Later, I sat with a drawing sheet and brush and colours till noon. It felt good to paint something after a long time.

I'd just had a wink of sleep after lunch when the continuously ringing phone forced me to get up. It was Tarun, an old friend from Baroda. We chatted for about half an hour. It felt good to know he was going to get married in the coming week.

'You'll have to attend the reception ceremony, okay?' He sounded ecstatic.

'I'll try,' I said in a low voice.

'What do you mean you'll try? You'll have to be here, otherwise I won't talk to you in the future. Do you understand?'

'Tarun,' I said. 'I seldom visit Baroda. And you know why . . .'

'I know,' Tarun said from the other end. 'Whatever happened to you was . . . anyway, I won't force you any more. I'd like to have you here.'

'Yeah. Congratulations in advance,' I wished him and made a mental note to call him up on the day of his marriage to congratulate him again.

'Thanks pal. Have a nice day!' he said, and hung up.

For a few seconds, I sat quietly with the receiver of the phone still in my hand and visualized Tarun—a fair, slender and short person, very conscious of his height. He believed that he didn't have a girlfriend just because of his height. Later, he had learned to ignore mocking remarks with, 'Actually, my brain is so rich and big that it didn't let my body grow under its weight.'

Tarun was really a super brain. He had always topped the class. He couldn't get a girl during college days, but now he was getting married! I wished him a fulfilling married life.

Tarun's call took me to the past when unlike the constrained atmosphere of the school, the free atmosphere in college gave us a new life. There was no burden of monotonous homework, no uniforms, no need to be punctual to catch the school bus and attend the classes, and no principal to keep a close watch over us. Those years helped me spread my wings as far as extracurricular activities were concerned. Though I wasn't the best, I played football, tennis and badminton at the college level, and the hobby that earned me prizes every year was painting. Tarun and I were friends since high school and he was the closest one until Krishna entered my life. Then I began to spend more time with Krishna without realizing that I was ignoring Tarun. I could recall every single thing I had done in my school and college life. It seemed like I was reliving my youth.

On the final day of our college, we had promised each

other we would all meet at least once a year—a mere consolation for our weeping hearts at that time for as time went by, nobody seemed to have any time for such reunions. Some of us, including me, tried to arrange a gathering for two years, but it wasn't possible for everyone to be at one place at one time. We drifted apart.

Vivek came at around 2.30 p.m. Before sitting down for studies, he went to the washbasin, washed his face and wet his hair. He then took a seat on my writing desk and I sprawled on the settee with Sidney Sheldon's latest novel, *The Best Laid Plans.* Although the book had a gripping plot, it didn't interest me at that time. I kept peeking at Vivek over the book. I always enjoyed watching him. Even a brief glimpse of his face could fill my heart with ecstasy. Vivek knew that I stared at him, but I didn't know if he ever had an idea why I did so. Maybe I was too clever to let him get an idea. Maybe he was too dumb to think that way. Had he been a bit cleverer, he would have understood my intentions. Had he been . . . or was he? I didn't know. I never knew.

I prepared tea for myself and hot milk for him at tea-time. I wanted to show him the painting that I had made in the morning, but since it needed a bit of finishing, I didn't talk about it. Waiting for him to finish his homework, I busied myself in ironing my clothes. And it was in the late evening that he was done. I had thought of going to the sunset point, but it was useless now since the sun had already set. So we set out for a walk through the little town of Valai. Discussing the recent leopard attacks and the previous day's defeat in cricket, we strolled from the library mid-town to the collector's bungalow at the far end of Valai, from the police station to the cathedral to the radio station up on the hill behind the water reservoir. He told me about how downcast he was with the result of the other day's match. And he also talked about girls. It was interesting to listen to him. Chandni was the kind of girl every boy would have liked to fall in love with, but she and Vivek belonged to different classes of society. She was an upper caste girl whose father was in a high post in a government sector, whereas Vivek belonged to the lower class and was the son of a poor farmer. Vivek felt that there was no future in their relationship and that was why he didn't want to get close to Chandni.

I didn't know Vivek was that mature since one rarely felt the same in his talk. That's why I was taken by surprise with what he had said. I liked that. Then he talked about the other girls he liked. One, Seema, lived in his village and he liked her but since his society didn't permit marriage with somebody from one's own village, he wasn't serious about her. The other girl, inferior to Seema and Chandni as far as looks was concerned, belonged to his neighbouring village. Her name was Mala and he had a soft corner for that dusky schoolgirl. He told me more about her, where she studied, who was in her family, how they'd met during Holi at Dang Durbar two years ago, and how they'd begun to like each other. Jealousy tore through me as I listened to him talk about his love interests, but I didn't let it appear on my face or in my voice. Instead, I pretended to be very interested in his love life.

'As we all know, many of the hostel boys have girlfriends in the girls' hostel. Don't you have one there?' I asked.

'No.' Came the quick reply.

'No . . .?' I frowned disbelievingly.

'In fact, I liked a girl when I was in class nine . . .'

'Nine!' I exclaimed.

'Yes,' he laughed. 'I was fourteen then. Didn't know much about love. Don't know now either. But it really was childish. She was older than me. I didn't want to propose to her or have her as a girlfriend. I'd just stare at her since I liked her very much.'

'Then?' I asked to get some more information.

'Then what?'

'Anyone else after that?'

'Not really,' he said judiciously. 'Physical attraction has happened many times, but not all the attractions necessarily result in a relationship.'

I liked what he had said and chuckled. For a long time, we remained silent till I caught sight of a young boy passing by on the road. The cap the boy had worn evoked the memories of Krishna within me and I whispered his name.

'Did you say something?' Vivek asked. *He had heard me whisper!*

'No,' I replied. 'The cap on that boy's head reminded me of how Krishna also liked to wear a cap.'

Vivek asked me about my love and I told him a funny incident that I recalled. It was a New Year celebration on the terrace of a four star hotel where I had gone with Krishna. The partying that had begun just before midnight was to continue till the wee hours of the morning. We ate and drank beer and danced for hours. While making merry, Krishna noticed that a good looking girl standing alone in a corner was staring at me constantly. He told me about her. My eyes on the other hand were on the two handsome guys who were dancing on the floor in the centre of the terrace. I didn't tell Vivek where my eyes and interest had been.

'Who cares?' I'd glanced at the girl for a second and busied myself in what I was doing. Krishna had no problem with my ogling at other boys. He went back to dancing with a frenzied vigour. A little later, when I was leaning against a pillar drinking beer, the pretty girl came and greeted me, 'Hi.'

'Hi,' I replied and looked at her face. She was slightly drunk. 'I'm Shirley. Would you like to go out with me?' She proposed boldly. 'I'm single and I guess we can be good friends.' Her cleavage clearly exposed, she leered suggestively and took a sip from her glass.

Before I could answer her, Krishna, who had his eyes on us all the time, came to my rescue. 'What's up, folks?' he asked in a sing song voice. The girl seemed to have no problem with his presence.

'She wants to go *out* with me,' I said and winked at him.

'Well, well . . .' Krishna replied. 'So why don't you? It will be fun.' Then he looked at her and said, 'But before that, there's something about him I'd like you to know.'

The girl turned her gaze to Krishna. I was sure of something obscene coming out of his mouth. 'He,' he pointed towards me, 'likes to mix his food and eat it like a dog.' He made ugly faces as he talked. 'He sleeps naked in bed and likes to come in the mouth.' As soon as those words came out of his mouth, the girl's face turned red. And Krishna's expressions were so funny that I couldn't help laughing.

'And above all,' keeping his eyes on the girl all the time, he slipped his hand around my waist and pulled me towards him, 'he's gay.'

How mean was that! At the end of that nauseating talk, Krishna nastily showed the girl his tongue and she could do nothing but escape from there.

It was fun. Krishna always did this kind of obnoxious and sickening things that left people stunned.

'I can't believe this really happened!' Vivek gaped at me incredulously. 'And how bold was that girl to propose to you! One can't imagine such things here.' Vivek laughed as the wayward incident really amused him. He looked even more handsome when he rolled with laughter.

'It's true and we cherished that particular incident for months,' I said.

'How could she believe you were gay?' Vivek asked. 'I mean . . . it's impossible! She should have understood that whatever your friend had said was a lie. How dumb of her!'

That left me speechless. He didn't believe I was gay. He couldn't think of me as a homosexual. He had no idea about who I was in reality.

'Krishna was fearless and outspoken,' Vivek said.

'Yes, he was. He was the one who had no hesitation in calling a spade a spade. Compared to him, I was more politically correct.' In an instant, I went back in time and relived the rest of the incident. After the party, Krishna and I had walked home hand in hand till day break.

Still inebriated, I had asked, grumbling, 'Why did you interfere between me and the girl?'

He stared at me. 'You were jealous, weren't you?' I needled him.

'Yes, I was,' he replied instantly.

'Why? What for?' I was enjoying putting him in an awkward situation.

'Because I hate you, damn it!' he spoke harshly and I laughed. *Because he loved me.* I knew. He was jealous because he loved me. *How blissful it is to know that someone really loves you!*

'Krishna was a great friend, wasn't he?' Vivek's question brought me out of my reverie.

'He was.' I sighed. *He was and is.*

While having a delectable meal at the Chinese restaurant, my mind compared Vivek with Krishna. I thought about the similarities and the differences between those two dearest men in my life. Both of them had a dusky complexion–Vivek was a shade fairer than Krishna and both had a brawny physique. They both didn't take life that seriously. Neither of them was irascible or squeamish. Vivek was so magnanimous and so were Krishna. I could call to memory that only once Krishna had taken my words amiss—I had been looking at my face in the mirror when he'd come from behind and put his chin on my shoulder to see his reflection in the mirror, trying to arrange his hair with his fingers. 'That wouldn't make any difference to your ugly face,' I had uttered, mocking him and he'd taken it to heart.

'Why doesn't my ugliness bother you in bed then?' he'd retorted and left. I had no idea that he would react like this, so I ran after him and apologized but he didn't talk to me properly for a few days after that. I had no such problems with Vivek probably because I still had not become as close to him as I had been with Krishna. Then from my break-up with Krishna, I had learnt that relationships are much like glass vessels—to be handled with care.

I had always been fond of eating, but I didn't have as big an appetite as Krishna's or Vivek's. They were hearty eaters and weren't fussy about food. Also both of them forgot things habitually and were latecomers. The most irritating thing for me was to wait, and the two people dearest to me frequently obliged me by giving me a chance to get miffed. Krishna freely uttered abuses and Vivek did the same, but not in my presence. Vivek was so much like

Krishna that the things he did reminded me constantly of Krishna. Time and again, I had told him how similar he was to Krishna. Even after falling in love with Vivek, I couldn't forget Krishna. Many of Vivek's habits, virtues and vices took me back to the memories of Krishna.

If I counted the differences, there were many. Krishna was taller and had curly, black hair, whereas Vivek was more handsome and had straight, brown hair. Vivek was a good singer, Krishna's singing was terrible. Krishna played soccer, Vivek, cricket. Though Krishna was inferior to Vivek as far as looks were concerned, he had so many other qualities Vivek lacked. Krishna had developed many hobbies such as skating, photography and sketching, Vivek was almost zero in everything other than cricket. That was probably also because Krishna lived in a sophisticated, material world where so much was available to encourage him, and Vivek had lived in a place where things came only in small packages. Krishna was shrewd, good at lying and making a fool of people, whilst those urban qualities hadn't touched Vivek. Again it was because of the different worlds they inhabited. Krishna was obviously what he was, in the fast paced life of Baroda where there was no dearth of fake, false personalities. Vivek's heart was as fresh and pure as the early breeze of winter. Krishna was such a good liar that he hid things very cleverly. His ever smiling eyes seldom reflected what was in his heart.

Then again, Krishna was great in bed, Vivek, I had no idea of as yet. Krishna was one person I could relate myself more with. Vivek was a person I was still learning about. Since Krishna was an intelligent fellow, I could discuss with him various subjects. Intellectually, Vivek wasn't as rich as Krishna, so I had to think before I gave any serious subject a go. Vivek was still not mature enough to understand everything I said. It was the age difference between us that didn't let me be as free with him as I was with Krishna. Krishna was a great soulmate, Vivek still hadn't reached that height. I missed Krishna so much because he was the one who understood me in every respect. He was ready to listen to even my stupidest talks. He was my punching bag. I could complain to him about anything, discuss with him my problems and cry before him without a feeling of shame or hesitation. I doubted if I would ever be that free with Vivek.

I found myself crazy about both of them, but one thing I didn't like in them was the lack of emotions. Neither of them had that emotional side which I expected in a person. They had feelings for me, but they kept their feelings under control and didn't express them. I still couldn't bare my heart to Vivek, but Krishna was the one who knew me through and through. With him I let my love and emotions pour out, but he seldom did so himself. That's what irritated me the most. I was at ease with expressing feelings, a quality very few men are said to have. In other words, it is a quality found mostly in women and I didn't hesitate to admit that I was a bit effeminate.

While getting back home after dinner, it started raining. Vivek and I enjoyed getting soaked. What a romantic evening it was! We had had a great time together and he made our walk back home even more romantic by singing a love song from an old Hindi movie. The entire time he had his hand in mine, giving an incredible satisfaction to my thirsty heart. This time reminded me of many such dreamy evenings I had spent at Baroda in Krishna's company.

Once home, I told him to change, but he said he was fine. I pushed him into the bathroom with a towel and when he got out, he had just the towel around his waist. What

Mayur Patel

a sexy body he had! I couldn't take my eyes away from his enticing upper body. The sight of his muscled physique aroused me and I found it difficult to fight the desire that burned in every part of my body. When he was dressing in my bedroom, I had an indomitable urge to take him to bed and do everything I used to do with Krishna. But I had to control myself. He put on my clothes that almost fit him and left with my umbrella.

I dropped on my bed as the hunger for sex was haunting me badly. There had been many such nights when my desire for sex had become uncontrollable. The cold bedspread turned into burning embers and fired up my body and soul. And even when sanity surrendered to necessity of bodily contentment, I wished to hold Vivek close to my body. I wished that the desire of kissing his lips and playing with his naked body for the entire night, would be fulfilled. Had I been a woman, I would have got him in my bed at any cost, by fair means or foul. There was only one way to satisfy the fire of my body on such thirsty nights. Imagining him with me in bed, I would masturbate. I frequently dreamed of having sex with him. I thought about him all day and he came in my dreams at night. Our hidden desires do come true in our dreams and my ultimate wish was to make love to Vivek.

As the simmering desire of having sex with Vivek haunted my body, I lapsed in time and relived every single second I had spent with Krishna in the bathroom that day. It was that third intercourse between us when I had actually enjoyed myself with all my senses alive. The clouds of penitence of having sex with my best friend had dispersed completely and I had accepted this new development in our liaison. As I cherished those precious moments I had with Krishna, my excitement was uncontrollable and my hand slipped within my undergarment. I was crazy about the way Krishna had kissed, bitten and caressed me. I could still feel the heat of his breath on my skin. We'd made love in every possible posture. The way he had made love to me that day in the bathroom, it seemed like he knew everything about taking his partner to the extremes of passion. The climax was delayed and finally, it was over. No, it hadn't been over. It had just been the beginning. The beginning of many more such passionate physical encounters.

thirteen

Though I had always been fond of fast paced thrillers, that day for a change, I picked up a romantic novel from the library. The novel had such a blissful narration of love and passion that I couldn't stop myself from getting romantic. Along with the real, outer world, I had been living in an imaginary, utopian world that I had created inside me since my adolescence. With Vivek, I had made a world of my romantic fantasies that was both unique and insubstantial, where there was no one to disturb us. I imagined us alone on a solitary island, a place beautifully crowned with tall, green trees. With bottles of beer and loads of fried chicken, we lazily rested on the white sands under the heavenly blue sky. Aromatic flowers lay strewn around us, colourful birds flew overhead, and foamy waves kissed our feet on the sloppy bank of the sea.

This pleasant atmosphere would last eternally. I would take his face in my palms and the kiss would be everlasting. *How romantic the experience would be!* My mind had created the same weird, surreal world when I was in love with Krishna. So many years had elapsed since then, but the madness of my younger days was still alive. Only the characters had changed. Then it was Krishna, now it was Vivek. Though I knew all that was impractical, I loved to indulge in my colourful fantasyland.

I'd always been a romantic person. Unfortunately, the men I fell in love with lacked the romantic gene. There was a chasm, not vast though, between us. Krishna foolishly tried to be romantic sometimes and ended up being the butt of my jokes. So far, I hadn't seen the romantic side of Vivek but I doubted if he had one because he had never sounded romantic even when talking about his girlfriends.

I loved Krishna so much and expected to get back the same sort of affection from him. The feeling that Krishna didn't love me the way I loved him disheartened me many times. It took me years to learn that there should be no calculations in love. Krishna couldn't open his heart to me. I was more expressive than was necessary and he was reserved more than was necessary. He loved me and took care of me, but the kind of devotion I expected from him was not there. His love was insufficient to me and that reality disappointed me.

'How much do you love me?' I had asked Krishna once when we were alone in his hostel room.

Instead of replying at once, he had stared at me for long. When I repeated my question, he'd asked, 'Is it necessary that I reply?'

I'd nodded and he'd asked further, 'You want a sweet answer or a true one?'

'The second option,' I said.

'Even though I don't know how to define the word "love", I like you very much. More than anyone else. What I feel for you I have never felt for anybody. And this comes straight from my heart,' he had replied passionately.

I was so touched with what he'd said and was about to say something nice when Jignesh, Krishna's hostel mate, cut in out of the blue. Though I welcomed him with a smile, I didn't like his intrusion in those few romantic moments of ours. Krishna seldom became romantic, so I knew how precious those fleeting moments were and I actually cursed Jignesh in my mind for violating the moments that might have led us to a passionate kiss. Well, the boy hadn't done anything, but I hated this disturbance. I liked what Krishna had said. The way those words had been spoken. Yes, he loved me, but it was always inadequate. I desired more and more.

Hypocrisy melts when a person gets physical with someone. With the denuding of the clothes from the body, the covers of hypocrisy melt. Other human limbs might be treacherous but the genital organs can't ever lie. The real person behind the mask appears in bed once the drape of shame and hesitation is cast off. Then there is no sense of guilt. To me, getting physical with my friend was not an aberration anymore. We got closer and closer to each other with each passing day as sex became an inescapable physical and psychological necessity for both of us. Many inexplicable things happen in life. Falling in love with Krishna was one such inexplicable but delightful thing. I had never intended to go as far with him as I had gone. But once love blossomed, I didn't know how to stop loving him. Love gives a meaning to life and Krishna had given my life a new meaning, a new hope and a reason to live my life the way I wanted.

In the beginning, the thought that I was getting physical with my best friend tormented me. *Why am I so? Why have I fallen in love with Krishna? Why do I have physical relations with him?* These questions haunted my thoughts. I even cried sometimes. But then I accepted that relationship just the way I had accepted my gayness. 'You are gay, accept it. You love him, admit it,' I told myself to get some peace of mind. And, in fact, it was Krishna who told me not to be bothered about the path that we two had mutually opted for. Being comfortable about his physical intimacy with me, he'd told me to refrain from attaching any kind of regret or shame or guilt to this new beginning in our relationship. He'd said it had happened because it had to happen. Such openness of thought from Krishna made me believe that it had all been planned by God and that He was the one who had brought Krishna into my life. Since then, there had been no regrets about getting intimate with him.

Before I met Krishna, my sex life had been zero. Except for that brief episode with my cousin Pranav, I had not slept with anyone. I'd liked a few men, but I was too shy and cowardly to approach them to get physical with me. It was frustrating because I was getting what I didn't want and what I wanted was out of my reach somehow. The thought that my youth and physical beauty would be wasted this way in waiting for the right man, disheartened me sometimes. And since I was good looking, people thought that I was the lucky bastard who was making the most of my charming personality by taking the most beautiful girls to bed at will. My friends never believed me when I said I was not seeing anyone. Some even tried to dig out my secret lovers, but they were disappointed because there were none. Still, not a single one of my friends believed me. They assumed I was too clever and was keeping my affairs totally private. I wished I was as clever as they thought I was. In reality, my eyes always remained in search of a man of my choice. Some male eyes did show interest in me but either I didn't like them or circumstances were not positive for a relationship. All I did was to fantasize about men and satiate my hunger for sex by masturbating. Then Krishna came into my life with a whole new definition of good sex and carnal ecstasy, and my forbidden sexuality sprang out of the closet. For years I had been waiting for someone like him and it was he who brought my erotic fantasies to fruition and changed all the equations of my sexually frustrated life. My boring and inhibited life was filled with colours of romance by his entry.

Once my relationship with Krishna had taken a different shape, we'd became shameless about getting physical, and what better place could we have for it but my home. He came to my place on the pretence of studying and stayed with me at night. Though our sexuality didn't need any outside props to be ignited, we sometimes watched porn films for a change. My family believed we studied behind the locked door of my bedroom. Krishna and I were so clever that nobody in my family had ever come to know about our sexual tendencies. Neither our college friends nor Krishna's hostel mates could ever suspect us to be homosexuals since we knew how to behave in public and how to keep a distance between us while going out with others. Our sexuality flared up only in a locked room or in desolate places. We spent countless erotic nights at my place and, before opening the door of my room in the morning, we made sure that the evidences of our sexual encounters were successfully hidden. It was all so much fun and the real thrill was to keep our copulations successfully veiled. We liked it, but sometimes the thought of being caught red-handed scared me. Our lives would be changed forever if that happened, so I prayed to God to not let that happen.

Krishna and I shared a relationship that lay somewhere between real friendship and true love. It was something I was unable to fathom, because to me, Krishna was the one I was in love with, to him, I was his for gratifying his sexual needs. Sex was an emotional demand for me and I was always more keen about kissing, touching and sharing the warmth of true love, whereas he was always more ardent about sensual contentment. He believed that whatever we did should just be plain sex and it indeed was just that to him way. He was a sexually confident man who discussed sex with ease, knew all about the sexual arithmetic and liked to try out new things in bed without any hesitation or feeling of disgust. Though he was gay, he'd never let his feminine self emerge. He was always so manly, liked to be aggressive and I was crazy about his virility. He never admitted it but the way he played adroitly with me in bed, I believed he'd had sexual liaisons with other boys before. My knowledge said that most homosexuals liked to be polygamous if they were not seriously in love. I doubted if Krishna had been monogamous because sex had always been only physical for him. For me from the very beginning, it had been more mental and less physical. We used to tell each other 'I love you', but the kind of affection I felt for him was missing in his attitude for me. In all, I could say I loved him and he liked me. He just 'liked' me. His love was only sexual. His feelings for me were always indistinct. Nevertheless, I was content with the notion that finally I had found someone of my choice. It felt great to have someone by my side, to love me. Loving means to have faith in the person we love and to love him just as intensely no matter what he does. So I loved him believing he was going to be with me forever.

The more intimate we got, the more difficult it became for me to live without Krishna. My obsession of being with him was all consuming. Even though he would stare at my face absent-mindedly, I became very fond of him watching me. When I would ask him what he saw in my eyes, he wouldn't reply but just smile. There always was an integrity in his smile, but I didn't know how to trust it. My mind couldn't dispense with the dreadful feeling that he was only interested in sex.

When you love someone, there's always a fear of losing your beloved. The feeling of insecurity ceaselessly gnawed at me when I was with Krishna. The dread that something dreadful might happen which would take him away from me forever, was always there in some deep, dark corner of my mind. The more we got close, the more that feeling increased. *Is he going to be with me forever? Will he love me till the end of my life?* This feeling of possessing him for the rest of my life never let me be in peace. 'Will you be with me forever?' I'd asked while sitting on the parapet of the hostel building one evening. I liked to put him in awkward positions by asking such questions.

He took his time before he replied, 'Why do you want to hold me forever? Hold me openly in your palms, not tightly in your fists. There should be no compulsions in any relationship. And please, please, please don't try to foresee the future of love. Just enjoy the present.' He continued as I listened, 'one should not expect so much from people as expectations kill relationships.'

Hold me openly in your palms, not tightly in your fists—was what Krishna had said. *So that you could leave me any moment*—was what came to my mind, but I didn't express it to him. Krishna was good at playing with words. I'd got the gist of what he'd said. The hidden insinuation in his words meant—'don't expect anything from me'. Neither was he true nor was I wrong. We invest feelings, love and time in our close ones and expect to receive the same from them. It's purely human and there's nothing wrong with it. We all are worldly-wise and this world relies upon feelings, love and expectations. Had it not been so, the earth would have been overcrowded with saints. I was dreaming about spending the rest of my life with Krishna, when he wanted to refrain from any kind of commitment. I wanted him to promise me not to leave me ever, but then, you can't *make* someone love you . . .

It is said that basic human nature is to always be dissatisfied. In the gratuitous anxiety over the unachievable, a man is unable to enjoy whatever he has got. I had Krishna who made my present special in every way, yet I worried about the future. What I got from him was not insufficient, it was my aspiration that was limitless. I had always expected too much from my close ones. I didn't know then that though it is human to expect, one shouldn't expect to be happy in love forever. There should be no conditions in love. With its divine feelings and sensations, love also brings sorrow, separation and suffering.

Though I enjoyed my gayness and had accepted it as an ordinary thing, sometimes I contemplated where it would take me. With Krishna, I had gone so far that there was no way back. Many boys in their teens explore same-sex relationships because of acute passion, lack of company of the opposite sex, and the curiosity to learn the first lessons of sex. Very few of them remain gay forever. I was one of them.

The main concern for most homosexuals is to have physical gratification, but that had never been the only objective of my relationship with Krishna. I needed him physically as well as mentally. Even at the peak of my relationship with him, I was attracted to other guys, but it was only bodily driven. The difference between those transient attractions and my vulnerability for Krishna was love. I loved him and wanted to be with him all the time.

I liked to be in his arms, I loved to be kissed, and I craved those passionate hugs, but it wasn't like I desired sex every time. And though my libido was not as strong as Krishna's, I had no problem with his voracious desire, so I accepted whenever he wanted to have sex with me. I didn't want to disappoint him in anything. I knew Krishna through and through. Sometimes, the pinching of his lower lip implied his desire. And I found myself always so responsive to his non verbal messages.

After finishing my studies, I had found a nice job as a teacher at a high school in Baroda. And since my sexuality was still a secret, I was a perfect bachelor in many people's opinion. Everybody used to keep telling me to get married. And after Smit's marriage, it seemed like all the people around me were there to marry me off. They brought me the photographs of the best looking girls from the best of backgrounds. Fortunately, I had a younger sister who was still studying, so I could turn the proposals down saying, 'I would think of my marriage only after Ridham's.' Only my family knew that I wasn't much excited about getting hitched. My father didn't take that seriously as always, whereas my mother told me about the benefits of a married life. My siblings laughed at me and Smit had once told me in private, 'When the body will haunt you, all your regulations and notions and beliefs will change. Take a girl to bed for once. I bet you'll be addicted to it.' He was clearly talking about sex. Yes, I was addicted to sex. But not with girls. I was addicted to being in bed with Krishna.

The same story was being repeated here in Valai time and again. The age of twenty-six is not considered too much for marriage in a place like Baroda but in Valai, it sure was high time to get married. Here, most of my colleagues, neighbours and well wishers frequently asked me when I was going to tie the knot. Thinking that an answer like 'I don't want to get married' might arouse other questions, I would reply, 'There is still time.' There was too much pressure. Marriage proposals from the upper classes of Valai had been continually pouring in since the day I had come here. I sometimes thought it was a good thing that I was born a man. Had I been a woman, and a lesbian, leading a solitary life without getting married would have been extremely difficult in this society where the standards for man and woman vary in many ways. No matter how great Indian culture is, the standards for the social status, responsibilities and duties of men and women have always been different in this orthodox society. Unlike Europe and America, our society doesn't accept same-sex relationships, otherwise I would have liked to marry Krishna. And once I had told Krishna so. And I still remember how pathetic and confused his expressions were on hearing this!

Sometimes, while making love, Krishna used to say, 'I wish you were a girl. I would have married you.' I had always been very imaginative, so when he stimulated my hidden desire, I began to dream that I was a girl and had married him. In any case, my feminine side had always been stronger. After Smit's birth, my parents wanted a girl, so until Ridham's birth, I was treated like a girl by my mother. She made me wear frocks and gave me a girl's name 'Sweety'. Besides, because of my father's strict temperament, I never wanted to be like him. In my opinion, it was my mother who lived an ideal life. I'd spent more time with her. When my father scolded me for minor mistakes, my mother came to my rescue. Growing up under her protective care, I began to idolize her for the love she showered upon me and for all the great values she had. I played tennis and football and was fond of all the games boys liked, but then, some of my hobbies and likes were similar to girls' such as cooking, shopping and dressing up.

I was different from the other boys of my class in many ways. When most boys uttered abusive words, didn't hesitate in getting involved in fights, passed vulgar comments on girls and talked about their private parts, I did nothing like that. I was not the only boy who refrained from all those things, but I was always so conscious about the fact that I had some attributes akin to girls. My emotions and instincts were stronger than other boys of my age. I was vulnerable, my face was fair, and the bone structure was tender, giving me a feminine charm. The thing I was the most concerned about was revealing my inner self. Some homosexuals are visibly gay, but I never let myself be one of them. I was conscious about not drawing attention to my true self. I made sure that I didn't look, sound or walk like a girl, especially at school for the fear of being teased by the boys. Hence, I couldn't make good friends at school. For years, I struggled with my sexual identity and couldn't let anybody get close to me. Smit had a great friend circle. Watching him, I wished for friends like his, but something from inside held me back and that something never let me earn good friends until I was sixteen. I was in the twelfth class when I had befriended Tarun and what a friend he was! He was the first guy outside of my blood relations with whom I had started to go out.

The feeling of being in love with Vivek was sensational and I wanted to share it with others, but there was nobody I could talk to about it. No one in this orthodox place would be able to understand my feelings. Not even Vivek. The only such person in my life was Krishna, but unfortunately, he was far away from me. Even though our relationship wasn't going to be what it used to be, I yearned to have that man back in my life. Many a time, I had thought of calling him on his old number but my ego held me back. Here in Valai, I had no one to pour my heart out to. Yes, Vivek was great company, but I was afraid of admitting the truth about my sexuality to him. I wasn't sure if he was mature enough to understand me. Thus, the frustration of keeping my love a secret built a certain resentment in me.

I was so immersed in Vivek's love and the desire to get him was so strong that every single knock on the door gave me the false impression of his arrival. And putting all my work aside, I would rush out to look for him. I found myself exultant when Vivek came and stayed with me, and hated the time when he took leave of me. I didn't want him to go away from me. Emotionally, I was so caught up with him that I wanted him to be with me for eternity. This led me to become possessive about him. Many times it had happened that Vivek was with me, and then one of his friends, especially Paresh, would turn up with something that would take him away from me. I just hated such a situation when someone disturbed us and stole him away from me. The same form of possessiveness had developed in me for Krishna in the past. I had become so attached to Krishna that I wanted to dominate him. I wanted to control him. I denied freedom to him. And it was my over possessiveness that had brought our relationship to an end. I didn't want the same to happen in my life once again.

I was in search for the right time to unveil my fondness for Vivek. Since I was unsure about Vivek's feelings for me, I asked myself 'What must Vivek think of me? Does he love me?' Never had his eyes conveyed the kind of love I was seeking. They expressed adulation and reverence. But not love. That way Vivek and I were so close, yet so far.

I had made up my mind that I would propose to him someday sooner or later. *But how?* That was a million dollar question. I had already told him that I had a secret to reveal to him and he had been eager to know at that time, but later, he had never asked me about it. It was possible that he had forgotten. The other possibility was that he was still interested, but wouldn't dare ask me. I had thought of taking a promise from him that he would keep my secret a secret. Taking him to a deserted place, I wanted to peel the layers from my innermost core and reveal myself to him. It wasn't going to be easy I knew, but I had to confess my love someday before he would leave Valai at the end of his schooling. I didn't know how he would react when my true colours would come out before him. Such an intense emotional revelation it would be that I doubted if he would understand it thoroughly! He might hate me for insulting our friendship and leave me forever in anger. I didn't want that to happen because I didn't want to lose his friendship, but then, neither was I ready to accept him just as a friend. I wanted more. I wanted from him what I had got from Krishna. All truths needn't be revealed always. But in my case, I had to unveil my truth to acquire my love.

Since the confession of my true feelings was to be a tough job, I had the option of getting drunk to help myself open up. I would probably cry and my tears might touch him since I knew he couldn't see anyone in pain. I thought that emotional blackmail was something that might work on that gullible soul. No matter what, I'd have to let him know what was welling up in my heart. There were two possibilities—he'd accept my love, or he'd refuse. I knew I'd have to be mentally prepared for both the situations. The urge to know what was in his heart for me, was getting more intense day by day, but I couldn't dare to open my heart to him for the fear of rejection. I could have played a nasty trick, but my position in his life held me from doing that. I felt I was too old for doing what I had once done to Krishna to test his love for me. I had sent him a message that I had had an accident, and in no time, he had rushed to my place. Finding me perfectly well on the couch in my room, he had stood agape at the door.

'It's not April Fool's day, is it?' he'd asked panting.

'I just wanted to see how much you love me,' I'd said teasingly.

He shook his head disbelievingly. I was elated at the thought that he truly loved me. That's why he'd rushed to me in a jiffy. He was one of the few people in my life who was happy in my happiness and sad in my grief. His feelings for me were genuine and that's what mattered to me the most. That is what had kept me hooked to him.

'You know something? You're a fool!' Taking a seat by me, he'd stared angrily at me.

'Yes, I am.' It didn't take me long to get romantic while being with him. 'I'm a fool. A fool in love. Your love!'

Suddenly, Krishna had become serious and stared at me. To get him out of his thoughts, I had snapped my fingers before his face and asked, 'Hello! Where are you?'

'Don't expect so much from me, Kaushik!' He'd said in the same vein. 'We never know what's hidden in the future.'

'Don't talk like that!' I'd complained with an optimistic smile. 'Nothing wrong would ever happen to us, I know.' By the time I was done, I had my arms around his neck. His lips parted to say something, but I hadn't give them the opportunity to speak. Krishna's solemnity had faded away with the magical touch of my lips. The kiss I had given him led us to what else but love making. *Passionate, divine love . . .*

Krishna and I used to wander around a lot. We would go for movies, outings and we loved to eat out. Since Krishna's financial condition was not that good, it was I who took care of the expenses. But that didn't mean anything to me. I liked to splurge when we were having fun. Krishna sometimes expressed his regret at not being able to pay the bills. At such times, I used to say, 'There shouldn't be anything like mine or yours. It should always be ours.' I said so because I believed it's not love if it is calculated. I did spend a lot of money on Vivek too. I never held back or calculated the expenditure when it was a question of making him happy. Even when his pockets were full, I seldom let him pay. And both, Krishna and Vivek, had been so warm and intimate that I had never felt they were with me just because I spent a lot on them. Their friendship was genuine.

An incident flashed in my mind about the time when Vivek had a bad cough and hadn't seen a doctor because he did not have the money for it. When I had asked him to go to the doctor, he had said it wasn't that bad and it would heal in a day or two. I had taken him to the doctor against his will. A few days later, when he'd come to pay the money I had spent for his medication, I had scolded him saying how could he think I would accept the money. He had apologized and I had calmed down. I was surprised to know how easy it was for me to forgive such a childish act of Vivek! Though Vivek had received a scholarship for his study, he was free to ask me for money for his personal expenses. And he borrowed from me when he needed. Considering his financial condition, I never expected him to return my money, but he always paid back. I was so obsessed with him that I wouldn't have minded even if he had exploited me for money. But the boy never did so. And that was one of the many reasons I adored him.

The apparent difference between the two love stories of mine was that with Krishna, I had become physical first and then love had blossomed. In Vivek's case, I had fallen in love first and was longing for sex now. But the feeling that I was doing something very wrong to Vivek bothered me often. I did repent falling for that innocent soul who respected me so much and thought of me as a great friend. It wasn't like I hadn't tried to stay away from him. I had tried seriously but failed. I had made efforts to cut the attachment but I couldn't keep myself away from him. It was tough for me to push him out of my mind. It would be tougher to go away from him. There was no such chance. I was so much hooked on him that I would relinquish anything for him.

In the beginning, I was guilty about falling in love with Vivek, but all those earlier regrets melted away once I realized that the boy was a godsend. The acceptance of the fact that he was a gift from the Almighty unshackled me from my remorse and I was free from the feeling of committing a transgression. The boy really was a gift because it was he who had brought back to my mundane life, the delight of adolescence which I had probably lost a decade ago. He got me out of my solitary confinement and filled my boring world with colours. With him, I became a child again and did many things that I had not done for years. We would sing aloud at the sunset point without giving a damn about the other people who looked at us mockingly. We would get soaked in the rain without worrying about falling sick, and we would go for outings without paying heed to the people who were jealous of our being together.

Spending time with Vivek always made my day blissful and I became even more romantic. Many times, I used to ask him, 'Why do I like you so much? Why are you so sweet?'

'I don't know,' he would reply. 'I really don't know what is so special about me.'

'That's something only I know,' I would reply. 'It's your innocence and your friendship that makes you so special.'

Vivek would smile at that. He always would.

Life teaches one a lot. Separation from Krishna and the aftermath of that disaster had taught me so much about life. I probably wouldn't have learned all that, had Krishna and I been together forever. I had become helpless in Krishna's love. One shouldn't be so helpless in love that the person he's in love with starts to take advantage of his helplessness. Krishna had never tried to take advantage of my blind affection for him, but then, the fact was that he'd never loved me the way I loved him. I had thought of having a permanent relationship with him, but our relations were just a way of passing time for him. He could dispense with me. I did let myself go weak in his love and suffered the pain of separation badly. I didn't want the same to happen in Vivek's case, but it happened. I made the same mistake of getting infatuated with a guy once again. I was retracing my own steps. I had dreamt of having a beautiful future with Krishna. It hadn't come true and had given me the biggest sorrow of my life. Again, I was on the same track of love and hope. Falling in love with Vivek, I'd committed the same mistake. But that's what we all do, don't we? Even though we know we're on the wrong path, we don't want to mend our ways. Falling in love with Vivek was one such error I didn't want to correct. I was neck deep in his love and he had become inseparable from my being. And I was ready for whatever destiny, the Master above had in store for me.

fourteen

The tender touch of the early morning radiance fell on my face through the window slits. I opened my eyes and felt excitement course through my veins. It was an early morning dream about making love to Vivek that had aroused me. Slipping under the bedspread, I put my mind to work and recalled the entire dream. Vivek was in my arms, I was pressing myself against his bare body and both of us were revelling in the joys that the union of our bodies had brought. With my eyes closed, I enjoyed that dream and wished it would come true someday. That was not the first time I had dreamt of getting physical with the boy. Having sex with him was my ultimate fantasy and it is rightly said that hidden desire came true through the medium of dreams. In the past, my sexual fantasies had circled around Krishna. Now they swivelled around Vivek.

When Sukhi brought me my morning tea, I asked her about Babu. She said that he hadn't done anything hateful since the day I had admonished him, but both of us knew that it wasn't going to last for long. He could behave like an animal any moment. And since I knew Sukhi wasn't going to get peace in her life while Babu was alive, there was nothing to be done.

At school that day, Vidya slipped a piece of paper in to my hand while passing by in the passage.

'What's this?' I asked urgently, attracting the attention of two students passing by.

'Find out for yourself,' Vidya said, merely looking back from the corner of her mischievous eyes, and walked away. Her gait signified something important. Still standing in the passage with the folded paper in my hand, I realized that the students were looking at me and the paper. So, quickly putting the paper in my back pocket, I walked away.

It was in the evening, after I came home, that I could open the paper Vidya had given me. It was as I had presumed—a love letter in Vidya's neat hand writing:

Dear Kaushik,

I decided to write this letter after long contemplation—It's something I've never done before. It takes a lot of courage to do such a risky thing, for one can end up getting defamed. I don't care because I'm unable to help myself anymore. It's taken me all this time to admit that I love you. It is love, it sure is, that I've found in your eyes. I fell in love with you the day I saw you for the first time. I'm sure it's not just physical attraction because I have had that experience in the past. Men have attracted me before, but not the way you have. It's you who occupy my heart. There's something so magnetic in your personality that appeals to the woman in me. I like everything about you, but the one thing that touches me the most is your sensitivity. I'm crazy about you and I think about you all the time. Love makes a person blind and I'm so blind in your love that I can't find a single vice in you even if I try.

Kaushik, I've never felt for anyone the way I feel about you. You don't know how your presence remains with me all the time. Your thoughts never let me be alone. I see you everywhere: in school, at home, while travelling. You're so deeply woven in my being that I can't pull you out of my mind.

They say love is an addiction. Yes, it is. I'm addicted to loving you.

Something happened deep inside my heart. I could reach myself because of you. Now I don't know what to do! In your love, I've lost my sanity. My mind is empty of all thoughts but yours. It's only you and nothing else there!

Thinking about you, loving you pains me, but that pain is the dearest and the most precious thing in my life right now. I want to marry you. I want to make love to you and I can do anything for you. Someone once said that marrying the person of your choice might bring you happiness or sorrow, but not marrying your beloved would surely bring you sorrow. And my heart wouldn't accept anyone else but you. Only you. Hope you will understand.

Love pains. Love kills. Love heals.

Now it's up to you to decide what I deserve.

Waiting for your, hopefully positive, reply

Vidya.

I had never thought Vidya would do something like this! I had assumed it was just physical attraction that had driven her to me. But now it seemed she really was in love with me! How unfortunate the poor spinster was that she had lost her heart to a homosexual! She was going to get nothing, but pain for loving me. Similar incidents had happened in Baroda. I still remember how frequently I had received love letters, gifts, red roses and greeting cards from girls. It was great to receive them but saying 'no' to those beautiful, charming girls was heartrending. Some girls were so attractive that I wished that I had not been gay . . .

This realization about my sexuality had closed many doors for me. Other than my mother, Ridham, Namrata and a few of my relatives, I preferred to stay away from women who seemed to have a certain kind of interest in me. It wasn't like I didn't like women. In fact, I adored women and loved to spend my time with them because I believed that a woman is more sensitive than a man and can understand a person in a better way.

Vidya was adorable and her sentiments for me were genuine, but I couldn't help the situation. I had always hated to do this but I knew I would be breaking her heart.

'Son, you want to join me?' Mr Desai called out from the road when he saw me having my evening tea on the veranda. I was jolted out of my reverie. To get over the slight tension Vidya's letter had caused me, I was thinking of taking a walk with Vivek.

'Where to?' I asked and he replied, 'To our Father's.' He addressed God as father. Just at that moment, the bell of the nearby temple chimed loudly and the old man responded. 'See? He's calling . . .'

I nodded smiling. 'Give me a minute,' I said, and it took me less than a minute to put my pants on and join him at the temple of Lord Shiva at the end of the residential area in the north. I'd thought that being at the temple would help me relax. We walked down the road discussing everyday things.

My mother, who was a great devotee of Lord Satya Sai Baba, had instilled spiritualism in us, her children. My family celebrated all the festivals very traditionally. I remember that as a child I used to go to the temples with my mother only for the prasad, the offerings to the deity that was distributed among the devotees. She used to tell us stories from the Mahabharata and the Ramayana. I wasn't fond of praying regularly, but I did it just for my mother's satisfaction. As I grew older, I became sceptical about the existence of God. In my adolescence, I had almost quit going to temples. It was just on festivals that I went there. I had felt that it wasn't necessary to go to the temples to seek God. I'd believed in the ubiquity of the Divine Force. Even today, my thoughts were the same—He, was within me. He lives in every single one of us; we just need to find Him. For his own convenience, man has imagined the Almighty in a human shape otherwise who has actually seen the Omnipotent. They say God lives up there in the sky but I believed something really very powerful exists around us. It is the unseen energy that gives us strength to face the hardships of our lives.

Mine was an agnostic home. The only picture of Lord Shiva I carried was in my wallet but I never deified it by offering flowers or incense sticks or anything else. I just saw the small picture whenever I needed to and that's all I did in the name of worship. Once Mrs Gavit had asked me about my not worshiping ritually. My answer had been, 'God lives in me and I don't need to search for him outside. You don't need to have the walls of your house decorated with the pictures of Gods and Goddesses.'

Later, the same question had come from Mrs. Desai. Obviously neither of the God fearing women had liked my answer.

After I had become close to Mr Desai, I started going to the temple of Shiva with him. That gave me a chance to know another aspect of the man whose image was of an abusive person. His knowledge of mythology was awesome and he was fond of the holy sermons Lord Krishna had given Arjun in the battlefield of Kurukshetra.

In one of our early meetings, I had asked him, 'Why do I need to go to the temples if I believe God is within me.'

He agreed with me on that and said very honestly, 'Along

with God, there's an evil too. God is within us when we are happy and honest. Evil takes control when we lie and commit sin. To slay the devilish element in you, you should go to the temple where no evil can spread his empire. The holiness we feel in the temples or in any other place of worship is something we can't have anywhere else. You just need to open your inner eyes to experience it.'

There he was! From him, I learned how to surrender myself to the Holy name. At the temple, we sat in the sanctum sanctorum in front of the Shivling with our eyes closed, experiencing the holiness of the divine place. Even at home while meditating, I would visualize the Shivling, the sacred symbol of Shiva, to help me concentrate.

Having paid obeisance to the deity, Mr Desai and I sat on a bench outside. Since I'd discussed my problems with him in the past, I was thinking of discussing with him about Vidya when he surprised me by saying, 'Don't hesitate. Talk freely.'

I looked quizzically at him, 'How did you know I have something to talk about?'

'*That* you will learn when you reach my age. Experience, intuition, whatever you name it. A sensitive man cannot be impervious to positive or negative energies around him. Especially, when it concerns someone he loves.' He smiled. 'Now speak up.'

I told him about Vidya's proposal and he said, 'You should go for this relationship. She's an attractive woman. Love is something that only lucky people get. It is God's blessing that he showers upon us through other people. Life's short and you don't know what's going to happen the next moment and how long your lifeline is. So why not take pleasure in what you've got at the very moment? The girl is pretty and I don't see any reason to say no. You should, must, go for it. If I were you, I'd have . . .'

I'd always tried to follow his advice, but in this case, there was no such likelihood. Neither could I tell him why.

That night, I thought about love. I had seen many love stories in films and read some romantic novels. And though I had liked and enjoyed them, the fact was that they were nothing more than perfect examples of nonsense for me—too melodramatic to be digested. Many writers and thinkers have given various definitions of love. Some have said that true love means to be ready to do anything for the person you love. Some have said that love demands sacrifice. Krishna used to call love 'rubbish'. In his opinion, nothing like love exists on this planet. It was just the necessities—physical, mental, economic, that drive two people closer to each other and they call it love. It probably was true in our case because both of us needed each other for physical satisfaction.

Once I had read in a newspaper that love is nothing more than a temporary infection of the body caused by the secretions of the sexual glands. If that was hundred percent true, and my affection for Vivek was only sex driven, then why was I ready to destroy myself in his love? Why was I ready to die for him? If that wasn't love, then what was it? The truth is that there is no specific definition of love. It varies from person to person. The most condemned word in the whole world is 'love'. People define this word at their own discretion. Love to me meant to be ready to sacrifice your life for your beloved. I wanted to die in Krishna's love. I had begun to have the same feeling for Vivek because being in love was the utmost, ultimate delight for me.

But like hunger and thirst, love is a basic need. Human nature varies from man to man. It entirely depends upon the person's nature whether to go towards growth and prosperity or towards deterioration and dissipation. Love has nothing to do with age. That was the notion that unshackled me from the guilt of falling in love with my student. I believed that love stabilizes the unsteady boat of life. Before meeting Vivek, my life was aimless. Now I had a reason to live. The faint hope of getting Vivek's love had brought new zest to my life.

Though we got along well with each other, Krishna and I used to fight a lot. Most of the time, Krishna's habit of arriving late caused strife between us. His memory was so poor that he would habitually forget things and couldn't keep his promises sometimes. Then he would come to me with lame excuses, apologize and beg for forgiveness to placate me, but it wasn't that easy because the most irritating thing for me had always been to wait for someone. Other than that we fought over trifles. For example, I liked performance oriented movies, whilst he preferred action flicks. Many times these small differences led to heated arguments over hundreds of subjects, be it beauty or sex, career, sports or movies.

We actually liked to argue with each other and that was the best part of our relationship. We quarrelled, didn't talk to each other for days and then one of us would make the first move to reconcile. Most times, it was Krishna who made the first move as, between the two of us, he was more inclined to forgive and forget. A humble, heartfelt apology with a genuine smile usually appeased my resentment, but when I was more vexed and an apology didn't seem enough, he had to go for a warm hug and a passionate kiss which I found impossibele to resist. He knew this very well, that I would get carried away while in his arms and all my dejection and anger did melt away in his embrace.

In my teens, I wasn't as calm and poised as I am today. I was moody. I suffered from mood swings that made me happy or sad in a split second. Every single act of Krishna would change my mood. When a touch of his hand or a blushing kiss would elate me, his ignoring me or getting displeased with me saddened me.

There was one such incident when I came to know that Krishna had been to the red-light area. This had upset me so much that I didn't go to college that day. Krishna came to my place after college to see if I was sick. The very thought that Krishna had been with a prostitute had irked me the whole day. I was in my bed with my head under the pillows when he came from behind and brushed my hips very gently, the way he did during foreplay.

When I asked him about his being to the red-light area, he said he had just passed by the place. He wasn't there to have sex, he swore. But he had lied. I doubted him. I knew he was good at lying. He had always been. My protest could have caused a fight, so I didn't drag the issue any further. However, I had a doubt in my mind that there was something he was hiding from me. The suspicion that he was visiting prostitutes, maddened me and left me in a puddle of uneasiness and insecurity. It wasn't that Krishna hadn't known my state of mind because it was apparent from my sullen face, but he didn't ask. Probably because he had been guilty. And I had worn the same expression of dreariness and melancholy for days because I wanted him to realize how badly one wrong step of his could hurt me.

Since the very beginning, I had known that Krishna wasn't totally gay but was a bisexual. I had no idea if he had had physical relations with girls in college, but one thing I was sure about was that he liked girls. When we went out, he would stare at girls the way other boys did. In the beginning, I didn't like that and envied those beautiful faces. It took me a while to accept it as a male attribute and then I had no problem with it. We hardly talked about girls, so I had a faint idea about his dream woman. He had been fond of Hindi film actresses and had their posters on the walls of his hostel room. The reason why he had chosen to get physical with me was that he was an average looking guy who couldn't get a girlfriend to satisfy his lust. It was I who was available. For someone like him, I was much better as far as looks were concerned. Still the fear that he might dump me for any girl someday had never let me relax. This anxiety had driven me to discuss the subject once. We had just had sex and were still naked in bed and I, expecting some sort of a commitment from him, had posed the question. 'Do you like girls?'

As always, he had taken his time to think about what to say. 'You want a sweet answer or a true answer?' He'd asked in reply. He would always ask this counter question whenever he thought his reply might hurt the other person. So I had known his answer was going to be unpleasant. Now it was time for me to think because a true answer was going to hurt me and I knew what that truth was.

'Begin with the sweet one.' My fingers played with his hair.

'The sweet one is "no".'

'And the right one is "yes", ' I said at once.

At that, he'd stared at me for long and then said, 'What do you want me to do? Hate girls? Close my eyes while passing by them? Crush all my dreams and desires?' His tone had turned suddenly bitter.

I had no answers, and averting his stabbing gaze, nestled my face in his armpit and said, 'Sorry. Let's not discuss this anymore.'

Pursuing the subject would surely have led us to argue and fight, and that's why I had ended the issue then and there. But one thing had become clear that he had his

Vivek and I

dreams, his own dreams, which were different from mine. He liked girls and there was nothing wrong with that, yet it had been tough for me to accept that he liked someone else other than me.

We used to exchange 'I love you' quite often, but I always felt that his utterance of those words lacked passion. They seemed plain, dry, and mechanical. I believed that he didn't admire me the way I did him. I was mad about him and wished he were just as crazy, which was never going to come true. But I rarely complained because whatever he had to offer was simply outstandingly marvellous. The sort of private time we had spent together was something I had never had before, and I doubted if I would have such wondrous moments ever again in my life.

It wasn't that only his own satisfaction mattered to Krishna. He did take care of me and treated me the way I liked. Once a month his hostel offered a feast and Krishna used to keep aside some really nice food for me. Then again how could I forget his anxiety and concern when I had a little accident! I had cut my finger while making salad at home one noon. Though the wound wasn't deep, it didn't stop bleeding. It had hurt, but watching Krishna's concern, I forgot my pain. He had grabbed my hand instantly, taken me to the washbasin, and held it under the running tap and bandaged it. While doing all this, he had complained that I should have paid attention to what I was doing with the knife. When I laughed he had scolded me even more. This incident had proved how concerned he was for me and how much he loved me.

Krishna was great in bed, but we had also made love out of bed sometimes. Whenever we found ourselves alone, he would be naughty or tickle me. It was always so stirring! He would embrace me from behind and pick me up to throw me on the bed and turn dirty. We would often have a pillow fight which would serve as foreplay and lead to sex. Sex had not been a quick and forgettable affair for either of us. We would take our time and revelled in the best possible way. We liked to remain nude in each other's embrace after an exhausting, gratifying session of sex.

I had made nude paintings of Krishna. I had them stored in my cabinet back home in Baroda. I wanted to make a nude painting of Vivek too since he had a good physique. But I doubted if the shy boy would ever be ready to bare before me. I liked nude painting since I believed that besides nature, a nude human body is the most beautiful thing in the world. It has unique language. Scientifically, it has been proven that physical touch of the person you like can do miracles. It heals and mends beyond one's imagination. Krishna and I had believed so and we used to touch each other quite affectionately. Though I had always been sceptical about his speaking the truth, I never suspected the touch of his body. It was genuine and real. Always. A tongue can lie—touch can't.

I used to confide in Krishna so much that I didn't hesitate to tell him how I had turned gay, but he kept a lot to himself. I never hid anything from him and wanted him to be as open and candid with me as I was with him. Knowing his mysterious personality, I doubted if I would ever get to know who he really was. Sometimes I felt I didn't know him at all! Then sometimes, I would express my discontent regarding his secretive nature. Whenever I asked, he would reply that he'd never had sex with any other guy before me. I could never believe that. We didn't hesitate to experiment in our sex life. He knew more about various postures and skills, and since he'd taught me everything about sex—from oral to anal and from being gentle to aggressive to sadistic—I strongly believed he must have had same-sex relationships elsewhere. When he did something new and exciting in bed, I would ask him where he had learned it from. He would just smile or try to divert my attention by doing or saying something else, but would never respond to my question. Behind that smiling face, there was a lot that was concealed. His secrets were never going to be made known to me. But I too had never compelled him to reveal his past. Maybe it had been terrible. Maybe there was something so aching behind those ever smiling eyes that he never wanted to recall it. There was a possibility that one of his close relatives had exploited him sexually in his childhood and he didn't want to remember all that. Whatever it was, I was never going to know. He would never let people know what was in his heart. Jovial by nature, he hardly took life seriously and believed in having fun all the time. He liked to make the most of everything around, lived in the present only and didn't care much for the future. I liked his style of accepting things the way they came to him in life.

A strange thing had happened to me while I was in love with Krishna. At the tennis club, I met a tall, well-built, young army man with a powerful sex appeal. My interaction with him in the beginning had been rather brief, we had exchanged smiles. I had begun to like him since our first encounter on court. He played superb tennis, and I became friends with him by complimenting his game. Actually, everybody at the club liked this soldier who shared his experiences of the army with us. His majestic figure and strong magnetism attracted me and soon I'd begun to feel drawn towards him. But I still loved Krishna and was confused about my feelings on loving two men at the same time. One day, I came to know that he had gone away. I was never going to see him again in my life. I missed him for a few days. I was in love with Krishna and at the same time I had become attracted to another man. *What had that meant? Wasn't this the two-facedness of my so-called true love?* I was able to reason it out, my liking the army man had just been physical attraction. Love had nothing to do with it. I felt it was human to get attracted to a good looking person while being in love with someone else. And so I forgave myself. My attraction to the army man had died away within a few days of his exiting from my life.

And the latest one-sided attraction in my life was Vidya. She was serious about a permanent relationship. Though not a great beauty, she dressed up well and tried to impress me with that. She wore makeup and perfume. She spent a good amount of her salary on saris. And she really liked to flaunt. Whenever she came to school in a new sari, she would ask me if I liked it or not. Her choice of colours was similar to mine, so I seldom showed disapproval. It was that auburn cotton sari that I liked the most and she wore it every week just because I liked it. The one with parrot green dots on white I disliked the most. Though the fabric was expensive, the design was a pain to the eyes. My frank opinion about that sari had disenchanted her from it and she never wore it again. Once, I had even asked her about the sari and had received a smile in return. I was never going to know. This was an example of how much my choice meant to her. She loved me so much that she didn't want to do anything I didn't like. She was ready to make changes in her life for me. She was ready to live her life on my terms. If that wasn't true love, then what was it?

Krishna had his own concepts about love. For him, it was 'rubbish'. I had no problem with that. But my heart said that I was truly in love with him. My idea of true love still is that if you can die for your beloved without asking the whys and the wherefores, you are a true lover. And Krishna was the one I could give up my life for.

Now I felt the same way about Vivek.

It is said that there is a thin line between true love and physical attraction. If what Vidya felt for me was not true love but just physical attraction, then what did I feel for Vivek? Was there no urge for sex? Oh yes, there was! I wanted to have sex with him. Then what was the difference between Vidya and me? Why blame her? I had no answer to these questions. It was just my acceptance of the fact that man keeps one standard for others and a different one for himself. He doesn't blame himself for his mistakes.

Whatever, I was going to say 'no' to Vidya.

fifteen

The first thing I had to do the very next day, was to meet Vidya and give her the love letter back. I knew that my denial was going to break her heart, but I had no choice. I just wished that she would understand me. Thankfully, she was alone in the staffroom at the end of the first period. I walked up to her and placed on the table the envelope that carried the same letter she had given me the previous day. She gave me a quick, radiant glance, her face aglow with expectation of a positive reply. She looked at the envelope that had only one word written on it, 'Sorry'. I had decided to explain my side of the story to her in person. I didn't want to admit I was gay, but wanted to assure her that she deserved a better man and I was not the proper choice for her.

She read the word and the glow on her face vanished. Unable to react or look up, she sat still in her chair. I walked away because I couldn't bear the pitiable look on her face. It definitely wasn't the time to talk because she seemed to be in a state where no words, no consolation could heal the sudden pang my denial had caused her.

The same day, the principal came to know that the Gavachi village school wanted to have the match on Saturday instead of Sunday. For some reason, they wished to have the match a day before the schedule. The principal talked to the sports teacher and the players, and only when they agreed, did they call Gavachi to let them know that we were ready to play at their convenience. Since there were less than twenty-four hours for the match, the players began practising.

While Vivek was on the grounds, I was in the staff room during the second recess. My mind was restive with unwelcome thoughts of Vidya, when I heard loud noises coming from the direction of the ground. Someone said that the students had had a scuffle, and I, along with two other teachers, rushed towards the ground. Surprisingly, it was Vivek who had engaged himself in a fist fight with another boy of his team. Desperate to knock each other down, the two could not be parted even by their team mates. Both of them were perspiring, their clothes soiled and torn at places, their hair dishevelled. I caught hold of Vivek from behind and Mr Bhatt did the same with Naman, the other student. Vivek, panting and shivering with anger, struggled to get rid of my grip to beat Naman up, whose nose was dripping with blood. His white uniform had blood stains. Vivek had bruises on his neck and there was a lump on the left side of his forehead.

By the time the principal reached there, we had managed to calm them down. Naman had covered his nose with a handkerchief Mr Sheikh had given him. First-aid had been administered to both of them right there on the ground and when they were able to talk, they were rebuked for their misconduct. Both of them were given time to put forward their side of the story and the other boys, witnesses to the clash, testified. The deduction was that Vivek had hit a lot runs off Naman's balls and Naman in frustration, had uttered abusive words about Vivek's sister. This had infuriated Vivek and he attacked Naman who'd fought back in self defence. Since Vivek was the stronger of the two, it was Naman who had received a severe beating.

The principal reprimanded Naman for speaking badly about Vivek's sister and admonished Vivek for assaulting Naman. He said that Vivek should have complained to the sports teacher. He was extremely angry with both the boys because never in the past had something like that happened. He expelled both of them from the team saying that there was no place for such misbehaviour. Then he left the ground in disgust. Everyone was worried about the next day's match since Vivek and Naman were both match winners for the team. There was little chance we could win without them.

Later, Mr Bhatt, Mr Sheikh and I met the principal in his office and requested him to reverse his decision of barring both the boys. He agreed to remit them on the condition that we would be responsible if they turned violent towards each other again.

That evening Vivek and his friends came to my place to learn about the outcome of our meeting with the principal. I was busy finishing the painting I had started the other day. The brushes, the tubes of colours and the rest of my artistic paraphernalia lay on the floor of my bedroom. Vivek rushed in, saw me painting, and requested me to come into the living room. Had he not been tense, he would definitely have liked to see what I was making. I left the things as they were and joined them in the living room.

'Is there any hope that I can make it for tomorrow's match?' Vivek asked pessimistically. The lump on his forehead seemed bigger now.

'Show me how badly he hurt you?' I asked him instead of replying. I wanted to tease him for a while. He stood close to me, so that I could see the lump and the bruises.

There was antiseptic ointment on the bruises and balm on the lump. The sight of those bruises on Vivek's neck reminded me of how I had received one such bruise when Krishna had bitten me on my neck in sexual enthusiasm. The reddish scar could easily be seen on my fair skin and though it hurt, I had liked it. After all, that love bite was the proof of our love! For several days, till it disappeared, I had to conceal it with the collar of my shirt. Whoever at my college had seen it, had asked about it and believed that it was a gift from some girl. The mysterious, playful look on my face only confirmed the belief of those ignorant people.

'It's not as bad as what he's got!' I said, referring to Naman and enjoying the look on his face.

'Certainly. A broken nose that he's going to remember for long.' He sniggered wryly.

'You hit him on the nose with your fist, didn't you?' I asked, sitting on the edge of my desk. He had strong hands.

'Hmm . . .' he replied and then tried to ask, 'What did the principal–?'

'And how did he hurt you?' I asked enjoying his uneasiness. I pretended to be looking for something among my books that lay in a disarray on the tabletop.

'With his nails.' His voice dropped to a whisper. 'Bastard!'

'Shhh . . .' I looked up at him from the books. 'No foul language!'

'Sorry.' He sat on the settee and asked desperately, 'please tell me what the principal's final decision about my expulsion is.'

I put the books aside, took off my specs and sighed heavily, all to make him believe that there was nothing positive. I shook my head in negation, and he closed his eyes. That disheartened his friends too.

'Okay, my destiny,' Vivek said sullenly. 'But I'm not sorry for beating that b–'

'Bastard?' I uttered the word he couldn't.

He got up, waved his hands in the air and started to walk towards the main door.

'Vivek!' I called out to him.

He stopped, turned and foolishly watched as a tantalising smile spread across my face. 'You are going to play tomorrow's match.'

'Really?' he asked aloud. A lively smile spread across his face. I nodded in affirmation and he ran towards me and I found myself in his arms. A pleasant sensation ran through my body as he hugged me tightly. It left me speechless. It was something I had never expected. It was something he had never done before. It was something I always wanted him to do. I enjoyed his body against mine. I wished the moment would last forever!

Vivek and his friends were ecstatic. Vivek thanked me for my attempts to convince the principal to take him back in the team. I said I wanted him to play his best game ever.

That was the first time I had seen Vivek's anger and I had been really surprised to see how violent he could become! I recalled his scowling face and aggressive behaviour that I had never seen before. For the first time I realized how severe he could be to defend his own people. What he did wasn't unusual. After all, it was a matter of his family's honour. I liked that in him. Krishna had the same courage. And I remembered what a coward I had been when it came to fighting for my rights. I had never fought anyone in my life. I preferred to stay away when my classmates indulged in brawls at school. Yes, I fought with Krishna and other friends of mine, but they could be called heated arguments and not fist fights.

The next day, all the students were in the cricket mood and the altercation between Vivek and Naman had been forgotten as if nothing had happened. Yet, I could see that the two boys were avoiding looking at each other. The sports teacher had taken a promise from both of them that their differences wouldn't affect the spirit of the game. Vivek looked perfectly well, but Naman's nose was still swollen. It still hurt him but he was so excited about playing the match that he was ignoring the pain.

My eyes were searching for Vidya in the crowd, but she was nowhere to be seen. It was the first time that she hadn't wished me 'goodbye' the previous evening before leaving the school. I actually had waited for her at the compound gate, but she hadn't appeared. I assumed that she must have left early to avoid coming face to face with me. My denial had affected her badly, but there was nothing I could do. Time would heal her wounded heart, I consoled myself.

Then she appeared on the ground with Ms Bhoye, after the match had started, looking extremely offended. She used to sit close to me usually, but that day she sat with other ladies, far away from where I was.

I had lost a friend.

It was perhaps good for her and probably for me too.

As always, Mr Bhatt's commentary made the game more interesting. The visiting team batted first and set a respectable target of 125 in ninety-six balls. Everybody was sure that our team would be able to chase the target, but the early fall of the opening pair made us tense.

'It looks like the visiting team is here to avenge their previous week's defeat and . . . there's an appeal for LBW but the umpire does not seem interested.' The commentary filled the atmosphere with anxiety.

Then came my hero Vivek, and it was a treat to watch his fours and sixes.

'Another bullet from Vivek's bat and it's a six! Ah, what a delight!' Mr Bhatt's commentary was in full form. 'Oh! What a desperate attempt for a catch! This could have been a turning point . . .'

Vivek made the fielders run in every direction and stuck to his position till the very last run. We won the match comfortably and all the credit was given to Vivek who was declared the Man of the Match for his unbeaten sixty-two runs. The boys lifted him up on their shoulders and danced. I congratulated him with a hug and the principal as usual, threw a party for the winning team. I was happy for Vivek and also for the entire team which now was being seen as a strong contender for the inter-school championship.

I could have had the chance to talk to Vidya by congratulating her for the success of our team, but she left immediately after the end of the match. She probably knew I would accost her and left without delay to avoid any kind of conversation. She hadn't talked to me, hadn't even given me a single glance. Never in the past had I seen her look so miserable. I felt responsible for the grief on her face.

At the principal's house that evening, the boys gorged on delicious chicken. Chicken with chapatti, salad and fried rice were a treat for the boys. We chatted as we enjoyed the spread. In the meantime, I asked Vivek to accompany me for an excursion to the famous forest of Mahal. It was Sunday the next day and everyone was in a relaxed mood. He had no reason to refuse. We planned the outing then and there and it was to be sponsored entirely by me. I had planned this trip to ease the stress of the split between Vidya and me.

Then Ms Ragini Bhoye asked me to join her when I was taking rice on my plate. Taking leave from the group of boys, I followed her and she took me to the far end of the yard where nobody could hear us.

'So, how are things going?' The fat, short lady with unattractive features began the conversation as we sat on a narrow bench.

'Great!' I put in a mouthful and started to chew.

'Has something happened between you and Vidya lately?' she demanded in a low voice, eyeing me through her spectacles.

I was aware that she might ask about Vidya and said, 'Don't tell me you don't know about it.'

The person Vidya got along so well with at the school was not I but Ms Bhoye. She trusted Ms Bhoye a lot and told her almost everything. Bhoye, a kind hearted, middle aged woman, possessed a nice house of her own near the post-office. Sometimes, Vidya stayed over at her place. She would have been at the principal's for the party had we not had the problem.

Ms Bhoye smiled. 'Vidya told me. You don't like her, do you?'

Since I knew that everything I was going to say, would reach Vidya's ears, I had to be cautious. 'I like her as a friend. What she wants from me is . . . you know . . .'

'She looks quite adamant about not getting married to anyone else.' Ms Bhoye continued, 'She has rejected many suitors so far. She likes you more than you can imagine.'

'You can't force someone to fall in love with you, can you?' I had already put my plate aside. 'She's your friend. You should make her understand.'

'I've already tried, but she's upset beyond words. Nothing will heal her lovesick mind,' she said with a sense of awareness of her loyalty to her friend. 'Who can be a better person to talk on this subject than me? I never told you myself, but I know that you know my story. Everybody does.' She seemed lost somewhere in her past life. 'Coming from a poor family, I have seen really bad days. Being the eldest child of my poor parents, I had to start working at a very young age. Along with that, I had to study too. When I joined our school, I was the only breadwinner of my family. I had a sick mother and a handicapped father and four young siblings to take care of. At an early stage in my life, I've had to play several roles. I've had to be the parent not only to my brothers and sisters but to my parents as well. I had my dreams and hopes. I had dreamt of a handsome husband. I had dreamt of children, my *own* children. But I had to dedicate my life for the better future of my family and I did. Without a single complaint I did it all. Killing all my desires at a marriageable age, I worked, earned for them, educated them, married them off and sought happiness in their prosperity. And by the time everything seemed to have settled in my dear ones' lives, I had lost my youth. Today, all of them have families and children. I live alone. My parents are long dead now.

'Thankfully, none of my siblings have forgotten my sacrifices and they are always with me in times of need. I feel relieved of all the responsibilities. Some people tell me to get married now. Now?' She scoffed at herself. 'At the age of forty-four? And look at me. I'm fat and ugly and I look older than my real age. Which stupid person will marry me?' she said sardonically. 'Sometimes, I think I deserve more than what I have got. I could have had a family of my own. The regret is not big, but yes, it is there. I could have–' The tears on her eyelashes sparkled in the moonlight, but she didn't try to conceal them. They reflected her fight against all the vicissitudes of her life. For a while, she was quiet. Then she asked, 'Could you please bring me some water?'

'Sure.' I went inside the house to fetch water. I took my time to let her shed her miseries in private. She was normal when I returned to her.

'Sorry for bothering you,' she said. I just smiled and waited as she drank some water. 'I told Vidya to choose a man and get married,' she continued with Vidya's story. 'I don't want her to lead the kind of life I'm leading. She's twenty-five already and within a couple of years, it would be tough to find a proper man. You know this place well. And also the orthodox mentality of the people here. I just wanted to hear it from you. Your final words. And I guess it is a no.'

I didn't say yes or no. I didn't have to.

'Whatever, I respect your decision,' Ms Bhoye's words hit me hard. 'But I don't think Vidya will find a better man than you.'

I took my plate in my hands and smirked. *Whoever Vidya would choose would be hundred per cent better than me.* I looked up at the moonlit sky and prayed. *May God find her the best man!*

The next day, we hired a jeep to reach the forest of Mahal which was about thirty-five kilometres from Valai. We were twelve including me and Vivek. We sang songs on the way and the boys were so delighted because I had become one of them. I told them tales of my college days and they quite enjoyed it.

The jungle of Mahal was the thickest in the entire district. It had a huge variety of trees and plants, but it was known for its enormous bamboo trees. The surprising elements were the circumference and height of the trees. Never could one imagine that bamboo trees could be this gigantic. And the foliage of the trees was so dense that sunlight barely reached the ground even at day time.

We took a new, uncharted path to venture into the thick stretch of the lush, green jungle. Vivek and I led the group as we made our way through the dense terrain of huge bamboo trees. It was tough to negotiate this unfamiliar path as it was full of overgrown weeds and prickly brambles. Trying to capture the scenic beauty around in my camera, I wished there was a clear sky. However, since early morning that day, it had been cloudy.

We had with us utensils, vegetables and grains. At noon we halted in a glade for lunch. Some went to collect dry branches to make a fire and some stayed with me to help clean the vegetables and grains. It didn't take us more than an hour to prepare *khichdi* and mixed vegetables. We ate in *baj*, a kind of a disposable plate made of the leaves of khakhro, bustard teak tree. After lunch, we rested for about half an hour since everybody was tired. The rest of the day was spent in exploring the forest which was at its best because of the monsoon. We spotted some deers and a hyena, and also had the opportunity to see a few rare species of reptiles crawling on the ground. In the company of the young boys, I enjoyed myself more than I had anticipated. All my miseries related to the recent fall-out with Vidya were forgotten.

It was afternoon when we decided to return. Instead of returning by the same path that we had set out on, we chose to take a different route for more fun and thrill. It took us a while to realize that we were lost. We were far from where we had started and none of us knew the way out. Most of us had been there before, but nobody had ever explored those unfamiliar parts of the forest. Most trekkers hired local hands who acted as guides because they knew the forest very well and were able to earn something. But we had thought we didn't need one since all of us were familiar with the geography and nature of the jungle. Whatever the reason, the fact was that we were lost in the middle of the jungle that was full of wild, carnivorous animals including the infamous man eaters. It didn't seem like a big problem in the beginning as we believed we would find the way out sooner or later. But we realized that the problem was bigger than what we'd thought because of the threatening sky ready to break into a downpour. Soon it started getting dark. After about two hours of futile attempts to find the way out, we were spent and perspiring and needed rest, but there was no time to relax. As darkness descended upon us, we began to get more nervous. The howls and roars of the animals we'd enjoyed spotting so far, began to frighten us. It was sure that we would be attacked by them unless we were able to make it to some safe place.

I don't know about the others, but I had inwardly begun to pray to God to show us the right way out. I was sure others must have been doing the same. Suddenly, we found a man carrying long, dry branches on his head and all of us cheered. We stopped him, and one of us who knew his dialect, told him about our problem. Fully familiar with the terrain, the angel helped us get out of the labyrinth of the jungle. As a reward I offered him some money, but he didn't take it. How relieved and happy we were when we reached our vehicle on the fringes of the jungle! It felt as if we had just stepped out of the jaws of the leopard. It was an experience not to be forgotten.

By early evening we were back in Valai. Vivek was the last one to get off from the jeep.

'Hey, Vivek!' I took him aside and whispered so that none of his friends could hear. 'Why don't you come to my house for the party I have arranged for you?'

'A party for me? Great. We'll be there.' He looked happy with the thought of having a party.

'No, no. Only the two of us,' I clarified. 'You and I.'

'Oh, okay, I'll be there. What time?'

'You are welcome at any time you like. Everything will be ready,' I said, expecting a nice night with him.

Later, I readied myself for Vivek's arrival. He was expected any moment. The early evening adventure had enervated me but I didn't want to look drained in front of Vivek. I took a quick, refreshing bath. Scrubbing my face with a face wash, I tried to get my skin fresh and glowing. Then I put on fresh clothes, a blue denim jeans and a white T-shirt. And when I looked at myself in the mirror, I couldn't help but praise my own appearance: *Darling, you look gorgeous!* Everything seemed to be just perfect. The clothes, the perfume and the unkempt beard. Just the way Vivek liked. After all, it had been done to impress him. *Who knows, it might drive Vivek to bed with me!* I'd had it in mind from the beginning. In fact the reason why I threw him this party was to create an atmosphere to take him to bed. The intoxication of beer might drive him out of control and the long awaited night might come true. That was what had happened to me and Krishna. I hoped the plan would work.

All I had to do now was to wait for Vivek. To subdue the anxiety generated by the dreamy thoughts of the night ahead, I sat on the cane chair in the hall with the newspaper. But it didn't interest me at all. I flung it on the settee and went to the veranda, my eyes steady on the road for the happy sight of my beau. The wind had lulled and the evening sky was laden with low hanging clouds. It is likely to rain, I thought. *Oh, it must. What a night it is going to be!* I buried myself in anticipation of the promising night.

Vivek came late.

'You are going to stay here tonight, okay? That's your punishment for coming late,' I said autocratically.

He said 'okay' with such simplicity that it enchanted me. I wanted to jump with joy. But the thought that it would seem weird didn't let me indulge in such stupidity. Sukhi had prepared chicken for us. The bottles of beer that had been there in the lowest drawer of my wardrobe for God knows how long, had already been placed in the refrigerator to chill. We arranged our seating in the middle of the hall. Vivek was fond of beer and chicken. I also liked beer and it was better to have it in such great company as Vivek's. We had had beer parties before. Earlier, I used to ask myself whether it was right to have such an alcoholic drink with someone who was a student and who was just seventeen? Wasn't I leading him onto become a drunkard? Well, I had never forced Vivek to drink. He had it because he liked it.

The drizzle outside turned into pouring rain as the night advanced. I had left all the windows wide open to let the cold breeze in and was sitting in a position from where I could see the terrible, destructive form of nature. The heavy raindrops seemed to be smashing into smithereens by the streak of frequent lightening. The wind was blowing with a vengeance, hurling raindrops into the room through the open windows. Vivek suggested the windows be closed to keep the rain water from getting in. I told him to enjoy the rain and not to worry. While drinking, I remembered how crazy Krishna used to be about beer. My capacity was no more than two bottles those days, whereas he could have five or six at a time and it didn't intoxicate him immediately. The beverage had been a great libido enhancer for us and we drank often. Needless to say, what followed was abundant sex.

From my bedroom, I fetched the painting I had been working on for the last few days. It had Vivek sitting under the neem tree with his eyes fixed towards the west. He was so surprised to see his picture, that he just gaped at it.

'You don't like it, do you?' I wanted him to praise my artwork.

'No, I mean . . . I like it very much. It's beautiful, but . . . I never posed for this one! How did you . . .?' His eyes were on the painting all through.

'I don't need you to be with me to make your painting. You stay with me all the time, even when you are away. Even with my eyes closed, I can visualize you any time.'

What I had said touched him and I could see that in his eyes when he turned towards me. He said nothing, just smiled. That was my reward! I got everything in that innocent smile. Time and again, I said emotional things to him so that he would realize how much I liked him and how much he meant to me. It was like a tender foreplay before admitting my real feelings to him.

While enjoying beer, we talked about different things. Remembering the scary experience of the jungle, we laughed. After such casual talk, I asked slowly, 'Have you ever had sex?' I knew my question was going to shock him and for a while, he really was dazed.

'No,' he replied, and I threw in my next question. 'Don't you have any addictions? I mean have you ever smoked or . . . you know . . . cigarettes or tobacco, wine . . .'

He looked puzzled, so I had to add immediately. 'I'm not going to judge you, and this isn't going to affect our friendship in any way. It is just that . . . I want to know. If you don't like, don't answer. I wouldn't mind.'

It took him a few moments to speak. 'I did try tobacco once, but it was tasteless. Don't know why they take it. And once, when I was a kid, my grandpa had given me a small dose of mild wine to cure my sick stomach. I don't even remember what that was like! Cigarettes, never. I like beer only.'

My eyes were fixed on his eyes as if they were examining if he was lying. But there was no sign of deceit. I felt heartened at his integrity. After a silence of a few seconds he asked, 'What about you?'

'You guess.' I could see perplexity on his face as I said, 'What do you think about me? Do you think I've experienced all these things?'

After a while, he spoke, 'I don't know. I really don't know . . .'

I tittered. 'I had tried a cigarette once when I was in the tenth class.' My confession made him frown. 'I was about . . . fifteen, I guess. Baroda is a big place where people are bolder than what you imagine, you know.' He nodded. 'I was on my way home with my school friends when we found a stub of cigarette on the roadside. The burning stub had a bit of tobacco still left in it. One of us picked it and asked who had guts to smoke. I also inhaled it with the others since it was a matter of prestige for all of us. Most of us, including me coughed badly because none of us knew how to do it. But it was fun.' I grinned. 'Then I smoked in college. A foolish imitation of my friends.' I grinned again.

'Alchohol . . .' I tried to remember. 'My father used to

keep expensive whiskies in his cabinet and I tried those with Krishna sometimes. I hate the smell of tobacco. Beer, as you know, is the only addiction now.'

He seemed to be thinking for long. Finally, he decided to ask. 'And what about . . . err . . .?' He hesitated to utter the word.

'Sex . . .?' I made it easy for him. He chuckled, somewhat embarrassed and nodded.

'It's something I had experienced at an early stage in life.' I couldn't tell him I was sexually abused. 'Baroda's a big city where everything happens fast. And sex is no exception, obviously.' I couldn't tell him whom I had sex with.

Vivek was in a great mood since yesterday's victory in the cricket match. I had my eyes on his charming face all the time. The night was getting stormy. We were chilled to the bones and the drinks had begun to influence our talk. And I had a keen desire to express my feelings. I had the three words, 'I love you' on my tongue, but I still couldn't dare utter than. Then intentionally I touched his hands several times to let him get some idea regarding my interest, but the boy didn't get it at all. Probably because he was drunk.

By the end of the fourth bottle, both of us were fully inebriated. He was not in favour of going for the fifth but I didn't listen to him.

'I'm done,' he said with heavy eyes.

'But I'm not,' looking into his eyes, I said suggestively. 'I'm still *thirsty!*'

Obviously he didn't get that as well, so I said, 'The bed is just a few steps away. Don't say no to *anything* tonight.'

He wasn't clever enough to gather the implications of what I had said. I wished he was. I wanted him to drink as much as he could. I wanted him to be out of control.

By the end of the fifth bottle, he was totally helpless. I had made him drink more than what I had taken. His stomach was so full of beer and chicken that he had no desire for dinner. Neither did I. Since he was unable to walk on his own, I had to help him to bed.

Very carefully, I put him on bed and stared at him for long. *How handsome he looks while sleeping!* I covered him with a quilt and returned to the hall to lock up the windows and the main door. As I stepped back in my bedroom, I took off my shirt and flung it on the floor. Vivek was in deep sleep when I went under his blanket. Slowly, I put my right arm around his neck and my head very close to his face. 'I love you,' I murmured in his ears in a quivering voice. I deeply inhaled the scent of his body. I liked his body odour. Krishna also used to smell good. I just loved to be in his arms and enjoyed the smell of his sweat. It was something that aroused me. Everything seemed just so perfect—the thunderous night, the intoxication that had taken control of my mind, the chilly weather, and the invigorating odour of Vivek's body. What a great feeling it is to have your beloved in your arms on such a cold, stormy night! How long it had been since I had a male body by my side in bed! The storm inside me was as fierce as the one outside.

My right hand slipped under his shirt and the heat of his muscled chest made me yearn for physical intimacy. My hand wanted to go down further but I couldn't for the fear of waking him up. 'Should I go for more?' I asked myself. *No way! He's my student.* Things were still not so positive. He was ignorant about what I was doing or was intending to do. He was so inebriated that he would have been unable to oppose it had I gone for sex. My body wanted to, but it was my mind that impeded me from going ahead. *Having* sex with him in such condition, would be equivalent to rape. And what if he comes to know about it in the morning? Oh, he would surely know. He's not that dumb. That might prove to be shattering for our relationship.

Then I concentrated on Vivek's face. How innocent! How guileless it was! I didn't want to ruin the happiness and innocence of his life. The boy trusted and respected me so much. How could I annihilate that trust? I was drunk, but could still make out the difference between good and bad. Finally, I made my decision. I slipped my right hand back to his belly, leaned over his face and kissed him on the cheek. He didn't move a bit. The second kiss that I dared give was on the lips. A mere brush. He still didn't wake up. I surveyed his face—the cheeks, the lips, the resting eyelids, and the forehead with the bulge. I moved a stray hair from his forehead and came back to his lips, touching them with my fingertips. I moistened my lips with my tongue and kissed his lips, this time more passionately. A sensational tingle ran down through my body as the touch of his lips was heavenly. My long cherished desire had come true. It had been years since I had experienced this. A kiss on the lips was something that took me to another world. Krishna had been a great kisser and knew very well how to kiss to give me pleasure. Remaining in that state for a while, I enjoyed licking Vivek's saucy lips until he moved slightly. I had to detach myself from him. What an exhilarating experience it had been! He was in deep sleep again. I put my arm on his chest, rested my head by his face and closed my eyes to sleep.

sixteen

I t is always so pleasant to open your eyes and find your sweetheart by your side in the morning. I watched Vivek through my drowsy eyes. How peaceful his face was! No stress, no worry, no anxiety. Just a plain face without any expression. I was staring at his enchanting face. As I remembered last night's fleeting moments of kissing his lips, an uncontrollable desire to have the same experience arose in me, but I refrained from doing so lest he wake up. We were so close that I could catch his stinking breath on my face. Krishna was the only person I had slept with like this. I remembered how we remained in bed for hours. Even if we were awake, we wouldn't leave the bed and stayed in each other's arms for long. Sometimes, we would have sex in the morning. Though I was never so excited about making love in the early morning, I never disappointed Krishna for whom the act of having spontaneous sex was always more exhilarating than a planned one. Such intercourses were always dominated by him.

The tender sunbeams of the aromatic winter morning intruded into the room through the window slits, and in the golden rays, Vivek's face looked fairer than it was. Normally, once awake, I didn't linger in bed, but Vivek was by me and I didn't want to get away from him. I whispered in his ears. *I love you, Vivek!*

Man makes a mistake one day and, instead of learning a lesson from it, repeats it the very next day. He does the same mistake again despite knowing that by doing so he would put his life on line. Separation from Krishna had gnawed at me more than anything else in the world and I had promised myself that I wouldn't ever fall in love again. This resolution had evaporated and I made the same mistake—of falling in love with Vivek.

I remembered the day when having found me thoughtfully gloomy, Krishna had asked the reason.

'Is it right what we are doing?' I had asked tentatively.

My question had made him reflet for a while. Sitting in front of me, he had taken my hands in his before he spoke. 'Why do you think that way? Don't you like it with me? If you like what we do, don't regret it. Don't judge yourself. It doesn't make you a bad person just because you like to sleep with a man. You are a nice human being, and I love you.'

Those healing words made me realize that I was special to him. Throughout the conversation, our eyes remained locked on each other's and I could see his were trustworthy.

I had unnecessarily believed whatever was happening between Krishna and me was wrong. The same thing hurt me in my relationship with Vivek. Sometimes, I thought it was a sin to expect Vivek to be mine. Several questions arose within me—*Is it a sin to love someone? What's the definition of sin and righteousness? And whose definitions are these?* And they got answered too—Man! A thing that's considered a sin in one society might be taken as normal in another. If loving someone is not sin then expecting sexual satisfaction from your lover is certainly not! Sex is divine, eternal. God wouldn't have made it a part of animal nature had it been bad. The thing that causes the birth of a life can't be damnable. Love is a blessing of the Almighty and I was thankful that he had sent an angel like Vivek into my life.

I noticed a change of expression on Vivek's face when he moved his jaws as if he was chewing something. I enjoyed that act as I enjoyed everything about him. A second later, he rubbed his forefinger on his left cheek and there was a small, red patch there. I wished to kiss his face, and at the same time I realized that I was feeling wet inside my knickers. I had had a night discharge.

Suddenly, I was fully awake and what I had done to Vivek the previous night, seemed distressing to me. I had no idea what exactly I had done to the boy next to me. Did we have sex? I asked myself. There was no visible sign. Neither on the bedspread nor on my body. But the discharge? I concentrated on recalling what had happened last night. All I could bring to mind was that I had kissed him once or twice and then I had slept. Nothing else. Nothing more. I concluded that the discharge had happened at a passionate moment in my sleep and that it had nothing to do with Vivek. Nocturnal discharges had happened even before. And with a relieved feeling, I slipped out of the bedspread at the earliest moment.

Vidya didn't seem interested in talking to me for several days. I had resolved not to make the first move for reconciliation since it was she who had chosen to be unfriendly. And I was upset with her. But my resentment evaporated like a wisp of mist within days as I began missing her. We take for granted people and happy moments, and only when they are gone forever, do we understand how important they were in making our life blissful.

Vidya was one such person whom I had always ignored

and disregarded, but when she started to ignore me, I couldn't take it. I always hated to be neglected by my dear ones. Being squeamish I'd taken it very hard when Krishna had overlooked me. While being in a group at the college, he sometimes behaved as if I didn't even exist. His talking to the other guys and taking no notice of me was frustrating and I became pathetically helpless and needy when things turned that way. Afterwards, I would complain about his behaviour to him and he would say it was not intentional, but I knew it was. Besides the fact that he liked to tease me that way, he wanted to know how much his attitude would make a difference to me. And whatever he did or didn't really did make a huge difference to me. I loved him so much that I wanted his attention at all times.

So it was now that I realized how much of a friend Vidya had been to me. I was in search for the right time to go and talk to her. It was something I couldn't discuss in others' presence, so I wanted the two of us to be alone, but she, who had earlier liked to meet me when nobody was around, cleverly avoided any kind of situation where we could be alone. I followed her for a chance to find some privacy, but she preferred to stay with other teachers all the time. I wanted to discuss the problem, but she seemed not to be interested in having any conversation. Fortunately, I found her alone in the staff room one day and approached her since the whole situation was getting unbearable for me.

'Why don't you talk to me?' I asked rather carefully.

She took her time, looked at me obliquely for a moment and asked angrily, 'You don't know?'

'We can be good friends . . . at least.'

'At least . . .' There was a sneer on her pale face. She was still not looking at me directly.

Was she ashamed of herself or was that hatred for me?

'I'd appreciate it if you'll try to see the whole situation through my perspective,' I said. You are being selfish by trying to force me to accept your love, those words were on my tongue but I didn't utter them.

'And what's your perspective?' she asked brusquely. I had no answer to this. I didn't have the courage to admit I was gay.

'Our colleagues are talking about our break-up and I don't–'

'So you want me to talk to you so that the others don't talk about us?' she retorted, looking at me irately. I couldn't face those stabbing eyes. Neither did I have any excuse.

'I want you to behave like a normal person.' I tried to propitiate her in as calm a manner as possible. 'I can't help you in the way you want, but we still can be good friends.' I was now almost begging. She was quiet, or was it the calm before the storm? 'Can't you just erase this episode from your mind? Just forget you ever loved me. It'll be–'

'It's not that easy,' she said, her eyes full of grief. 'Not for me at least.'

All my attempts to soothe the anguished woman were of no avail. Unwilling to face the harsh reality, she left me alone in a pensive mood. *She's right. It's not that easy . . . could I ever forget Krishna? Could I erase his memories from my mind? It's not that easy . . . not for anyone . . .*

I had lost a friend. I mulled over it while strolling around with Vivek that evening. The boy was talking about something, but my mind was somewhere else. My conversation with Vidya that noon kept echoing in my mind. Vidya was a nice person and our friendship could have lasted longer, but her expectations were not viable. She had always searched for a lover in me and I had never thought beyond a healthy friendship. The whole situation was hopeless. It was she who would have to compromise with her expectations and dreams since there was no chance of me having second thoughts about the sort of development that she wanted in our relationship. I remembered how frankly she had told me all about her past. It was interesting to listen to her past crushes.

Though I had always liked her company, I had preferred not to be seen with her alone so that no rumours about the two of us would spread. I had evaded her at times and now her avoidance was irritating me. I wanted to have a chat with her in private and now it was her turn to show no interest. She preferred not to look at me or to come near me. In school, she pretended to be normal and happy as if nothing had happened. She wore a fake smile before others, but she was not so good an actress that she could hide her frustration and dejection from me. I knew very well how much grief was hidden in those plain eyes. I could have helped her out of her miseries, but she wanted to be left alone. She had probably set her heart on throwing me out from her life. *How could someone end a relationship like that? How could you expect someone to be what you want?*

One mustn't expect too much from a relationship because when expectations don't come true, it can be devastating. The expectation of living my entire life with Krishna had been an absurd imagination of my lovesick mind. I had expected the impossible, and that had punished me a lot. After my break-up with him, I had decided not to expect anything from anyone. History had however, repeated itself and I had fallen in love with Vivek. This had again shoved me into the same inescapable circle of hopes and expectations. Vidya too had done nothing different. In fact, her expectations were more sensible. I had no right to blame her because I was also on the same track. And it's human to expect things from the people around you.

The only way to save my relationship with Vidya was to accept her love, which was impossible for me. I consoled myself and hoped that the day would come when she would forget everything, her wounds would heal and she would talk to me again.

'Sir, where are you?' I heard Vivek's loud voice.

'Hmm . . .?' I tried to pay attention to what Vivek was saying. 'Did you say something?'

'I've been talking for many minutes, but I'm sure you have no idea about what.' Vivek smiled innocently. I had been so preoccupied that I had not paid attention to what Vivek had said. But he had taken nothing amiss—a quality I greatly appreciated in Vivek. Unlike me, he never expected too much from people.

'Oh, I'm sorry. I was . . .' I apologized. 'Tell me. What is it all about?'

'Ah . . . nothing important, but . . . I think we're far enough now.'

He was correct. We had reached very far from the residential area and it was getting dark. It was dangerous to be out at this hour because of the leopards.

'Oh, we must turn back now,' I said and we started to walk back home.

Thoughts about Vidya didn't let me relax the entire next day too. I was so lost in her thoughts that I didn't even notice Vivek's arrival. I was surprised to see him sitting by me.

When I asked, he replied that he had been there for about fifteen minutes or so. He hadn't disturbed me, but busied himself in a magazine.

'Sorry, I didn't realize,' I apologized.

'That's okay. Why don't we go to the sunset point?' he asked. 'I haven't been there for quite some time.'

The idea didn't thrill me as it had always done, yet I nodded in approval. But even the pleasant breeze of the evening couldn't heal my pensive mind which was still disturbed about Vidya's rejection of my friendship. I was almost quiet during the entire walk and it was Vivek who talked about this and that to bring my mood back.

At the sunset point, we sat on a rock, staring at the sinking sun.

'Life's like this sun. You never know when it will set,' I spoke with a heavy sigh.

'Thank God, at least you talked!' Vivek said with a broad grin. 'You've just said three words since we had started from your place.'

'What?' I asked quizzically.

'"Yes", "okay" and "well" are all you have uttered in the last half an hour.' His calculation brought a smile to my drawn face.

'That's how I like to see you. Cheerful. Smiling.'

Vivek seldom talked emotionally, so those few words touched me, but I couldn't respond since my heart was still morbid.

'Life teaches us to move ahead, don't you say always,' he said jovially. 'Forget the pain and enjoy what you have in your hands. You'll always find them full. Am I correct?' he asked in a manner as if he was playing a part in some epic, historical play. It was all a repetition of what I had said to him in the past. 'Look at the sunset, at the flock of birds flying in the distance, and at the colours in the sky.' He stood up on the rock, stretched his hands in the air and continued to mimic me, 'how pretty the sight is! How pleasant the breeze is! Do they seem gloomy to you? Do they?' He went on and on like that, and I smiled, giggled and finally laughed at his mimicry. I had never known he was that good at mimicking.

'Stop making a fool of yourself.' I pulled his hand, still laughing. 'The people around will jeer at you.'

'Who cares?' He sat back and looked at me. 'That's what I wanted to see.'

I became serious. We looked into each other's eyes for longer than ever. How beautifully the ever smiling face glittered golden in the last rays of the sun! How bewitching his brown eyes were and what a captivating face he had! *Oh God, I love this boy more than anything else in the world!*

Vivek's sweet mimicry had changed my mood and cheered me up. In the meantime, the clouds that had been gliding aimlessly so far had quickly gathered and began to shower us with rain.

'See, even the rain's happy,' Vivek said instinctively.

We remained there talking, until darkness started to engulf the place. It was just the two of us along with the drizzle and the pleasant breeze. Both of us were wet, cold, and the desire to kiss him blazed within me so badly that I went back to my past. I had become dependent upon my past. To get whatever I didn't get from Vivek in the present—love, warmth and physical intimacy—I travelled to my past where I got it all from Krishna.

Krishna and I used to hit the road on my bike for long rides in the rain. It was one such noon when we were roaming aimlessly and rain had started to pelt down. I was driving and he was hugging me from behind. 'Take me to some deserted corner,' he had demanded and within a minute, we were in the woods by the highway.

Mayur Patel

We parked the bike in the bushes and unable to restrain our passion, we started getting physical. The cold breeze, the solitude, the raindrops filtering through the canopy of the trees and wetting us, and his hot lips pressed against mine—everything had been just so magical! There under the cluster of eucalyptus trees, we made love in a rhythm that was timeless and ecstatic. It was like being in some miraculous world. Instead of being hasty and aggressive as he used to be most of the time, Krishna had been slow and gentle.

When I thought about that time, I wondered how bold and daring we were to have sex under the open sky. Driven by acute passion for physical satisfaction, we had even forgotten that someone could have seen us there in that bare condition. The memory of that treasured experience got me excited and I wished to have such moments of bliss with Vivek. Solitude can drive two people crazy and I tried to find a suggestive gesture in Vivek's eyes, but there was none I could take as an invitation. They were as pure and innocent as they had always been.

Maybe he's waiting for me to make the first move, I thought. Words went through my mind but I couldn't dare utter them. *What if he had no such intentions at all? How terrible would it be for him to find out that his teacher was gay?* I couldn't dare. I wouldn't.

On our way down the hill, I asked him to sing the same song he had sung the other rainy evening. He sang in a mellow voice and I was enjoying it until I accidentally spotted Jalpa with the same boy I had seen her with a few days ago. They were standing alone in a deserted place behind a derelict house at the base of the hillock. We stopped in our tracks. We could see them in the moonlight, but they didn't see us.

'Do you know that guy?' I asked Vivek.

'Uh . . . huh,' Vivek was quick to respond. 'Marcus. That's his name.' He knew more than what I had expected. 'He's a Christian. Doesn't do anything for a living. His father has enough money. I've seen him with other girls before. A perfect ruffian, you can say. A good choice for Jalpa.' *Vivek knew what kind of a girl Jalpa was!*

So my perception hadn't been wrong, I thought. *The girl is really stupid to have such a boyfriend.* Marcus was tall, dark and slim, but not that attractive. *What had she seen in him? I must have a chat about this with Mr Gavit before the damn girl does something wrong! And my God, how bold is she to be with her lover in a place like this late in the evening!* I was determined to let her father know.

'You didn't know about her secret boyfriend, did you?' Vivek's question pulled me out of my thoughts. He repeated the question and I shook my head.

'They have been seeing each other for quite some time now. It's not a secret anymore.'

She has been seeing him and that's why she has almost stopped visiting me lately, I thought. Well, good for me.

'By the way, her secret reminds me of your secret.' Vivek changed the topic. 'Remember, once you had told me that you have a secret you want me to know? Is it still not the time to reveal?'

'Certainly not,' I replied at once and asked, 'why didn't you tell me about Jalpa's affair before?'

The boy did say something to that, but I was unmindful of what he was saying. I was worried about Mr and Mrs Gavit. What nice people they were! I wished Jalpa wouldn't bring them disgrace.

When it was time to say goodbye, I held his hands in

mine and thanked him. 'Thanks for making my day. You changed my mood.'

He just smiled and his face looked so pretty in the moonlight that I wished I could hold his smiling face in my palms and kiss him. Instead, I murmured, 'I love you.'

'What?' He looked bemused.

'I said I love you.' Then seeing the expression of shock on his face, I had to make myself clear. 'I love you as a good friend, a nice human being. What did you think? That I'm seriously in love with you?'

'Nobody has ever said that to me, so I was–' It was easy for him to reply. 'Sorry for not getting it right.'

Will you ever get it right? I thought and said aloud, 'It's okay. I know you have never met someone like me, right?'

'Right,' he said. Then wishing me goodnight he vanished down the lonesome, shaded path towards his hostel. And I sighed. *I want you to get it right, Vivek.*

When I got into bed that night, I was cold to the bones. I put on my socks and sweater and wrapped myself in a pair of quilts to thaw out my frozen body. I wished I wouldn't get sick because I had already begun sneezing.

'If things can go wrong, they will,' says Murphy's Law. Once again, it came true when the next morning I found myself ailing—my head aching, nose blocked and body feverish. I was unable to talk because of the infection in my throat. Getting wet in the rain had caused the problem but it wasn't the first time that I had been in the rain for that long. Never had I become so sick since I'd come to Valai. I had had fitness problems in the past, but never so serious as to compel me to take complete bed rest.

I had to take sick leave from school. Vivek was the first one to come and see me. I wanted to talk to him, but my sore throat didn't support me. Then came Mr Desai, uttering abusive words as always, 'Stupid fellow, don't you know about the epidemic spreading through the place nowadays?' He was irritated about the fact that I had been in the rain last evening. It was his affection for me that was coming out of his mouth in the form of abusive words. He sat beside my bed and filled my ears with God knows how much advice.

Sukhi was equally worried about my health though I was not seriously ill. It was just that I couldn't talk properly because of the pain and swelling in my throat. Otherwise the fever was gone after I had taken the first injection and the first dosage from the prescription. In spite of that, my inability to talk bothered her.

Seeing her worried, I remembered my mother. *How overwrought she used to be when I fell ill!* She would take great care of me. She would do everything to perk me up. She would prepare nice food for me, sit by me and watch TV, and bring me whatever I asked for. How concerned she used to be for her kids. Even after the three of us had grown up, she treated us like kids.

I wished she was with me. It had been days since she had phoned, so a call from her was expected any time, but I wished she wouldn't call until I was able to talk at least. I didn't want her to know about my poor health.

When I was alone after lunch, I remembered Vidya. She must have come to know about my sickness. She must be worried, I thought and hoped that she'd come to see me in the evening after school. I eagerly waited for her, but she didn't appear. Does she hate me so much? I asked myself. *No, she can't. She can't ever hate me.* I was sure. I had hurt her, broken her heart, then why was I expecting her to be there?

Mr Desai visited me again in the afternoon. With him was Mrs Desai who brought with her some Ayurvedic medicines which in her opinion, were more efficacious than the allopathic medicines prescribed by the doctor. She added some Ayurvedic powder in boiled water and prepared a kind of tepid decoction which I had to drink despite its awful taste. She instructed me to take some more of it at night and also directed Sukhi about what my diet should be. Then she showered me with the same advice Mr Desai had given me in the morning.

I was expecting Vidya after school, but she didn't turn up. That disheartened me, but soon the disappointment dissapeared as Vivek came and produced an envelope that carried the photos I had taken on our expedition to the Mahal. I had given the negatives at a photo studio and had paid in advance. Vivek had done a good job by collecting them. The photos brought a big smile to my ailing face. I tried to talk, but couldn't. Vivek told me to keep mum. Traces of worry could be seen on his face. *Oh, he is perturbed about me. My sickness has troubled so many people except Vidya.* Had she not been offended, she would have come here immediately, I thought. *Very well. Fine. If she doesn't want to keep a healthy friendship, let it be so.* I tried to get rid of her thoughts, but it wasn't easy.

seventeen

When I opened my eyes the next morning, I heard someone talking to Sukhi in the kitchen. I tried to figure out who it was, it wasn't Jalpa's or Mrs Gavit's voice. It was, as I recognized a bit later, Vidya's. I called Sukhi's name and the face that appeared at the door was Vidya's.

'Good morning!' She walked up to the window and threw the curtains open. 'How are you feeling now? Better?' she asked and stood by the bed.

The medicines had really worked and I was able to talk comfortably. 'Much better,' I said and added intuitively, 'because of your presence.'

'I'm flattered,' she said and helped me get up. Though I didn't need it, I let her help me. I got fresh and she busied herself in preparing breakfast for me.

We had tea with biscuits, boiled eggs and idli. Vidya had brought idli for me. I liked this steamed rice snack, with tomato sauce. She knows what I like, I thought.

Having finished breakfast, we both sat in the hall and chatted and I showed her the photographs I had taken of the forest of Mahal. As she busied herself with the pictures, I thought how caring she had been of me! Despite the fact that I had broken her heart, she had come to see me, prepared breakfast for me and behaved as if nothing had happened between us. I suddenly felt remorseful for what I had done.

'Thanks for coming,' I said when she was about to leave.

She just smiled and left with a promise to be back in the evening. Her visit made me feel so good that I felt I was recovering faster.

When Vidya was gone, I sat with the latest issue of the *India Today* magazine which had an interesting survey article about same-sex relationships. The article reminded me of an incident from my past. Having spent a nice evening with Krishna when I had returned home, I found Mr Trivedi, my father's old friend, at home. Mr Trivedi lived in the United States of America and visited India occasionally. It was the month of January, a year back when he had come to India with his wife and only daughter. He and my father were best friends. Father hardly talked about him, but my mother had told us how close they were since their youth. The two men were in the study room and when I went there to pay him my respects, they stopped talking. Trivedi uncle replied to my greeting, but I could sense that it was passive. I saw there were streaks of tears on his cheeks. Puzzled, I went to my mother in the kitchen where she was busy preparing dinner. When I asked her about the air of seriousness in the study room, she hadn't answered at once. She asked me to go to ask Smit, my brother about it.

Smit told me that Mr Trivedi's only daughter, Piya, owned an Indian restaurant in San Francisco. The Trivedis also had good jobs in Los Angeles. The three of them were very happy with their lives. The only thing that bothered them was that Piya, who had turned thirty-two by then, was not in favour of getting married. They had given her the freedom to live her life her own way, but they also wanted her to have a family of her own. Like most other parents, they had dreamed of their daughter marrying the perfect Indian man and having kids. Piya was beautiful and rich so she could have any man of her choice, but she was strictly against marriage. Many times, her parents had questioned her about her decision of not getting married, but she had never given a satisfactory answer. She had always said that she had nothing against men, it was just that she didn't want to get married. She had even been asked if she had a boyfriend she wanted to get married to. Since she was getting old, her parents were desperate. An Indian man would have been given priority, but then they were ready for even an American if she so wanted. Mr and Mrs Trivedi did their best, but Piya was not interested in tying the knot at all.

One day, Mr Trivedi received a letter from Piya. She had written that she had married the person of her choice. It was shocking that she hadn't cared about telling her parents. But the real shocker was that she had married a woman. Yes, Piya had been a lesbian since her young days and she had chosen to live the rest of her life with a white, American woman named Michelle. Piya was so smart that she had never let her parents get any idea about her being a lesbian. There was no chance that Mr and Mrs Trivedi would have approved of this marriage. How could they have? Their daughter had brought them such humiliation that they were unable to cope with it. Within days, they decided to leave America forever since Piya's marriage had been the talk of the town in the Indian community there. They had returned to India a week ago and this is what he was discussing with my father.

Mr Trivedi didn't stay for dinner. My father was so

angry with Piya that he loathed the stupid girl for what she had done to her parents. He said that such useless children should be shot and that it's better not to have any children than having one who'd earned their parents shame and disgrace. Hearing him, I was petrified, thinking what would happen if he came to know about my homosexuality. How terrible would it be for him to accept the fact that his son was gay! Would he stick to his words and shoot me? No, he wouldn't. He loved me. He wouldn't kill me but I would probably die of shame. I was terrified since I knew how bad his anger was. I wished that day would never come.

But the evil day did come and ravage my life.

It took me two more days to recuperate and to get back to my job. Vivek, Vidya, Mr Desai, and Mrs Gavit were the people who visited me every day. The way they showered their love upon me, I felt I was lucky to have such nice people in my life. Every single one of my colleagues and many of the students came to see me during that short period of illness. All of my students wished the same thing, that I get well soon because they didn't like my absence at the school. That was the first time I realized how much the people around loved me. The sickness had indeed come as a blessing in disguise.

It was the month of September when the first exams were held. Vivek was busy with his studies and I was involved with paper setting which kept us apart for about a fortnight. It wasn't like we didn't meet each other, but we couldn't have those leisurely meetings in the evenings. I didn't know if he missed me or not, but I sure missed having those conversations with him. Finally, when the exams were over, we decided to spend a whole day together. We took Mr Gavit's bike and strayed towards the remote ends of the district. Such a fine excursion it turned out to be as there were just the two of us and no one else to interfere. I wished I could drive Vivek away from the rest of the world, leaving every thing behind. I wanted to elope far, far away with him if he was ready. I knew that not each and every wish comes true and that which is forbidden is most desirable.

Since we didn't have any food with us, we stopped at a small village the name of which I couldn't pronounce correctly. I asked the village men if they could arrange some food for us. As they were not fluent in Gujarati, Vivek talked to them in Dangi, the local language. For a while the old shepherds looked at each other and said something which was beyond my understanding. One of the men decided to cook for us at his home when I offered him some money. Herding the flock of his sheep and goats, the shepherd, all skin and bones, took us to his place. His house was a small hut, the walls were made of bamboo sticks, coated with mud and dung, and the roof was made of coconut leaves woven tightly together. Through the open entrance, I could see that inside the hut there was almost nothing in the name of furniture. All he owned was a small worn out cot, a large cylindrical vessel made of mud and dung, and a few other things which I didn't know what they were used for. I pitied them, but then, that's the way they lived. Washing our face and hands, we sat on the raised platform made of clay around a pipal tree in his backyard. We had asked for chicken, so he caught one of his hens and slaughtered it by cutting its throat right before our eyes.

While the man sat with us to talk, his woman was busy inside her kitchen. Vivek conversed with the old man in his language, whilst I listened to the pastoral song being sung sweetly by a woman in one of the neighbouring huts. The aroma of the chicken filled our nostrils and enhanced our appetite. Half an hour later, we had before us a vessel full of spicy chicken and a pile of rotlas, like chapattis, along with salad of salted onions.

On seeing the pile of rotlas, my first reaction was, 'What do they think of us? Gluttonous giants? I doubt if we'll finish even half of this pile.'

'Don't worry, I'll do that for you,' Vivek said and started eating at once, but I felt awkward in the presence of that rustic man. He was squatting right in front of us with his eyes gliding between our faces and our food. I didn't like someone staring at my food or at me when I ate. So I asked Vivek, 'Would you please ask him to leave or to have some chicken from this plate? Be polite, make sure it doesn't embarrass him.'

Vivek said something to the old man and a smile appeared on his weather beaten face. Making some incomprehensible gestures with his hands, the man left in no time. He went towards his livestock which were grazing at a short distance on a sloping land. He was to return only after we finished our lunch.

'What did he say?' I asked Vivek.

'He asked us to savour the meal and also that he has already had his lunch,' Vivek replied.

'Was he laughing at me?' I asked uncertainly.

Vivek grinned, 'No, but he probably understood that you didn't like his presence.' Then he added, 'Don't bother. These people don't know how to take things amiss.'

He was right. These people were too innocent and humble to take things to heart. I compared these uneducated, neglected people with the highly educated people of Baroda who lied and betrayed, and were experts in playing mean games in their daily life.

The chicken was very tasty, but I couldn't eat much. Vivek devoured most of it and I liked the fact that he didn't hesitate. He ate well, but couldn't finish the pile of rotlas. We decided to leave after taking a brief respite under the pipal tree. Vivek was more than happy to be with me that day. While getting back to Valai, I asked him if he wanted to drive and he did. I had taught him to ride a bike. I liked to sit behind him with my chest touching his back and my nose close to his shoulders, hair and neck to enjoy the smell of his body. His body odour filled my mind with unusual sensations.

In the middle of the jungle, I asked him to halt to watch the sunset. We parked the bike on the roadside, climbed a nearby hill and sat on the grassy land. To my surprise, we noticed small, thatched houses below, along the other side of the hill which were not visible to the passers-by. Without a word, we watched the sun go down. The tall teak trees on the edge of the mountain at the opposite end of the narrow valley grew pale with the approaching darkness. A small flock of wild cranes flew over our heads in the ruddy sky and though they were at a distance, the flutter of their wings could be heard easily in the dead calm of the evening. What a magnificent canvas of natural spectacle it was!

'Aren't they beautiful?' I asked, breathing deeply and keeping my eyes on the flock till they disappeared. 'We search for God in temples and mosques and cathedrals but the fact is that God resides in a place like this.' I was drinking in the surroundings. 'People ask where God is. I say He's here in the wind, in the trees, in every single element of nature. We just need to open our eyes to all these things that are unarguably more real and clean and sinless than the places that man builds for the Gods.'

When I realized Vivek was staring at me, I turned my eyes to him and shook my head questioningly. 'What?'

'Where do you get such unique thoughts from?' he asked. 'There's nobody like you, not in my acquaintance at least!'

I smiled and said nothing, but stretched my hand and ruffled his hair. For some more moments, I feasted my eyes on the beauty of the scenery around.

'What a wonderful day we've had!' I looked into his eyes and took his hand in mine. 'I will never forget this day. Thanks for making this trip special. Thanks for being in my life and making me feel good. Thanks for everything. I've been addicted to you. Hope the addiction won't be a pain.' I doubted if he understood the last two sentences. *I wish we'd never have to part.* I didn't utter that. *One thing I'm sure about is that you're the person I'd love to spend the rest of my life with.* I wished he could hear that. I wished he could read my eyes and reach the bottom of my heart where profound love lay for him. Without uttering a single word, he kept smiling through the conversation that was dominated by me. Talking like that was an attempt at stirring his heart, but I had no idea how much he got of whatever I'd said.

Sitting by Vivek that evening, I remembered Krishna with whom I had spent the best days of my life. Besides daily outings, we used to go for long holidays. We had gone to Goa, visited the entire Saurashtra and the desert of Kachch, but the best holiday I had in his company was when I had gone to his village in Kerala. Krishna's family lived in Surat, and he had told them a lot about me. His family had invited me to their place in Surat and they had been happy to meet me. All members of his family were so friendly that it didn't take me long to mingle with them. On the festival of Onam the following year, I joined them in Kottayam, Kerala. Those holidays had proved to be the best vacation of my life! I'd celebrated the biggest festival of the Malayalees. I'd learnt to make rangolis from flowers, eaten delicious food and enjoyed village life fully. But the most exciting things I had done was to swim in the backwaters and to ride the elephants. And the worst, that still makes me laugh, was to get dressed in traditional clothes of the Malayalees. I believed I looked very funny in the fine, thin dhoti that felt as if it would blow off in the wind any moment! Everybody there said I looked nice, but only I knew how uncomfortable I was.

Had Krishna been in Vivek's place, we would be having fun—kissing or maybe doing something more exciting! I smiled. That's what we did when alone. The man in me got hungry and I wished that the boy by my side was gay.

We sat there until darkness descended upon the picturesque landscape. By the time we set out for home, it was late. The moon had appeared early that night and the entire expanse was bathed in moonlight. More than once that day, I had thought of expressing my feelings to Vivek openly, but the fear of being rejected, held me back. It's not the right time, I thought.

Vivek was not sure if he would pass in the subject of psychology. I told him to have faith but Murphy's Law came true once again—'When things can go wrong, they will'. He failed. He said he had done his best, but it hadn't been good enough. I told him not to worry so much and promised that I would help him study the subject for the next exam. Even I had disliked psychology in my school days, but I had never failed. I had made a promise to console Vivek, but I had no idea that it was going to be nightmarish for me to go through the subject again after so many years.

Vivek's failure reminded me of the time when I had seriously fallen in love with Krishna. My performance had weakened in one exam. I hadn't failed, but had obtained very low marks. Having no idea regarding my failure, Krishna had asked me the reason. When I said I couldn't concentrate on my studies because I thought of him all the time, he had scolded me and took a promise from me that our relationship wouldn't affect my studies. And he'd said he wasn't going to go away from my life.

'I'm not going to go away from your life.' The memory of those words of Krishna brought a tragic smile on my face and my heart heaved a silent sigh. *But you did leave me, pal.*

Soon after the exams, the practice for the Inter School Cricket Competition began. The sixteen selected students were being coached by Mr Sheikh. The festival of Diwali was close and a three week long vacation was to follow, so the coach wanted the players to be on the ground as long as they could be. The players were told to keep playing cricket at home during the vacation too. I had no intention of going to Baroda, but since Vivek was also going home, I made up my mind to go visit my place. Before the holidays, I wanted to have a nice time with Vivek, so we took a trip to Sapttara. We took Mr Gavit's bike and had great fun together.

Before leaving for his home, Vivek invited me to his place during the vacation. I said I would think about it, but couldn't promise. I went to bid him goodbye at the bus stand where I gave him a tight hug before he boarded the bus. From his face, I knew that he had liked my hugging him. But when the bus sped away, an ominous thought hit my mind, someday, he'll leave me like this forever! I couldn't deal with that terrifying thought. I dreaded it happening. Somewhere deep in my heart a prayer rose that that day should never come.

Back home, I received a warm welcome because my family hadn't seen me for the past four-five months. Everyone except my father behaved normally as if nothing had happened and it seemed that they all had forgiven me. I had thought it would be a boring vacation, but to my surprise, it wasn't bad at all. For about a week, I visited my relatives and friends. All of them were happy to see me, making me realize that they still loved me. Though I wasn't at ease with some of my elders, it wasn't difficult for me to mingle with my cousins and friends. With them, I wandered all over Baroda, went for late night movies and visited a few new restaurants. I enjoyed my time the way I used to when I was in college. I also visited my college, but there were no familiar faces except for some professors. They liked that I had taken up teaching.

The memories of Krishna followed me wherever I went. There were innumerable places where we had spent time in the past. All the places took me back to my old days, and I had to push myself hard not to think about the bygone time. Though I was with my friends and Krishna was nowhere around physically, I could sense his presence all the time. I doubted if the city of Baroda would ever let me forget him. I had no idea where on earth he was. He must have settled somewhere else. Probably, Bombay. He liked the city and had talked about settling there since the place had so much to offer. Or he might have gone back to his home town. *Did his family know what had happened between us? What must he be doing for a living?* None of us had ever tried to contact each other since we separated. He must have been waiting for my call, just the way I had been waiting for his. It was our egos that had kept us from calling each other. Otherwise, there had been no one, nothing to stop us. I was curious, but I was afraid of making inquiries about him lest my family came to know about it.

While Krishna's memories saddened me, Vivek's brought zest. Many times, I wondered what he must be doing at home. My guess was that he was busy playing cricket, roaming with his village friends in the jungle, giving a hand to his father in his farms or milking his cattle with his mother. It was fun to think about that young boy. I oscillated between the thoughts of Krishna and Vivek during the holidays.

I met my cousin, Chhaya, and apologized for not being with her on the auspicious day of the inauguration of her boutique. She fought with me for more than half an hour before she finally smiled. I took her to dinner that night, and as a punishment, I had to listen to her incessant talk until midnight. But it was fun. Since I had been away from all of them for so long, I had no reason to complain and enjoyed their company. I went to parties, discotheques and outings almost every day. And the sadness that had overcome my entire personality after the disclosure of my being gay, had completely vanished. During the last two years, I had been to Baroda more than once, but never could I be what I used to be. The realization that the people around me knew my secret had held me back from indulging myself. All of a sudden, my life, like a widow's, had become solemn, insipid and worthless. I had wanted to go out, but couldn't because my friends and cousins seemed to be hesitating in being seen with me. It had been so frustrating and torturing. It was now that I again started to enjoy life here in Baroda. The festival of Diwali, which had been my favourite festival since childhood, went off well. It was after two years that my family was celebrating the festival traditionally. I attended the pujas, went to the temples, and helped my mother in making colourful rangolis. But the best part was relishing the sweets and other homemade snacks that were prepared only on the festival of Diwali. I bought firecrackers and sweets for the street children and tried to bring a little joy into their lives.

The time that I had anticipated would be tiresome, had turned out to be such fun that I didn't even realize when the vacation was over. Throughout my stay at home, I had hardly talked to my father because he was still upset with me. When I was to leave, I received five words from him. 'Travel safe and take care.' He gave me a hug and that was enough for me. It probably was the beginning of his acceptance of my gayness.

eighteen

When I returned to Valai with the pleasant memories of the time I had back home, I was impatient to talk to Vivek about them. Surprisingly, he was there at the bus station to greet me. Seeing him after so many days, my heart leaped with joy and I wondered how he was there. As he drew nearer, I stretched my arms and he happily let himself be hugged. Wishing the hug to be everlasting, I held him close for a while.

'Happy Diwali and a Happy New Year,' I whispered in his ears joyfully.

He also wished me. Dressed in a white shirt that gleamed in the sunlight and neatly ironed blue trousers, he looked so good that I couldn't help myself praise him 'You're looking so *sexy.*'

He smiled shyly. The sight of his ever smiling face was such a relief to me that the fatigue of my long, tiring journey faded in an instant.

'Mrs Gavit told me that you're coming today,' he said even before I asked.

Two days ago, I had phoned Mrs Gavit to inform Sukhi about my arrival so that she could clean the house before I came. It was great to see Vivek. *He really cares for me.*

I gave him my handbag and we walked to my place. On our way home, I told him that I had a lot to talk about. He said he'd love to hear about everything.

'Back home everybody from my family wants to meet you,' he began talking. 'I've told them almost everything about you and they all are so impressed with you. I wish you could have been at my place this Diwali. I missed you.'

He'd missed me!

'I would love to hear what you have told them about me.' I found it interesting that he had talked about me. Also, I wanted to know his thoughts on me.

'Well, I told them that you are such a nice person, such a handsome man, such a nice soul, a very good friend and, above all, a great human being.'

I began to laugh. 'What?' he asked, confused.

'Is that what you think about me?' I was still laughing.

'Yes, why?' he looked puzzled.

'I'm not *that* good, you know?' I replied, but actually I was happy that he thought so well of me. I was too damn happy.

'I know what you are.' He looked at me lovingly.

I stopped laughing and looked at him with gratitude.

'Tell me, when will you be visiting my house?' he asked.

'We'll plan that,' I answered.

'We'll take Mr Gavit's motorcycle, okay?' he loved to ride the bike.

'Sure.'

'When?' he asked smiling.

'Right now if you say,' I said, miming his drawl and then added, 'Actually it better be some other time. I'm tired.'

'But *when*?' he was insistent.

'Vivek . . .!' I threatened him with my eyes.

'W—w— when?' he asked imitating.

'We shall. We shall. It's a gentleman's word.' I relented.

We talked about some other things. I asked him about his cricket practice and he said it was going well. He and all his team mates had arrived back in Valai five days before the school was to start. It was because the Inter School Cricket Championship was just a fortnight away and the coach wanted them to spend as much time as they could practising.

The door of Mr Gavit's house was closed. I was surprised. It was never closed at that hour in the evening. They all must have gone somewhere, I said to myself.

'You don't know, do you?' Vivek asked from behind as I opened the door of my quarter to get in. It took me a while to realize he was talking about the Gavits.

'What?' I asked without curiosity.

He took his time, breathed deep and then blurted, 'Jalpa has eloped!'

'What?' I was stunned.

He nodded in reply.

'Damn that silly girl!' I sat on the settee and cursed.

'It was going to happen someday . . .' Vivek sat by me. 'It's the same guy we had seen her with the other day. Marcus, if you remember. It's been four days and her parents are so ashamed that they are hiding in their house all the time.'

I shook my head and went to the washbasin. *I should have spoken to bhai about Marcus.* I would have, had I not fallen ill. But because of my illness, the incident had got erased from my mind. Having washed my face, I tried to relax. It wasn't Jalpa I was worried about. It was Mr and Mrs Gavit I was concerned about. *How terrible a time they must be having! I must go to see them.* I told Vivek to come later and when he was gone, I went to meet the Gavits.

Their faces were wreathed in grim smiles. Mr Gavit took me inside with a faint greeting in his swollen eyes, while Mrs Gavit began to sob. I took a seat by her. 'Have you gone to the police?' I asked Mr Gavit. To my surprise, he shook his head in denial. 'Why?' I asked. I believed the police would have been helpful.

'I don't want her back in this house.' Mr Gavit was struggling to keep an even tone. 'The sort of disgrace she has brought to us is unforgivable. I won't let her in . . . ever!'

When I asked them if they had any idea about Jalpa seeing Marcus, the Gavits again shook their heads. *What ignorant parents!* When Mr Gavit learnt that I knew about his daughter's affair, he told me in a shocked tone that I should have told him. To mollify him, I apologized, saying I didn't know she would go this far. And I genuinely didn't have any such idea even though I knew, from personal experience, of Jalpa's fondness for men. I also mentioned that because of my sickness I had almost forgotten the incident. It seemed Mr Gavit had believed me.

I asked him if he had met the parents of the boy. He said they didn't seem much worried. After all, he was a boy and society always points a finger at the girl in such cases. Everybody in Valai knew that the boy was a ruffian. And he was much older than Jalpa. She was only fifteen. I tried to persuade Mr Gavit that if we filed a case against the boy, he'd be in trouble, as running away with a minor girl was against the law. Even though Jalpa had fled with him willingly, he'd be charged with misleading and exploiting an underage girl.

But Mr Gavit thought it'd be useless to punish the boy when his own daughter was equally to be blamed. He was not in favour of going to the police. Neither was he doing anything himself. What was he going to do then? When I asked this, he said that for them, Jalpa was as good as dead. She wouldn't get her life back even if she returned.

The stupid girl had stolen some cash and her mother's jewellery. I was sure that as soon as the money was spent, they'd be back home. Nothing else happens in such cases. They'd wander from place to place, make merry, have fun and then return home empty handed. Valai was such a small place that even a minor thing became the talk of the town, so it was obvious that by now everybody had come to know about the scandal. People I knew kept asking me about her since I was her neighbour. I told them, 'I only know as much as you do.'

About a week later, two young boys came to meet me at the school. They introduced themselves as Marcus's friends. They told me that Marcus had called them that morning. He and Jalpa wanted to return home. The boys had informed Marcus's family and they had no objection. Now they wanted me to talk to the Gavits as I was the closest one to them. That evening, I talked to bhai. He said nothing. I tried to urge him to forgive Jalpa. Yet, he remained silent. He had been adamant about not letting his daughter into his house again, but all the bitterness I had seen in him lately was gone. Never before had I seen him so helpless. After all, he was a father who loved his child more than anything else in the whole world. He didn't utter a single word. He didn't need to. I took his silence as his assent and met Marcus's friends the next day morning.

Later that afternoon, Marcus's friends came to me to let me know that Jalpa and Marcus were to arrive late that night. I was with Mr and Mrs Gavit in that critical time period. In the dark hours of midnight, the couple arrived. I got a phone call from Marcus's friend who informed me about the rendezvous. I took Mr Gavit's bike and left for the place where I was asked to go. On the outskirts of the town, I figured out from a distance, five blurred figures in the dim moonlight. Pulling up by the roadside, I watched them momentarily. They were Marcus, his three friends and Jalpa, who seemed to be so ashamed of what she had done that she couldn't even look into my eyes. When I looked at Marcus, even he averted his eyes from me. That was the first time I had a closer look at that ruffian and not a single thing was remarkable about his looks. Nothing was there to say or to do. Jalpa sat on the backseat of the bike and we drove home. I was angry about what she had done to her parents, but there was no point in rebuking her at that moment.

Jalpa's parents were waiting in the living room. Mrs Gavit looked at her daughter but Mr Gavit had his eyes fixed on the blank wall all the time. Jalpa flinched to get in for fear of her father, so I held her by her hand and took her to her room. Then I returned to the living room to the Gavits and said, 'Get some sleep. It's late.'

I was back in my house but was still anxious lest something unpleasant happen. I was alert in case Mr Gavit or Mrs Gavit did something wrong like reviling, or beating up Jalpa. When nothing seemed to be happening, I was able to go to sleep.

The following days were not going to be normal. Neither for the Gavits nor for me. The fact that Jalpa had brought with her an incurable stain on her character had stolen the peace from that fun loving couple. The sweet bickering over trifling issues, the blithe conversations while having the evening tea, and the merriment that filled the air all the time was all gone! Life became tasteless. The stabbing eyes of their acquaintances, mental torture, and the ceaseless brooding over the transgression of their daughter was what the Gavits reeled under. Jalpa had landed them in such a predicament that they preferred to stay locked in their home most of the time and I could no longer chat with them. It was all so frustrating, but I couldn't help the entire situation. Nobody could. Jalpa was not allowed to go out. Neither of her parents talked to her. She was paying for her mistake. After a day or two of their homecoming, Marcus was seen in public as if nothing had happened. He had got his life back. When I saw him passing by on a bike with his friends one evening, I cursed him in my mind. *Had bhai taken legal action, the bastard would have been behind bars.*

The incident didn't make any difference to Marcus or his family. For the Gavits, things were not to change for months.

Vivek had to give most of his time to cricket and had little time for anything else. I had to go to the playground to see him. It was only after dark that he could find some time for me, but I didn't complain as he was doing his best to make me and our school proud. Those were the days I really spent alone. I went to the sunset point, sat under the neem tree and talked to myself, but I liked nothing in his absence. I remained half-hearted during the day too, but didn't let it show on my face when I went to meet him at the ground. The more the days of the cricket tournament neared, the more busy he became. He apologized for not being with me and vowed that he surely would have leisure time with me later. That was enough for me. *He wants to be with me. He misses me. He likes me.* It just takes a single thought to make you feel good beyond your imagination.

I found ways to enjoy myself alone. I had to because I had no other option. I tried to keep myself occupied with the books at the public library. I preferred to be at Mr Desai's for hours and then I decided to give my little garden a new life since the rainy season was about to end. The gardening, fortunately, took much of my time and I quite enjoyed it. Seventeen kilometres from my place at a village called Subir, there was a nursery from where I decided to buy new plants. There was such a huge variety of plants that I was confused about what to pick and what not to. I would have bought them all had my garden been big enough to hold all of them, but I selected only a few. To me, they were like children and friends. I actually talked to them in my mind as I worked. I wasn't short of time, hence I could arrange them in the most elegant ways. And when it was all done, it looked really pretty.

One morning, when I was busy in my garden, Jalpa came to see me. I hadn't seen her for days, so it felt good to see her. She looked sapped from being locked up in her house all the time. Mr Gavit was out at that time, while Mrs Gavit was in the bathroom. Since she was not allowed to go out of doors, Jalpa had little time for what she had to say.

'I'm sick of being imprisoned,' she spoke slowly. 'I was wondering if you could talk to my father to allow me to go back to the school.'

'I will,' I said thoughtfully, and then she was gone. 'Aren't you ashamed of what you did?' I wanted to ask her. She wasn't, I was sure. She had been out with that boy for twelve days. They must have had sex. After all, that's what they had eloped for. I hoped they had used contraceptives. Jalpa had courted enough humiliation for her parents, so I wished there would be no more.

The next day, I met Mr Gavit and talked to him to allow Jalpa to attend school. I tried to make him understand that

Jalpa was in the tenth class and it was a crucial year for her studies. I urged him to forgive her. He remained quiet until I was done.

'I'll think about that,' he said in the end. I felt sorry for the man. How I hated to see that gloomy face which used to be joyous all the time! Life's so unpredictable. Sometimes things happen in a way that change the course of one's life. The same had happened to the Gavits.

When it was time for school the next day, I had my eyes on the Gavits' house but Jalpa was nowhere to be seen. I was disappointed, but I didn't lose hope. The next day, my eager eyes gleamed with joy when they caught Jalpa in her school uniform on the veranda of her house. She looked at me and smiled her thanks, and after days, I could see her face lit up with a beautiful smile.

In the meantime, something unexpected happened. I was passing by Vivek's class during the recess one day, when I saw him sitting with Chandni on the last bench. It was a shock for me because I had never anticipated that something of this sort would ever happen. I was not sure, but I thought they were aware that I had seen them together. For the entire day, it kept bothering me that something was going on between the two of them. I decided to ask Vivek, but he didn't come that evening. It was only the next evening that I happened to meet him in private. I was thinking how to bring up the issue. 'Don't you want to tell me something?' I began to pry after some casual talk.

'What?' he asked in reply.

He won't tell me unless I ask openly. I asked directly. 'About Chandni. Don't tell me you're not seeing her.'

He remained speechless for long.

'Come on, you can tell me. But if you don't want to then . . .' I knew that would make him talk.

'It's not like that.' He sounded quite hesitant. 'I have been talking to her only recently.'

I didn't like that, but I was wary. The fake smile on my face didn't fade.

'She proposed to me through her friend and . . . my friends also told me to say yes . . . and it happened.'

'So you said yes?' I asked though it was clear.

He nodded. I could see that he seemed puzzled by my enquiry.

'She proposed to you?' I asked. 'How?'

'One of her friends came to me and asked if I would talk to her.' He blushed.

It amused me that Chandni had proposed to Vivek by asking a question like, 'Would you talk to me?' Actually people in a small place like Valai had the mindset that if a young boy and a young girl were talking to each other, they were in love. That's why instead of asking 'would you like to be my friend?' they asked, 'would you talk to me?' Talking to someone of the opposite sex meant you liked that person. Unlike Baroda, a healthy friendship between a boy and a girl, was impossible in this conservative society. Maybe that's why some people questioned my relationship with Vidya. But who cared? I didn't give them any importance! Neither did Vidya.

'Then what would happen to the others?' I was in a mood to needle him. He didn't get me until I spoke out the names of his other female interests. 'Seema and . . . err . . . what's her name? Mala, yes.'

He laughed out loud. 'There's nothing serious going on with them.'

'How serious are you about Chandni?' It took me a while to ask since I realized he really liked the girl.

'Not much because I know there is no future with

her. She's out of my reach.' He was looking in the other direction, while I kept my eyes on his face to study his expressions. 'The good thing is that she also knows. Before getting into this relation, we had discussed that. It's just that we like each other's company. I want to be with her till I can. It'll be a good experience, wouldn't it?' He sought agreement from me.

'It sure would!' I replied with caution so that my displeasure wouldn't appear in my tone. There was a long silence before I said, 'You two are wiser than you appear. Such thinking is rather unexpected in adolescence. Good for you. Good for her!' I took a deep breath and sighed.

Ceaseless thoughts about Vivek's new love interest didn't let me relax that entire evening and night. The thought that he had started to like someone increased my tension. Though I knew it was nothing but a teenage physical attraction, I couldn't deal with the fact that my love was attached with someone else. I was actually jealous of Chandni! I had been in search of a chance to admit my infatuation for Vivek, but this latest development in his life had disrupted my plan completely. I thought of keeping my eyes on them. It was necessary. I wanted them to separate before Vivek seriously fell in love with her. I had to think of something, and quickly.

nineteen

S ix major schools had been chosen to host the Inter-School Cricket Competition and ours was one of them. A total of thirty-two schools were divided into eight groups. Each group had four teams, of which only the top two were to make it through to the next round. Each school was to play three league matches with the opponents in its group and the organizers had made sure that no team had the chance to play on their own school grounds in the first round. The school was to continue as usual during the tournament, but I was to travel with the boys as they really wanted me to be with them for moral support.

Our schedule for the league matches started on Saturday when we were to take on a qualifier team. It was a comfortable victory for us since we demolished our opponent who batted first and ended up making a total of merely forty-seven runs. The next battle was on Monday and the opponent was going to be stronger this time. But we conquered them with an unbeaten half century by Vivek who was declared the winner of the Man of the Match award. The last league match was scheduled for Tuesday at a distant venue called Zaghadamba. Our boys won that match too and topped the group. Every single person in our school was buoyant with that superb start, and before the pre-quarter final round began, we were among the top three favourites to win the tournament. Vivek emerged an allrounder by taking four wickets and scoring 107 runs in the three league matches.

Our team got a break of two days before the beginning of the second round. The atmosphere at the school was charged and Vivek was the one everybody was talking about. He was getting adulation from everyone and expectations were getting higher. I found him nervous when I went to see him on the ground.

'Sir, I'm feeling tense now. The expectations . . . you know. The major matches are to start and if I fail–' He held his tongue. There was a reflective pause.

'Don't think negatively. I'm sure you'll do better in the following games.' I tried to motivate him. 'I believe in your abilities and you're going to make all of us proud. Everything will be fine, so don't worry, and concentrate on your game.' My words seemed to have motivated him and he genuinely thanked me.

Henceforth, the tournament was to be a knockout. One failure and our team would be out of the competition. In the next two rounds, our team was to confront teams that were inferior to us. And that was the problem. We would be under pressure for a sure win, whereas the opponents had nothing to lose. Being clear favourites puts a lot of pressure in any field because when you lose, the blame is always more heightened than the praise you get when you are triumphant.

Within five days, forty-eight league matches were played at six different venues, and sixteen teams were through to the pre-quarter final round.

The second round began on Thursday. We were to play our match on Friday and were supposed to register a comprehensive win. It went off smoothly as our boys defeated the competitor. Every win was celebrated in our school campus. Four fascinating victories in a row put everyone of us in high spirits and it seemed like our team was going to do what we had done two years ago—win the trophy. Though the next match was not tough, it was highly anticipated as we were going to play on home ground.

The ground was packed to capacity that Sunday afternoon, and though we prevailed, the opposite team fought well, better than what everybody had anticipated. Our boys had to give their best shot. This was the first match that was so on the edge that our team had to fight body and soul to register a victory. Vivek was out for just eight runs in that match. As usual, the unhappy boy came to me and I consoled him that he would do better in the semi final that was against the Jakhana High School, a much stronger team and the defending champion.

A holiday was declared for the school and the principal organized a bus trip for the students to reach Pimpri, the village where we were to play the semi final match. Our school was given none of the semi final matches since we had the final match on our grounds. Everybody thought that if we could defeat the defending champion, the title would be ours because of the advantage of playing the final on home ground. I knew the semi final was going to be tough, but it turned out to be more thrilling than I or anybody had ever imagined.

Batting second, and chasing the score of 151 in twenty overs, we lost wickets at regular intervals, but it was Vivek who held on at one end and kept the scoreboard rolling. The bowlers and the captain of the opposite team tried hard to get his wicket, but Vivek played the way he'd never played before. He kept taking singles and pushed the score to 143. It was the last over—we had just one wicket in hand and nine runs were needed for a win. Vivek was at the crease and he knew that he couldn't afford to take singles any more because the tail-ender at the other end was weak in batting and the opposite team was in search for his wicket. The fielding was so tight that Vivek had to go for a big hit. He missed the first ball, the second hit could have given a single run, but he didn't risk it. With every ball, my heart skipped a beat as did that of most other supporters of our team.

The third delivery Vivek hit in the air. The fielder on the boundary ran for the catch but, it was out of his reach. This six brought a wave of thunderous applause and cheer amongst our supporters and the match turned even deadlier. Three balls and three runs. *Come on Vivek, you can do it!* I was praying to God. Vivek ran to take a run on the fourth ball and he got only one run, but the wicket keeper couldn't control his throw from the fielder and we got an extra run. The scores were equal now. A great applause ran through the spectators of our school. The final run came smoothly as Vivek just played it to the gully. And all of us—shouting, cheering and clapping, ran towards the pitch. I was among the first of them with the coach and the team mates. In raptures, I hugged Vivek tightly and kissed him on his cheek. There was no sexuality here. It was just plain jubilation at winning a great game. He was amazed at my action. Our joyous eyes met for a split second.

Soon a horde of students jumped in and almost suffocated Vivek with their hugs and handshakes. His team mates picked him up on their shoulders and brought him to where the principal was seated. The principal and the entire staff congratulated and praised him on his incredible innings of seventy-one. Predictably, he was declared the Man of the Match with a special mention from the coach of the host school that his had been the best innings of the tournament so far. That really was encouraging and the graph of expectations from Vivek's bat went even higher.

The final battle, the biggest game of all, was to happen on Friday and we were the clear favourites with the advantage of playing on home ground. The opponent, the Saraswati Vidyalaya of village Galkund, had created history by defeating another former champion and reaching the final for the first time. They had some fine players in their team, but we were confident of our strength. I believed Vivek's bat would pour runs again and he'd win the Man of the Series award.

What an awesome atmosphere we had at the ground! People from far off villages had come to see the final battle. The spectators were cheering for both the teams. Ear splitting noises of cheers, drums and whistles had turned the whole atmosphere electric. The match began in our favour as our captain won the toss and elected to bowl first. Our boys were good chasers, so it was obvious that he had chosen to bowl first. The opposite team started off slowly, but once they picked the pace, they seemed unstoppable. They had it in mind to score as much as they could because they knew very well how good our team was at chasing big scores. They risked and experimented with their batting order beyond our understanding. After the opening pair, they tried a combination of a good batsman with a tail-ender and shocked everyone at the ground because never before had anybody witnessed such experimentation in the game of cricket.

The principal, sitting by my side, had even jested in the beginning, 'They're going to regret this stupidity.' I had agreed with him, but it seemed as if the ugly combinations had started working! When the regular batsmen were hitting

Mayur Patel

only ground strokes to save their precious wickets, the tail-enders were batting frantically. They had a plan to muddle our bowling order that way. They knew they had a small chance to win against us, so they had taken a risk and it worked out well for them.

Initially, one of the openers and the first two tail-enders were out soon, and it looked as if the awkward strategy wouldn't work in their favour. But the next tail-ender, a hefty boy with broad shoulders, turned the tables as he started to hit sixes all over the ground. His strokes were so powerful that there was no chance he could be caught at the boundary. He didn't linger for long, but his innings of thirty-five runs in just seventeen balls hiked up their run rate. After him, came the wicket keeper who normally came third in the batting order. At the fall of every wicket, we tried to predict the next batsman and we were wrong everytime. The coach, as if he had gone mad, experimented more than expected. The batsmen from the middle order were nowhere to be seen. Our captain didn't know whom to bring in to bowl. The bowler who bowled well against the stronger batsmen went weak against the hard hitting tail-enders. And even though Vivek didn't allow the regular batsmen much space to bat well, he too was helpless against the tail-enders who were hitting big shots at regular intervals. Moreover, the unbeaten opener, Mehul, was a headache as he calmly played masterstrokes throughout his splendid innings of sixty-two.

All the four tail-enders were out by the end of the fourteenth over, and three batsmen from the middle order were left. From 119 runs in fourteen overs, they had taken their score to 187 in twenty overs, adding a whopping total of sixty-eight runs in the last six overs alone. No other team had thrashed our bowlers this badly in the entire tournament. The game plan of the opposite team that had seemed impractical in the beginning had turned out to be unbelievably advantageous for them. Their coach had reserved the middle order to make the most of the final overs. Their bowlers, not known for good batting, freely played gigantic strokes.

Normally, what happens in the game of cricket is that the tail-enders can't bat well in the final overs as they are under pressure. Here, what worked for the opponents was that the batsmen did not have to worry about saving their wickets. They played freely as there were better batsmen at the other end. The entire gimmick resulted in great success for them and left our team dumbstruck. Our boys were good chasers, but the asking average of 9.40 was not going to be easy at all. Moreover, the opposite team was known for their good bowlers. The feeling that we were surely going to win the title seemed to be fading away as we realized we had to deal with the second highest score of the championship! No other team in the past four years had successfully chased such a big total.

During the break of twenty minutes, all of us tried to inject confidence into our players. When I saw anxiety in Vivek's eyes, I told him, 'Don't doubt your strengths. Just go for it. You'll do better than you've ever done!'

The confidence level had diminished not only in him, but in all the other players too. On the other hand, the opposite team was fully assured of their victory for the reason that they had done the unexpected. The million dollar question was—would our players live up to our expectations? Nobody knew. We needed a miracle.

From the beginning, our team was under pressure to keep the scoreboard rolling. The run rate average didn't touch the necessary figure of 9.40. It was the third over that brought in some hope as Vivek and Sagar, the openers, hit thirteen runs in six balls. But before the celebration of the good beginning ended, we lost Sagar as he was caught behind the wicket. Later came the bigger blow when Vivek, attempting a six, was caught on the boundary line in the fourth ball of the next over. While the supporters of the opposite team celebrated the superb catch that was meant to be a six, a cloud of great dejection engulfed our supporters. Vivek couldn't leave the crease for a while as it was hard for him to believe he was out. Though we had other good players in the middle order, it was almost over. The hero of our team was out and the fact was going to affect the rest of the batsmen. Had Sagar still been playing, we could have hoped for the best as he was also a match winner. With the fall of Vivek's wicket, our enthusiasm began to ebb.

Vivek was so ashamed of his performance—he had scored only seventeen runs, that he couldn't even look anybody in the eye. He sat by Sagar without a word. The two of them were sitting away from the others. I went to them and tried to console, 'It happens. You tried.' But I knew it wasn't going to mollify their anguish and frustration.

The rest of the boys tried to fight back, but no one played up to the mark. It was as if the mammoth score had scared them. The loss of Vivek's and Sagar's wicket led to the collapse of the rest of the batting order. The entire team caved in on a pitiable total of ninety-eight with two overs still left. We lost but the way we did—by eighty-nine runs—was really shameful. Vivek was the top scorer of the tournament with a total of 233 runs, but it was Paras, the fast bowler of the winning team, who grabbed the Man of the Series award for taking a remarkable twenty-six wickets in seven matches. He was also given the Man of the Match award for taking six wickets in the final. As a consolation, Vivek was awarded with the Best Batsman of the Tournament award, but he had surely missed the bull's eye.

The tournament was over, we had lost and what a shameful disaster it had been! We had got the chance to win the title after two years and we had just let it slip from our hands. Negative thoughts surrounded Vivek for a couple of days and he remained gloomy. No consolation could pacify his acute agitation. He had wanted to win the trophy for his school, he had wanted us to be proud but he hadn't accomplished his goals. He was so remorseful that he didn't come to school on Saturday and remained in bed. I went to the hostel to see him in the evening. He hadn't shaved, and unlike me, he didn't look good in a stubble that had grown in an irregular fashion. But it wasn't the beard that was making him look bad, it was the sadness on his face.

I simply hated to see him like that.

'You're still in the mood of yesterday's debacle?' I asked as I sat by him on the bed. 'Or are you sick?'

He didn't answer. He looked at me for a second and shook his head in negation.

'It's really hot here. Let's get out.' I stood up, held him by his wrist and pulled. He hesitated to move.

'Come on, let's get going,' I said somewhat authoritatively and he had to follow my directions since he was not in a position to say no to me. I took him to the terrace where we sat on the parapet.

'It's much better here, isn't it?' I asked, feeling the breeze on my face. 'Now let's talk.'

He still remained silent, so I had to begin with something else. 'You know what this reminds me of?' I wanted to take his attention away. 'I remember Krishna with whom I used to sit on the mossy, ancient walls of the fort in Baroda. We would just sit there and talk till the end of the day. It was so peaceful there.' I recalled how an aged woman had caught us lip locked in a damp corner of that castle. And we had to escape from there in no time since she had started to scream and call the other women working in the fields at a distance. For days, we had laughed remembering that particular incident. *Such a nice time it was!* Before I could get lost in the past, I forced myself back to the present.

'Vivek, you've lost just a game. It's nothing that you can't live without, okay?' I offered him words of solace. 'Cheer up, young man. Things *do* get unpleasant sometimes. What will you do when you have to face bigger difficulties in your life? We should learn to accept the defeats the way we accept victories. So—'

'It's not that easy,' he interrupted me, but I'd liked that he had spoken.

'I know it's not that easy, but you'll have to accept the fact.'

'I won't have the chance to play for our team the next year. I had my chance and I blew it. I could have made my school proud. I let you and everybody down and I feel terrible about that.' His eyes were on the horizon. 'All of us had prepared for the ultimate celebration and I just couldn't . . .'

'You *did* make your school proud. I *am* proud of you. You batted well throughout the championship and the award you received is the proof. Cricket is a team effort and it's not your fault that you didn't win, so please don't think of it as a personal failure. The entire team is responsible. You better stop decrying your efforts and blaming only yourself.' I put my arms around him for a while and patted his back.

He still remained silent.

'You know something? You are a handsome, young man but you look really ugly with such pathetic expressions on your face.' I tried to make him smile. 'Come on, give me a smile.'

He smiled awkwardly for a second.

'A little broader, just a little.' My smiling face brought a wide smile to his face. *How should I say how much I love this smiling face of yours? I want this smile to be on your face for eternity!*

'Let's make this evening special by eating dinner outside.' I asked, 'Chinese?'

He nodded and we set out for a pleasant evening.

At the restaurant while eating, I kept talking about this and that so that he would stop thinking about his failure in the match. And I really changed his mood. He looked happy and stress free in a while. When he seemed to be thoughtful, I asked, 'What're you thinking about?'

'Ah . . . nothing.' His attention was suddenly back on me.

'Oh, yes. You were.' I was more intelligent than he could assume. 'Chandni, right?' I knew I had got that right. 'Come on. It's in your eyes. You don't need to hide it from me.' *I want to know how deep you have got into this shit.*

For a while, he stared at me and then said, 'Yes.'

I knew it. Keeping a smirk on my face, I asked, 'Tell me something more about her.'

He chuckled and started. 'She's good. I like to spend my time with her. She's the kind of girl any boy would like. And the best thing about her is that she doesn't show off her wealth. She's a sweet girl indeed.' His face was flushed. 'Sweet and demure. The way I like.' A reticent smile flickered across his face.

My appetite had already died. I had to keep smiling to hide my jealousy. I wanted to know more. 'So what do you talk about?'

'We talk about different things'. He was eating and talking as well. 'She's a chatterbox, so I let her speak. She talks about what she does at home, about her family and asks me about my life. Valai is a small place, so we can't meet outside. What we have is just the recess, so we try to make the most of it. And our friends are so supportive that they leave us alone.'

I felt something burning inside me, yet I had to wear a mask of fake happiness.

'One thing I still don't know is what she has seen in me!' he asked.

Even though he didn't seem to want an answer, I didn't miss that opportunity to praise him. 'If that's the thing you really don't know about, I suggest you start looking in the mirror. You have a captivating, charming face and an attractive personality, hard to be ignored by anyone who understands beauty. As far as I know, you are still a virgin. Am I correct?' He nodded, grinning. 'I bet you wouldn't be a virgin had you been in Baroda!' He frowned at that. 'The atmosphere there is irresistible. Such a sharp face and strong body! Girls would have gone crazy for you!'

Both of us laughed—his was real, mine, fake. The thought that he was getting serious about Chandni was troubling me inside. I hadn't thought that he'd ever fall in love. According to me, he wasn't the kind of man who could be sensitive enough to understand true love, but then love needs no teaching. It just happens.

As a result of my frustration, I couldn't help but say, 'Believe me, Vivek, if I were a girl, I swear to God that I would have fallen in love with you.' Hearing that, he gaped at me. 'Honestly. You've got something very positive and special in your personality,' I added.

'Really?' he asked and I nodded.

'Just like you?' he asked, I nodded again.

'Besides, women don't give much consideration to physical beauty in men. It is important, but not the way men expect beauty in women. Actually, nobody knows what a woman sees in a man. It's probably inner beauty that matters the most to them. Fortunately, you have got both—a lovely face and a beautiful heart.' I had no interest in the noodles and manchurian now, yet I was eating.

A bit later, I asked, 'How far have you guys gone?' It was tough to suppress my curiosity.

He hadn't understood me. He was frowning stupidly.

'I mean . . . did you kiss her or . . .?' Not sure of an answer, I wished it would be a 'no'. *Just say no . . .*

'No, no,' he spoke up at once. 'I . . . just holding hands and . . . that's it.'

I could see innocence in his eyes. There I saw nothing hidden. *That's it! It mustn't be more than 'that's it'. I'll have to do something before he goes deeper into this relationship.*

twenty

_____

On a breezy Saturday afternoon of early winter, I found Vidya at my door. 'May I come in?' she asked sweetly.

'You don't need to ask, do you?' I asked in a similar vein.

'Of course, I don't.' She got in and gave me what she had brought for me. It wasn't the first time she had brought me home cooked food. Her mother had sent a kind of sweet for me that I had never tasted before.

'This is awesome!' I said, putting one piece in my mouth and feeling it melt.

'Like it?' she asked as she took a bit from the box in my hand.

'Love it!' I said loudly and ate some more.

She looked happy. I had been surprised by her appearance because whenever she wanted to visit me, she would inform me beforehand. When I asked her the reason, she told me that she had been to Ragini ma'am's home after school and from there she'd come to mine. Then without asking, she made her way into my bathroom. Well, she didn't need to ask for my permission, I mused. When she came out after a minute or two, her face was wet. The dripping tresses dangling from one side of her forehead enhanced her beauty. Tiny rivulets of water, streaming down her neck, had soaked her blouse. She looked at me with a seductive smile. A smile that would have excited any heterosexual man. Though I was gay, I adored beautiful women and Vidya was lovable. Momentarily I forgot I was gay and for that brief second, I wished I could take that sizzling woman to bed.

Instead, I asked her if she had a lunch. She said no. Since I had already had mine, I told her to eat whatever she could find in the kitchen. There wasn't much. She found two chapattis and some cooked spinach. I asked her if I could make her an omelette but she refused and said she'd manage with whatever was there. I then made some salad and apologized for not being able to give her a good meal. As she ate, I sat with her on the dining table and asked how she was going to spend the three days of Christmas vacation. She replied that she had nothing to do unless I had some plans for the two of us.

I had always liked to look into people's eyes while talking. I believed that it helps to create a good chemistry, understanding and bonding between two people. In Vidya's case, I preferred not to do so for the fear that she'd take it some other way. During casual conversation, she sometimes gave me a *certain* kind of look that used to disturb me and I had to take my eyes away from her. She liked to give our conversation some romantic angle. Whenever I felt she was trying to be romantic, I would change the topic of discussion. She seemed somewhat irritated with such behaviour, but never complained. I only hoped that she wouldn't do something that might harm our friendship.

'Aren't you afraid of spending an afternoon alone with a young lady in your house?' she asked biting her lower lip seductively. We had shifted to the living room to relax after she'd finished her lunch.

'I don't have to fear anyone. Neither should you. If we're guiltless, nobody can harm us,' I said unhesitatingly.

'I like it,' she said and started to talk about our colleagues and it was quite interesting and amusing to listen to what she thought about them. In the meantime, I went to my bedroom to look for the photographs I had taken while touring during the cricket tournament. And I had no idea when she came and stood behind me. I realized it only when she put her hands on my shoulders. Startled, I turned back to face her.

She took my hands in hers and spoke gently, 'Oh, Kaushik. How can I tell you how much I love you?'

I knew she was going to start the same story once again, so I wanted to pull my hands away from hers. But I don't know why I couldn't. It was perhaps the fear of hurting someone who really, genuinely loved me. She was pressing her body against mine and I was vainly trying to find a way to escape. Her face was so close that I could easily feel her breath on my neck, but to evade a kiss and more intimacy, I was holding my head tight, upright.

'This is not . . .' words barely escaped from my mouth as she put her head on my chest.

'I tried to forget you,' her lips were touching my chest and I felt her breath on my skin. 'I tried hard not to let your memories take control of my mind, but I have failed.' She looked at me, her lips pouting in invitation. 'The more I tried to forget, the more you were on my mind. I can't bear this pain any more. I simply can't!' Her voice was filled with emotion. 'I want to be yours for ever and ever . . .'

Our bodies were so close that the proximity would have made any man give up.

'I can't . . .' I held her hands tightly and pushed her back slightly.

Vivek and I   257

'Why? Why not?' She asked urgently and came closer again. This time I managed to keep her away from my body. Her tearful eyes gave her face such a pathetic look that I couldn't bear to look at it. I had always found it difficult to see people cry. For a moment, a strong urge of telling her the truth arose in me, but I repressed it. There was a possibility that she might not be able to digest it. She would probably think that I was just making it up to keep her away. *And what if she disclosed this secret of mine?* She was a friend, but then, a woman wounded in love could do anything.

While I was thinking of avoiding her, she did something I had never imagined even in my wildest dream. She slipped her sari from her shoulder, revealing her heaving cleavage. Pushing herself close to me, she caught the collar of my shirt in her hands, closed her eyes and said boldly, 'I can do anything to please you. Take whatever you want from me. I'm completely yours. Do whatever you–'

'Vidya!' I screamed holding her by her shoulders and shaking her violently. 'Stop being over emotional and behave yourself!' I scolded her. 'Shame on you! I never thought you could be have like this . . . you've insulted our friendship . . . and me too.'

She was petrified since whatever I said was quite unexpected to her. Her face ashen, and eyes brimming with tears, she opened her mouth to speak but words didn't come out.

'Please, leave, ' I pointed my finger to the door.

Unable to comprehend my anger and rudeness, she froze in that traumatized position. Tears glistened in her eyes as she gazed at me.

'Right *now*.' My voice hardened. She started sobbing and ran out of the room. For more than a minute, I stood still, trying to cope with whatever had just happened. *What has she done?* I grinded my teeth in fury. *Stupid woman!* Since last night, I had been tense about the blossoming love between Vivek and Chandni, and Vidya had increased my stress level by doing this obscene act. I was angry with her and myself as well. In my anger, I hurled a pillow at the wall. Then with my eyes shut tight, I lay on the bed, trying hard to forget this unbelievable incident.

'Is anything wrong?' Vivek inquired. He was perceptive enough to notice that my mood was off. He had come to my place in the evening wanting to go out.

'Not really.' I was sure that my answer didn't satisfy his curiosity.

I constantly thought about the ugly scene with Vidya and they weren't going to stop pricking my mind, so I thought it was better to go out with Vivek. Instead of our usual destination, the sunset point, we went towards the jungle in the north. Under a tall teak tree, I sat on a stone. Vivek sat on the stump of a tree, looking in the direction of the deep valley ahead. The tree tops were gently swaying and there was no sign of clouds overhead. But the perfect atmosphere didn't interest my troubled soul. I had chosen to go out to get some peace of mind, but my mind was so occupied with inexorable thoughts of my conflict with Vidya that nothing, neither Vivek's presence nor the scenic beauty around, grabbed my attention. With a slender twig that I had picked from the ground, I started to make incomprehensible figures in the dust.

'Look at that squirrel!' Vivek tried to distract me. 'Isn't it beautiful?' He whistled to catch its attention.

I glanced at the squirrel disinterestedly and looked away. Vivek sensed the apathy of my reaction. He knew I was a great nature lover. I would have enjoyed the innocent frolicking of the squirrel under normal circumstances. Even when it was frisking around the trunk of the nearby tree, I didn't smile. Vivek understood that something very wrong had happened. He seemed curious to know the reason of my sadness, but apart from being good friends, we shared the relationship of a teacher and a student and that perhaps held him back from asking me again.

He was a confidante who could keep a secret, so I was not hesitant to tell him, but it took me a while to do that. And he was appalled to learn how Vidya had behaved with me. 'It's hard to believe she did that!' For a long time none of us said anything. He must be thinking why I didn't take advantage of that young woman, I thought. *Is he thinking I'm impotent? He must be.*

'You know,' his words dragged me out of my thoughts. 'What you did was right. It's hard for any man to . . . you know . . . control in such situations. But you did it. I admire that.'

I looked at him. *He didn't think I'm impotent? Is he that innocent or stupid enough not to think I'm gay? Should I tell him the truth about my sexuality? Will he understand that?* Countless questions arose in my mind and left me feeling uncertain.

Before getting into bed that night, I meditated to extricate myself from the agitation that had bothered me all day after Vidya's visit. But it was useless as I couldn't keep her out of my mind. I pondered over how my relations with Vidya had soured. Such a stupid, desperate attempt to gain love! She had behaved like a woman possessed. What had she thought of me? Did she think I was just like others? An easy target to be seduced with the nakedness of a female body? If that's what she thinks of me, she's insulted me. She insulted me and our friendship! I was so dejected with the whole situation that I had skipped dinner.

I wished what happened hadn't happened, but then, it was not my fault.

I knew all about Vidya's squeamish nature, so it was apparent that she was not going to talk to me because of the way I had rejected her. I could understand what kind of humiliation she must have felt because I, myself, had been in a similar situation in the past. Then I had been in Vidya's place and in my place was Krishna. My old sores were revived as I remembered the most heart rending day of my life.

Krishna had decided to marry a girl and he had hidden it from me so that I wouldn't jeopardize his marriage. Somehow, I came to know about his engagement and in no time, I'd rushed to his place where his parents greeted me gleefully. They were ecstatic about getting their son married. I felt sad for them, and for a while, I thought of getting away from Krishna's life forever, but my possessiveness and selfishness didn't let me.

Later, when Krishna and I were in his room, I sat on a stool while he chose to remain standing. For a while none of us spoke . . .

'Is it . . .?' How hard it had been for me to ask that! 'Is it true that you're going to get married?' There was fear in my tone. I was feeling suffocated. My heart beat became faster and my palms began to perspire. Though I had known the answer to my question, I wished it to be the exact opposite.

After a prolonged silence, Krishna nodded slightly. And something started to burn inside me instantly. I was unable to handle this extremely arduous situation. My mind was reeling with negative feelings of betrayal, resentment, fear, hatred, jealousy, rage . . . I had loved Krishna so much and put all my faith and hope in him, so what he had done was pure injustice to me. In a second, my life had begun to feel vain and pointless. I didn't know what to do, how to react. I wished he would do or say something sympathetic, something that might lessen the intensity of the bitter reality that stood between the two of us. But he did nothing.

Krishna's behaviour had been different for the past few days. I had become aware that his feelings for me were on the ebb. We had been meeting, but the enthusiasm from his behaviour was gone. He had not been his usual self. I'd got the feeling that he had gone out with me only because of my strong insistence. It was as if I was continually running after him and he had been trying to avoid me all along. I had asked him if he was sick or had any problems, but he had evaded my question. I now knew the real reason for his changed behaviour.

'Why?' I'd asked, studying his colourless face. 'Why didn't you tell me about your engagement?'

'I was going to tell you . . .' He tried to placate me as if I was a kid, 'It happened so quickly that I couldn't even invite my relatives from Kerala . . . you know . . .'

I hadn't believed him. 'You kept me in the dark so that I wouldn't be able to spoil your engagement. Isn't that the truth?' I had asked angrily.

'No,' Krishna stressed his answer in a whisper.

'Yes, it is,' I'd said stubbornly.

Krishna shook his head in disagreement. His eyes wandered around before settling back on me.

'And you never even talked about your interest in marriage!' Subduing my frustration, I had struggled to sound polite.

'It was all done by my parents. As I said, it happened in haste. They saw the girl, liked her and they want me to get married to her.' He tried to explain.

'They want me to get married . . .' A sneer flickered over my face on hearing the lame excuse. It wasn't hard to understand what it meant. 'I'm not concerned about anyone else but you. Tell me what do *you* want,' I asked, knowing the answer already. 'Are you being compelled to get hitched?'

'No,' he replied cordially. 'I also like her. She's nice.'

It had been an ordeal for me to accept that he liked someone other than me. Again the air was wrapped in uncomfortable silence and it took me a while to talk further.

'She must be pretty, isn't she?' I vainly tried to conceal jealousy from my tone.

'She is, yes.' Because of his guilty conscience, he was trying to avoid looking into my eyes.

I had asked him about his fiancée and he had replied evasively. The nervousness in his conversation was intolerable. He was a different person who was embarrassed about what he had done. He knew that I was trying to reach a conclusion, something he didn't want to face. That's why he was distracted, doing unnecessary things such as giving attention to the bonsai by the bookcase, studying the calendar on the wall and arranging the bedspread on his bed which was already in perfect order. Not once did he dare look at me.

'Krishna, none of us is a fool. Why don't you sit here and just talk to me?' Although I was sick of his pretentious behaviour, I'd asked in as calm a manner as possible.

'I'm talking to you.' He didn't take his eyes away from the calendar.

'Counting the days to your marriage or what?' I'd asked, sarcastically.

He'd looked at me for a second or two and then busied himself with the calendar again. When I couldn't tolerate that, I walked up to him and put the question directly, 'What will be the future of our relation after your marriage?'

He looked at me, trying to find proper words, trying hard not to hurt me.

'I don't have any problem with your marriage . . .' I had spoken even as my heart was welling up '. . . actually I have, but I'll accept it for the sake of your family. But . . . I just want you to keep the same relationship with me.'

'We will be good friends,' he'd said in a futile attempt to smile.

'I'm not talking about friendship.' I'd put my hands on his shoulders. 'We share more than just friendship. I want us to have it even after your marriage and–'

'That's not possible!' he had exclaimed suddenly.

'Why? Why not? We wouldn't ever let anybody know.' I caught his face in my palms and made him look straight into my tearful eyes. 'I can't live without you, Kris–' Words refused to come out of my chocked throat. I put my head on his shoulder and let myself go. We stood there. He had his arms around me until I stopped crying.

'It would be injustice to Aastha and I can't . . .' he had whispered. 'I love her. I really do.'

'You love her, she loves you.' I had smiled painfully, my face smeared with self pity. 'What about me?' He had no answer to that. 'What is my place in your life?' He'd just stared fixedly at my wet eyes.

'You're being selfish!' I'd accused, pulling myself away from him. I was dismayed that he was being insensible to my misery.

'You should learn about the temporariness of relationships.' Whilst I was attacking him with harsh words, he was philosophizing, keeping himself composed. 'What you have today, won't be with you tomorrow. Tomorrow you'll have something else, that's not with you today. Nothing's permanent. No belief, no transgression, no joy, no relation. Not all the things and circumstances and people in our lives can be under our control all the time. You'll have to forget whatever happened between us. It's not tough, believe me. Just give it a try and you can–'

'I don't want to listen to your sermons!' I'd said in rage and protest.

He still didn't look vexed. He stood silently with his eyes on me. The expressions in his eyes made me whine with helplessness, 'You drove me into this and now . . .' I wasn't in a mood to listen to him. 'I . . . you've no idea how terrible it would be for me to . . . Now you can't . . .' I'd found myself unable to talk.

'Stop it yaar!' The anguish of his heart had finally forced him to yell at me. As he saw me stunned into silence, he tried to control his anger by inhaling deeply. 'There is my family down there. If they listen to this . . .' The exhaustion in his voice was apparent. 'What do you want me to do? Ruin my life and my future for you? What reason would I give to my family for not getting married?' I had no answers to his questions and he went on trying to explain to me, 'You have a brother, I've none. Even if you leave your family for me, Smit is there for your parents. My family has a lot of expectations from me and I am their only hope. And you know how orthodox and conservative they are! We had a great time together, but then, life is all about moving ahead. And let me be frank that I too want to have a wife and kids.'

Shaken by the truth, I'd suddenly felt sick and sank down on his bed. The pursuit of gaining Krishna's true love had proved a failure. I had been running after a mirage that was intangible. Krishna was right. He was mature and I was childish because I was unable to understand the transience of life. Only after getting a little older and richer in experience could I understand the ultimate, supreme truth that nothing is permanent. Things do change with time and nobody can help it. We mustn't try to bind people with us. Krishna's words had been full of wisdom but they didn't bring any solace to my frustrated mind. Something withered deep inside my heart. The reality that I had lost my love made me pathetically vulnerable. Krishna couldn't face those pitiable expressions on my face. He came near me, sat beside me and tried to soothe me, 'I can do anything for you but not what you ask for. Not anymore. I'm committed to Aastha and . . . well, I don't want to lose a friend like you.' His last words had been like a last ditch attempt to save our relationship.

I lifted my eyes, watched him for a moment, and then had said rather stubbornly, 'You have, already.' And I got to my feet abruptly. 'You're free to do whatever you want. I promise that I won't be back in your life to bother you anymore.' There had been finality in my tone. Leaving him in despair, I'd stormed out of the room. So angry and dejected, I had decided not to see him ever again.

My break-up with Krishna had gnawed at me beyond imagination, so I could understand what Vidya must be feeling. It is hard to forget your love and even worst to be neglected by the one you once loved more than anything else in the world. Krishna hadn't been as harsh to me as I had been to Vidya. I had been cruel to Vidya's sensibilities and was sorry about hurting her, yet I couldn't get myself to apologize. After all, it was she who had insulted the purity of our friendship by asking me for a physical relationship.

She had used her body to seduce me. The thing she was calling 'love' was nothing but lust. Deeply disturbed and hurt over that distasteful episode, I had made up my mind that I would talk to Vidya only after she made the first move.

Was she angry about what I had done to her or was she ashamed of her deed? I didn't know, but she didn't talk to me. She didn't even look at me. It was as if I was responsible for the mess in our relationship. She probably wanted me to feel bad and guilty about whatever had happened, but I wasn't ready to convict myself for the rift. I thought that I had had a very wrong impression of her in my mind till now.

I had considered her my best female friend in Valai. Then I thought that it was natural for a human to fall in love and make stupid mistakes. I was ready to forgive her had she apologized, but her ego was perhaps bigger than mine. She behaved as if I didn't even exist. Neither did I try to approach her. The staff and the students could easily see the detachment between the two of us, and within days, it was well known that something very wrong had happened between us. Some of my colleagues asked me about the reason for the discord and I had to avoid the discussion by saying that there was nothing serious. They kept guessing, and as far as I knew, only three people knew the real reason, Vidya, Vivek and I.

I missed Vidya. I missed talking to her, listening to her frivolous prattle. But she behaved so heartlessly as if there was no place for me in her life any more. I didn't blame her for whatever she'd done. It was human and any wounded person would do so. However, it is really tough to accept rejection from the person you love with all your senses. After my break-up with Krishna, I had thought I would die without him. But I lived, survived and though it was tough, I managed. I learnt a great lesson—nobody dies because of anybody. Time heals every wound, no matter how deep and excruciating it is. I knew it would take time, but I was sure that Vidya would realize her mistake sooner or later. I prayed to Lord Shiva to soothe the wounds of her heart and bring her back in my life. I was ready to welcome her with open arms any time because I didn't want to lose such a friend. But I was unable to give her what she wanted and she was not ready to accept me as just a friend. So I left it on time and God and decided to wait for the storm to settle.

twenty one

Continual neglect from Vidya left me in a deep well of suffering and the day that brought back some happiness was Vivek's birthday. Yes, it was his eighteenth birthday on 13 December. I still remembered the day I had asked him about his date of birth. Before answering he had asked, 'Do you also believe, like most others do, that thirteen is an unlucky number?' I had frowned and smiled somewhat jokingly. Then I had become careful all of a sudden lest he take it ill. *Yes, I do,* I had on my tongue, but I lied, 'No, not at all!'

'But you laughed,' he had looked at me momentarily and said in a somewhat offended tone.

'I didn't laugh. I just . . . smiled,' I said and he gave me a long, cold stare. 'I didn't mean to be derisive. Believe me!' I added.

'It's okay,' he'd said despairingly. 'Everybody does.'

That was the first time I found him offended by my remark.

'Come on, Vivek. It's not like that. I just . . .' He didn't seem interested, so I had to steer the topic in a different direction. 'So how do we celebrate your birthday?'

On Vivek's birthday, I bought cake and candles, and in the evening, we set out on Mr Gavit's bike for the river Ambika where we sat in the sand and ate the cake. I gifted him a T-shirt. That's what Krishna and I used to gift each other on our birthdays since both of us were fond of clothes of the latest fashion. Lying on the cold sand, Vivek counted the stars and I told him how I used to enjoy my birthday in my younger days. I told him about how I used to give a nice treat to my friends, and take them to the cinema and the discotheque. The revelry lasted until the wee hours of the morning. That was also how all my friends celebrated their birthdays. Krishna had been the only one who refrained because he couldn't afford to throw a treat on his birthday. On his birthday that was 6 February, he used to take me to a restaurant. He never wanted to celebrate his birthday with anyone but me.

Vivek liked to hear all those stories of my past. My birthday was on 26 May, the time when we had our summer vacations in school. Vivek did mention it many times if we could be together on my birthday too. I never told him that I had stopped celebrating my birthdays since Krishna's exit from my life. Vivek and I talked and stayed there until it was dark. *What a moonlit night it was!*

Back home, while we were having beer and chicken, I found him staring at me.

'What are you looking at?' I asked.

'Nothing,' he said, shaking his head in denial.

I knew that he had something on his mind. I started guessing what it could be. There was nothing negative, so I assumed that he must be thinking something nice about me. Something that he didn't want to tell me. *Is it just about my giving him such a good time? Is it something that he can't say openly? Or is he falling in love with me?*

Before leaving, he mentioned that his birthday had never been celebrated this way. He thanked me for making his day special and I thanked him for filling my life with bliss.

I was unable to sleep that night. Having had a nice

evening with Vivek, I had been happy, but all of a sudden, a thought struck me from nowhere and left me uneasy. Somewhere in the dark corners of my mind, there always was something unpleasant to upset me. *Would these happy times last for ever? Will he be with me till the end? What if something takes him away from me? Would I survive the pain caused by his exit from my life?* I couldn't get rid of the chain of such unwelcome thoughts. My closeness with Vivek troubled me whenever I thought that this time would not last. Life without him seemed impossible and the more I knew him, the more I would get obsessed with him, the more it would trouble me in the future. I tried many times to get rid of my feelings for Vivek, but had failed every time I had attempted to do so. Then I thought, who had foreseen the future? Whatever my destiny would be, I'll have to accept it. Then why should I spoil my present by worrying about the future? It's all about the present and I wanted to make the most of it. God had given me a chance to live some unforgettable moments with Vivek and I didn't want to miss them. So I decided to enjoy this beautiful time. But no matter how positive I tried to be, the ambiguity of the future of my love never let me relax for long.

My restive mind slipped from Vivek to Krishna. A desire to see Krishna drove me to the cupboard that had his pictures. While going through all the photos, my eyes came to rest on a particular picture in which Krishna and I were seated in an ice-cream parlour. That was probably the last photo we had taken. I gazed at the picture and my mind went back in time.

The college years had rolled by and we had finished our studies. Now it was time for Krishna to get back to his family in Surat. I didn't want him to leave me and he too was interested in staying in Baroda, but he had to go back. I didn't like it without him and itched for him so desperately that I called him up every day to tell him to come back to Baroda. In the meantime, something pleasant happened. He got an interview call from a high school in Baroda and he returned to me. He cleared the interview with flying colours and got the job of a teacher. While he was happy about getting a job, I had been happier with the thought that we were going to be together again.

Krishna had stayed at my place till he found a small but nice apartment on rent. I was also teaching at a local school and the daily routine of our meeting wasn't disturbed. Every evening, I would go to his place, pick him up and we'd have fun on my bike. We would eat out, party, go for movies and generally have a good time. Our day would end in the bed at his place as there was no disturbance there. I stayed there at night many times and nobody ever came to know what kind of relationship the two of us actually shared. It continued like this for months until his family shifted to Baroda to live with him. Their arrival wasn't as unplanned as Krishna had told me earlier. They were there to get Krishna married!

After my break-up with Krishna, I had wanted to cry in a desolate place and what better spot could I have found than the old fort that had witnessed our love. How devastating it had been for me! Before the thoughts of my break-up could sicken my mind, I returned to the present where I had such an exquisite present—Vivek.

Since my break-up with Krishna, nothing terrible had occurred in my life. I had been fortunate not to have had any shattering events that I couldn't cope with. However, one terrible tragedy was set to take place in my life which was going to tear my heart apart. It was the month of January. As Valai was set on a higher elevation compared to the neighbouring districts and towns, the climate turned extreme in winter here. On that portentous day, Valai was engulfed in white wreathes of mist since morning. Mrs Desai had a joint problem and the cold weather had made her knees stiff and painful. She couldn't walk properly and had to keep her knees strapped up with heated bandages all the time.

On that evil evening, the wind was blowing like a hurricane. Mr Desai had gone to the market and their maid wasn't at home. Mrs Desai heard some noise in the backyard, and from her bed she could see through the window that a few dogs had intruded into the compound and were messing up the plants of chillies and tomatoes that her husband had cultivated so well. Though unable to walk properly, the old woman, when she realized the dogs were going to ruin their little garden, risked going out to shoo them away. The house had a shed of corrugated concrete sheets in the backyard. Mrs Desai picked some stones from the ground and tried to hit the fighting dogs but they wouldn't run away. In the meantime, their neighbour, Anish, a young boy in his early twenties, came to see what was happening. From his compound, he tried to hit the dogs with stones, but the dogs were so engrossed in fighting that they didn't bother about the stones.

Finally, when Anish realized that they were not going to leave so easily, he jumped over the boundary wall which separated his house from Mrs Desai's, and attacked the dogs with a thick bamboo stick. He started to hit them violently and Mrs Desai watched him, both of them unaware of what was going to happen in a few seconds.

A tall jackfruit tree by the compound wall couldn't fight the cyclonic wind for long and suddenly gave up, falling straight towards the shed that Mrs Desai was standing under. The shed couldn't resist the weight of the heavy tree and collapsed. One of the broken parts of the concrete sheet hit Anish on the back, throwing him to the ground. By the time he realized what had happened, it was too late. Forgetting his aching back, he hastily removed the scraps of concrete sheets only to find the old lady lifeless. The accident had taken her life instantly. The neighbours rushed in and found that the roots of the killer tree had rotted, and that's why it had yielded to the storm. Not only the shed, but also a part of their kitchen had collapsed. One of its walls was completely destroyed and the water tank by that wall was also damaged. Someone took Anish to the doctor since the sheet had hit him so badly that he was deeply wounded and bleeding. The young guy, as he narrated the incident later, was fortunate to be standing away from the shed. Alas, Mrs Desai wasn't as lucky!

By the time I reached there, the doctor had already pronounced her dead. In the living room, Mr Desai sat by the body that had been wrapped in white cloth. His eyes were fixed on his wife's face which looked so peaceful, already on her way to the final destination. He was deeply pained, but had no tears in his eyes. But I wasn't as strong as he was. I had lost a motherly figure and was unable to control my tears. I sat by Mr Desai and cried. 'You won't be here even the day I die!' her prophetic words reverberated in my ears.

Mr Desai put his hands on my head and tried to console me silently. I hugged him and let my feelings pour out.

The funeral was to take place the next morning so that their children could come from Ahmedabad. Along with his friends and neighbours, I sat awake with Mr Desai for the entire night. There were no more tears. What remained were the reminiscences of that kind hearted woman. I had such an exceptional relationship with Mrs Desai that every now and then she reminded me of my mother. When I used to tell her how similar she was to my mother, she would say, 'The feelings and love every mother in the world has for her child is universally the same.' True. Very true. That's why I always saw my mother in her. I remembered that she wanted to meet my mother. I was sorry that I had not fulfilled this wish of hers.

When her children and relatives from far off places arrived early next morning, the bier, bedecked with flowers, was taken to the crematorium in the outskirts where Mrs Desai's eldest son consigned the body to the flames. Before that, I bowed my head and touched the feet of that benevolent soul resting on the pyre. The image of the pyre on fire left a lasting impression on me. Mr Desai still had no tears in his eyes. He hadn't reacted much, neither had he uttered a single word since the time he had seen his wife's dead body. He remained silent even when his children hugged him and cried. It was late in the evening when he finally spoke.

A thick layer of mist had swallowed the surroundings and, though it was cold, Mr Desai wanted to sit outside. Bhavin, his younger son, and I were with him in the yard when he slowly said, 'I'm not complaining about her exit but the way . . .' His eyes were fixed somewhere in the dark sky. 'She shouldn't have gone this way. You know, when her joints pain became more than she could bear, she used to say the malady was going to kill her someday. The realization that it could come true someday always scared me and I would remain in its dread until the winter was over. I wouldn't let her work. I gave her knees the necessary exercise and massaged them. Bandaged them. I'll miss all those things. She should have given me a chance to at least talk with her one last time. I wanted to fight with her. And I wanted to thank her for tolerating me all these years, for being with me through thick and thin, and for making my life so precious . . .' He choked with emotions, his face was a piteous sight and the eyes finally gave in as they began to pour. Neither Bhavin nor I could control our tears. Even the cashewnut tree near the compound gate seemed to be shedding tears as the dry leaves were falling off its branches in the hissing wind.

twenty two

Mrs Desai's demise was so heart rending that I remained mournful for days. I visualized her sympathetic face and heard her mellifluous voice in my mind. How compassionately she used to call me 'son'! How much she liked to cook for me! And how she complained when I didn't visit her! All that was gone and I was going to miss her for the rest of my life. To get some peace of mind, I went to the temple of Lord Shiva and meditated. In that critical time, I missed my mother a lot. I wanted her to be there with me. I thought of taking leave from school for some days, but the second exams for the year were due to start in just a few days, and I was going to be busy. There was no possibility that I could take leave. Vivek was the only person I could share my feelings with. He was the one who understood my feelings. He helped me get out of the depressed state.

Mr Desai's children stayed with him till all the rituals were done. When they were leaving, they asked him to go with them, but he didn't want to leave the place where he had spent a large part of his life. I promised his children that I would take care of him. For days, I ate with him and slept at his place so that he wouldn't feel alone. I still remember that evening when I had seen tears in Mr Desai's eyes. I had never thought a strong man like him would ever shed tears, but the loss of a loved one can melt even the stoniest heart. Everybody knew how close I was to the Desais, so all my colleagues offered their condolences. Vidya was also one of them. She attended a condolence ceremony one evening, and that was the day we talked to each other after about two months. Our relationship was never going to be the same again, but the walls of our egos had definitely been broken.

To help Vivek study psychology for the upcoming exams, I went through his books and found that it wasn't as tough, incomprehensible and boring as it had been in my school days. Yet, I had to meet Mr Rajput, the psychology teacher, when things were beyond my understanding. He had always been helpful. One day, when I went to him with one such problem, he asked me, 'Whom are you studying this for?'

'It's Vivek, class eleven B,' I replied. 'He's got some problem with . . .'

'I know him, that pretty boy. Is he a *friend*?'

I felt his tone was suggesting something else. 'Yes, why?' I asked.

'No, just asking.' He jeered, 'I've seen the two of you together—many times.'

'So what?' I now understood what he must be thinking.

'Nothing. Not–' He tried to change the topic as he knew I was getting him right. 'Where were we? In the book of course!'

Had he guessed Vivek and I were more than just good friends? I thought on my way home. *Had he seen it in my eyes? Did he get some information from Baroda?* These questions distressed me for a while and I decided that if Mr Rajput would talk like that again, I would give him a piece of my mind!

Mayur Patel

Later, I thought about it in another way. I decided to talk about it to Vivek to know what his reaction would be if he was taken to be emotionally attached to a man. But this was not the proper time. Something like this would drive his attention away from his studies and I didn't want him to fail again. So I reserved the discussion for future.

He came to my place to study because there was no peace at his hostel. And I was impressed and happy to see that he was really taking his studies seriously. It was one such evening when he was studying in the living room and I was busy with my job of setting question papers. He came to me, talked about few unimportant things, and then said, 'My friends have asked me to ask you if . . . hmmm . . . if you could give us some . . . some questions that are likely to be in the paper.'

I was shocked. 'Sorry, dear,' I responded sternly with an unfriendly smile. 'We are friends, but that doesn't mean I can do this.'

He nodded hastily and got back to his studies. Obviously, my reaction had been totally unexpected for him. When he was going to leave, I called out, 'Vivek!'

'Yes,' he sounded apprehensive. He must have thought I was going to scold him.

'I can do you a little, a very little favour,' I said. 'The essay you should be studying is "Visit to a Railway Station". Better keep it a secret.' As he nodded smiling, I didn't miss reprimanding him mildly, 'If you focus on your studies rather than on *anybody* else, you wouldn't have to ask for a favour.'

I didn't know how much of my sarcasm he got, but those words definitely stole the smile from his face. He had most probably understood who my remark was aimed at.

By the end of January, the exams were over and I got leave. Finishing corrections of the answer sheets, I left for Baroda. I talked to my mother about Mrs Desai's loss. It felt really good after talking to her. I came back after five days.

Vivek had cleared all the subjects, and though he wasn't great in psychology, he had managed to get passing marks in the subject. I made him promise that he'd fare better in the annual exams. My relations with Vidya remained the same. I didn't know whether she was ashamed of what she had done or whether she was still upset with me for not accepting her love. She chose to stay away from me and I respected her decision.

One Sunday afternoon, Vivek and I were sitting under the neem tree. Our bodies were bathed in the sunbeams that had made their way through the dense grove of the tree.

'Unlike Baroda, people here are simple and not conspiring. Had we been in Baroda, our friendship would have been questioned since we do spend a lot of time together.' I suddenly veered to this delicate subject of homosexuality from the usual chat that we had been having. Vivek seemed not to understand what I was up to, so I went ahead. 'We have been seen together. Such friendship between a teacher and a student is not usual, you see?'

'I know that. Even some of my classmates and hostel mates are jealous of our friendship.'

I had no idea about that so I asked, 'Really?'

He nodded and said, 'I have never told you, but it's been long since they have been talking about us. Nobody has ever talked abut it to my face but back biting can hardly be concealed. My well wishers told me about the discussions they had heard. I don't give a shit unless they dare to say so to my face.'

I liked his fearlessness. I tittered and asked questions to make him talk more on the subject. 'People might take us to be homosexuals. What if somebody actually believes us to be gay?'

'I'll hit him on the face and make sure that he loses all his teeth!' he spoke up belligerently.

'What?' I laughed. 'Are you serious?'

'Of course! I won't entertain something like that. I don't like it if someone tries to disgrace me.'

So he doesn't like it. Then I asked, 'But what if it actually happens to you? I mean suppose you get physical with one of your friends or someone else and it's in the air, and people start to talk. Would your reaction be the same?' I wanted to know how positive or negative he was about homosexuality.

'Yes, my reaction will be the same. And by the way, I wouldn't ever get physical with a man.'

'Even if he is good looking?' I had my eyes on him.

'Yes, whatever.' He was serious. 'For me, that would be the last thing I would do on earth.'

He's not an easy target. But people change. They do. I'll change his thoughts, gradually. Someday, he wouldn't be immune to my feelings. Someday, he won't resist my love. And someday, he'll be in bed with me. Someday . . .

It was 6 February, Krishna's birthday. I relived the past that night. The memory of the few brief blissful moments spent together were replaced by the bitter remembrance of our break-up. *How isolated I had let myself become after my split with Krishna!*

It's better to end a relationship when it becomes a burden. After our moving separate ways, I was determined not to meet him ever, but it isn't that easy to forget the person you love. I had fallen into deep depression. I liked nothing and cried often. I had cursed and hated Krishna for being so insensitive to me. I had brooded over the loss. The loss of everlasting love that I had expected from him. I had not been ready for what he had to offer me and he was unable to fulfil my desires any longer. None of us was ready to give in.

To rescue myself from that despondency, I had taken the support of liquor. At a private party one night, I drank like never before. Though I was heavily drunk, there was no sign of sleep in my eyes. I couldn't stop thinking about Krishna. I had loved that man so much that I believed he should have remained faithful to me and that I had to possess him. Freedom is the breath and soul of love but I didn't want to let go of him. I had become so selfish that I wanted to tie him with me forever. The truth was that the moment my mind had created a hedge around him, love was gone. The integrity and truthfulness was gone. What had remained was this disillusioned, ugly but intense feeling of possessing him.

Trying hard to fight the emotional tumult of my sick mind, I had made a phone call to Krishna from my room at midnight. When he came on line, I started to babble about my condition. He tried to make me understand that such conversation shouldn't be held on the phone and that he was ready to meet me, but I was out of control. Broken hearted, I had cried my heart out like a child and tactlessly whined about how important he was to me and how barren my life would be without him. Since there was no one else to listen to my plaintive grumble, I had blurted out everything that I had suppressed in my heart for days. After about fifteen minutes I had ended the conversation with a promise from him to meet the next evening. I was happy that he had listened to my outpourings, and was ready to meet me because I wanted to tell him in person how precious he was to me. One more time I was going to try to convince him to continue the same relationship with me. At that time, I had no idea that a terrible thing had happened. Standing right behind me was my father who had overheard every word that I had said on the phone.

'You pervert . . .!' he yelled at the top of his voice and slapped me so hard that I had stumbled to the floor. The knowledge that his son was gay had maddened him. All the intoxication had evaporated from my head with that one hard smack. Never before in my life had I suffered from such embarrassment and shame! My father had abused me for what seemed like hours and I had stood there crying and shivering, not even daring to ask for mercy. Unable to face his stern expressions, I had kept digging at the floor helplessly. Behind him had stood my mother and brother in a dazed state, not knowing what to do. My mother was too shocked to react and had soon slumped into the sofa. It was my brother who had stayed with me the entire night so that I wouldn't take any wrong step. And that day, I was so ashamed of myself that I would have done something drastic had he not been with me.

That night I had buried myself in bed and cried over the tragedy that my life was. Not only had I lost my love, but my family had also segregated me from their lives. And that had just been the beginning of my punishments. The aftermath was going to be even more harrowing.

Krishna must have waited for me the next day, but I was not allowed to go out. Neither had I been permitted to receive any phone calls. He had called me, but the reply he had got every time was 'wrong number'. My family had been so shocked to know that I had had physical relations with none other than Krishna whom I had called my best friend and whom my family had adored and always considered a very sincere boy. Without telling me, Smit met Krishna to know his side of the story and told him what had happened at my place. Krishna told Smit how I was against his marriage. To my family, I was more guilty of the two, since it was *I* who was trying to hinder Krishna's marriage. It was *I* who didn't want to end whatever we had between us.

Krishna had confessed to my brother that he adored me as a friend, and that he had never been in love with me. It was just bodily pleasure that had driven him to me every time. Though I had known it to be almost true, I wanted to hear the same from Krishna's mouth. Smit let me attend Krishna's phone and he repeated what he had told Smit. It was so heart rending to realize that Krishna's love had been just a fantasy. It had been just his sexual dependence that had kept him attached to me. And now, when he had found a girl of his choice, he needed me no more. He didn't think of me; didn't care about me. How selfish he had been! I had been so maddened by his statement that I had even thought of calling Aastha to inform her about my relations with Krishna, but I didn't dare. It would have finished their marriage but wouldn't have brought Krishna back to me. I had lost the man I had loved.

Many times, Krishna had told me not to be very serious about our relationship. I knew then why he had said so. His feelings for me had been fake, only sexual and they had nothing to do with true love. He had never wanted us to be together forever. What a fool I had been to imagine being with him till the end of my life! How the hell had I not perceived that my vain pursuits and expectations were going to bring me nothing but grief, pain and tears! The realization that the man I loved the most had never wanted to spend the rest of his life with me exasperated me at first. But when I ruminated about it, I concluded that I had no right to compel him to do anything. Loving someone doesn't mean it gives you the right to decide the future path of your beloved's life. All the decisions taken in love should be mutual and in my case, Krishna had never cared about my thoughts or feelings. He had his dreams, had responsibilities towards his family, and there was no way I could have him in my life the way I wanted. The only thing I could do was to let him go. But it hadn't been that easy. Neither had I been that mature at that age. I couldn't take the reality positively since Krishna had given me wounds that were never going to heal. That was that. It was the end. I murdered my feelings and it was all over . . .

. . . or so I'd thought. I had believed all this had only been between me, my family and Krishna, and the shameful story was never going to come out. But I had been wrong. Even the walls have ears. Somehow, it got out that I was gay. I later suspected our maid who must have let the cat out of the bag. My relatives and friends circle came to know about my reality. Nobody dared to ask me directly, but it was in their eyes that seemed to mock me. Most of my male friends had begun to keep me at a distance to avoid being suspected as my gay interest.

Those had been the worst days of my life.

I was almost left alone by my family and all my kith and kin. The thing I called love was inconsequential and alien to them. Being a homosexual was a sin to all of them, no matter how progressive and modern they claimed to be. Thankfully, the people at my workplace had no idea about what was going on in my life. I could be relaxed only at work. Any other place, the thought that people around me knew my secret, wouldn't let me be at ease. So

I quit going out unnecessarily and would be in my room all the time. For months, my parents didn't talk to me. It was only Smit who, after days of my isolation, started to behave supportively.

One fine day, I found a piece of paper in one of the drawers of my wardrobe. The address of the Jeevan Bharati School of Valai was written on it, and I recalled that months ago, I had turned down their offer. It had become really tough to live in Baroda and I had been desperately looking for an escape from my agonizing past. What better option could I have had at that time? Though I was not sure of a positive response as the offer had come long ago, I phoned the principal and humbly asked if I could have the job I had been offered earlier. To my surprise, the principal called me to Valai for an interview immediately. By God's grace, I passed the interview with flying colours. None of my family members had an objection to my taking a job in Valai then. My mother, brother and sister knew it would be better for me to shift somewhere else, whilst my father seemed to be no longer interested in my life. None from my family said a proper goodbye to me when I left my home. How could they? The wounds I had given them were still fresh and aching. I slept fitfully thinking of the ugly past.

twenty three

It was the middle of autumn. Most of the trees had sloughed off their leaves and wore a skeletal look. Even the neem tree had become barren, and although I didn't like it in this avatar, there was the hope of a new blossoming.

In such time of natural ebb, I was chatting with Mr Desai in the public garden when he told me that he had decided to move to Ahmedabad. For a second the news shocked me because as far as I knew he had always wanted to spend his last days in this land of the Dangs. Sitting on a bench in the park, the still grieving man told me that everything he had here was connected with his wife and after her demise he had been feeling an emptiness in everything. The barrenness of his house, of what used to be home when his wife was alive, stung him every day. His bewildered eyes searched for her in every corner. His children were constantly calling him and he had finally made the decision. The ever present smile on his face had faded away. Here, it was impossible for him to forget the happy times he had with her. In Ahmedabad he felt, his miseries would lessen in the presence of his children and grandchildren. So the idea of going over was right for him, but tough for me. I had already lost a mother figure, I didn't want to lose him too. The thought of departing from him pained me deeply, but I didn't let him know. I told him to follow his heart. The very idea of losing a dear one had always grieved me and now one more person was going to be away from me forever.

Though I kept a smile on my face when he left for Ahmedabad, he knew that I was weeping inside. To raise my spirits, he promised that he would be back if he didn't like it there. But I knew that it was an empty consolation. He was never going to come back to Valai. Watching their car receding in the distance, my eyes brimmed with tears and I felt my heart break.

I found myself staring at the neem tree which by far had become a mirror image of my life. It was solitary and secluded. Just like me.

Mr Desai was gone. I could have stopped him, but I didn't. He needed his family. But now, when he was away, I realized that I, too, needed him in my life where he had played a great role. More than a friend, he had been a fatherly figure from whom I had learned how to better my life. He abused me several times, but I never took it to heart as it was not meant to hurt me. It was an interesting aspect of his character that he reviled all people and situations. My own father couldn't be a friend of mine, but Mr Desai had been a good companion. Even though he had no idea about my homosexuality, he was aware that I was in love with someone. Interestingly, the old man had asked me about my girlfriend once or twice, but when he realized that I didn't want him to know about my love, he quit asking. He, who didn't know that it was Vivek, thought the girl I was in love with must be lucky. He knew about how strained my relations with my father were! In his opinion, there was little I could do to improve our relationship since, he had said this unhesitatingly, my father was an obstinate person who lived immersed in self importance.

I used to visit temple with him and it was he who had

given me books on meditation—books that had helped me control my anger and heal my grief. And attending a party at his place was something I had simply adored. Unlike him, I was never a great cricket fan, but I accompanied him because he liked my company while watching cricket. I remembered how I bought things for Mr and Mrs Desai—cakes, pastries, ice-creams, chocolates. They would say that they were too old to eat those things but I would insist that they have the food. Mrs Desai used to say on such occasions that I had brought them their childhood again. They were away from their children, and I longed for my family and that's what made us a perfect family. Moving away from my dear ones who had satisfied my emotional needs was something that had always pained me. The loss of the Desais from my life was heart breaking since they had been invaluable to me. It would take me days to get accustomed to life without them.

God had tested my abilities of tolerating grief time and again. Losing the Desais was bad, but I had had worse. Earlier, it had been my break-up with Krishna that had grieved me insufferably. Knowing that people knew about my homosexuality, a sort of uneasiness had developed within me and I opted to stay alone all the time. People talked about me and it was impossible to shut them up. It was all so depressing. I would go to work, come back home and stay in my room until the next morning. Facing the outer world was not as big a problem as it was facing my family. Unable to look into their eyes, I was so embarrassed that I couldn't even ask for forgiveness. Only because of me, dark shadows of invincible negativity had prevailed over the positive atmosphere of my home. There was so much of tension that none of my family members talked to one another unless it was really required.

It had been an unwritten rule in our family that we all ate dinner together. It was only because of me that that rule had been broken. I couldn't take my meals with them. I would take my food to my room and eat alone. I would try to exchange a few words with my family, but they would ignore me most of the time. During that most frustrating period of my life, I had received no emotional support from my family or anyone else. I had felt like committing suicide several times. I thought I had troubled many souls, and my life was useless and I did not deserve to live. Once, in the bathroom I had tried to end my life by cutting my veins, but my shaky hands didn't let the razor touch my wrist.

It was Smit who forgave me first. Having seen my condition for days, he had started talking to me, and accompanying me for dinner in my room. He was the one who'd hated me the most when the truth about my sexuality had been brought to light. We had never been friends and he had always been the typical elder brother, but I was thankful to him that he had forgiven me and brought back some moments of hopefulness in the toughest times of my life. Namrata, my sister-in-law, had been at her father's place in Pune for a holiday, when the secret about my sexuality had been revealed. Smit must have told her about that shameful episode, but she never stopped talking to me. Neither was her behaviour with me any different. In fact, she was the least troubled person in my family with the revelation of my homosexuality. She behaved as if nothing had happened, and I was so grateful to her for not making me feel bad or humiliated in any way. That time I realized how good a human being she was! Next was Ridham, my younger sister. She was the one who spoke to our mother about forgiving me. Slowly, all of them began to behave

Mayur Patel

normally with me and it seemed like I had got my life back, but father was still angry with me and nobody in my family had the guts to go talk to him about me.

In the meantime, I tried to forget Krishna, but it was in vain. He had become an inevitable part of my existence that I couldn't put him out of my lovesick mind for even a single second. Memories of the heavenly time I had spent with him would come back to me time and again, and submerge me in tears. Never before had I experienced such loneliness and I had no idea how terrible it could be. When the object of my love was gone, was no longer there, I realized that loneliness kills. It really kills when loneliness silently creeps upon you and there is no way to go beyond that phase.

Krishna was the man I had depended on physically and psychologically, and not having that companion with me anymore almost paralysed me. Since the beginning of our relationship, I had thin hope of his being with me forever, yet I had let myself depend on him. I felt so empty without him.

I wanted to completely erase his memories from my mind, but couldn't and when it became increasingly difficult to get rid of the shadows of my past, I tried yoga and meditation, but even that didn't help much. The more I tried to forget him, the more his memories gnawed at me. Then, ending my vain efforts to forget him, I left it entirely upon God and decided to live my life as it was. With the pleasant memories of Krishna, I started my day and earnestly prayed to the Almighty to bring him all the success and happiness possible. I had a faint hope that, leaving all other things behind, he would return to me someday. But he didn't. Days, weeks and months went by. I kept waiting, but he didn't come. Sometimes I felt it was I who'd left him.

Krishna had tried to sustain our friendship, it was I who wasn't ready to compromise. I had told him that he was being selfish but my introspection made me realize that *I* was being selfish by not letting him marry the girl of his choice. I would have been ready to accept his marriage had he agreed to carry on with our relationship even after his marriage. And that, as I had realized later, was immoral. I had been responsible for our break-up. But I had been helpless. How could have I accepted him as just a friend? He was more than that. He had always been.

When the situation we get pleasure from becomes a burden to the one we love, we have to let our beloved go. Krishna had wanted to end the relationship with me, so I had set him free. He wanted to be happy in his married life.

One fine evening, Krishna had surprised me by paying me a visit at my workplace. I had been happy to see him after months but I didn't let it show on my face. I behaved as if I didn't need him in my life anymore. He wanted to talk to me and I, pretending not to be too interested, had agreed to meet him after school hours. On a windy evening the same day, we'd met at the Nimeta garden. We chose to sit on a bench in a far corner. I could immediately feel the difference when he kept a distance from me on the bench. In the past he used to sit close to me all the time.

The two of us had sat there, silently staring at each other. Then he'd broken the silence, 'How are you?'

In reply, I had asked, 'How should I be? Happy?'

He hadn't taken it amiss. He knew me. He knew I was still dejected. From his shirt pocket, he pulled out an envelope and gave it to me. I knew that he was going to get married next week at his hometown Kottayam in Kerala. It pained me but I managed to hide my grief. I smiled.

'This might be our last meeting, but I'm your friend

and will always be.' There was a pause. 'There's a letter inside the . . .' he'd pointed to the pink envelope in my hand '. . . and my phone number also. You can call me any time.'

I had resolved that I wouldn't give into my feelings before him, but then, I had found it hard to control my tears. He got closer to me, took my hands in his, and asked, 'Won't you say something? I would like to hear.'

There was so much to talk and whine about, but it all would have been for nothing, therefore, I suppressed it all in my heart. 'I'll be happy for you.' I'd found it hard to be able to talk. 'I just want you to be happy.' That's what I had told him a thousand times.

'I'm sorry for hurting your sentiments,' Krishna had said. I knew that had come straight from his heart. I said nothing. There was nothing else to be discussed. We stayed in that state of speechlessness for a while.

When leaving, he'd asked me, 'Can I get a hug?' There had been a mist of tears in his eyes.

For a while, I'd remained silent and then nodded. I was probably waiting for something like that. We stood up, he embraced me tightly and my eyes had welled up. For a few moments, we'd remained in that position. He had given me a kiss on my cheek. One last kiss. The kiss that had lasted briefly but brought alive all those memorable moments of our passionate past. Receiving that hug and kiss, I had let myself get lost in that beautiful fantasy where time stood still.

'Have a good life,' I wished him in the end.

'You too,' he had murmured and walked away.

With a sinking heart, I'd watched him leave. Nothing under the sun was more terrible than the feeling that the man I'd loved more than myself, was leaving me forever. I watched him until he was out of sight. I wanted to cry and scream in pain, but couldn't since it was a public place. Instead, looking down, I'd blinked and let the saline drops fall on the ground. The rest was to happen at night back home in my locked room where there would be no one to listen to me crying. I unfolded the letter.

Dear Kaushik,

I don't know about you, but you still are dear to me and will always be. I know that you're angry with me and your anger is valid. I've hurt you, been bad to you, and I am apologetic about that. It's up to you to forgive me or not. It's okay even if you don't accept my apology.

You brought me so many pleasant moments that I will cherish for the rest of my life. Thanks. You helped me financially and mentally. Whatever we shared was beyond being heavenly. But every good thing has to end someday. I don't want to lose you since your friendship is precious to me. I want to keep that friendship, but on one condition that it would only be a healthy friendship and nothing more than that.

Call me if you are positive about my proposal.

Krishna.

Our companionship was precious to me too, but I couldn't be *only* a friend after what we had for a long period. There was no chance I could accept him the way he wanted. There was no chance. I was not to give him a call, ever.

The back of the envelope had on it printed—Life doesn't

end with the end of one relationship, no matter how strong a relation it is.

A sarcastic but pained smile had flickered over my face. *You say so because the end of this relationship will not be as grievous to you, as it will be to me. It might not make any difference to you, but it sure will change my life forever.* I had wanted Krishna to listen to the laments of my blistered heart, but he was long gone. What difference would it have made anyway?

That had been the last time Krishna and I saw each other till fate brought us face to face again.

It was a Saturday afternoon, when I saw Vivek standing with Chandni at the school gate after school hours. They were busy talking, while their friends were keeping an eye around. All of them, seven in all, saw me and knew that I had seen them. I obviously didn't like the sight, yet I smiled at Vivek and he smiled back somewhat hesitantly. Feigning not to be bothered at all, I just passed by.

They've started to meet outside. I'll have to do something. I was too damn jealous! I had talked to Vivek about not dreaming about her seriously, since there was no match between him and Chandni because of their divergent family background and financial condition. Apparently, Vivek hadn't paid heed to his own advice! The mess in my relationship with Vidya and Mrs Desai's demise, and then Mr Desai's recent departure had taken my focus away from what was going on in Vivek's personal life. In the meantime, Vivek seemed to have developed a great rapport with Chandni. It would now not be easy, if not impossible, to separate him from the girl. But I was determined to keep Chandni away from stealing my love interest. I had survived all of my recent tragedies, and now I wanted to put all my energies and efforts in separating the immature couple.

That unpleasant sight of the two of them together, niggled me that entire afternoon. I ate and sang songs and watched TV, but nothing helped me forget that sight. Vivek came to me at around 3.30 p.m, looking exultant. I welcomed him and we sat in my bedroom. Ever since, he had confessed to me about his feelings for Chandni, he was at ease in telling me all about her. He needed just a little nudge to reveal all. So, after some loose talk, I came to the point, 'So, what's happening in your love life?'

He blushed and answered earnestly, 'It's going great. Today was—' He suddenly became quiet.

'What?' I asked impatiently. 'What happened today?' I couldn't conceal the anxiety in my tone.

'I don't know how to describe this.' He was hesitant. I was eager.

'Come on, you can tell me. We're friends, aren't we?' I egged him on.

'In the recess today . . . when we were seated on the bench . . . last bench . . .' On my insistence, he described it with difficulty. 'I had her hand in mine and . . . and after a while she took my hand to her . . . leg and . . .' He broke off.

'To her leg?' My eyes widened in curiosity.

'Hmm . . . to her leg . . . err . . . thighs.' He looked in the other direction and murmured.

I was stunned. 'What?' I was suddenly alert. 'What did you do then?' I asked, my pulses racing.

'I was stunned for a moment because I . . . I had never . . . you know.' He gulped. He was so embarrassed that he couldn't look into my eyes, yet he went on. 'Then I . . . kept it where it was and it felt . . . it . . . felt good.'

'It was the first time, wasn't it?' I asked. I knew he must

have felt around her thighs, but he was too uncomfortable to talk about it.

'Hmm . . . it was,' he said. We remained silent for a long time. Then I looked at his face. Finding me staring at him he asked, 'You want to say something?'

'Yes . . . no,' I stammered. 'Ah . . . yes actually. But this might make you feel bad. And I don't want to spoil your day.' I did want to spoil his day. Any procrastination in poisoning his ears against her could be disastrous for me.

'No, no. Just say. I won't take it ill.' He said in a normal tone. I knew he was the kind of person who never took anything amiss.

I chose my words carefully. 'You are in high spirits and I don't want to kill your excitement, but as a friend, I think I must talk to you about this.' I cleared my throat. 'As far as I know, you two have not been seeing each other for more than a month. Right?' He nodded and I asked further, 'So don't you think, what you did, touching her thighs and all that, was a bit too soon?'

He suddenly became serious. 'I don't want to put this into your brain, but I think she's not as innocent as she looks. I mean no girl would let a guy go this far in such a short period of time. And in your case, as you said, it was she who took your hand to her thighs. That's something I am unable to digest. You understand me?'

Vivek became thoughtful. That's what I wanted. I continued to poison his brain, 'You might not agree with me, but I think that she must have had such an experience even before. With someone else. Otherwise, it's unusual for a girl to approach things the way she did. You are getting my point, right?'

The way he nodded, my words seemed to have had an impact on him. I was pleased from inside. 'Well, I have no problems with her, but since you are my friend, I told you what came to my mind. Now it's up to you how you go ahead with her, okay?'

The Vivek who left my place, was not the same as the one who had come. He was more serious and quieter and more thoughtful now. I hated to see him like that, but then it was necessary to manipulate his mind. I was happy that I had successfully sown the seeds of suspicion in his brain. I thought it was going to work out the way I wanted it to. Vivek would suspect her, which might lead to their separation.

Two days later, I told Vivek to ask Chandni if she had an affair in the past. Although I knew Vivek wasn't intelligent enough to figure out my licentious intentions, I was careful not to sound jealous.

I knew I was playing my cards brilliantly. My obsession with Vivek was getting more and more intense, and after Chandni's entry in his life, it had turned into possessiveness. To get Vivek's love, I planned to target Chandni. Was I afraid of the girl? For a second, I thought I wasn't. But the fact was that I was. Even if I didn't like to admit it, I really was afraid of the girl. She could steal Vivek from my life.

The more I came to hear and know about the young duo, the more my evil intentions grew, only to leave me restless. Eventually, a kind of repugnance for Chandni began to develop in me. I wished to punish and rebuke the girl in the presence of her class. Misusing my position as a teacher, I thought of giving her a lot of writing work so that she couldn't find time to sit by Vivek. But then, thinking that something like that would hurt Vivek, I refrained from doing so. I hardly punished any of my students, so punishing Chandni might make Vivek suspicious. The fact that my beau loved someone else irritated me beyond my tolerance. I envied Chandni, and I felt helpless and insecure all the time. So much of repulsion accumulated in me, that I shunned looking at the face that was stealing my love away. I had thought of expressing my love to Vivek, but now, I had to abstain from doing so because I knew that the chances of the acceptance of my love were lesser in Chandni's presence. That girl had indirectly begun to test my patience. I knew I'd have to expel her from Vivek's life.

A few days went by, and Vivek and I were at the sunset point one evening. I was in a good mood, so I praised the blue jacket Vivek was wearing. 'Nice jacket. Looks good on you.' Praise, in my opinion, was the best thing to strengthen a relationship.

'Thanks. It's my friend's,' he said. 'Chandni also likes it very much.'

My mood died with that. I wished I had not been so forthcoming with my praise.

'I had asked Chandni if she had someone in her life before,' he said suddenly.

I was dying to know the answer. *The girl must have become angry. She must have fought with him.* That's what I wanted.

'She said she used to like a guy who lived in her colony . . . about a year ago . . . he had also liked her, but their relationship didn't last long as both of them were afraid of her father. She said she still talks to him sometimes, but neither of them is serious about their relationship anymore.' And, before I could make something out of it, he said happily, 'You know what's the best thing about her?' He looked at me. 'She doesn't lie. I mean she could have kept it a secret, but she didn't. She told me the truth, that means she trusts me.'

Damn! I cursed her, trying to control the heavy sigh of disappointment. *That's a blunder. It backfired—her confession drove him closer to her. How stupid of me!*

My super brain came to my rescue in a while as I made at least something out of it. 'That proves her father is a strict man. And she most likely wouldn't go against his wishes.'

'Seemingly,' Vivek said judiciously. 'But she is crazy about me. The other thing she said was that she wants to elope with me, she wants to marry me.'

I gaped at him as he continued, 'So stupid of her! It's fun to imagine something like that. Running away with your lover. Very filmi. But where would I keep her? What would I get her to eat? I have no money.' He seemed to be lost in his dream world. 'When I asked her these questions, she said that she knew nothing but the fact that she loves me and wants to be with me forever.' He chuckled and kept chuckling to himself for a while.

'Well, I don't want you to be too serious about this relationship. I don't see any future in it. And you know that, don't you?' He nodded as I continued to dissuade, 'Dreams pain us beyond our endurance. Please refrain from dreaming so that it won't hurt you severely when the time comes to end the relationship. Dreaming about getting married to your beloved is one thing and making it possible is something else. You have a family to think about. Be careful, and don't get serious about whatever comes out of her mouth.'

Whenever I told him something like that about Chandni, his face would turn pale. I disliked this visage of his, but it was necessary to keep him close to reality.

'You are right. I'll have to be careful,' he said gloomily.

'You better be.' I felt like a winner. 'You are my dearest friend here.' I started to flatter. 'I do care for you.' My eyes were on him as he listened to me attentively. 'I can't see something bad happening to you. I just want you to be happy.'

That wasn't a lie, but the truth was that I wanted myself to be happy first. My happiness meant the most to me and Vivek was all I wanted. I was ready to do anything for him. He reminded me of Krishna, the love I had lost, and yet he was so different—young, innocent, totally oblivious to the ills of the world, unmindful of my deep desire to possess him, make him my own . . . It was all consuming, this need, this craving . . . I had no idea how far I would go.

twenty four

A m I getting possessive about Vivek? I asked myself. *Yes, I am. So what? I love him and I'll do whatever it takes to take him away from Chandni. But even if I succeed in doing so, will he be mine? Will I be able to tell him how I feel about him?*

I was sceptical whether Vivek would end his relationship with Chandni or not. For several days, I kept telling him things that might deter him from going ahead with the relationship, but nothing seemed to be working in my favour. Vivek agreed on everything I said and it looked from the solemnity and thoughtfulness on his face that he would not try to meet Chandni more often, but it was all quite useless. That girl had really cast her spell on him. Recess was the only opportunity they had to sit close and talk, otherwise there was no chance Chandni could risk being seen with him. It was weird, but I loved Vivek so much and was so desperate to separate the duo that I tried very hard to influence his innocent brain. Since the beginning, I knew I was in the wrong, but I consoled myself that everything's fair in love and war. I was madly, deeply in love with Vivek, and one can't be in love and be wise at the same time.

The desperation of getting Vivek was so intense that I had started to plan something big, something that would end their relationship permanently. I thought of asking Vivek to ask Chandni if she had had sex with the guy whom she admitted she'd liked a year ago. Vivek belonged to an orthodox society where virginity still meant a lot. I needed to indoctrine his brain that Chandni was not a virgin. It was like firing in the dark and the chances of hitting the bull's eye were fifty–fifty. There were many probabilities. Chandni could say 'no' and the matter would end there. Secondly, she could get angry with Vivek for suspecting her loyalty, which might create strife between them. But if the poor girl had had sex before, and trusted and loved Vivek so much that she wouldn't lie to him, he'd definitely dump a girlfriend who had already lost her virginity.

But then, I also felt it would be too sordid to do something like that. Attacking Chandni's character that way might result in Vivek hating me instead, and that I didn't want at any cost. I had to go for some other option that could be as effective, but not dirty. And the devil in me cooked up one masterstroke.

The same day that Vivek came to my place, I executed my plan. 'Getting fearless in love, huh?' I asked with a cunning smile. 'Sunset point was never so beautiful, was it?'

He didn't understand what I was talking about. 'What? I don't–'

'Oh, come on! You can't hide it from me!' I laughed as if I had caught him red-handed.

'What?' he asked, frowning.

'You want me to narrate the entire scene? What I saw?' I was surprised that I was as good a liar as Krishna was. It was just that I seldom practised it.

Still unable to understand my insidious intentions, he smiled dubiously.

'Okay, let's hear it from me then.' I clapped in the air. 'The two of you . . . Chandni and you . . . I saw you at the sunset point last evening. Had a great time? Oh, you must . . .'

The smile on Vivek's face faded. His brow became furrowed.

Enjoying his perplexity, I asked innocently, 'What?'

'Something must be wrong! I was at the hostel the entire evening. How could I have been at the sunset point?'

'You don't have to lie, dear. I won't talk about this to anyone.'

'I'm not *lying!*' he replied vehemently, 'I was at the hostel all the time. You can ask my roommates. In fact, I had thought of seeing you in the evening, but you had said you were too busy with something else. That's why I didn't show up here.'

Now it was my turn to act puzzled. 'Oh, yes. I had to go with bhai to meet someone. The meeting was cancelled, so we ended up at the sunset point where I believed I saw you and Chandni.' Every word of mine increased the confusion and anxiety on Vivek's face. *You're on the right track, Kaushik.* I couldn't help praising myself. *What a great actor you are!*

The nervous little chap stood gaping in uncertainty, so I spoke expressing my doubts, 'Well, then I must have seen someone else. It was probably because the boy and the girl I mistook for you and Chandni were seated far away, and I didn't get a chance to see their faces. I thought since I was not going to be with you, you two had decided to meet. I didn't want to disturb the two of you. Neither did I mention it to bhai.'

I paused to see if Vivek had anything to say. His face was not as tense as I had imagined but the concocted story sure had bothered him. His expressions were a mix of confusion and disbelief.

'The couple was sitting close under a tree.' I went on embellishing my tale. 'I didn't notice the colour of the girl's dress, but she looked so much like Chandni. The shirt the boy had worn was white, similar to the one you have. But they must have been somebody else. The boy seemed to be taller than you, but I'm not very sure since they were seated at a distance. Maybe my eyes have gone weak. But it wasn't foggy. Neither was it that dark. But then . . . it must be someone else.' I had done what I had planned to and the result was before my eyes. Vivek's face had turned pale and he must have been thinking what I had wanted him to think. *Chandni was seeing someone else . . .*

Throughout the conversation, I acted as innocent as a child. Never before had I fudged that way. And I was feeling guilty for doing so to the young man I called my friend and the object of my affection. But then, I had followed my heart.

The plan had been contrived carefully. The previous evening, I had told Vivek that I was not going to be at home since I was busy with something else. In reality, I had nothing to do. It wasn't necessary that I go out but I did lest Vivek should come by my place and disrupt my plans. Mr Gavit had accompanied me to the sunset point, where I had seen nobody like Vivek or Chandni. It was just that I wanted to incite Vivek against Chandni by generating mistrust in his mind about her loyalty. Vivek had blind faith in me, so I was sure that he was not going to ask Mr Gavit whether what I had said was true or not. I also knew that he was going to ask Chandni about her being at the sunset point with some other guy. Chandni would obviously deny the story, and Vivek would think she was lying. End result? A quarrel. So far, everything was going the way I had planned.

Vivek still looked too perplexed to believe that Chandni was playing fast and loose with him. Despite a strong urge, I didn't carry on with the topic any longer lest he sense my cruel intentions. It was better to leave the entire matter at that point since the seeds of infidelity were already sown in his little brain. Though he didn't try to refute whatever I had said, from his face I knew that he wasn't convinced about my story. The poor boy didn't know whom to trust. On one side it was me, his teacher, guide and friend who he believed would never mislead him, and on the other side was Chandni, the girl he was in love with. But if he had to choose between Chandni and me, I was sure, he would choose me. As far as I knew, I was the person he trusted the most in Valai.

The glee he had on his face when he had come in had faded, and I hated to see that crestfallen look on his face, but then, it was necessary. It was important in order to gain my love. I had told Vivek not to tell anybody about whatever I had discussed with him and he kept his promise well. I trusted him so much that I was sure Chandni or nobody else would have any idea what I was trying to do with Vivek. I told him that it wasn't love that had driven the two of them closer, it was just physical attraction which was normal at his age. My advice to him was to take the relationship lightly, so that it wouldn't hurt him so much when it ended. I talked in a manner as if I was sure about the death of their affair. I reminded him that he was a student and had to concentrate on his studies, and that he had so many responsibilities back home and that his family should be his priority. All that I had said was a part of my conspiracy, but the poor lad was so naïve that he believed I was his well-wisher. He actually thanked me for showing him the right path. Though all my advice was wise and true, I knew I was just being selfish in love. I was taking full advantage of my astuteness and Vivek's blind faith in me. Tough, indeed, is the game of love. Tougher is to play it with cleverness.

The second half of my plan didn't go as I had envisaged. I had expected him to tell me about what had happened between Chandni and him, but he didn't broach the subject. Neither did he seem upset. The eagerness to know what must have happened between them bothered me for a few days, and I remained uncertain whether to ask Vivek or not. Finally, when it became impossible for me to tolerate the situation, I asked him. I was shocked to know that Vivek hadn't asked Chandni about her being at the sunset point with the other guy. He said that he trusted her and didn't want to spoil their relations because of a trifling suspicion. He added that even if she was there with somebody else, it didn't bother him since he wasn't going to spend the rest of his life with her. This disheartened me because the climax of that false story had been way too different from my expectations.

Vivek sometimes behaved impatiently, but in this case, he had behaved like a mature man. He either was afraid of losing Chandni by suspecting her character or truly didn't believe she was the one I had seen at the sunset point. Maybe their relationship was not as weak. Maybe my story had been weak. I should have said I was sure the girl was Chandni. Better luck next time, Kaushik! I consoled myself. It was too early to hatch a new plot. I would have to wait for a chance. A better chance.

As far as I knew, there seemed to be nothing happening between Vivek and Chandni except for sitting on the last bench of the class during recess and touching each other. I was sure that Vivek was going to get bored with just that because, even if he hadn't admitted it, I knew for sure that like most men, his ultimate intention was to get physical with Chandni. And it was natural.

I thought of playing some masterstroke that would separate them forever. I thought about informing Chandni's father about his daughter's affair through a phone call or some other way, but on deliberation, decided against it. I was still thinking about another plan when one evening, alone under the pleasing shade of the neem tree, a thought just hit me—*What are you doing, Kaushik? What are you doing?* I had the answer. I was trying to contaminate the present and the future of two innocent souls. We get the birth of a human being only once, and Vivek had the right to live his the way he wanted. I had no right to do whatever I was doing. *How could I stoop to deceiving Vivek who trusted me more than anyone else?* He considered me a friend, a philosopher and I was trying to betray and ensnare him. Such a diabolic act was the worst sin that I could commit! *How could I be so sacrilegious?* Being in love doesn't mean you start playing havoc with your beloved's life! Love demands sacrifice but my love was a mere example of selfishness. My tryst with my inner self made me hate myself for being devilish with Vivek who, as a friend, loved me unconditionally and without any expectations. *Oh God, how could I have degenerated the way I had?* Fighting my conscience was proving to be difficult, and I had never been so vulnerable since the disclosure of my homosexuality.

I realized that Vivek liked the girl so much and really wanted to be with her. He was so crazy about her that despite all my wrong advice and conspiracies, he hadn't stopped seeing her. Also, I thought that bothering Vivek all the time to end his relationship with Chandni would affect our own relationship too. So I almost quit telling him about what to do and what not to do. After all, it was a mere teenage infatuation which wasn't going to last long. Vivek, so far, had known how to go on with that relationship. He had agreed with me in not getting very serious about this girl. His adolescence needed the company of the opposite sex, and he had one of the better ones, so why not let him enjoy! He'd surely learn something from it. I needed to leave him on his own, and that's just what I did.

The innocent, smiling face of Vivek flashed before my closed eyes and I made a decision that I wouldn't interfere with his private life any more. That was the thought that brought me back some self esteem. From that day on, I gave up telling him this and that about Chandni. As just a mute onlooker, I decided to watch the growth of their relationship.

It was soon, Holi, the biggest festival of the Dangs, and the entire town was once again thronged with people from all directions. Valai wore a festive look on the celebration of the Dang Durbar, an event that brought back all the familiar faces to Valai. Jaydeep, Mr Gavit's son, arrived home and it was fun to be with him since he was a knowledgeable guy—such a rare commodity in a place like Valai! I met all my colleagues at the fair, and hoped that Vidya would leave behind all hard feelings, but she didn't. She came to the fair, stayed at Ms Bhoye's place for three days, and whenever we came face to face, ignored me. She pretended to be happy without me, but I knew that she was miserable inside. She acted as if she had enjoyed the fair, but she couldn't hide the streaks of dejection on her face. It didn't upset me because she seemed to be even more disheartened. I had other people to share my joy with. There was Vivek and his entire gang of happy young men who made my day. But the real surprise was the arrival of Mr Desai who came to Valai on the fourth day of the celebrations. I was surprised because I had not expected him at all since we had talked over the phone a week ago, and he hadn't even mentioned anything about visiting Valai. I was so glad to see him.

He was to stay in Valai for about a week or so, and I was excited about getting an opportunity to spend time with him. Although he had so many people to meet, he preferred to be with me for a considerable time. We and his old friends had a good time. We partied and enjoyed and he talked about his life in Ahmedabad. I was glad to know that he was happy with his family. Had he stayed here, he would have been so lonely in Mrs Desai's absence. I was sad when he left after eight days.

Teenage affection blows strong in the beginning and fades away gradually. I was waiting for such a thing to happen to Vivek and Chandni, and I didn't have to wait for long. Vivek came to my home with a long face one day.

'What's wrong?' I asked, lifting my brows.

'How do you know something's wrong?' he asked in reply.

'I read faces. And yours is a kind of mirror where nothing can be hidden.' I blinked with an honest smile.

Vivek sighed heavily, took his time and then said, 'It's about Chandni.'

Tell me you fought with her, tell me. I wished devilishly. 'What about her?' I asked immediately, hiding my eagerness successfully.

'This morning I was talking to another girl, at the school gate. Mala—I'd told you about her if you remember. She had come here to see one of her relatives at the civil

Mayur Patel

hospital. Then she came here just to see me, and I was talking to her when Chandni saw us together. Since we were alone, she suspected us and enquired about Mala when she and I were together during recess. I told her that Mala was just a friend from my neighbouring village, but she didn't believe me. She has fixed it in her mind that I am interested in Mala. I was angry at her suspecting me and got away from her in no time.' Then he asked, 'You tell me, was that fair? I mean, she doesn't trust me at all! And that makes me angry.'

Yes! I was elated. *That's it*. That's what I wanted. A fight between the two of them. That's exactly what I had wanted.

'Well, I would take your side here.' A troubled soul needed some sympathy. My virtuous resolution of being just a witness to Vivek's puppy love melted away instantaneously since I didn't want to miss that great opportunity to vilify Chandni. 'Trust, in my opinion, is the basic, integral thing every relationship relies on. Having faith in your beloved's word is the first and the foremost thing for the success of any relationship.' My scheming brain philosophically added fuel to the flames. 'And it's worthless if she doubts your faithfulness in such a trifling matter. She shouldn't have done so.'

He nodded silently. I thought he was happy that I had taken his side. 'Did she say something insulting to you?' I had a little more to say against the girl.

'Uh . . .' Vivek was thoughtful. I was concentrating now, eagerly waiting for something to come out of his mouth that might help me raise another ghost in his mind against her. 'She got angry in a way that I have never seen before and . . . said that I was just like the other guys. All the boys are same. Yes, that's exactly what she said,' he said icily.

'That means she compared you with other boys. How many guys does she know?' I blurted out and then realized I shouldn't have said that. That was like attacking her character. 'I think she wants to dominate you. She must be driven by her beauty and richness. Superiority complex, that's what it is called. She must be thinking she's superior to you and you must only do what she likes. She —'

'It wasn't like that,' he interjected. 'Her wealth was no issue. She wasn't particular about dominating or . . . you know. She was just angry.'

That made me cautious about whatever I was going to say. I didn't want to sound too biased against Chandni. 'You know I've seen and experienced all this back in Baroda. I belong to an upper middle class society where people like to show off their wealth. They look and sound humble until they get into a fight. And wealth always shows up when it comes to covering up their misdeeds and deficiencies. People use it like a weapon to dominate those who are less wealthy. Chandni might be doing the same by suspecting you and not giving ears to your explanations.' Vivek had his eyes on me. 'Dear, you are too innocent to understand these things. But she has inherited this from her supercilious father. You might forget about the issue this time, but it'll surface in the future again. You are a person with some self esteem. It's up to you how far you should go with this type of a girl! Had I been in your place, I wouldn't have forgiven her for suspecting my fidelity.'

He meditated for long. I let him be by himself and didn't disturb. I had done what I had intended to. Now I was curious as to how much my words had affected him.

'I think you are right,' he spoke. 'She has no right to suspect me like that, to get angry with me and not to listen to my explanations.' He nodded. 'I won't forgive her for that. I won't talk to her unless she apologizes.'

Bingo! I had hit the bull's eye. But I didn't let my elation appear on my face. 'What you should do is, stay away from her, ignore her and let her feel sorry for her reprehensible behaviour. And make sure you don't look gloomy in the class even if you are. Pretend that you're not upset or tense. Act as if she doesn't matter to you. Okay?'

He nodded. He seemed to be convinced. Such a stupid fellow! A sign of immature love, what else? The poor boy had no idea what my intentions were. All the compunctions I had earlier against playing villain in Vivek's love story were gone and the devil in me was back with a vengeance. I had an opportunity to create a rift between Vivek and Chandni, and I didn't want to miss it. All I had to do now was to play my cards carefully. Vivek had blind faith in me and I wanted to make the most of it. I knew I was in the wrong. I could have subdued the Satan in me, but I chose not to. I couldn't help myself. Love knows no sanity and I had gone mad in love.

twenty five

After Vivek's fight with Chandni, I kept asking him what was going on between the two of them. Ignoring the diktats of my conscience, I enjoyed misdirecting Vivek by telling him what to do and what not to do. I successfully led him by the nose and tried my best that they don't find a middle ground. There are many things in life that are unethical, yet one goes ahead with them. My feet were getting deeper in the slough of evil doings and I was right on track to earning my transgressions.

Vivek confided in me so much that he unhesitatingly gave me the latest updates in his love life. He told me minute details about how he avoided and ignored Chandni and enjoyed her discomfort. Earlier, they used to sit together and chat during the recess, but now, Vivek had begun to leave the classroom with his friends. By not allowing her to contact him in any way, he had made her life miserable. Within days, she realized what she had done to Vivek was wrong. She had sent messages through her friends for reconciliation, but Vivek, strictly and stupidly complying to my advice, didn't show any interest in reconciling. Being indifferent to the person we love can sometimes be fun. Krishna and I used to play the same game by ignoring each other. Vidya had done the same with me by keeping her distance from me and now Vivek was doing the same to Chandni.

As the days went by, Vivek began to dislike the whole situation. The way the radiance from his face had dissapeared, it was obvious that he hated to be in that situation. He was a sweet boy with a very friendly nature and he didn't like to be upset with anyone, more so Chandni who was his love interest. He wanted to end the discord, but it was I who told him to hold himself back for some more days. I fooled him that their relationship would strengthen after this temporary estrangement. I had thought Chandni would ask for forgiveness in some days, and then would get fed up of it seeing that Vivek was disinterested. She would jilt him forever and by the time Vivek would realize the seriousness of the matter, it would be too late. Even if he would try to compromise, the girl wouldn't give him another chance. This was what I had planned but, I had no idea that neither of the two was as egoistic as I had thought them to be.

Chandni kept approaching Vivek through his friends, and finally, Vivek gave in. He sat with her and she apologized, teary eyed. She promised that she wouldn't ever suspect his loyalty. And everything then became as normal and pleasant as it used to be. Not for me though. On the day of their reunion, I found him elated when he came to see me in the evening. He told me about his conversation with Chandni and like always, I listened to him with a fake smile. He let me know how genuinely she had apologized and how cordially he had forgiven her and . . .

Suddenly, he stopped, his face blushed with shame. He wanted to say something but couldn't.

'What?' I asked. He shook his head immediately.

'*What*?' I had to ask even more emphatically. 'Come on, you can tell me. How many times will I have to remind you that we are friends?'

He took his time, gulped, and breathed deep before he spoke in a low tone. 'When I forgave her today . . . in the recess . . . we were alone in the classroom and she . . .,' I was aching with curiosity, '. . . she came near me and . . . kissed me.'

'Did you say *kissed*?' I couldn't believe him.

He looked away, nodding happily. I felt terribly jealous. Thankfully, he wasn't looking at me otherwise, he would have seen on my face the feelings of envy and antipathy. *This is not what I had imagined would happen!* I sighed in frustration. I realized that after this, it would be tough to poison Vivek's ears against Chandni. I cursed Chandni for kissing Vivek and for spoiling the state of my mind.

'That's fine, but,' I advised, 'both of you should focus on your studies. The annual exams are nearing.' What else could my frustrated mind have said! All my weapons had been ineffectual.

Soon after the exams, a seven week vacation was to follow. Since my relations with my family and others were on the mend now, I decided to spend my summer holidays at home. Last year, I had spent only two weeks of summer holidays at home because things hadn't been positive then. After about five months, I was leaving for home with hopes of enjoying my days there since my last Diwali vacation had turned out to be unexpectedly delightful. My relationship with Vidya was still the same and it was entirely up to her whether to make-up with me or not. My assumption was that she was never going to get back to being friends with me. That's why I kept my distance from her. I had already forgiven her and was ready to accept her as a friend, but had no courage to ask her to call off this cold war between us.

It was a lethargic summer afternoon and the winds had

ceased to blow. The annual exams were still a week away and I was looking at the English question paper I had prepared for class eleven. There was a knock on the door. Vidya was standing there at the entrance with a serious face. For a second, I couldn't believe my eyes. Then I welcomed her, we exchanged greetings and sat before each other in the living room.

I had no idea why she was here. I chose to remain quiet. She started with an apology, 'I am here to ask for forgiveness. Will you forgive me?' she asked in a normal tone.

'Come on, Vidya. It's all in the past now. I have forgotten everything. It happens,' I said offering my sympathy. I was cautious not to hurt her sentiments any more.

'No, but I really wanted to apologize to you and–' Visibly suffering from pangs of guilt, she suddenly found it difficult to talk.

'We are friends and it happens in friendship, okay? I have nothing to complain about anyways.' I wanted to take the conversation away from being serious.

'You say so because you are such a nice human being. And I just don't want to lose a friend like you.' She fought back tears, her lips tightened. 'I'm so sorry for behaving childishly and for hurting you so badly.'

'You needn't . . .'

'Please let me finish, Kaushik,' she interrupted meekly. 'I've been thinking of saying this for days and weeks but something . . . something from inside was stopping me.' I listened carefully as she expressed herself candidly. 'After that incident, I couldn't sleep for nights. For the first time in my life, I had truly loved someone and the realization that that man was out of my reach made me angry. The rage I felt against you for not accepting my love, turned against myself when I realized what a terrible mistake I had made. I am so ashamed of myself for insulting our friendship, but believe me, it was not planned. It was one, just one moment of passion that came like a storm and swept me and I got carried away. I want you to condone me for my injudicious behaviour and I promise I won't trouble you anymore in the future.' Then she cried like a kid. I got up and gave her a hug. We hugged till she stopped crying.

'Now, let's have a non serious chat, some tea or coffee, whatever you'd like, your majesty,' I said laughingly. She grinned. We made tea and noodles together, and sat at the dining table. She stayed with me for more than an hour and we talked about this and that. We hadn't talked for weeks, so there was a lot to catch up on. It was fun.

When she was about to leave, she said, 'I have a request if you allow . . .' I nodded positively, she went ahead after a deep breath. 'Kaushik, I loved you and I still love you and I don't think I will ever be able to stop loving you. You can't forget the person you love, can you?' We were looking straight at each other. 'Please don't tell me not to love you any more. It is something I can't do even if I want to. As I promised earlier, I won't bother you. We'll be friends forever, okay?'

I managed a relieved smile and shook hands with her. She left and I went back to my room. *I love you, Vidya, because you are a valued friend*. I had always enjoyed my homosexuality, but that day I wished I had not been gay. She was the woman I would have loved to love. But I was happy that the real Vidya was back in my life. After that lovely meeting, I felt light hearted and thanked God for repairing our friendship.

In the following days, Vidya appeared to be a happy person, but I knew she was pining for my love. A queer thought sprang up in my mind many times that I should let Vidya know about my homosexuality. But then I asked myself if she will be able to understand this. I was sceptical if this small town girl would understand my condition. Would she be able to bury my secret in her heart and not pour it out before others? I was afraid of that possibility. My life in Baroda had already been messed up and I didn't want the same to happen in Valai. The fact that things could change adversely for me in trying to make Vidya happy loomed large. I couldn't let that happen at any cost. I had earned enough disgrace and I didn't want anymore. Not again. Not at all.

Since Vivek couldn't study well at the hostel, he chose to come to my place for the preparation of the final exams. I helped him as much as I could, and I liked the fact that he was serious about his studies. And to concentrate further, he had decided not to meet Chandni.

The exams went off well and Vivek was confident about successfully passing all the subjects. The summer vacation was to begin soon after. It was the day of Vivek's last paper and he was to leave for his village the next day, so I called him to my place to accompany me for a stroll and to have a nice dinner at our favourite Chinese restaurant. It was a gorgeous spring evening and I was seated in the yard waiting for the boy. With the advent of spring, the gulmohar was dressed up in an enticing orange sheen. The flowers of the gulmohar were glowing in the radiance of the evening sun.

I had anticipated that Vivek would be late as always. On the contrary, he arrived early. I was surprised. 'What's wrong with you?' I asked. 'You're on time today. In fact, before time. Is everything all right?'

Vivek smiled nervously. I didn't know why. He is up to something, I thought but didn't ask. He was looking nice in a scarlet T-shirt. Through the V-shaped neck of the T-Shirt I could see his chest hair.

'By the way,' I said, 'you're looking good in this T.'

He smiled, his nervousness still apparent. I wanted to ask him the reason for his uneasiness, but couldn't. Something from inside me held me back. We went for a walk, spent nearly an hour at the sunset point and ate at the restaurant before getting back home. Through the evening, I felt as if he had something to say. Usually, I would have asked him directly, but that day, I don't know why I didn't ask. After beating about the bush for the entire evening, he finally came to the point. 'Sir, I want you to do me a favour.'

I nodded in approval and he breathed deeply before he said, 'I want to meet Chandni . . . but the problem is—as you know—we can't meet outside. So I . . . I was thinking if . . .' He was hesitant.

'Go on,' I said.

'I was thinking if you would allow us to meet at your place . . . just for a few minutes.' He looked at me expectantly.

I had not thought that he would ask me for something like that. Now I knew the reason for his nervousness. That was why he had come to me before time. He had thought of everything. I was Chandni's teacher and she would come to my place pretending to have some problem with her studies and nobody would have any idea about their meeting at my place. It was a good plan! I didn't want them to meet, but I had to say 'yes' to please him. Besides, he seldom made any demands, so I couldn't refuse.

The next morning, Chandni came to my place and they sat in the living room hand in hand. I was in my room, and had left the door open just a little so that I could listen to the conversation between the two of them. However, except for some whispers, I couldn't hear anything. Later, Vivek told me that they didn't talk much, but just looked at each other. He wanted to remember her face since he was not going to see her for the next seven weeks. When Chandni was gone, Vivek gave me a hug and thanked me for arranging their meeting.

'You are in love, aren't you?' I asked, trying not to sound jealous. We were seated before each other. He didn't say anything, but managed a shy smile. That said everything.

'What can you do for her? Can you die for her?'

'Yes, I can.' He didn't take even a second to think.

'Can you kill someone if she demands?' I was getting to the point.

'If necessary, yes.'

'Can you leave your friends for her?' That was what I was interested in knowing. That's the way I liked to dig out people's hearts!

He remained silent for a while, then said, 'No. That's probably the only thing I wouldn't do.'

'Why?'

'Because friends are more important to me. I can have another girl, but friends . . . real friends are not easy to find,' he said earnestly.

I liked the answer. I really did. That was what I had expected. Chandni was not more important than friends which included me. *Me*.

At home, I enjoyed my vacation as happy days were back in my life. No one seemed to be bothered about my gay status any more. My father didn't talk much with me, but other than that my family had no complaints against me. I let myself go, with visits to pubs, movies, restaurants and parties for a change. Since it was the marriage season, I attended many marriage functions too. I had quit celebrating my birthday since my break-up with Krishna, but my friends organized a small party for me and I couldn't disappoint them. I did everything I couldn't do in Valai. In the midst of these activities, playing tennis and swimming, I didn't realize how quickly the vacation got over. When I came back to Valai, I was eager to share my happy experiences with Vivek.

Vivek came to Valai a week later. He gave me a hug and wished me 'happy birthday' and presented me with a beautiful pen as a gift. 'It's not very expensive,' he said. 'But that's all I can afford.'

'Shut up or I'll slap you,' I admonished him with a smile. 'You are killing my joy by saying so.' He smiled as I spoke, filled with emotion, 'This is special and you can't imagine how much. I'll always preserve it. Thanks.' I was so happy to have received a present from him.

Vivek passed the annual exams with flying colours. To celebrate his success, I arranged a dinner at my place. We talked for hours. Listening to how great a time I had had in Baroda, Vivek expressed his regret over never having had such fun in his life. I felt sorry for him and suddenly thought of taking him to Baroda the next time I go. But before I could tell him about it, I realized something like that would be a mistake. The people in Baroda would take him to be my gay interest. After so long, my life seemed to be back on track and I didn't want it to be derailed again.

Another year at the school started as usual. Vivek was in class twelve now and the students of class tenth and twelfth, were not allowed to take part in school cricket as they had to appear for the Board exams. But Vivek couldn't quit playing cricket because he adored the game.

He played in the hostel with his friends. He was such a brilliant player that the school team was going to miss him. The sports teacher had even said that if he were allowed to choose one player to have back in the team, it would unarguably be Vivek. Everybody wanted him back, but a rule is a rule. Vivek was not going to play for his school again. That's why he had desperately wanted to win the cup last year.

My relations with Vidya were good, but I still could see the hope in her eyes. As far as Vivek's love story for a change was concerned, it was on a roll. He had kissed Chandni a couple of times when they were alone in their classroom during recess. He told me that despite knowing the fact that she wouldn't be with him forever, he couldn't help himself falling in love with her. The girl also knew it, but she too was helpless. They had less than a year. Once they passed the twelfth class, there was a very small chance that they would do college together. So they just wanted to enjoy this time as much as they could. But destiny had planned something cruel for them.

One day, Chandni's father somehow came to know about his daughter's interest in Vivek. The next day, he was in the principal's office and the principal sent for Chandni and Vivek. There, Chandni's father insulted and then warned Vivek to stay away from his daughter. The entire staff witnessed the scene and since Chandni's father was a rich and powerful man, nobody stood by Vivek. The helpless boy had his eyes lowered all the time, while Chandni couldn't control her tears. I wanted to speak in Vivek's support that if loving someone was a crime, Chandni was equally guilty and she should be scolded the same way. But I was stopped by the principal and I couldn't disregard his order.

Vivek was so humiliated that he remained distraught for several days. He was very frustrated with whatever had happened and tried to find out how the hell Chandni's father had come to know about them. He suspected some of his classmates who he knew envied him for having a girl like Chandni. But he had no idea who the real culprit was! So much resentment had accumulated in his heart that he swore to God in my presence that he would give the informer a severe beating if only he knew who it was. Chandni wouldn't dare to talk to Vivek after this. I believe she was threatened by her father that if she talked to Vivek, he would receive the punishment. The poor girl knew what a devil her father was! I had wanted their friendship to end but not this way. It was useless this way because they still loved each other.

Vivek said he could push Chandni out of his infatuated mind only while playing cricket and while being with me, otherwise she stayed with him all the time. He wanted to forget Chandni, but it wasn't that easy. He could have forgotten her had she been away from him, but unfortunately, she was there right before his eyes in class. He saw her every day and that didn't let him forget the pleasant memories of the time they had spent together. Chandni was having the same trouble and it was visible on her sullen face. Meanwhile, Chandni's birthday came on 8 August. Vivek had planned to gift her something, but at the moment, he couldn't even wish her. I felt sad for both of them. I had wanted them to have an irresolvable dispute so that they would dislike each other and slowly forgot each other without any regret. But here they were pining for each other right before my eyes. Since I myself had been in a similar condition, I understood how terrible it was to get separated from your beloved. When I had broken up with Krishna, I had thought I would die because I could not imagine life without him. I had even tried to kill myself. That incident had changed me in many ways. Cheerfulness had vanished from my nature and I had grown serious overnight. I had become calm and mature and had realized later that it had been good for me. I expected the same thing to happen to Vivek. Time heals everything. No matter how deep the wounds are! He would forget his love in some time.

I told him one evening, 'Vivek, nothing happens without a purpose. God must have something in store for you that is more exciting. You will find a better girl.' I tried to console him, not knowing how healing my words were going to be. 'So don't worry. Just concentrate on your studies and you will forget her in time.'

He grimaced agonizingly and asked, 'Have you forgotten your first love?'

I was speechless. Something deep inside me stirred because I felt, to some extent, I was responsible for Vivek's piteous condition. For the first time I had seen tears in his eyes otherwise, he was mentally so strong that he had never let himself cry no matter how dreadful the situation was. Be it his failure in the championship match of school cricket or the humiliating incident of being insulted by Chandni's father. He'd never let his vulnerability emerge, but the separation from his beloved broke him down. I believed that the negative energies and the evil wishes of my mind had brought him such a miserable time. I was guilty, and unable to face the bitterness and gloom that his eyes were full of. I asked myself—*Have I forgotten Krishna? Would I ever be rid of his memories?* The indisputable answer was, *no, not in a million years!* Krishna was so merged into my existence that I wouldn't ever be able to efface him from my mind. He was an indispensable part of my being. Vivek was right.

twenty six

Vivek and Chandni found it hard to forget each other but something unexpected happened which turned out to be a blessing in disguise. Chandni stopped coming to the school suddenly. At school, everybody thought she must be sick, but the truth was that she wasn't even in Valai. When even after days of her split with Vivek, she had carried on with a sullen face, her father had realized that she wasn't going to forget Vivek. So he had sent her to one of his relatives in Bombay to continue her studies. Vivek came to know about it after many days. He didn't react much. Whatever had happened was good for both of them. The geographical distance would help them forget each other.

When I asked him how he felt, he replied, 'I will be fine. I loved her so much but then . . . there are other important, more valuable things in life to deal with—family, studies. This is not the end of my life.'

The answer impressed me. I was actually amazed at the way in which he had handled the situation. At his age, I wasn't as mature. He was brave. He didn't break down. Unlike me, he didn't think of self annihilation. He accepted his destiny. What he said was very true. *This is not the end of my life.* After all, life doesn't end with the end of one relationship.

Yet Vivek remained sad for days and didn't talk much. Though I didn't like to see him depressed, from inside I was happy that Chandni was gone from his life for ever. I thought that the biggest encumbrance of my life had departed and now there was no one between Vivek and me. Will the separation from Chandni bring Vivek closer to me? I asked myself. *Vivek's been intimate with a girl, won't that make it tougher for me to turn him gay? He sure would like to find another girl instead of a gay companion. Chandni's exit from his life doesn't mean he's available for me. It's not going to be easy for me to make him develop gay interest in me.* The yearning of an impossible dream had made me stoop low. I was deluding myself with the false hopes of succeeding in my love life. The feeling that I had defiled the sanctity of our friendship started to sting me once again. Sitting alone on a bench in the garden in mist-laden dusk, I regretted following this path. Looking at the full moon, I apologized to Lord Shiva for demeaning myself. I was not sure whether I would be forgiven or not, but my confession certainly made me feel better.

As time went by, the pain in Vivek's heart died down and he came back to his original form. He regained the cheerfulness in his nature and then he hardly talked about Chandni. I was happy that he was single again. I thought of proposing to him before he fell for another girl. I actually rehearsed it—how to unveil my feelings to him—in my mind but then, I postponed it to the next day every time and that next day never came.

Vivek grew very serious about his studies. He came to my place to study, took his meals with me and joined me for evening walks. In the meantime, I visited his place once and stayed there for a night, which gave me an opportunity to experience village life. I actually had been there before, but this was the first time I had spent a night there. It was fun to talk to the old men of Vivek's village as they told me about their customs and rituals and few other things I never knew about. They were in turn surprised by my friendly behaviour, especially since almost everyone looked at me as if I was from an alien world. Vivek told me that it was because they had never had a guest like me who belonged to the upper class and still had no problem with their poverty.

Though most of them were extremely poor, they lived a full and happy life, free from all the ostentations of the urban world. And it showed on their faces, in their talk. I thought how different these complacent souls were from the disgruntled, insatiable spirits I knew in my hometown. There I learned, from Vivek's mother, to milk a cow. This act which looked simple actually needs a lot of practice to do it correctly and efficiently, and also it fatigues ones fingers. I sat by that kind woman as she prepared for me, kheer, a sweet dish made of milk, rice and sugar, and rotla of bajri, a kind of grain they grew in their fields.

After a delicious dinner, Vivek and I, lay on a string bed, the khat, in the backyard and watched the twinkling stars in the sky until midnight. The reception I received had been overwhelming, and I thanked Vivek for giving me such a memorable day.

In reply, he said, 'It is nothing compared to what I've got from you.'

'Do tell me what you've got from me?' I asked.

'Is it necessary?' he asked. 'You know I am not as good as you are at expressing my feelings.'

I smiled and said, 'You don't need to. I can see it in your eyes.'

He turned his face to the stars.

'Why are you so sweet and nice?' I asked as I had done earlier.

And his reply was the same, 'I don't know.'

We talked until midnight. When Vivek felt sleepy, he said, 'Let's get inside and sleep.'

'Why don't we sleep here?' I asked.

'Here?'

'Why? What's wrong in sleeping here?'

'This khat won't be comfortable. I mean, you're not used to it.'

'I'll be fine. Just sleep. It's great to be under the open sky.'

He agreed to my wish and brought a quilt for us. There, on the khat, we slept together. It was great to be with him under a single quilt.

Weeks after Chandni's departure, Vivek told me that her memories didn't bother him anymore. He just wanted to concentrate on his education and nothing else. I was glad that he was on the right track. I had helped him in his studies and he seemed to be under an obligation to me. As far as my life was concerned, I was very happy. Things were normal back home, the Gavits seemed to have recovered from the infamy their daughter had earned them, Vidya continued to play a sweetheart, and Vivek was by my side always. I couldn't ask for more from God.

The first exams went well and Vivek was sure about not only passing, but also getting good marks. I left for Baroda during the Diwali vacations. These holidays were going to be my most memorable in recent years since I had the opportunity to celebrate Diwali in Nepal. Together with my brother, sister-in-law and five cousins, I spent twelve days in that beautiful country. I missed Vivek a lot and wished he was with me to make my happy days happier. I took many photographs of the mesmerising landscapes and also captured with my camera glimpses of the culture of the Nepalese. I was eager to show Vivek those pictures and to talk to him about my trip.

From Nepal, I had purchased a woollen sweater for Vivek. Hoping to have a good time with him, I was anxiously waiting for his arrival in Valai. He was to come on the last day of the vacation. Chandni's memories had almost vanished from his mind, so this was the best time to admit my love for him. It was now impossible for me to stay away from him. Then there was also the danger of his getting attracted to someone else, so it was better that I confessed the truth about myself. But, since it wasn't going to be easy, I thought of putting my feelings on paper. There were still two days to his arrival, so I had plenty of time to pour my heart out in writing. I took my time, chose the best words to give my writing an emotional touch and expressed everything that I had always wished to tell him. Before putting that eight page letter in an envelope, I went through it twice and rewrote some parts. Then the envelope lay hidden in the drawer of my cupboard, waiting for his arrival. All the excitement of talking to him about my holidays in Nepal and the photographs and the sweater apparently faded before the letter which held the key to my future. Finally, the much awaited day came.

Standing alone on the edge of the sunset point, I was enjoying the cold wind that was ruffling my dry hair. The last rays of the evening had lit up the far edges of the mountain ranges in a golden glitter. Everything appeared to be just so perfect until a stray black stain of a huge cloud wafted out of nowhere and shrouded the sinking sun. All of a sudden, the pleasant evening breeze changed into a merciless wind. Dark shadows engulfed the atmosphere and plunged the surroundings into a murky wilderness. The air went arid, the light turned faint and broad clefts formed on the barren land. Before I could understand what was happening, my eyes caught sight of the neem tree just a few feet away from where I was standing. Bereft of the thick grove of fresh, green leaves, the crumpled, naked branches of the tree looked hideous! The dry neem leaves strewn on the ground under the tree swirled as the wind blew. The old roots of the tree appeared and then disappeared under a thick layer of yellow. I gazed at the tree without knowing how ominous it all was!

In a while, the wind picked up again and changed into a whirlwind. It took with it all the dry leaves resting at the foot of the neem tree. The swift vortex swirled towards me and in no time, before I could do anything to help myself, it hit me badly, tossing me up in the air and flinging me off the edge of the cliff. I found myself helplessly falling into a bottomless, infinite abyss. Plunging in that darkest well of death, I felt giddy and before my body hit the bed of the valley, I fainted.

Suddenly I was wide awake, and realized it was just a horrible nightmare. Bathed in sweat, I sat up on the bed for a while and then moved to the window to breathe in fresh air. I took a deep breath as I watched the neem tree bathed in moonlight. Thank God, it was just a nightmare, I said to myself. *Or was it an ill omen of some impending pitfall to occur in my life? Hopefully not.* I went back to sleep, but the dread wouldn't let me sleep.

The sense of foreboding was still there with me when I woke up the next morning. I had a sinking feeling that something wrong was about to happen. I was shaving when Vivek came in with Paresh. Seeing him I immediately began to hope for a nice time, but his face seemed to be telling another story. He looked drained. I was suddenly gripped with the feeling that something deeply wrong had happened. All my enthusiasm to meet him faded. As I went near him, I could see tears in his eyes and knew that something very wrong had befallen him.

'What?' I asked apprehensively.

He embraced me tightly and wailed loudly. I could feel the tremors in his body. My heart was racing.

'What's wrong? What happened?' I asked him in consternation, and looked at Paresh for the answer. He, too, was unable to speak and had tears in his eyes.

Vivek was a strong boy, so the way he's crying, I knew the reason had to be extremely serious. With my arms around him, I let him cry and kept patting his back gently. Moments later, he spoke with difficulty, 'My father—' His voice was choked and he couldn't talk further.

'What about your father?' I asked in apprehension.

In a trembling voice, he uttered, 'He . . . he's no more . . .'

I was shocked. My jaw fell open and suddenly tears rushed to my eyes. 'How did this . . .?' I left the question unfinished. Suddenly, it struck me that what I had seen last night wasn't just a nightmare. The premonition had come true.

'My father's gone . . .' Vivek uttered. He was finding it difficult to stand. Paresh and I helped him sit. I fetched a glass of water for him. We sat on either side of him.

'How did it happen? Was he sick?' I asked slowly.

He shook his head and told me all about it. The tragedy had befallen a fortnight ago. The evening before Diwali, his father had been busy in his field when a poisonous snake bit him and he fell unconcious. He was taken to the doctor but it was too late. While all that was happening and Vivek was in deep grief, I was making merry in Nepal, wishing for the boy's company. *Oh, God! I should have been here with him.* I regretted not being him when he needed me the most.

Vivek had arrived in Valai that morning and was to leave in the evening itself. I asked him if he could stay for a day, but he said his family was alone back home. And he was the only man in his family now. He didn't show any interest in having lunch, but I made him eat. He, Paresh and I ate together. He stayed at my place for the entire day and felt good after talking to me. All my excitement about telling him about my vacation had evaporated after hearing about his father's demise. I didn't show him the photographs I was so thrilled about. Neither did I give him the sweater I had purchased for him. And there was no chance I could give him the letter I had written for him. He was aggrieved and suffering, so this was not the right time to give him another jolt. We sat in my room and talked until it was time for his bus.

Vivek had come to collect his luggage from the hostel since he had decided to discontinue his studies. The entire responsibility of his family was on his shoulders now, so there was no chance he could go on with his education. One of his maternal uncles had called him to Rajkot to work with him in a garment factory and it was almost fixed unless he got some other job in close proximity. Though his mother and sisters didn't want him to go so far off, he was left with no choice. Making good money without higher education in Dangs was highly impossible. This place had lesser opportunities. However, Rajkot was a place where he could make money despite his low qualifications. And it was very important for Vivek to earn and save since his younger sisters were getting old enough to marry. He'd have to save for their marriages. With all the responsibilities on his shoulders, the young boy had become a man overnight. He was healthy and would be able to do a physically demanding job. I was sure that he would become what his father was to his family.

I understood the plight he was in, but the idea that he was to discontinue his studies displeased me. I didn't earn much, but had some savings since my necessities in Valai were limited. I had an offer for him. 'Vivek, whatever you're thinking for your family is very good, but I was thinking if you could finish your studies first. You already get the scholarship which, as far as I know, is enough for your education here. The issue is, livelihood for your family. What if I wish to help you with my earning? Would you take it?'

'No, sir. I can't.' That was an expected answer. I was ready for that since I was aware of his high self esteem. I needed to convince him.

'Look, you can pay me back any time in the future at your will. Consider it a loan.'

'I appreciate that, but I don't think that's an idea my mother would agree to. Besides, it's not only about my studies. My grandmother is asthmatic. My younger sisters also study. Then they'll get married someday. It's going to be too much. My father laboured in our farms like an animal. And now God has put me in this condition to test my abilities. I'll have to take my father's place. I also want to study, but it seems impossible now.'

'At least you can finish your twelfth. That would help you get a better job. Later, you can do graduation through correspondence with a job.' My suggestion seemed to have worked as he looked thoughtful.

'That's nice but . . .' he said with uncertainty. 'I'll have to talk to my mother.'

'Yes, you should.' What else could I say?

When he was about to board his bus, I reminded him again. 'Think about my proposal. Give me a call or write. I'll wait.' In truth, I was terrified at the thought of losing him.

'I shall.'

His positive reply fuelled my hopes. I looked into his eyes and I could see the promise of moving forward with this hope in them. I gave him a tight hug which was much needed for both of us in this time of uncertainty. My eyes suddenly flooded as the bus slowly disappeared in the evening fog. Looking up in the sky, I said a silent prayer with a sinking heart. *God, show him the right path.*

twenty seven

The following days were full of uncertainity for me since I was doubtful about Vivek's coming back. I was also feeling helpless in dealing with the mounting nervousness of losing my love. I was ready to help him financially and had done my utmost to convince him, but it was entirely up to him whether to accept my proposal or not. Not knowing what was written in his and my destiny, I was hoping against hope to have him back in my life. Everyday, I prayed to God to bring him back to me. When I remained agitated because of the uncertainty of the future of my love life, I decided to visit him.

There at his place, I first paid my condolence to his mother and sisters over the tragedy, and then I asked Vivek what he had thought about my proposal. He said he too wanted to pursue his studies, but the circumstances were not supportive. He told me that his maternal uncle had fixed a job for him in Rajkot and he didn't want to disappoint his elders. His uncle felt that completing class twelve wouldn't be of much help in finding a better job. I asked if I could confer with his uncle, but Vivek said there was very little hope. I could have talked to Vivek's mother on that subject, but it was of little use since the poor woman seemed entirely dependent on her brother. Very disappointingly, Vivek said he would have to go by what his elders had decided. He thanked me for my gesture, and I had to give up in the end. It was done. God had been cruel not only to Vivek but also to me. The obstacle named Chandni was history, but who knew it would be his father's death that would set us apart. The tragic death of the man had really sabotaged all my dreams.

I gave him the sweater that I had purchased for him from Nepal. He promised me that he'd visit me before leaving for Rajkot, and I returned home with a heavy heart. I had tried my best to convince him to accept money from me, but my attempts had proved futile. The same thing had happened to me when Krishna had decided to get married. I had chased him, while destiny had cruelly driven him away from me.

When I thought about the entire situation, I realized that I was just being selfish. Vivek was recovering from the loss of his father and all I was worried about was the future of my love life. Seemingly, my offer that I wanted to help Vivek financially, so that he could finish his schooling, was a noble one, but the truth was that I didn't want him to go away from me and that's why I had tried to help him in every possible way. *How could I have been so selfish! How terrible it is to lose your dear one! How could I not think about Vivek's family!* His family needed him to work, to earn and to take his father's place. And what I was doing was selfish. I had wanted him to be with me and for that I had tried to use my money. This thought left me disconsolate with an overpowering sense of guilt and self hatred. Being with me longer would have cost Vivek something very precious for a man. Sooner or later, he might have ended up becoming a homosexual in my company. It felt as if God had saved him from me. Neither of us liked the separation, but it probably was the best thing that could have happened to him. The other notion that hit my brain was more logical. Separation from Vivek was the punishment God had given me for playing the villain between Vivek and Chandni. I didn't let Chandni have her love, God didn't let me have my love. That's what I really deserved.

All the fun from my life was gone in Vivek's absence. I realized how important a role he had played in my life! There were other people around me who were important to me. The Gavits and Vidya. But Vivek was Vivek. No other person could take his place. I missed him each and every moment.

It was past nine and I was making my bed when my heart—I don't know why, began to beat irratically with a premonition all of a sudden. I felt uneasy so I went to the window and opened it to inhale some fresh air. I tried to relax, and looked around. A murky moonlight was faintly lighting the quiet surroundings and the neem tree looked like a sage seated motionless in meditation for years. Suddenly, the dead wind picked up and the leaves of the tree rustled. The breeze relieved me of my agitation and I stayed at the window until the phone rang. It was Vivek.

'What a pleasant surprise! How are you?' I was so elated to hear from him.

'I'm fine. Thanks. Uh-huh . . . I'm sorry but I'll have to leave for Rajkot tomorrow,' he said. This was no less than a blow for me.

'How come?' My elation faded away in no time. 'It just doesn't make any sense!'

He replied, 'It was not planned at all, sir. I just got a call from my uncle this afternoon and . . . sorry I couldn't come to see you.'

Damn you! I cursed his uncle in my mind and spoke irritably, 'I wanted to see you so badly. For the last time . . .' I felt my throat choke and it was getting tough to go on talking.

'Same here, but . . .' I could hear a heavy sigh over the phone. 'It seems impossible now.'

'Tell me how will I live without you? What will I do in your absence?' I fought back my tears.

'I don't know. Even I am hating this . . . I don't want to go away from a friend like you, but I'll have to.' He was sounding equally low. 'Find yourself a friend. I'm sure you will. I'll pray to God to help you get a nice friend.'

'Oh, yes.' I tried to control my emotions. 'I might get another friend, but I won't get one like you. There's no one like you. No one can be like you. No one can take your place in my life.'

There was no response from the other end. He had been touched by what I had said. Probably, no one had let him know how important a person he was in their life. His heart was welling up just like mine.

It took me a while to ask, 'When do you leave?'

'My bus is at 5 a.m.'

'Okay. What else can I say but, take care!'

'You too. Bye.'

'Bye.'

He hung up and I, utterly dispirited, stared at the receiver until the tears gushed out from my eyes. I wiped them away and lay on the settee. *Vivek*, I whispered into the silence. I wanted to cry out of pain but I couldn't. *I just want to meet you once. One last time. God knows when you would return. I wish I could . . .*

I was grieving about not having a chance to see him until my mind hit upon an idea. I was overjoyed. I decided to go to Vivek's place to bid goodbye to him. It was 9.30 at night and Vivek's village was nearly thirty-five kilometres from Valai. I reckoned that there was plenty of time to reach his place. Obviously, there was no night bus available for that route. The last one had left at 7.45 p.m. It was no big deal. I rushed to Mr Gavit and took his bike. He gave me the keys and asked, 'Where to? At this hour?'

'I'll tell you later. Be back in the morning!' I replied and got back home. Had I told him I was going up to the Kurkas, he either wouldn't have let me go or would have asked to accompany me since travelling alone through the jungle and the mountain passes at night was not safe.

Taking into account that it was night time and the ghats were dangerous, I calculated that it would take me nearly two hours to reach Vivek's place, so I decided to leave at 2 a.m. but sleep had vanished from my eyes. The realization that Vivek was going to leave me had shattered me. But I was happy that I was going to see him before he left. During that long wait of nearly four hours, I prayed again and again to God to make it possible for him to meet me. Finally when the clock showed 1.45 a.m., I put on my jeans, T-shirt, leather jacket and shoes. I took a torch and a metal rod with me, for safety. While getting dressed, I remembered the letter in the cupboard. For a while I contemplated giving it to Vivek, but then I realized that it still wasn't the best time. So many tragedies had happened in his life that he needed a break from anything unexpected. The turbulence in his life must settle down first. The secret of my true feelings should only be revealed once he gets back to normal life.

It was the first time that I was driving after midnight in the Dangs and the experience was scary. It was the beginning of winter and hence I was continually being hit by strong gusts of freezing wind. After driving for a few kilometres, I was chilled to the bones and wished that I had put on something else beneath the jacket. In the absence of the moon, I could only see what the headlight of the bike lighted up. No help would be available if the bike broke down in the middle of the daunting jungle. Then there was the danger of coming across a leopard. I had risked beyond anyone's imagination, but then it was all for Vivek. I so desperately wanted to meet him that I was ready to court death.

Throughout that formidable drive of two hours, I kept praying to Lord Shiva to be with me and make my daring attempt to meet Vivek a success. I reached Vivek's village safely. The dilapidated bus stop on the outskirts of his village was deserted. It was not 5.00 a.m. as yet. I had reached before time and since there was no point in waiting there, I decided to go to his house.

Before knocking at their door, I wondered what Vivek would think of my visit. He will surely be surprised, I thought, breathing hard, I then moped my perspiring palms on my pants, and knocked. It was his mother who opened the door. She was so surprised to see me that she even forgot to invite me in. She went inside to call Vivek who was getting dressed. Vivek was equally astonished to see me at his door.

'I just wanted to meet you,' I said, looking directly into his eyes.

'Don't you know how risky it is to travel at night in the Dangs? And that too alone?' he asked as his eyes checked out if there was somebody behind me.

'Anything for you.' He liked my answer. I sat inside with him until he was ready to leave. While Vivek's sisters stayed at home, his mother and cousin joined us to see Vivek off to the bus stop. There were still five minutes to go, so we had a chance to talk.

'I'll wait for your letter,' I said with a heavy heart. 'Write to me about your life there. And take care of your health. Don't give up exercising.'

'I shall,' he replied with an affectionate smile.

From the pocket of my jacket, I took out an envelope that contained two thousand rupees.

'What's this?' he asked as I placed it in his hand.

'Keep it,' I said. 'You'll need it.' I was still holding his hand. Between our palms was that envelope. It didn't take him long to understand there was money inside.

'No, sir. I can't take it. It's . . .' he hesitated.

'Please.' My eyes met his.

'But I . . . I have enough money. I don't think I need more. Really.' He was still hesitant but looked adorable as he smiled.

'Take it as a gift from a friend.' He still didn't seem positive, so I had to say, 'Please, Vivek. Accept it for the sake of our friendship.'

Vivek looked at his mother for her permission.

'She wouldn't say no,' I said, turning my head to his mother. 'Would you?'

The woman smiled and nodded. I looked back at Vivek and he finally put the envelope in his bag. He then talked to his mother and cousin until the bus arrived. He touched his mother's feet and shook hands with his cousin and me. He was about to board the bus when I called him from behind. He turned towards me and I gave him a tight hug. Separation from my dear ones had always pained me so much and only I knew how hard it was for me to control my tears on such moments. 'I'll miss you.' I managed to speak with a choked throat, in a mawkish tone.

'Me too,' he croaked. 'You've been such a friend, philosopher and guide that I'll surely miss you.'

Whatever he said meant a lot to me. It made me realize my importance in his life. 'I love you,' I whispered in his ears so that no one else could hear it.

'Me, too,' he murmured in my ears.

We didn't separate until the conductor spoke aloud, 'Make it quick!'

He boarded the bus, took a seat by the window and gave me one last look, his eyes expressing gratitude. Our eyes met for a brief second and we exchanged smiles before he glanced at his mother and cousin, and waved. The next moment the old bus rattled down the stony road. The whirr of the bus could be heard even after the vehicle had vanished into the distance. To conceal my tears, I looked in another direction, took my spectacles off and wiped my unseen tears. Then I bid goodbye to Vivek's mother and cousin, and set out for Valai with the lasting image of Vivek's smiling face. I thanked God for making our meeting possible. It was still a little dark and I was driving alone, but nothing intimidated me. I had got what I wanted. I was so lucky that I could meet Vivek on time. At the same time I was sad that I wasn't going to see him again for very long. All I had to do now was to live with the memories the boy had left behind. As I remembered his parting words, tears trickled down my cheeks and froze in the chilly wind.

Life became insipid after Vivek's departure. After Krishna's episode, once again I encountered the same dilemma of isolation from my soul mate. How frightening the loneliness was! How tough it was to overcome the agony of solitude! Unable to fight, I accepted the loneliness as an unavoidable part of my life. I persuaded myself that I needn't run away from the weary emptiness that Vivek's departure had caused. I couldn't escape from the affliction of separation from my love. Neither did I need to. I had to accept all the miseries of my life with open arms just the way I had accepted and welcomed all the joyous times. But it wasn't that easy to live without the person who had been a part of my existence for so long.

Without Vivek, I didn't like anything. I found myself unable to push him out of my mind even for a second. I talked to him in my mind and nursed the memories of the happy days that I had spent with him. Even at school, when I taught Vivek's class, my eyes tried to search for him amongst the boys. Again and again, they turned to the place where he used to sit. Finding someone else in his place, I would get disappointed. When all that longing and brooding became unbearable, I cursed myself about letting him go. Why hadn't I stopped him?

Not physically, but in my mind he stayed with me while eating, bathing, sleeping and in doing practically everything. So much so, that it began to affect my health. His absence had created a vacuum in my life and had affected my food habits and sleep patterns. I lost weight and my cheeks became sunken. I became as thin as I used to be in my college days. And when people started to ask me the reason for my drained look, I made up my mind to stop brooding over my lost love, but it wasn't easy. All the excitement had been sucked out of my life. Now, it was about waiting all the time. Endless waiting.

I was so excited the day I got a letter from Vivek. He had written that he was fine at Rajkot, liked his job and was satisfied with his salary. I was glad to know that he was getting along with his uncle's family pretty well. He wrote that he remembered me everyday and missed the life he had in Valai. Then he asked me to let him know my secret. I sat on my table and wrote to him right away with the pen he'd gifted me on my birthday.

Dearest Vivek,

Life without you has turned drab. It is tough. I wake up, get ready for school, do my job, get back home and sleep, that's about all. I don't remember you because I don't have to remember you. We have to remember them who are away from us, out of our memory. You have become such an inevitable part of my existence that you stay with me all the time, no matter what I'm doing. I miss you so much that I've actually started talking to you in my mind. I discuss my day with you and try to cajole myself into believing that you are with me all the time. I have given up Chinese food since I don't like it without you. I seldom go to the sunset point now. When I meet your friends, I ask them about you, but they know as much as I do. I pray to God for your good health and for showering blessings upon you.

I'm dying for your company and it's hard to live without you, but I'll have to manage somehow. You are not with me, but I have the memories of the pleasant times we shared. Thanks for those precious moments you gifted me and thanks for making my life so special. As far as the secret is concerned, it's still not the right time for the revelation.

Take care and keep writing to me at your convenience. Give me your contact number. Do let me know when you will pay a visit to your home. I'll come to see you if you can't come to Valai.

Missing you all the time.

Kaushik

I could have written more, but thought that would be enough for a first letter. Now all I had to do was to wait for his reply.

Mayur Patel

twenty eight

Earlier the neem tree used to be just an object, I had now personified it as a female friend after Vivek's departure. Now I could relate myself to the tree more so because, like her, I too was alone. I got used to sitting under the tree and actually started to talk to her in my mind. Then I thought of giving the tree a name. For several days, I searched for a proper name that would do justice to the beauty of the tree. Maya—the name flashed in my mind. It means affection, attachment, and fondness. I had affection for many people in my life and I always found it hard to liberate myself from such attachments. Maya, the name I had given the tree was both feminine and perfectly signified the beauty and nature of the neem tree.

Almost every day, I sat under her shade and talked to her. I asked her how she was and told her about my life. And soon, she knew the whole story of my life. I talked to her about Vivek and told her how much I loved him. *Maya, I got a call from Vivek last night. He is happy there. It was good to talk to him. It has always been. I wish he would have everything he's ever dreamed of. He's the most special person in my life since Krishna. I really love him so much.* My thoughts would go on and on and on. After all, she was the only one to whom I could confess my true feelings. But I was cautious that it all went on only in my mind lest someone found me talking to a tree and took me to be insane. Without using my lips and tongue, I talked to her. And I felt she responded by flapping her leaves. I would ask her something that could be answered in 'yes' or 'no', and then wait for the fluttering. The wind would blow, the neem leaves would flutter and I would make out the answer at my own discretion. For example, I asked, 'Will I have Vivek back in my life?' And she always gave a positive answer. It was a silly thing to do—such wishful thinking! Whatsoever, Maya became a good friend of mine and I liked to bare the secrets of my heart to her.

Vivek called me up the day he received my letter. We talked about a lot of things and he told me not to stop visiting the sunset point and not to quit eating Chinese food. I asked him about how he was doing with his job, and he replied that, though it was not a tough job, he was getting bored of the monotony of his work. It made me sad, but then he had to cope with whatever he had in his hands. He asked me about Valai and our school and his hostel and his classmates and friends and teachers. I talked pleasantly about it all those things and the people, and he was happy to hear about it all from me. It felt good to have a chat with him and I had really laughed after days. His departure had stolen the joy from my life and only he could bring it back.

To learn to live without Vivek was the toughest ordeal I had ever faced in my whole life. Each and every moment I had spent with him was as fresh as the morning breeze in my mind. I would close my eyes and his smiling face would flash before me. Remembering the pleasant time I had with him, I would smile and then, with the thought that that time will never be back, I would cry. I tried to keep myself busy, but I couldn't keep him out of my mind even for a single second.

He in turn, kept writing to me and shared with me the experiences of his new life. Though he was busy in Rajkot, he never forgot to reply to my letters. That proved how much he cared for me. Many times, I had thought of posting him that special letter but the fact that it carried disturbing, unpleasant secrets of mine kept me from doing so. What if someone else would come to read it!

Living in extreme solitude, I was leading a tedious life. I started to give much of my time to meditation and yoga. I meditated and prayed to God to give me strength to survive the pain Vivek's leaving had caused me. To fill in the emptiness, I started to spend even more time with books. The library was a great relief and it was only reading which kept Vivek out of my mind. I chose to spend my mornings and evenings at the library since there was no one to go out with. Sometimes, Mr Gavit accompanied me, but he hardly found time from his travelling job.

In the meantime, Vivek's birthday came and I remembered how we had celebrated Vivek's last birthday. The location we had chosen were the banks of river Ambika. How we had struggled to light the candles in the wind! And how naughtily I had stuffed a big piece of cake in his mouth! How emotionally I had wished him 'Happy Birthday'! I had hugged him tight and remained in that state longer than necessary. Such an exquisite celebration it had been! I wished he was with me on this birthday too to have the same fun. In fact, I had asked him if he could come to Valai for the auspicious day. Even though he wanted to, he couldn't. Early morning on 13 December, I gave him a call and wished him. I missed him the most that day. The same day, I purchased a nice shirt for him and sent it to Rajkot.

I missed Vivek every second and whenever his memories saddened me, I went to Maya and talked to her, or I sat with the photo album and looked at his pictures. Time heals everything and geographical distance helps you detach yourself from the memories of your close ones. Had Vivek been away from me for long, the memories might have faded. But we happened to see each other at regular intervals and that didn't let me forget him. The way Vivek had taken Krishna's place in my life, Vivek's place might have been filled had I fallen in love with someone else. But there was no one like Vivek. I had no idea about the future of my love life but one thing I was sure was that I wasn't going to forget him, no matter what happened. I loved him so much that to detach myself from him was next to impossible.

Once or twice a year, we met and spent some memorable time together. Whenever he came to his place, he paid me a visit. He stayed at my place and we did everything we used to do when he was in school—sitting at the sunset point for hours, going for lovely excursions on the bike, and having Chinese food. It was great to talk to him about old times. Every time he visited me, I would make up my mind to give him the letter, but something always stopped me. And I would console myself that there always would be a second chance. I waited for the right time.

Often, he told me to visit Rajkot, mentioning that there were so many beautiful places worth a visit. So, I went there during the Diwali holidays. I stayed with him for a week and he became my guide as we travelled through the land of Saurashtra. That was the best vacation I had since the tour of Nepal. Again every time we met, I'd make up my mind to express my real feelings, but I didn't dare for fear of losing his friendship.

Years elapsed this way. Almost every year, someone close to me got married. Vidya Parmar got married to a civil engineer. I was glad that she had finally found the man of her choice. I attended her marriage with my colleagues. There was a smile on her face that everybody could see, but her eyes told a different story. Perhaps only I knew what that was. Without uttering a single word, she let me know through her eyes that the marriage was no more than a tender compromise. There still was love for me in those eyes. After marriage, she settled in Bharuch. I missed her a lot too. We talked over the phone occasionally. My sister, Ridham, also married a professor in Baroda. I didn't know how much Karan, Ridham's husband, knew about my past but he was such a decent man that he never made me feel uncomfortable by asking me anything unpleasant. He was so gracious that he hardly interfered in anybody's personal life. Ridham was lucky to have a spouse like him.

In between, news of Chandni's marriage hit my ears one day, and I told Vivek about it over the phone. For a moment or two, there was complete silence at the other end and then, he started talking about other things. He completely evaded the issue without giving it any importance. He was hurt, I knew he was. Otherwise, he would have talked, asked about her. He still hadn't forgotten her. He still hadn't forgotten his first love.

Three years later, Vivek's younger sister got married in a nearby village. That occasion gave me a chance to stay with Vivek for three days and we thoroughly enjoyed the marriage. Since I was not his teacher any more, I once again told him to call me by my name, but he wouldn't do so. He continued to address me as 'sir'. Vivek's skin had turned a shade darker because Rajkot is a warm place. But who cared?

Though looks mattered, I loved the man behind that skin. I loved his soul which was so pure and innocent like a dew drop on a winter morning. Physically, he'd changed a lot. Whenever I met him, I found him healthier, taller and more muscular. But from inside, he was still the same, as child like as I had known him years ago. The innocence I had found in him at the age of seventeen, was still there at twenty-one.

I turned thirty and my marital status started to bother my mother because everyone around, even the younger ones, were getting married. She must have thought that during the past six years, my sexual preference would have changed. But since it was still the same, I told her to put the thought of my marriage out of her mind and not to worry about my future. But she was a mother. She dreamed of seeing my happy family before closing her eyes forever. The poor woman was dreaming of something that was totally impossible.

Life is full of surprises. Not always does it go according to plans. One sombre evening, when I got back from school, an envelope was waiting at the door of my house. It was an invitation of marriage. Vivek's marriage!

When I read his name on the envelope, I suddenly felt sick as if I was having a cardiac arrest. I felt dizzy and had no clue about how to deal with those paralysing moments. When it became difficult for me to stay on my feet, I sank into the chair in the veranda. *Vivek is getting married.* I was bewildered. *How come he never told me? How could he keep me in the dark about this?* For confirmation, I read the name again. It was Vivek. I rapidly went through the entire card and found the names of his mother and uncles and aunts. It was them all right. It was *my* Vivek's marriage. For many minutes, I didn't know how to react.

And when I realized, it was too late to do anything and that he was out of my reach now, I cried.

After letting my frustration pour out, I decided to give him a call. I washed my face and dialled his number in Rajkot. When he came on the line, I asked him about it and he told me how it had happened. Throughout the conversation that lasted for about twenty minutes, I was cautious not to sound disheartened. I had to act and sound as if I was excited about the news of his marriage.

Vivek was just twenty-two and he wasn't convinced about getting married at such a young age, but people got married early in his caste. It was his elders who had chosen the girl and arranged everything had believed that since Vivek's youngest sister was still unmarried, there was no chance of his marriage, as was the custom in his village. That's why I had always thought that I still had time to express my feelings to him. What actually happened was that his youngest sister being good in studies had expressed her desire to study further. Vivek wanted her to fulfil her dream since he had not been able to do so himself. That's why he agreed to get married before his sister.

Standing by the window of my room, I looked at the tree. The fall season had stripped Maya and made her look gaunt and ugly. I never liked that bleak appearance. I compared myself to her. Without Vivek, my condition would be the same. Vivek's presence in my life was the only reason for me to smile, and now when even the thinnest hope of having him in my life had died, I was in no better state than the tree that stood naked, ruined and forlorn on the hill. It was as if the barrenness of the tree symbolized that my condition would be similar without Vivek.

All the whimsical dreams I had woven had smashed on the land of bitter reality and were now shattered to pieces.

The dreams of the future I had envisaged with Vivek were buried in some deep and dark pit of despair. The silent scream that had arisen from some ruined corner of my torn heart carried unbearable pain. I found myself left in a dark hovel of depression with all the doors locked. There was no direction to take. Clouds of solitude and dejection engulfed me and no streak of light or hope was visible. Demeaning myself, I had earned uncountable transgressions in the chase of the impossible dream that someday I'd attain Vivek's love. What I got after all the conspiracies and intrigues was nothing. I found myself empty handed. I was left with the residues and dregs of all the hopes, dreams and desires that Vivek's company had brought into being. The feeling of failing in love for the second time left me half dead. Life seemed meaningless, futile, and my mind was choked with suicidal thoughts. Alone at the sunset point, I tried to measure the depth of the valley.

Crestfallen and jaded, I would have led myself to self destruction. I might have searched in alcohol the remedy for the pain of losing my beloved. But I didn't do anything of that sort. I let my eyes shed tears, I tried to squeeze gloom out of my broken heart. Then a thought that I should meet Vivek and tell him everything I had buried in the depths of my heart, crossed my mind. But I stopped. I knew it was too late for that too. I had already lost him as a lover, but I didn't want to lose him as a friend. I had no choice but to seek my joy in his happiness. Vivek had the right to live his life the way he wanted and with the person he liked. And that person was definitely not me. I had no right to spoil his present and future.

Burying all my dreams, I attended Vivek's marriage much against my will. It was organized at his village and I stayed with Vivek throughout the celebration that lasted for three days. From inside, I was totally broken, shattered, but I didn't let it appear in my behaviour. Wearing a fake, wide smile, I behaved as if I was in high spirits. My bruised heart was groaning in acute pain, but I managed to play the opposite like a good actor. His wife, a nineteen year old girl from a nearby village, was slim and beautiful. Vivek and she made a perfect couple. I blessed the newly wed couple and retreated into my own world of misery and emptiness.

Locking myself up in the bathroom, I stood under the shower with all my clothes on and cried the way I had never cried in my whole life. It was rage against God, against Vivek, and against myself that streamed out. Like a child, I complained to God for snatching away my love once again. I had always believed that Lord Shiva was with me all the time, in everything I did. Even in the meanest deeds of mine, I deemed that He was there with me to help. In Vivek's case, I proposed mean desires and He disposed them all. It is said that God punishes silently. I had played devil in Vivek's love life and what I received from God in return were invisible, incurable lesions. I howled and asked Him why he brought Vivek into my life, why He had made me fall in love with him if He didn't want our destinies to be one. I tore my shirt, hurled it on the floor and hit the walls with my fists in anger. I fell on my knees when I felt too weak to stand. I didn't even know for how long all that crying and complaining went on. When no more tears were left, I looked into the only mirror in the bathroom and saw reflected the most piteous image of me. I hated the very sight of myself as I thought how bad a person I had become. After indulging in all the conspiracies, depravity and evilness, I did not deserve to be alive. Sinister thoughts of ending my life took control of my brain again and I found it hard to fight them. The despondency was far more acute than it was when I had broken up with Krishna. I thought I should have nipped my feelings in the bud. But how could I have? Vivek was so nice and sweet and likable that I hadn't been able to. It had been my destiny to regress into the same heart rending pain of failing in love once again.

I stayed in the same frame of mind for several days. It was tough to put on the act of being a happy person throughout the day, even more tough was to spend sleepless nights. I found it hard not to let my heart weep over the desolation that Vivek's marriage had brought upon me. *Someday he'll leave me forever.* I had thought that once and the fear had come true. Vivek had left me forever. There was no chance I could get him back ever. The letter that held the truth about my sexuality and love still lay in the drawer of my cupboard. I pulled it out and started to read it, but couldn't go beyond a few lines. It blinded my eyes with tears and I had to set that useless bunch of papers to fire. It was not the papers that were burnt that day, it was my dreams, expectations and optimism that died that day.

In that tough time of loneliness and melancholy, books on positive thinking came to my rescue. I went through them and also read the *Bhagvad Gita,* and learnt that self annihilation was no remedy for the despair I was dealing with. The sermons Lord Krishna had given Arjun on the battlefield of Kurukshetra led me to spiritual enrichment, and helped me get out of the sick state of my mind. Isn't it enough that I've loved someone? I asked myself. *Why should I expect to receive the same sort of love from Vivek? What if he doesn't love me? What if he isn't going to be with me? And how could the two of us live together forever? He has*

no future with me. God has bestowed me this beauteous
feeling of love—the greatest of all in the universe. Then
why should I cry over the issue as if it was a failure? My
relationship with Vivek is one of the best things that ever
happened in my life. When I accepted him as a blessing
of Lord Shiva, then taking our relationship to be a failure
would be like insulting the Almighty. I mustn't do that.
This thought process made me feel better and relieved. I
consoled myself that at least I loved a person who had
been loyal to me. I was content with the feeling that I had
loved a good human being, a nice soul.

This was the second time that all those scriptures had
helped me ease my suffering. The same had happened after
my break-up with Krishna. Then, I had tried to search for
the joy of life in the people around me, but what I had learnt
from those books was that we must not expect happiness
from others because no one else can make us happy but
we, ourselves. The key for being happy is inside us. We
just need to find it.

Vivek paid me a visit with his wife after marriage and
I welcomed them with a fake smile, and put on an act of
being exultant. He was happy with his marital life and that
showed in his attitude. That quirky, boyish appearance was
gone and he looked like a grown man now. They didn't
stay for long since they had to leave for Rajkot after two
days and they had plenty of other people to meet. Having
visited the school and hostel, he left for his village. And
before leaving, he asked me to get married too and I smiled.
I just smiled. I wished he could fathom the pain behind that
smile. He also told me to call and write to him. I nodded,
but I was determined neither to phone nor to write. I just

wanted him to be out of my life completely. I just wanted to forget him. But the big question was—would I? Had it been that easy, I would have forgotten Krishna by now. Even after falling in love with Vivek, I hadn't forgotten Krishna. Then how could I forget Vivek? It was something that I would never be able to do. Krishna and Vivek were indelible parts of my being. And now, I had to learn to live without Vivek. I had to.

twenty nine
─────────

In life not all dreams come true. My desire of getting Vivek was one such unfulfilled fancy. It was not going to come true. Ever.

Surrounded by an indescribable burden of grief, I didn't know where God was planning to take me. One by one, He had separated me from my close ones. Forever gone was Mrs Desai who had been no less than my own mother. Forever gone was Mr Desai from whom I had learned so much about life. And now, forever gone was Vivek, the apple of my eyes. I lost my interest in life and had no idea about what to do, where to go. All the places in Valai—the sunset point, the neem tree, school and hostel buildings, the Chinese restaurant—reminded me of Vivek. I saw him everywhere, and to escape this insufferable situation, I even thought of leaving Valai. I seriously contemplated about shifting to a city to lose myself in the life that I had left behind long ago. But I doubted if that would be helpful since Vivek's memories still gushed in my blood and it was impossible to efface them completely.

Vivek continued to call and write, and I continued to reply. The grief of losing him might have healed in the long run, but staying in touch didn't make that possible. After talking to him on the phone and reading his letter, my heart always wept. My situation was terrible and I had no idea how to cope with it. Ceaseless brooding over the failure of the relationship caused me to have a nervous breakdown. Unable to fight the terrible wretchedness any longer, I lost my appetite and sleep and lost considerable weight. The deep insights I had gathered from the books on positive thinking were washed away. Seized by negative energies, I fell ill. My close ones in Valai were worried about me and I had no reason to give when they asked me about my sickness.

Our grief appears to be larger and severe in solitude, away from our nearest and dearest. Though there were nice people in Valai to take good care of me, I desperately needed someone who I was really close to. I longed for my mother, and finally, when the situation became truly unbearable, I had to take a long leave to go to Baroda. I was so pale and thin that my mother couldn't recognize me at first. A warm hug from her was a great relief. I couldn't tell her the real reason for my poor health. Having seen my condition, the principal had given me permission to stay in Baroda until I was perfectly well. Everybody thought my problem was just physical, but only I knew it was mental. Secretly, I consulted a psychologist and it was he who helped me get out of that nervous breakdown.

When I was on the mend at home, I got a call from Michael, an old friend from college who was a writer and had recently won one of the most prestigious awards in literature for his third book. He invited me to Mumbai for the celebration he had organized. Although I accepted the invitation, I had no intention of going there. However, just before the day of the party, I thought it would be fun to be with an old friend after so long. I might even be lucky to meet some other friends too. Moreover, I hadn't visited Mumbai in years so I packed my bags and left for the city.

There, I had fun as expected. For old time sake, Michael had invited many of his school and college friends, but only a few had come. Sneha, Binita, Vibha and Javed were pleased to see me. Michael was a great host and we had the luxury of staying in a four star hotel for three days. Back with my old friends, I once again became what I used to be in my college days, careless, talkative and vibrant. We partied, watched movies, shopped, talked about myriad memories of our college days, and ate the best food available in Mumbai. In their company, I forgot all my miseries. During that happy time, I learned that everybody was happy in his life except for me. And all I had to do was to pretend to be happy with my life too.

On the last day of my stay in Mumbai, Michael insisted that I stay with him for one more day and I couldn't turn down his request. That day, he took me to a mall for shopping. We were in the middle of our shopping when he got an important phone call. I didn't know what the matter was—didn't want to know either—but he had to go meet the caller in no time. He apologized to me and told me that he'd be back within half an hour. After he left, I busied myself in roaming all over the place.

Life's unpredictable. The unexpected breaks into life without the slightest warning. And the unexpected was about to happen to me. I was trying to find something nice for my mother in the sari section, when some impulse made me raise my eyes from the rack and I saw a couple standing just a few feet away. The couple, busily going through the saris displayed in the glass window, was looking in the opposite direction and I could only see their backs. For a second, I thought I knew the man as his physique seemed to be familiar. Is it . . . Krishna? I asked myself.

Then I stood still, my eyes on the man, waiting for him to turn so I could see his face. Krishna? No, I told myself. *It can't be him. It can't . . .* I was about to turn away when the man turned his face to the woman by him and I saw the profile of his face. Yes, it was Krishna! *Krishna.* I was stupefied. My breath froze in my throat. I didn't know how to react. I didn't know whether to be happy or not. I didn't know if I should go meet him or not. I was completely lost.

The elation that had been generated with the sight of one time soul mate seemed to be fading away as I figured that the woman with him was his wife. I was going to turn my face in the other direction to hide from him, when he saw me. Our eyes met and froze. I forgot to blink. His reaction was no different. He was equally shocked at seeing me after so long.

We remained in that state of bewilderment until the woman touched Krishna's hand to direct his attention towards her. I was still uncertain about what to do. Escaping from there would have left questions about me in her mind as she had seen her husband look at me.

'Come,' I could hear Krishna say to the woman. They both came to me and Krishna stretched his hand to shake mine. In the past, we'd always greeted each other with a hug. But the present was different.

'Kaushik!' He looked surprised, and glad.

'Hi!' I gave my hand in his. It was a firm handshake.

'Meet my wife, Aastha.' He gestured to the attractive woman next to him and introduced us to each other. 'Aastha, this is Kaushik, a friend from college.'

He didn't say 'best friend'. I probably was never his best friend. I was more than that. I always was.

Aastha and I exchanged smiles. For a while, I stared at

that attractive lady, smartly dressed in a purple sari and a sleeveless blouse. Thin in built, she had waist long black hair and wore a warm smile on her fair, egg-shaped face. When I remembered Krishna, sometimes I would think of Aastha. *How beautiful would she be? Must be pretty.* I had no idea she would be so beautiful. Krishna was a lucky man to have such a woman.

'It's been a long time,' Krishna said. He looked more relaxed than me.

'Seven years,' I said and smirked to mask my uneasiness.

'Seven years?' he spoke in surprise as if he had no idea about it.

'That's a long time, indeed,' Aastha intervened. 'By the way, Krishna talks a lot about you. Good things. Praises. And I always wanted to meet the person Krishna calls his best friend. It indeed is a pleasure to meet you.'

I chuckled at what she had just said, 'Krishna talks a lot about you'. *Did he?*

'Dear, if you don't mind, would you excuse us for a while,' Krishna asked his wife.

'Oh, sure,' Aastha said. 'I've a lot to do with my shopping yet. You enjoy talking about old times.' Before she left us alone, Krishna told her to meet us at the restaurant on the ground floor, after she was done shopping.

'You enjoy talking about old times'. Aastha's words reverberated in my mind. There was nothing to enjoy about the old times.

Krishna and I sat across the table in a corner of the restaurant and he ordered some refreshments. I watched him as he was going through the menu card. He looked different from what he used to in college. His muscles had disappeared under layers of fat, his cheeks were puffed and a double chin had begun to appear, but the thing that shocked me was his tummy. It was not a pot-belly, yet it was clearly visible through the loose cloak he had worn. Age had affected him. He looked older than his age. In his comparison, I was fit and young. I bet nobody could guess that we were of the same age.

'Are you sick or something?' he started the conversation with a query.

'I was,' I replied. 'Much better now. How did you know?'

'Your eyes have gone deeper. And there are dark circles around them.' He was watching my face carefully.

He still observes the details of my face. Just the way he used to, years ago. After all, this is the face he was crazy about.

'But you look healthier,' I scoffed at the fat he'd put on. 'I had never expected you to be in this shape.'

'I've turned lazy. No exercise. I don't have time for it now, you know,' he said unenthusiastically. Seeing me snigger, he added, 'Okay, fine. It's a poor excuse.'

My smile changed into laughter. He showed me his tongue and said, 'Yes, yes. You can laugh at me like always.'

It seemed as if we had started to get back to our old form. He asked me about Baroda and our old friends. I told him about Michael and he was surprised to know that I had been with Vibha, Sneha, Binita and Javed. He regretted not getting a chance of meeting them. When I expressed my surprise about his absence at Michael's, he reminded me that the two had never liked each other in college. I remembered that despite being in the same group, Michael and Krishna had never been friends. They had some problems they could never resolve. We talked about others.

'Where's your cap?' I asked.

'I'm not ashamed of my curly hair any more.' He

touched his hair and smiled. The same positive attitude. I had always liked it.

'What have you told your wife about me?' I asked.

'I told her about what good buddies we were in college. And about some other things.' Suddenly, the smile vanished and he grew serious. 'I never forgot you. You were always there with me and will always be for the rest of my life.'

I was quiet for a while, then whispered adoringly, 'Same here.'

A minute or two passed in silence. 'Do you still believe that love is rubbish?' I asked as the waiter brought us our order.

'Not any more,' came the reply. 'I misjudged the word "love".'

Oh, yes. You did. I wish you had thought so years ago. I gazed at him longer than was necessary. 'How's your married life going?'

'Good. Ah . . . It's fun.' The way those words were spoken, I guessed it was not the complete truth. And he knew that I knew. 'Actually, it's sort of boring. Routine. Nothing exciting, honestly. But I'm happy nonetheless.'

'I think I'll have to talk to Aastha about this,' I said jokingly.

'Oh, sure. With great pleasure.' He was a bit loud. 'She knows it all. I've already told her many times.'

I laughed again. 'You're still the same,' I said sipping the pineapple juice from my glass.

'You too,' he said, biting into a cheese sandwich. 'We don't need to change ourselves, do we?'

'It's not you who changes yourself. It's life that does so.' The air was serious again.

'What's new in life?' he asked to steer the conversation from becoming serious.

'Ah . . . nothing special.' I tried to smile.

'It's okay. If you don't want to tell me . . .' he said, giving his lips an ironic curve.

'I've fallen in love again.' I said promptly and silenced him.

He had known I was hiding something. He could still read my face. I had my eyes fixed on him. In his heart, he was still the same. I was hesitant about telling him about Vivek. But then, he was the only person in the world whom I could disclose my secret feelings to and who could better understand my condition. Finally, I decided to pour my heart out to him.

'His name is Vivek.' Then I told him everything about Vivek and he listened to me carefully. When I was done, I asked him, 'I can't forget him. Neither do I have any chance to get him. You tell me, what should I do?'

Krishna was silent for long. Then he spoke, 'The crisis of being indecisive, of deciding what to do and what not to comes in every one's life. Right now, you are going through the same phase. Some people keep crying over spilt milk while others knit new hopes and move towards the future. The choice is yours. What you want to do is entirely up to you. Select the best possible way. We waste our energies and precious time in the wrong directions. As you know, I was a good football player in college, and had my mind set to make my future in that sport. Unfortunately, I couldn't forge ahead in that field because of the financial condition of my family and I still regret it. Circumstances snatched from my hands a chance to prove my abilities, of doing something big and extraordinary. You wanted to become a teacher and you achieved it, but now it's time to look back and dig out your past. There must be some wish that's yet to be fulfilled.

'Think and concentrate and see if you can find that. There surely would be something dormant in the dark corners of your heart that's still waiting for you to give it a call. What you need is to find it and put all your efforts into making it a success. You might find a new aim in life. Life brings us a lot of opportunities. You just need to wait for the right one and grab it. Keep your senses alert. It can strike from anywhere.'

Whatever Krishna said was worth paying heed to. It was time to turn a new leaf. Before we could talk more, Aastha appeared, her hands laden with shopping bags full of nappies and tiny, colourful clothes. Watching me stare at all the stuff, Aastha asked, 'Didn't he tell you?'

I looked at her, she looked at Krishna, and Krishna apologized to me, 'Sorry, I forgot. We're expecting a baby.'

For a second, I found it difficult to react. Perhaps, the possessiveness for Krishna was still there in me. And Krishna too knew, that's why he hadn't told me about the baby before. He must have known I wouldn't like the news. He was probably right. The news didn't thrill me, yet I smiled and congratulated them. I couldn't accept the fact that someone else possessed Krishna.

'I'm really hungry,' Aastha said and ordered. There was no chance Krishna and I could discuss the subject we had been on any more, so we talked about other trifling things until Aastha finished her meal. She talked a lot, but I liked that she was friendly.

When we were leaving, the lovely lady insisted I pay them a visit. Krishna gave me his card and said, 'Give me a call any time, think about what I said, take care of yourself and have a great future.' He stretched his hand. A strong wish to give him a hug arose for a second, the next second it was suppressed.

I saw them leave. Krishna is lucky to have such a wonderful wife, I thought. *That's what he deserves. May God bless them and their child!*

That meeting with Krishna had been productive in many ways. Having talked to him about my feelings for Vivek, I felt relieved. His words kept reverberating in my mind for the rest of the day. Later, while having dinner at Rosemary's, Michael told me about the subject of his next book and about his plans for the future. I listened to all that disinterestedly and nodded at everything without paying much attention. My mind was reeling with what Krishna had said. It was time to give my life a push into a new direction, but I was ignorant about the possible route.

Until midnight that day, I remained in search of that *something* Krishna had told me to keep my senses alert for. I had pondered over most of my childhood dreams and thought about those that were yet to be fulfilled. As a kid, I had dreamed about being a pilot and fancied flying in the sky. But it was just a dream. There was nothing in it that would change the path of my life. At the same time, I was so impressed with Krishna's words that I was sure that something would strike me sooner or later. But, that something was still mysteriously hidden.

Next morning, Michael drove me to the railway station to see me off. He was talking about a lot of things and I was just nodding and saying 'yes' but my mind was occupied with Krishna's thoughts. It had felt good to see him after such a long time, and I wished we could have chatted for longer. There still were things to be talked about, his parents, his village and his profession. So much had been left unsaid. *Do you still play football, make sketches?* And so on . . .

While I was in my reverie, at a traffic signal, two children dressed in rags appeared at the car window and started begging. Michaels's face distorted with dislike and repugnance as he searched for coins in his shirt pocket. He gave a five rupee coin to each and they moved towards another car. Their piteous faces looked so helpless and hopeless that I was shaken from inside. I couldn't take my eyes off them until the signal turned green and we moved on. Leaving those unfortunate souls behind, our vehicle made its way through the busy streets of Mumbai. *Something should be done for them,* the epiphany suddenly hit me. 'Keep your senses alert. It might strike from anywhere', I recalled those words.

Yes, this is it. The street children. They need to be helped. Something within me was suddenly awake. Krishna's words rang in my ears, 'You just need to wait for the right opportunity and grab it.' This is what Krishna had talked about. *This is the opportunity I was looking for! This really is it.* All of a sudden, I was exultant.

When the car stopped at the entrance of the Victoria Terminus station, I was determined about what I wanted to do. Michael asked me the reason for the excited glow on my face. I told him that I would let him know soon. Then I gave him a hug and boarded the train. When the train caught speed, the objects outside the window were left behind. A new sun of hope and zeal was rising.

thirty

I was never a philanthropist, but I had always had this feeling of sympathy for the poor, especially the children. When I was a kid, my mother used to take me to my school which was no more than half a kilometre from my house. On the way, we would pass by a slum where I would see many kids playing. Observing their dirty bodies and threadbare clothes, I'd ask my mother several questions, 'Why don't they dress like I do? Why don't they go to school? Why are they so unclean?'

I had no idea how hard my mother would have found it to answer. She would reply, 'They don't have what you have.'

'Why don't they have what I have?' would always be the next question.

'Because they are poor.' Mother had always been ready to satisfy my eagerness.

'Why are they poor?'

'Because their parents don't earn much.'

'Why don't their parents earn much?'

'Because they are not educated.'

'Why—?'

The questions emanating from my little brain had been countless but mother never got fed up of them. She was always so concerned about giving her children the right lessons. On the contrary, when I had bothered my father with such questions, he would get irritated and send me to my mother.

At that time, I had pitied the street children and had thanked God that I was not one of them. I had wanted to do something for them but felt I was too young to do anything appreciable that might better their lifestyle. Occasionally, during my college days, I would buy fast food for them from my pocket money. But the quantity was never enough. The food packets I bought for them were always less than the hands that stretched towards me. It was so difficult to satisfy the hunger of each one of them. Whoever got the food would be happy, but the dejection on the rest of the faces would make me sad. I wanted to see smiles on all the faces. But that wish had never come true.

That desire for doing something big for poverty stricken people had always remained in some deep corner of my heart, but it had never taken any form. Then Krishna had come into my life and become the centre of my existence. And I slipped into self merriment. Then break-up had changed the course of my life and I had shifted to Valai.

In Valai, the desire to do social work had arisen in me when I had come across the tribals. Their lifestyle told me that much was needed to be done for them. The funds from the government poured into the Dangs but most of the money was embezzled by the officials and hardly any help reached where it should have. The people in the farthest corners of the district were deprived of not just the facilities such as education and medicines, but also the basic necessities such as food and clothing. Again my main concern had been the children. There were primary schools in every other village and the children also went to primary schools in good numbers, but when it came to higher studies, most of them discontinued studying because of their financial condition or the absence of high schools and colleges nearby.

I had wanted to help them and mend the situation but once Vivek became the priority of my life, I had forgotten about everything else. It was now that I was free from all the attachments. It was all thanks to Krishna that I was ready to explore this desire of my life. He had showed me the right path just when I needed it the most. He was the man who always came to my rescue. I also owed a thanks to the children at the traffic signal. It had just taken the sight of those children in tatters to provoke my conscience and to ferret out the desire to do something for them within me.

On my way to Valai, I planned everything in steps. I met a few of my colleagues, the principal and Mr Gavit, and told them about my intentions and asked for their advice. Most of them responded positively and promised to back me up with whatever they could do. I started a Non Government Organization, which was to work for the welfare of the poverty stricken. The organization was named 'Udaan' which means 'flight'. Some of my well-wishers chipped in financially, and some joined my NGO as volunteers. We started concentrating on the children who had left schools because of several reasons. With my group of volunteers, I began visiting the remote villages and met those who wanted to study further, but couldn't. We surveyed the most backward of the tribal areas and studied their lifestyle. Only that way could we learn about their necessities and problems. Our salient concern was to help the needy in the best possible way.

Most people in my life were happy to know about this endeavour of mine. It really made me feel good since I was sceptical about getting support from many of them. They contributed and encouraged me more than I had anticipated. I talked to my mother over the phone about the NGO and she appreciated my mission. Ridham and Smit also sounded positive, but I didn't know whether they really liked my idea, because they were more like my father—career driven, ambitious and somewhat self centred. As far as my father was concerned, I was sure he would take this as one more stupid scheme of mine. That's why I held myself back from talking to him directly. I told my mother to tell him about my NGO.

Then I phoned Michael and updated him about the latest in my life. He was thrilled to know that it was in his company that I had decided to go in for this venture. He congratulated me and instantly talked about donating fifty thousand rupees to my NGO. I gave Krishna a call and he too was glad to know about my getting into social work. Before I hung up, I thanked him for exhorting me. Then I called up Vivek. For the first time since his marriage, I had no feeling of despair when I talked to him. He was equally excited about coming to Valai and seeing what I was doing for the Dangies. And sure enough, he paid me a visit a few weeks later, stayed at my home for three days and helped me in my work. I still liked him, loved him, but the urge to possess him mentally and physically didn't exist any more. All my vigour and abilities had been allotted to my work.

Earlier, most of my energy was spent in daydreaming and remembering the past. I used to live in worthless reveries. Now I was free from all those thoughts, both past and present, that were of no use. My mind had been the real cause of all my problems and most of my wounds had been self inflicted, therefore, instead of changing the world outside, I worked to amend the world inside me. I became conscious about my own insufficiencies and tried to reform them. I stopped looking at Vivek the way I used to. I stopped daydreaming and liberated myself from mental stress. I completely surrendered myself to Lord Shiva, and this understanding of my spirituality helped me control my carnal desires. I prayed for an invisible companion to be with me all the time and to show me the right way.

It took me a while, but I finally realized that 'nothing is permanent'. Indeed I had learnt this only after losing the two men I had been in love with. Fortunately, there were no more misgivings about not attaining their love forever. I had loved and lost twice, but I took all those bitter-sweet moments as learning experiences. I had learnt a lot from the mistakes of my past. I couldn't change the past, so I had changed my attitude towards it.

Now I don't remember my wrongdoings, neither do I regret anything any more. I don't miss my home or Krishna or Vivek because the boundaries of my life now extend far beyond them. My prime focus would be to enrich my present and future. Where I am today is because of those two wonderful men in my life. Had either of them been in my life the way I had wished, I wouldn't be here today. I would have to express my hearty thanks to them for making my life worthwhile in every way. I am glad that they are still in my life, guiding and helping me through this new venture.

Many times in the past, I had thought of leaving this material world, of getting rid of all the attachments and walking away. Had it been so easy, every second man on earth would have been a saint. There was no need to become a monk because I had found a better goal in my life. A goal that was greater than my own personal desires.

For a long time I had been living a shallow life. Now it had some meaning. A meaning that had led me to inner fulfilment.

Earlier, I used to seek happiness in people, in things. I used to think that happiness could be found through something, somebody. My moments of bliss relied upon others. But now, there was no dependence upon anyone because giving held the key to my spiritual contentment and lasting happiness. A considerable part of my time was consumed by this new activity that brought me great relief from all the miseries and frustrations of my past. I never knew that being helpful to people would bring such satisfaction. All this had filled my heart with so much delight that I felt that so far, my pursuit of happiness had been entirely focused in a wrong direction.

There was a time when acquiring the love of the people was the aim of my life, now it was all about helping needy people and bringing joy into their lives. Flitting from one attachment to another, all I did was to demand from the people around me. Not knowing the fact that people start to turn away from love when we start making demands, I demanded things that people were unable to fulfil. My indecent demands had murdered my relations with Krishna and caused me to separate from my family. Fortunately, nothing like this happened with Vivek. Now I don't demand anything from anyone. All I seek are opportunities to give.

The longing for physical intimacy with a man is a thing of the past now. I have now started to accept things as they come. I have quit planning for my future. The only thing that matters to me, is to better the future of 'Udaan'. So far, in my life I had stayed in touch only with near and dear ones, but now, I have dedicated my life to those I don't even know. Earlier, I hardly let people get into my life, now every human being is welcome. This sacred cause has changed me and my priorities the way I had never imagined it would. It has helped me grow poised and serene, and I have successfully left behind all my gloominess and issues. It has given me an opportunity to look at life from a different perspective. The drastic changes in my disposition surprises me when I look back into my past and an introspection tells me how immature I have been till now!

At last I realized where God had intended to take me. By taking my kinsmen away from me, He wanted to deliver me from the bonds of relationships so that I could reach ultimate salvation. Before drawing me into philanthropy, He wanted to unleash me from all my agonies and sorrows. He washed away all my sins and transgressions, and I feel redeemed. God had planned for me this new route.

All my woes have melted away and there is no more the regret of doing something wrong. Meditation, yoga and prayers have helped me find a better person inside me. The reading of the holy books taught me to be calm and collected. I always believed I knew myself very well but the truth was that I had never come across this *other* Kaushik that was within me.

The only affection I couldn't cast aside was Maya's. Whenever I find time, I go to her, sit in her lap and talk to her. It always feels very soothing in her company. Time passes, seasons change and Maya keeps wearing her various looks with charm and elegance. She blossoms in a season and sheds in another. What I learn from her is that life is all about celebrating what we have, when we have it. The assurance about the tree is that unlike people, she is never going to leave me alone. I am afraid of falling in love one more time because it has always earned me pain, yet I chose to fall in love with the tree because I am sure that she will never betray me. Our relation is to be eternal and forever young.

Acknowledgements

I would like to thank the editorial and the design departments in making this book look crisp and beautiful. I owe a hearty thanks to my literary angel, Vaishali Mathur, for handling this sensitive subject so maturely and effectively.

Though I had been alone in the process of writing this novel, I have to thank my friends, Manish Vaghela and Sanjay Parmar, for their support and for belief in my abilities. They have always encouraged me for making the most of my talent. Thank you ever so much guys!